Best Short Stories

Middle Level

10 Stories for Young Adults—
With Lessons for Teaching the
Basic Elements of Literature

Raymond Harris

Jamestown Publishers
Providence, Rhode Island

Best Short Stories, Middle Level

10 Stories for Young Adults— With Lessons for Teaching the Basic Elements of Literature

Catalog No. 793
Catalog No. 793H, Hardcover Edition

Copyright ©1983 by Jamestown Publishers, Inc.

Cover and Text Design by Deborah Hulsey Christie
Illustrations by Robert Brun, George Lawrence,
James Watling and Deborah Hulsey Christie

Printed in the United States of America

8 9 10 11 12 RM 96 95 94 93 92

ISBN: 0-89061-321-4
ISBN: 0-89061-322-2, Hardcover Edition

Contents

Acknowledgments

Acknowledgment is gratefully made to the following publishers and authors for permission to reprint the stories in this book:

"First Confession" by Frank O'Connor. Copyright © 1951 by Frank O'Connor. Reprinted from *Collected Stories* by Frank O'Connor, by permission of Alfred A. Knopf, Inc.

"Raymond's Run" by Toni Cade Bambara. Copyright © 1970 by Toni Cade Bambara. Reprinted from *Gorilla My Love* by Toni Cade Bambara, by permission of Random House, Inc.

"Chocolate Pudding," from the book *Dear Bill, Remember Me?* and Other Stories by Norma Fox Mazer. Copyright © 1976 by Norma Fox Mazer. Reprinted by permission of Delacorte Press.

"The Moustache" by Robert Cormier. Copyright © 1975 by Robert Cormier. Reprinted from *8 Plus 1* by Robert Cormier, by permission of Pantheon Books, a Division of Random House, Inc.

"Another April" by Jesse Stuart. Copyright © 1946 by Jesse Stuart. Reprinted from *Tales of the Plum Grove Hills*, E.P. Dutton Co. By permission of the Jesse Stuart Foundation, Morehead, Kentucky.

"Sucker" by Carson McCullers. Copyright © 1963 by Carson McCullers. Reprinted from *O'Henry Awards 1965 Prize Stories*, Doubleday & Co. Reprinted by permission of Candida Donadio Associates.

"A Sound of Thunder" by Ray Bradbury. Copyright © 1952 by Ray Bradbury. Reprinted from *The Golden Apples of the Sun*, Doubleday & Co., 1966. Reprinted by permission of Harold Matson Co.

"Naftali the Storyteller and His Horse, Sus" by Isaac Bashevis Singer. Copyright © 1973, 1976 by Isaac Bashevis Singer. Reprinted from *Naftali the Storyteller and His Horse, Sus and Other Stories*. Reprinted by permission of Farrar, Straus & Giroux, Inc.

"The Lucid Eye in Silver Town" by John Updike. Copyright © 1964 by John Updike. Reprinted from *Assorted Prose* by John Updike, by permission of Alfred A. Knopf, Inc.

Christine Powers Harris has been a companion author for all four *Best-Selling Chapters* and *Best Short Stories* books. Teachers will once again recognize her critical insight and appreciation for literary technique in the following units: Unit 1, The Short Story; Unit 4, Setting; Unit 5, Theme; Unit 6, Use of Language; Unit 8, Science Fiction; and Unit 10, Judgments and Conclusions: Discussing Stories.

To the Teacher

Introduction

Most students who use this book will become aware for the first time that stories don't just happen—that they are created with great care and diligence by people with a special talent. For this reason you will find that the lessons often refer to the visual and performing arts, in order to show students the various ways in which feelings and ideas are communicated through the things that people create.

Students can often intuitively appreciate the colors in a painting or the majesty of a tall building, though they may not understand what it is about those art forms that evokes a response in them. But these same students may not be able to appreciate a well-drawn character or story setting without some guidance. They must first recognize and understand the basic elements of literature—character, setting, plot, tone and theme—and how they are used in a particular story, before they can understand and appreciate the ideas and feelings embodied in the story.

To help students understand that the ideas and feelings that exist in literature are *created*, just as the ideas and feelings in other art forms are created, consider beginning your literature course by exposing your students to a wide range of graphic, structural and musical arts. Your school's woodworking shop, for example, would be a good place to start. Follow this with a visit to the art and music rooms. Explain the planning, feeling and craftsmanship that go into any creation. Point out some of the ideas and feelings that can be communicated through artistic craftsmanship. A table, for example, may be severely practical or luxuriously ornate; strong and massive, or delicate, with flowing lines. Music may be stirring or soothing, depending on the composer's intent. And don't overlook the world of movies and television. Even the poorest sitcoms hold valuable lessons in elementary plotting, setting, theme and character development.

Young readers must also have good reading skills in order to readily appreciate literature. It is essential, therefore, that readers continue to practice their reading comprehension skills while they are learning new literary skills. To this end, each unit in the book contains a set of comprehension questions. The students' reading comprehension scores can be plotted on the charts at the back of the book, making it easy for you to see improvement or difficulties students may have in the five comprehension areas. As a student's reading comprehension skills improve, you will probably also notice an increasing appreciation for literature.

The stories in this book have been carefully chosen to give students as broad a reading experience as possible. They range from the uncompromising ferocity of Jack London to the delicate poetic quality of Jesse Stuart's writing and the visionary folk style of Isaac Bashevis Singer. All the authors are masters of their craft and have proven themselves favorites with millions of young readers.

We hope that you and your students enjoy working with the stories, lessons and exercises as much as the authors have enjoyed preparing them.

The Contents of a Unit

The book is divided into ten units. Here is what you will find in each unit:

1. **An Illustration with Questions for Discussion.** Each unit begins with a two-page illustration that depicts the characters in a key scene from the story. This illustration enables visually oriented readers to easily place themselves in the story situation. The page that follows contains questions based on the illustration.

   You will notice that the picture serves as an introduction to the lesson as well as to the story. The questions that accompany the picture also direct the students' thinking to essential ideas that they will encounter in the lesson. In discussing the questions, students will be previewing both the story and the accompanying lesson. This activity will heighten students' anticipation of participating in the story (because they will be anxious to know if their interpretations of the illustration are correct) and will sharpen their perception, as they read the story, of the literary concept that will be discussed in the lesson.

2. **Introduction to the Story.** Each unit contains a brief, three-part introduction. The first part sets the scene and explains a bit about the characters and the story situation. Things that are alluded to in the story and which may be outside the experience of most young readers are explained. For example, the Catholic confessional and some Irish colloquialisms are explained in the introduction

to "First Confession." This part of the introduction also provides information about the author and suggests other books and stories by the author that the students may want to read.

The second part of the introduction defines the literary concept to be studied in the lesson. This is done simply and concisely.

The third part of the introduction consists of four questions intended to call the students' attention to particular passages in the story that are used to illustrate the four major points discussed in the lesson. The students should keep these questions in mind and look for the answers to them as they read the story.

3. **The Short Story.** Each of the ten stories in the book is complete and unabridged. These stories were chosen both for their literary excellence and for their proven appeal to young readers. Each story is particularly suited to illustrate the literary concept taught in the accompanying lesson.

4. **The Literary Lesson.** Each lesson begins with a general explanation of a major literary concept. Then four major elements of the concept are discussed individually, and each is illustrated with an appropriate passage from the story. After the literary element is explained in relation to this passage, the students are presented with a second passage from the story that illustrates the same element. This passage is followed by two questions that allow the students to practice what they have just learned.

Six of the ten lessons deal with elements of literature: plot, character, setting, theme, language, and tone and mood. Three lessons serve as an introduction to genre. The first lesson in the book introduces the short story as a special kind of literature. Later lessons examine two types of stories that are popular with young readers—science fiction and the folk story. The last lesson in the book—Judgments and Conclusions: Discussing Stories—is an easy first venture into criticism and critical thinking.

5. **Skills-Oriented Comprehension Questions.** Fifteen comprehension questions that follow each lesson provide a quick check of five major reading skills: recognizing words in context, recalling facts, keeping events in order, making inferences and understanding main ideas. Each question is labeled according to the skill it tests. A Comprehension Skills Profile is provided at the back of the book so that you can keep track of the kinds of questions each

student misses most often. There is also a Comprehension Scores Graph that can help you keep track of overall progress in reading comprehension.

6. **Discussion Guides.** Through nine discussion questions in each unit, students are asked to consider three aspects of the story: the literary concept emphasized in the lesson, general ideas and implications of the story, and the author's technique or special relationship to the story situation. Answering these questions will encourage students to a thoughtful review of their reading and will give them practice in discussing literature.

7. **The Writing Exercise.** The writing exercises have proven to be one of the most popular elements in both the *Best-Selling Chapters* and *Best Short Stories* books. You will find that the writing exercise in each unit is directly related to what has been presented in the lesson. For instance, following the lesson that deals with setting, the students are asked to create a setting of their own.

How to Use This Book

This book has four major objectives:

- To help readers understand basic structure and the elements of literature
- To sharpen reading comprehension skills
- To encourage critical reading
- To give readers an opportunity to make a conscious effort to introduce elements of literary style into their own writing

Following are suggestions for ways to use the various parts of each unit:

1. **Discuss the Illustration Using the Accompanying Questions.** Ask the students to look carefully at the illustration. On the page following the illustration there are a key question and several supporting questions. Read the key question aloud. You can have the students respond spontaneously or ask them to hold their opinions until they have discussed the supporting questions.

   Have either an open class discussion or small group discussions of the supporting questions. Then return to the major question and ask the students to respond to it in light of the answers they have arrived at in their discussions. Emphasize the importance of supporting or clarifying their opinions and conclusions by pointing out supporting details in the illustration.

Questions help students focus on both the story they will read and the lesson that follows. Read the story and lesson first yourself so that you can direct the discussion of the illustration to assure that it is a good preview of the story and lesson.

2. **Have the Students Read the Story Introduction.** You may wish to add information to the introduction from your own experience with the story or the author. Be sure the students are aware that the author has written other works that they may want to read. Some of these are mentioned in the introduction.

Call attention to the four questions that conclude each introduction. These are questions that the students should keep in mind as they read the story. Point out how each of the questions is related to the definition of the literary concept given in "What the Lesson Is About." Discuss what the students should look for in the reading selection in order to be able to answer the questions. The questions are designed to guide the students, as they read, toward an awareness of the literary concept that will be discussed in the lesson.

3. **Have the Students Read the Story.** Tell the students that you want them to enjoy the story for its own sake, but point out that you also want them to read the story carefully. (With some students you may want to use the word *critically* and explain what critical reading is.)

In order to keep the students' attention focused on the literary concept they will learn about in the lesson, you may want to have them keep a copy of the questions from the introduction beside them as they read. If the students will be reading the story in class, write the introductory questions on the chalkboard. Also, remind the students that they will have to answer comprehension questions about the story later—another reason for reading carefully.

4. **Explain the Lesson.** Each lesson is divided into five parts. It begins with a general introduction to the literary concept that will be dealt with. After the students have read the introduction, some discussion will be in order to assure that they have a general understanding of the concept. Then have the students read and study the other four sections of the lesson, one at a time. Each explains a different element of the major literary concept on which the lesson is focused. The students should also complete the exercise at the end

of each section. After they have finished each section, pause for a discussion of the lesson so that the students can find out whether their answers to the questions in the exercise are right or wrong, and why.

5. **Have Students Answer the Comprehension Questions.** In classes in which reading comprehension is the primary concern, you may want to have the students answer these questions immediately after reading the story. They should answer without looking back at the story. The comprehension questions focus on five important reading skills:

   a. Recognizing Words in Context
   b. Recalling Facts
   c. Keeping Events in Order
   d. Making Inferences
   e. Understanding Main Ideas

6. **Have Students Correct Their Answers.** Students can check their answers to the comprehension questions by using the Answer Key that starts on page 451. Students should be encouraged to correct wrong answers and to consider why one answer is wrong and another right. Have students count the number of *each kind* of question they get wrong and record these numbers in the spaces provided at the end of the comprehension questions.

7. **Have Students Record Their Progress.** Students should plot the number of *correct* answers they got for each story on the Comprehension Scores Graph at the back of the book. Instructions for how to use the graph are given on the page with the graph. When students use the graph, a visual record of their progress quickly emerges.

   Students should mark the number of *wrong* answers they got in each comprehension skill area (there are three questions related to each of the five skills) on the Comprehension Skills Profile on page 463. This will show at a glance which skills a student needs to work on. Students usually enjoy keeping track of their progress, especially when they are allowed to manage this task themselves. Seeing visual proof of improvement in scores invariably provides the incentive to strive for even more improvement. You should also monitor the students' progress, so that you can recognize any problems and deal with them early.

8. **Spend Time on Discussion.** There are three kinds of discussion questions for each story—nine questions in all. The first three questions focus on the literary concept studied in the lesson. These questions give students a chance to demonstrate their new skills and allow you to expand upon the lesson if you wish. Questions four through six are more general and allow students to use their imaginations and apply themes in the story to their own experiences. Finally, the last three questions deal with the author's experience and technique, and focus attention on the subjective aspects of literature.

9. **Have the Students Do the Writing Exercise.** The writing exercises at the end of each unit are designed to allow students to improve their writing through imitation. Each writing exercise asks students to apply what they have learned about the literary element discussed in the lesson. In order to make use of the truism that we learn to write by reading, encourage students to imitate the authors of the stories, if they wish. But an individual, freewheeling style may also be encouraged, especially among the better writers in a class.

To the Student

If you follow the adventures of Snoopy, the world's most famous beagle, you know that one of his ambitions is to become an author. He sits on top of his doghouse with a little typewriter and begins:

"It was a dark and stormy night . . ."

And that's where he gets stuck. He just wasn't meant to be a storyteller, it seems.

The same is not true, however, of Snoopy's creator, author/cartoonist Charles Schulz. Schulz is a first-rate storyteller. The "Peanuts" gang, created from the author's imagination, is known all over the world. Through the antics of these characters, Schulz is able to entertain millions of people everywhere. And there is something else he does, as well. Through his stories and his characters, Charles Schulz is able to communicate his own thoughts and feelings to a vast audience. It's as if he had some magical power to charm people into listening to him. In a way, he does.

Storytelling is an ancient art. Stories were told around campfires long before anyone thought they could be written with pictures, symbols or letters. And people who could tell stories were usually considered very special. Such people must surely have a gift from heaven, it was thought. Today we call this gift *talent*.

You have probably read many stories in your life. You have also had other people read to you. And you have seen many stories on television and in the movies. Everyone still loves a good story today, just as people always have. In this book you will find ten stories which we hope you will enjoy. You will have a chance to see *how* the stories were constructed, or created, by their authors. You will also learn just what it is that makes stories so interesting and enjoyable.

Each story in the book is preceded by an introduction. Be sure to read it. The purpose of the introduction is to help you understand more about the story you will read and about its author.

Lessons that follow the stories take you inside the author's head, in a manner of speaking. You will learn about the things that early people thought of as "magic" in the art of storytelling—how characters are created and used in the story, how the story is made to hold your interest, how the author makes you feel what he or she wants you to feel, and how the author passes along ideas and influences your thinking.

Lesson exercises, questions, discussion guides and a writing exercise round out each unit in the book. These will help sharpen your reading and reasoning skills.

As you become used to reading and thinking carefully, each story unit will be easier to work with than the one before it. So this may be the first textbook you've ever used that becomes easier instead of harder as you go along. And you will find that the skills you learn here will be useful throughout your life, not just for reading, but in any situation in which you have to think and deal with people, their feelings and their ideas.

Unit 1   The Short Story

First Confession
BY FRANK O'CONNOR

About the Illustration

How would you describe
what is happening in this
scene? Point out some
details in the drawing to
support your response.

Here are some questions to
help you think:

☐ What kind of place are
these people in?

☐ Who appears to be the
main character in the
drawing?

☐ What does the expression
on the little boy's face tell
you about how he feels?

☐ How do you think the girl
feels? What details make
you think that?

Unit 1

Introduction   What the Story Is
About/What the
Lesson Is About

Story   First Confession

Lesson   The Short Story

Activities   Comprehension
Questions/Discussion
Guides/Writing
Exercise

Introduction

What the Story Is About

An important milestone in the religious life of young Catholics comes when they make their first communion. This happens when the children are about seven or eight years old—old enough to know the difference between right and wrong. The occasion is a special one. The boys wear suits, the girls don fancy white dresses and white veils. Pictures are taken. A special breakfast may be prepared for the children. There are gifts of rosary beads, prayer books and the like. In church, on this special Sunday, the children are the center of attention as they march down the aisle, two by two, to receive communion for the first time.

This happy event, however, comes only after the children have cleansed their souls by confessing their sins. Adults tend to remember their first communions and forget their first confessions. But that first confession looms large in the mind of a small child. First of all, there's the shame of having to recite all of one's sins, or wrongdoings. Every child is sure his are worse than anyone else's. Equally worrisome is the thought of entering that dark, mysterious confession box.

The confessional, the cubicle in which the priest hears confessions, is divided into three compartments. The priest sits in the middle one. On either side of the priest's box is an adjoining compartment. A small screened opening covered with a sliding door connects each of these with the priest's box. A Catholic wishing to confess his or her sins enters one of these boxes, kneels down and waits for the priest to finish with the person in the compartment on the other side. When the little door finally slides back, the person begins his confession with the words "bless me, Father, for I have sinned . . . ." If this is his first confession he goes on to say, "This is my first confession and these are my sins."

It sounds simple enough. But when you are a small child, the whole process can seem filled with complications. How do you know if the priest is in there? Is he *always* in there? What if you walk in on somebody making his confession? What if somebody walks in on *you*? The chances of embarrassing oneself seem enormous.

That is the situation facing Jackie, the small boy in Frank

O'Connor's story "First Confession." Jackie is hardly what you'd call a little angel. At home he conducts running battles with his grandmother, whose coarse ways distress him no end, and with his older sister Nora. Nora is a bossy young girl who likes to think she is better than anyone else. What with fighting the two of them, Jackie figures he has broken all of the ten commandments.

Out of this minor childhood crisis the author fashions a lighthearted story that will have you doubled over laughing.

O'Connor was an ardent Irishman, and his stories reflect the small-town lives of the Irish people. So you will notice many Irish expressions in "First Confession." These give the story an Irish flavor. Imagine, if you can, the whole story told with an Irish accent—it adds to the fun.

Other short stories in this book have their own local flavors. One story is set in the Kentucky hills. Another is set in Harlem. And a third is set in Poland during the last century. Each has its own expressions that add a special interest and flavor.

Here are some expressions you will find in "First Confession." You can probably figure out the meanings of most of them yourself from the way they are used in the story.

> **a jug of porter.** Porter is a dark brown ale.
>
> **sucked up to the old woman.** Played up to the old woman.
>
> **I was heart-scalded.** We usually say heartsore or heart-sick.
>
> **half-crown.** a British coin, worth almost a dollar at the time the story takes place.
>
> **dirty little caffler.** Much like saying dirty little beggar.
>
> **Begor.** Also *begorra*; an Irish way of saying "by gosh!"
>
> **the screech of trams.** A tram is a trolley car.
>
> **Father gave me a flaking.** (See if you can figure this one out for yourself.)

Frank O'Connor (1903–1966) wrote other, equally humorous stories about children. Yet his own childhood was far from funny. His family was very poor, and he received almost no education, except what he could pick up on his own. Yet by the age of twelve he had turned out his

First Confession

first collection of writings: poems, biographies, and essays on history. "I was intended by God," he once remarked, "to be a painter, but I was very poor and pencil and paper were the cheapest . . . . Literature is the poor man's art." After reading "First Confession" you will probably want to read some other stories by Frank O'Connor. One of his most popular collections is titled *"My Oedipus Complex" and Other Stories.* You can find this collection in most libraries.

What the Lesson Is About

The lesson that follows "First Confession" is about the short story as a type of literature. The short story is an art form. It is a story that presents a complete human experience in the space of about ten pages.

It takes great skill to create characters, build a plot and get your point across in such short order—and, of course, entertain the reader at the same time. Frank O'Connor does all of this. *How* he does it is well worth a closer look.

The questions below will help you spot some important elements of a short story. Try to keep them in mind as you read "First Confession":

1 How does the author grab your interest right from the start?

2 How does the author make Jackie and his sister Nora seem real?

3 How does the mood of the story change as Jackie comes closer and closer to his moment of truth—his first confession?

4 What is it about the end of the story that leaves you with a satisfied feeling?

First Confession

Frank O'Connor

All the trouble began when my grandfather died and my grandmother—my father's mother—came to live with us. Relations in the one house are a strain at the best of times, but, to make matters worse, my grandmother was a real old countrywoman and quite unsuited to the life in town. She had a fat, wrinkled old face, and, to Mother's great indignation, went round the house in bare feet—the boots had her crippled, she said. For dinner she had a jug of porter and a pot of potatoes with—sometimes—a bit of salt fish, and she poured out the potatoes on the table and ate them slowly, with great relish, using her fingers by way of a fork.

Now, girls are supposed to be fastidious, but I was the one who suffered most from this. Nora, my sister, just sucked up to the old woman for the penny she got every Friday out of the old-age pension, a thing I could not do. I was too honest, that was my trouble; and when I was playing with Bill Connell, the sergeant-major's son, and saw my grandmother steering up the path with the jug of porter sticking out from beneath her shawl I was mortified. I made excuses not to let him come into the house, because I could never be sure what she would be up to when we went in.

When Mother was at work and my grandmother made the dinner I wouldn't touch it. Nora once tried to make me, but I hid under the table from her and took the bread-knife with me for protection. Nora let on to be very indignant (she wasn't, of course, but she knew Mother saw through her, so she sided with Gran) and came after me. I lashed out at her with the bread-knife, and after that she left me alone. I stayed there till Mother came in from work and made my dinner, but when Father came in later Nora said in a shocked voice: "Oh, Dadda, do you know what Jackie did at dinnertime?" Then, of course, it all came out; Father gave me a flaking; Mother interfered, and for days after that he didn't speak to me and Mother barely spoke to Nora. And all because of that old woman! God knows, I was heart-scalded.

Then, to crown my misfortunes, I had to make my first confession and communion. It was an old woman called Ryan who prepared us for these. She was about the one age with Gran; she was well-to-do, lived in a big house on Montenotte, wore a black cloak and bonnet, and came every day to school at three o'clock when we should have been going home, and talked to us of hell. She may have mentioned the other place as well, but that could only have been by accident, for hell had the first place in her heart.

She lit a candle, took out a new half-crown, and offered it to the first boy who would hold one finger—only one finger!—in the flame for five minutes by the school clock. Being always very ambitious I was tempted to volunteer, but I thought it might look greedy. Then she asked were we afraid of holding one finger—only one finger!—in a little candle flame for five minutes and not afraid of burning all over in roasting hot furnaces for all eternity. "All eternity! Just think of that! A whole lifetime goes by and it's nothing, not even a drop in the ocean of your sufferings." The woman was really interesting about hell, but my attention was all fixed on the half-crown. At the end of the lesson she put it back in her purse. It was a great disappointment; a religious woman like that, you wouldn't think she'd bother about a thing like a half-crown.

Another day she said she knew a priest who woke one night to find a fellow he didn't recognize leaning over the end of his bed. The priest was a bit frightened—naturally enough—but he asked the fellow what he wanted, and the fellow said in a deep, husky voice that he wanted to go to confession. The priest said it was an awkward time and wouldn't it do in the morning, but the fellow said that last time he went to confession, there was one sin he kept back,

First Confession

being ashamed to mention it, and now it was always on his mind. Then the priest knew it was a bad case, because the fellow was after making a bad confession and committing a mortal sin. He got up to dress, and just then the cock crew in the yard outside, and—lo and behold!—when the priest looked round there was no sign of the fellow, only a smell of burning timber, and when the priest looked at his bed didn't he see the print of two hands burned in it? That was because the fellow had made a bad confession. This story made a shocking impression on me.

But the worst of all was when she showed us how to examine our conscience. Did we take the name of the Lord, our God, in vain? Did we honour our father and our mother? (I asked her did this include grandmothers and she said it did.) Did we love our neighbours as ourselves? Did we covet our neighbour's goods? (I thought of the way I felt about the penny that Nora got every Friday.) I decided that, between one thing and another, I must have broken the whole ten commandments, all on account of that old woman, and so far as I could see, so long as she remained in the house I had no hope of ever doing anything else.

I was scared to death of confession. The day the whole class went I let on to have a toothache, hoping my absence wouldn't be noticed; but at three o'clock, just as I was feeling safe, along comes a chap with a message from Mrs. Ryan that I was to go to confession myself on Saturday and be at the chapel for communion with the rest. To make it worse, Mother couldn't come with me and sent Nora instead.

Now, that girl had ways of tormenting me that Mother never knew of. She held my hand as we went down the hill, smiling sadly and saying how sorry she was for me, as if she were bringing me to the hospital for an operation.

"Oh, God help us!" she moaned. "Isn't it a terrible pity you weren't a good boy? Oh, Jackie, my heart bleeds for you! How will you ever think of all your sins? Don't forget you have to tell him about the time you kicked Gran on the shin."

"Lemme go!" I said, trying to drag myself free of her. "I don't want to go to confession at all."

"But sure, you'll have to go to confession, Jackie," she replied in the same regretful tone. "Sure, if you didn't, the parish priest would be up to the house, looking for you. 'Tisn't, God knows, that I'm not sorry for you. Do you remember the time you tried to kill me with the bread-knife under the table? And the language you used to me? I don't know what he'll do with you at all, Jackie. He might have to send you up to the bishop."

I remember thinking bitterly that she didn't know the half of what I had to tell—if I told it. I knew I couldn't tell it, and understood perfectly why the fellow in Mrs. Ryan's story made a bad confession; it seemed to me a great shame that people wouldn't stop criticizing him. I remember that steep hill down to the church, and the sunlit hillsides beyond the valley of the river, which I saw in the gaps between the houses like Adam's last glimpse of Paradise.

Then, when she had manœuvred me down the long flight of steps to the chapel yard, Nora suddenly changed her tone. She became the raging malicious devil she really was.

"There you are!" she said with a yelp of triumph, hurling me through the church door. "And I hope he'll give you the penitential psalms, you dirty little caffler."

I knew then I was lost, given up to eternal justice. The door with the coloured-glass panels swung shut behind me, the sunlight went out and gave place to deep shadow, and the wind whistled outside so that the silence within seemed to crackle like ice under my feet. Nora sat in front of me by the confession box. There were a couple of old women ahead of her, and then a miserable-looking poor devil came and wedged me in at the other side, so that I couldn't escape even if I had the courage. He joined his hands and rolled his eyes in the direction of the roof, muttering aspirations in an anguished tone, and I wondered had he a grandmother too. Only a grandmother could account for a fellow behaving in

28   First Confession

that heartbroken way, but he was better off than I, for he at least could go and confess his sins; while I would make a bad confession and then die in the night and be continually coming back and burning people's furniture.

Nora's turn came, and I heard the sound of something slamming, and then her voice as if butter wouldn't melt in her mouth, and then another slam, and out she came. God, the hypocrisy of women! Her eyes were lowered, her head was bowed, and her hands were joined very low down on her stomach, and she walked up the aisle to the side altar looking like a saint. You never saw such an exhibition of devotion; and I remembered the devilish malice with which she had tormented me all the way from our door, and wondered were all religious people like that, really. It was my turn now. With the fear of damnation in my soul I went in, and the confessional door closed of itself behind me.

It was pitch-dark and I couldn't see priest or anything else. Then I really began to be frightened. In the darkness it was a matter between God and me, and He had all the odds. He knew what my intentions were before I even started; I had no chance. All I had ever been told about confession got mixed up in my mind, and I knelt to one wall and said: "Bless me, father, for I have sinned; this is my first confession." I waited for a few minutes, but nothing happened, so I tried it on the other wall. Nothing happened there either. He had me spotted all right.

It must have been then that I noticed the shelf at about one height with my head. It was really a place for grown-up people to rest their elbows, but in my distracted state I thought it was probably the place you were supposed to kneel. Of course, it was on the high side and not very deep, but I was always good at climbing and managed to get up all right. Staying up was the trouble. There was room only for my knees, and nothing you could get a grip on but a sort of wooden moulding a bit above it. I held on to the moulding and repeated the words a little louder, and this time something happened all right. A slide was slammed back; a little light entered the box, and a man's voice said: "Who's there?"

" 'Tis me, father," I said for fear he mightn't see me and go away again. I couldn't see him at all. The place the voice came from was under the moulding, about level with my knees, so I took a good grip of the moulding and swung myself down till I saw the astonished face of a young priest looking up at me. He had to put his head on one side to see me, and I had to put mine on one side to see him, so we were more or less talking to one another upside-down. It struck me as a queer way of hearing confessions, but I didn't feel it my place to criticize.

"Bless me, father, for I have sinned; this is my first confession," I rattled off in one breath, and swung myself down the least shade more to make it easier for him.

"What are you doing up there?" he shouted in an angry voice, and the strain the politeness was putting on my hold of the moulding, and the shock of being addressed in such an uncivil tone, were too much for me. I lost my grip, tumbled, and hit the door an unmerciful wallop before I found myself flat on my back in the middle of the aisle. The people who had been waiting stood up with their mouths open. The priest opened the door of the middle box and came out, pushing his biretta back from his forehead; he looked something terrible. Then Nora came scampering down the aisle.

"Oh, you dirty little caffler!" she said. "I might have known you'd do it. I might have known you'd disgrace me. I can't leave you out of my sight for one minute."

Before I could even get to my feet to defend myself she bent down and gave me a clip across the ear. This reminded me that I was so stunned I had even forgotten to cry, so that people might think I wasn't hurt at all, when in fact I was probably maimed for life. I gave a roar out of me.

"What's all this about?" the priest hissed, getting angrier

than ever and pushing Nora off me. "How dare you hit the child like that, you little vixen?"

"But I can't do my penance with him, father," Nora cried, cocking an outraged eye up at him.

"Well, go and do it, or I'll give you some more to do," he said, giving me a hand up. "Was it coming to confession you were, my poor man?" he asked me.

" 'Twas, father," said I with a sob.

"Oh," he said respectfully, "a big hefty fellow like you must have terrible sins. Is this your first?"

" 'Tis, father," said I.

"Worse and worse," he said gloomily. "The crimes of a lifetime. I don't know will I get rid of you at all today. You'd better wait now till I'm finished with these old ones. You can see by the looks of them they haven't much to tell."

"I will, father," I said with something approaching joy.

The relief of it was really enormous. Nora stuck out her tongue at me from behind his back, but I couldn't even be bothered retorting. I knew from the very moment that man opened his mouth that he was intelligent above the ordinary. When I had time to think, I saw how right I was. It only stood to reason that a fellow confessing after seven years would have more to tell than people that went every week. The crimes of a lifetime, exactly as he said. It was only what he expected, and the rest was the cackle of old women and girls with their talk of hell, the bishop, and the penitential psalms. That was all they knew. I started to make my examination of conscience, and barring the one bad business of my grandmother it didn't seem so bad.

The next time, the priest steered me into the confession box himself and left the shutter back the way I could see him get in and sit down at the further side of the grille from me.

"Well, now," he said, "what do they call you?"

"Jackie, father," said I.

"And what's a-trouble to you, Jackie?"

"Father," I said, feeling I might as well get it over while I had him in good humour, "I had it all arranged to kill my grandmother."

He seemed a bit shaken by that, all right, because he said nothing for quite a while.

"My goodness," he said at last, "that'd be a shocking thing to do. What put that into your head?"

"Father," I said, feeling very sorry for myself, "she's an awful woman."

"Is she?" he asked. "What way is she awful?"

"She takes porter, father," I said, knowing well from the way Mother talked of it that this was a mortal sin, and hoping it would make the priest take a more favourable view of my case.

"Oh, my!" he said, and I could see he was impressed.

"And snuff, father," said I.

"That's a bad case, sure enough, Jackie," he said.

"And she goes round in her bare feet, father," I went on in a rush of self-pity, "and she know I don't like her, and she gives pennies to Nora and none to me, and my da sides with her and flakes me, and one night I was so heart-scalded I made up my mind I'd have to kill her."

"And what would you do with the body?" he asked with great interest.

"I was thinking I could chop that up and carry it away in a barrow I have," I said.

"Begor, Jackie," he said, "do you know you're a terrible child?" "I know, father," I said, for I was just thinking the same thing myself. "I tried to kill Nora too with a bread-knife under the table, only I missed her."

"Is that the little girl that was beating you just now?" he asked.

" 'Tis, father."

"Someone will go for her with a bread-knife one day, and he won't miss her," he said rather cryptically. "You must have great courage. Between ourselves, there's a lot of

First Confession

people I'd like to do the same to but I'd never have the nerve. Hanging is an awful death."

"Is it, father?" I asked with the deepest interest—I was always very keen on hanging. "Did you ever see a fellow hanged?"

"Dozens of them," he said solemnly. "And they all died roaring."

"Jay!" I said.

"Oh, a horrible death!" he said with great satisfaction. "Lots of the fellows I saw killed their grandmothers too, but they all said 'twas never worth it."

He had me there for a full ten minutes talking, and then walked out the chapel yard with me. I was genuinely sorry to part with him, because he was the most entertaining character I'd ever met in the religious line. Outside, after the shadow of the church, the sunlight was like the roaring of waves on a beach; it dazzled me; and when the frozen silence melted and I heard the screech of trams on the road my heart soared. I knew now I wouldn't die in the night and come back, leaving marks on my mother's furniture. It would be a great worry to her, and the poor soul had enough.

Nora was sitting on the railing, waiting for me, and she put on a very sour puss when she saw the priest with me. She was mad jealous because a priest had never come out of the church with her.

"Well," she asked coldly, after he left me, "what did he give you?"

"Three Hail Marys," I said.

"Three Hail Marys," she repeated incredulously. "You mustn't have told him anything."

"I told him everything," I said confidently.

"About Gran and all?"

"About Gran and all."

(All she wanted was to be able to go home and say I'd made a bad confession.)

"Did you tell him you went for me with the bread-knife?" she asked with a frown.

"I did to be sure."

"And he only gave you three Hail Marys?"

"That's all."

She slowly got down from the railing with a baffled air. Clearly, this was beyond her. As we mounted the steps back to the main road she looked at me suspiciously.

"What are you sucking?" she asked.

"Bullseyes."

"Was it the priest gave them to you?"

" 'Twas."

"Lord God," she wailed bitterly, "some people have all the luck! 'Tis no advantage to anybody trying to be good. I might just as well be a sinner like you."

The Short Story

Just what it is that compels people to make up stories and other people to read or listen to them is hard to pin down. Yet stories hold us spellbound. They always have and always will.

Among the earliest stories are the *myths*. Myths explained the sometimes tangled affairs of the gods and goddesses who were once believed to rule the earth and heavens. Like human beings, they were apt to be jealous, lovesick, greedy or power-hungry. Their various activities, which were told about in the myths, helped people find reasons for the ups and downs of human existence, because the things the gods and goddesses did affected nature and the people on earth.

Two other early forms of storytelling are the *fable* and its cousin the *parable*. Both are stories that teach a lesson. They set down rules of conduct and codes of behavior—right versus wrong. Like the myths, these kinds of stories helped people find order in a world that often seemed to be without rhyme or reason.

The modern short story exists simply for the sake of telling "a good story." It too carries a message for the reader. But the author's main purpose in writing it is to share an idea by telling of an experience.

Because it is a *short* story, it tells of a single situation or a single experience. There is one story, one plot line. The story usually takes place over a short period of time, and there are only one or two main characters.

Yet, within the space of only ten pages or so, the author manages to recount an incident or an experience that strikes a common chord in all who read it. And when you have finished, you are left with the satisfied feeling that you have stood in another person's shoes, if only for a little bit, and shared a significant experience in that person's life.

This is all accomplished in an orderly manner. A situation is presented, characters are introduced, things start happening. How an author does this is what this lesson, in fact this whole book, is about.

Let's look at how Frank O'Connor goes about the process of building a story in "First Confession." Along the way we'll mention some specific storytelling elements that will be the focus of later lessons. Right now, however, let's begin by looking at the story as a whole, from start to finish.

Most short stories can be discussed by considering how the author has accomplished each of the following things:

1 Setting up the story

2 Developing the characters

3 Building toward a climax

4 Winding things down

The first few paragraphs of a story are very important because they must do several things. Right from the start, the author must set the mood, or frame of mind, he or she wishes the reader to share. He must introduce important characters without delay.

He must hint of conflict, or troubles, to come. Above all, he must "hook" the reader—grab your interest so that you will go on reading the story.

Look at how Frank O'Connor does all these things in the opening paragraph of "First Confession." As you read it, ask yourself, "Who is talking?" "What do we learn about this character?" and "What might be in store for us in this story?"

> All the trouble began when my grandfather died and my grandmother—my father's mother—came to live with us. Relations in the one house are a strain at the best of times, but, to make matters worse, my grandmother was a real old countrywoman and quite unsuited to the life in town. She had a fat, wrinkled old face, and, to Mother's great indignation, went round the house in bare feet—the boots had her crippled, she said. For dinner she had a jug of porter and a pot of potatoes with—sometimes—a bit of salt fish, and she poured out the potatoes on the table and ate them slowly, with great relish, using her fingers by way of a fork.

This is a young child speaking. (We learn in the next paragraph that it is a boy and, later, that he is seven years old.) He is the one who is telling the story. It is his voice saying, "All the trouble began when <u>my</u> grandfather died and <u>my</u> grandmother . . . came to live with us." We are hearing the story as the boy sees it, from his point of view. This is worth keeping in mind, because you may not want to take everything he says as the whole truth and nothing but. There may be other ways of looking at the situation he describes.

Clearly, the little boy is going to be an important character in the story. And what have we already learned about this character? We know two things: (1) he has a grievance against the newest member of the family, his grandmother, and (2) he feels "put upon." He feels he is being made to suffer by her presence in the house.

There are hints of conflicts to come: "Relations in the one house are a strain at the best of times," he tells us. This gives us good enough reason to read on; it's interesting to read about other people's small domestic squabbles.

You might think from all this that the grandmother is going to be a main character in the story. As it turns out, she isn't. What *is* important here is how the boy sees things. His attitude toward his grandmother is an example of this. Her manners, her clothes and her habits probably haven't changed in fifty years. To the boy, she looks different and, therefore, threatening. He sees things from a child's limited point of view.

This, by the way, is what makes the story so funny. It's the difference between a small boy's point of view and your own that makes you chuckle, even laugh out loud at times.

In Exercise A, you'll see Jackie's attitude toward another member of the family—his older sister Nora.

Exercise A

Read the following passage and answer the questions about it using what you have learned in this part of the lesson.

When Mother was at work and my grandmother made the dinner I wouldn't touch it. Nora once tried to make me, but I hid under the table from her and took the bread-knife with me for protection. Nora let on to be very indignant (she wasn't, of course, but she knew Mother saw through her, so she sided with Gran) and came after me. I lashed out at her with the bread-knife, and after that she left me alone. I stayed there till Mother came in from work and made my dinner, but when Father came in later Nora said in a shocked voice: "Oh, Dadda, do you know what Jackie did at dinnertime?" Then, of course, it all came out; Father gave me a flaking; Mother interfered, and for days after that he didn't speak to me and Mother barely spoke to Nora. And all because of that old woman! God knows, I was heart-scalded.

First Confession

Put an *x* in the box beside the correct answer.

1. Here we meet Nora, the other main character of the story. Based on her part in this dinnertime battle, you could say that Nora is

☐ a. an innocent victim.

☐ b. a peacemaker.

☐ c. a substitute mother.

☐ d. a little tattletale.

2. One sentence toward the end of the passage tells who Jackie thinks is to blame for the whole family quarrel. Find this sentence and copy it on the lines below.

_____

_____

_____

Now check your answers using the Answer Key on page 451. Correct any wrong answers and review this part of the lesson if you don't understand why an answer was wrong.

The Short Story

2 **Developing the Characters**

Before long we get to know the main characters better. Like real people, they have a "public" side and a "private" side. Your public side is the side that strangers and people you're trying to impress see. When you are in public you are usually on your best behavior. Your private side is the side your family, and maybe your closest friends, know about—it reveals the personal things about you. This is the side of you that can be sensitive, selfish, insecure, impatient, catty, and other things you may not be proud of. Authors try to show both sides of main characters. This makes them seem more rounded, more real.

Take Jackie, for instance, the little boy telling the story in "First Confession." He would like you to believe that he is a splendid chap. Any small failings on his part are always someone else's fault. Throughout the story, however, there are little hints that suggest otherwise.

In the following passage, Jackie tells us about Mrs. Ryan's little game with the half-crown (a British coin worth almost a dollar at the time when the story takes place). How does Jackie depict *his* role in this little scene? What, perhaps, might be closer to the truth?

> [Mrs. Ryan] lit a candle, took out a new half-crown, and offered it to the first boy who would hold one finger—only one finger!—in the flame for five minutes by the school clock. Being always very ambitious I was tempted to volunteer, but I thought it might look greedy. Then she asked were we afraid of holding one finger—only one finger!—in a little candle flame for five minutes and not afraid of burning all over in roasting hot furnaces for all eternity . . . . The woman was really interesting about hell, but my attention was all fixed on the half-crown. At the end of the lesson she put it back in her purse. It was a great disappointment; a religious woman like that, you wouldn't think she'd bother about a thing like a half-crown.

Remember, this small boy is always trying to make himself look as good as possible. He declines to hold his finger in the flame, he says, because he "thought it might look greedy." What is more likely is that he was *afraid* to put his finger in the flame. His excuse is the kind of little white lie that makes us smile. Secretly, we know we might make the same weak excuse ourselves.

It next becomes clear that, contrary to what he tells us, Jackie is very greedy indeed. Mrs. Ryan is using the coin to drive home a lesson about the terrors of hell. But Jackie couldn't care less about the point she is trying to make. As he says, "My attention was all fixed on the half-crown." He watches with great regret as the old woman puts it back in her purse.

These little bits of information about Jackie's thoughts and feelings help round out his character. We see not only his public side, but his inner, private self too. And the scene is not only funny—it's realistic. It shows the way people are; they try to present only their best side to the world. We all do the same thing. By telling us about this incident and revealing Jackie's thoughts, the author has succeeded in developing a character we can believe in.

There are two sides to Nora as well. See if you can spot them in Exercise B.

Exercise B

Read the following passage and answer the questions about it using what you have learned in this part of the lesson.

"Oh, God help us!" she moaned. "Isn't it a terrible pity you weren't a good boy? Oh, Jackie, my heart bleeds for you! How will you ever think of all your sins? Don't forget you have to tell him about the time you kicked Gran on the shin." . . .

Then, when she had manœuvered me down the long flight of steps to the chapel yard, Nora suddenly changed her tone. She became the raging malicious devil she really was.

"There you are!" she said with a yelp of triumph, hurling me through the church door. "And I hope he'll give you the penitential psalms, you dirty little caffler."

Put an *x* in the box beside the correct answer.

1. In the first part of the passage, Nora seems to

   ☐ a. reassure Jackie.

   ☐ b. wash her hands of Jackie.

   ☐ c. be angry at Jackie.

   ☐ d. sympathize with Jackie.

2. In the last half of the passage, Nora does a complete turnabout. Now we see a side of Nora that she usually tries to hide. Find the sentence that describes this unpleasant side of Nora, and copy it on the lines below.

   _____

   _____

   _____

Now check your answers using the Answer Key on page 451. Correct any wrong answers and review this part of the lesson if you don't understand why an answer was wrong.

By now the reader knows that Jackie is in a tight spot. He is about to make his first confession. Yet his sins are so dreadful (or so he imagines) that he is afraid to tell them to the priest. But if he holds anything back, he'll have made a "bad confession" like the poor man in Mrs. Ryan's story.

The Short Story

3 **Building Toward a Climax**

This kind of situation, in which the main character is faced with a problem, is called the *conflict*. There is a conflict at the heart of every story. Without conflict, a story would be rambling and pointless. Conflict gives a story its focus. How the main character deals with his conflict, or problem, is what the story is all about.

As the main character comes closer and closer to the heart of his problem, suspense builds. Finally, he must solve the problem or the problem will crush him. This moment in the story is the point of greatest suspense. It is called the *climax*. (And, because it is a turning point in the story, it is sometimes called a *crisis*.)

In "First Confession," the climax approaches as Jackie enters the confession box. You can see it coming, you can even *feel* it coming, as Jackie steps inside:

> With the fear of damnation in my soul I went in, and the confessional door closed of itself behind me.
>
> It was pitch-dark and I couldn't see priest or anything else. Then I really began to be frightened. In the darkness it was a matter between God and me, and He had all the odds.

It is dark, Jackie is scared and confused. He feels helpless. The reader shares his anxiety. At this point the tension is so thick you could cut it with a knife. Either Jackie is doomed to roast in the everlasting fires of hell, or he will be forgiven for his sins. But one way or another, something's got to give, because the crisis is always a turning point in the story. But there is also humor in the situation. The humor comes from knowing that things are hardly as bad as the poor little boy imagines.

In Exercise C, Jackie finally meets the priest through the little sliding window of the confession box.

Exercise C

The place the voice came from was under the moulding, about level with my knees, so I took a good grip of the moulding and swung myself down till I saw the astonished face of a young priest looking up at me. He had to put his head on one side to see me, and I had to put mine on one side to see him, so we were more or less talking to one another upside-down. It struck me as a queer way of hearing confessions, but I didn't feel it my place to criticize.

"Bless me, father, for I have sinned; this is my first confession," I rattled off in one breath . . . .

"What are you doing up there?" he shouted in an angry voice, and the strain the politeness was putting on my hold of the moulding, and the shock of being addressed in such an uncivil tone, were too much for me. I lost my grip, tumbled, and hit the door an unmerciful wallop before I found myself flat on my back in the middle of the aisle.

Put an *x* in the box beside the correct answer.

1. Why is this a turning point in the story?

☐ a. It seems that the worst possible thing has happened to Jackie.

☐ b. It shows that Jackie is doomed to hell for making a bad confession.

☐ c. It makes fun of the priest.

☐ d. It is an interesting anecdote.

2. In a humorous story, the climax is often the funniest part. Two main things are funny here. Briefly, in your own words, tell what these two things are.

_____

_____

Now check your answers using the Answer Key on page 451. Correct any wrong answers and review this part of the lesson if you don't understand why an answer was wrong.

The Short Story

4 Winding Things Down

Finally, after bringing us breathless with suspense and laughter to the edge of our seats, the author proceeds to wind things down. This part of the story is called the *resolution*. The feeling of suspense has passed. The conflict has been worked out, and the crisis is over. All that is left for the author to do is to tie up the loose ends.

A good short story leaves the reader with a sense of completion. This includes getting a parting glimpse of the main character after the crisis is over. Has he changed at all? Has he learned something as a result of his experience? What, in the end, has the story been all about?

If you can answer these questions, then you have more than likely found the *theme*, or main idea, of the story. The theme is the point of the story, the underlying lesson that the story holds for us. (In the fable and the parable of olden times, the theme was always neatly stated as a moral—a lesson about right and wrong—at the end of the story.)

Look at the following passage, taken from the last part of "First Confession." What mood do you sense here? Does Jackie seem a little bit different—older or more mature—than when you first met him?

> He [the priest] had me there for a full ten minutes talking, and then walked out the chapel yard with me. I was genuinely sorry to part with him, because he was the most entertaining character I'd ever met in the religious line. Outside, after the shadow of the church, the sunlight was like the roaring of waves on a beach; it dazzled me; and when the frozen silence melted and I heard the screech of trams on the road my heart soared. I knew now I wouldn't die in the night and come back, leaving marks on my mother's furniture. It would be a great worry to her, and the poor soul had enough.

You can almost hear a big sigh of relief at this point, and that is the mood—relieved. "My heart soared," says Jackie as he comes out of the church. The ordeal is behind him, and it wasn't so bad after all.

But there's more to it than that. Jackie has learned something. "I knew now I wouldn't die in the night and come back, leaving marks on my mother's furniture," he says. In the space of an afternoon he has outgrown Mrs. Ryan's, and his sister's, limited idea of religion.

First Confession

Religion was never meant to frighten people into being good—the young priest has shown him that.

As we leave Jackie, we feel that we have shared an important experience in his life. And that ability to make the reader feel that he or she has been truly involved in the events of the story is the essence of a good short story.

There's a "kicker" at the end of this story, whereby Nora gets her well-deserved "comeuppance." In other words, she gets what's coming to her for being so self-righteous and so cruel to Jackie. Go on to Exercise D now, and savor with Jackie his moment of triumph.

Exercise D

Read the following passage and answer the questions about it using what you have learned in this part of the lesson.

> "What are you sucking?" [Nora] asked.
> "Bullseyes."
> "Was it the priest gave them to you?"
> " 'Twas."
> "Lord God," she wailed bitterly, "some people have all the luck! 'Tis no advantage to anybody trying to be good. I might just as well be a sinner like you."

Put an x in the box beside the correct answer.

1. After finishing this story, the reader is left feeling

☐ a. angry and amazed.

☐ b. pleased and satisfied.

☐ c. puzzled and mystified.

☐ d. sad and depressed.

2. One reason Nora's last speech is so funny is that she has everything backwards. She suggests that she is good and her brother is a sinner. In your own words, explain what is wrong with her thinking.

_____

_____

_____

Use the Answer Key on page 451 to check your answers. Correct any wrong answers and review this part of the lesson if you don't understand why an answer was wrong. Now go on to do the Comprehension Questions.

Comprehension Questions

Answer these questions without looking back at the story. Choose the best answer to each question and put an *x* in the box beside it.

Recalling Facts

1. Who, according to Jackie, was responsible for all the trouble in his household?

   ☐ a. Nora

   ☐ b. Father

   ☐ c. Mother

   ☐ d. Grandmother

Recognizing Words in Context

2. Jackie says, "When I was playing with Bill Connell ... and saw my grandmother steering up the path with the jug of porter sticking out from beneath her shawl I was *mortified*." To be *mortified* means to feel very

   ☐ a. shy.

   ☐ b. surprised.

   ☐ c. embarrassed.

   ☐ d. proud.

Recognizing Words in Context

3. Jackie says that when his father found out he'd hidden under the table with a bread-knife he gave Jackie a *flaking*. Judging from the way it is used, *flaking* must mean

   ☐ a. reward.

   ☐ b. spanking.

   ☐ c. penance.

   ☐ d. piece of advice.

4. It is safe to say that Mrs. Ryan, the woman who prepared the children for their first confession, succeeded in

☐ a. showing them God's love and mercy.

☐ b. scaring them half to death.

☐ c. helping them understand their religion.

☐ d. teaching them right from wrong.

Understanding
Main Ideas

5. How does Jackie feel about making his first confession?

☐ a. He is looking forward to it.

☐ b. It is a big joke to him.

☐ c. He dreads it.

☐ d. It means very little to him.

Making
Inferences

6. On the way to the church, Nora keeps reminding Jackie of all his past sins so that

☐ a. when the priest hears how bad he was will give Jackie a big penance to do.

☐ b. he won't make a "bad confession."

☐ c. he will thank her when it's all over.

☐ d. the devil will not get his soul.

Keeping
Events in
Order

7. At what point in the story does Nora try to make herself look saintly?

☐ a. When she escorts Jackie to the church

☐ b. When she helps Gran around the house

☐ c. When she walks up to the altar after going to confession

☐ d. When she questions Jackie after he comes out of the church

8. The first time Jackie talks with the priest in the confession box, the priest is

☐ a. angry at him.

☐ b. kind to him.

☐ c. amused by him.

☐ d. afraid of him.

9. When Jackie falls out of the confession box and into the aisle, Nora

☐ a. helps him up.

☐ b. leaves the church.

☐ c. slaps his head.

☐ d. pretends she doesn't know him.

10. At what point does Jackie begin to feel better about making his first confession?

☐ a. As Nora talks with him on their way to the church

☐ b. As he watches the other people go into the confessional

☐ c. After the priest tells him to wait until he's finished with the others

☐ d. When he is on his way home again with Nora

11. Jackie tells the priest that his grandmother drinks porter, "knowing full well from the way Mother talked of it that this was a *mortal* sin." A *mortal* sin must be

☐ a. a very serious sin.

☐ b. a past offense.

☐ c. an unintentional sin.

☐ d. a very small sin.

12. From the priest's manner as he listens to Jackie's first confession, the reader can infer that the priest is

☐ a. shocked by what he hears.

☐ b. amused by what Jackie tells him.

☐ c. saddened at the boy's sins.

☐ d. bored with the youngster's problems.

Recalling
Facts

13. What penance did the priest give Jackie after he'd heard his sins?

☐ a. Three Hail Marys

☐ b. Five Hail Marys and five Our Fathers

☐ c. The rosary

☐ d. The penitential psalms

Understanding
Main Ideas

14. How does Jackie feel about himself by the end of the story?

☐ a. He feels that he is a terrible sinner.

☐ b. He is ashamed of himself.

☐ c. He feels good about himself.

☐ d. He feels proud of being bad.

Understanding
Main Ideas

15. How does Nora feel at the end of the story?

☐ a. She is annoyed that everything went so well for Jackie.

☐ b. She is pleased and proud of her little brother.

☐ c. She is sorry she gave Jackie such a hard time.

☐ d. She is worried about her brother's soul.

Now check your answers using the Answer Key on page 451. Make no mark for right answers. <u>Correct</u> any wrong answers you may have by putting a checkmark (✓) in the box next to the right answer. Count the number of questions you answered correctly and plot the total on the Comprehension Scores graph on page 462.

Next, look at the questions you answered incorrectly. What types of questions were they? Count the number you got wrong of each type and enter the numbers in the spaces below.

Recognizing Words in Context	_____
Recalling Facts	_____
Keeping Events in Order	_____
Making Inferences	_____
Understanding Main Ideas	_____

Now use these numbers to fill in the Comprehension Skills Profile on page 463.

Discussion Guides

The questions below will help you to think about the story and the lesson you have just read. If you don't discuss these questions in class, try to think about them or discuss them with your classmates.

Discussing Short Stories

1. This story is told from Jackie's point of view; we see everything through Jackie's eyes. Should we believe everything he tells us? Find something in the story that might be only half true.

2. Dialect is a manner of speaking that marks a person as coming from a particular area or background. What are some examples of Irish dialect in "First Confession"? What do they add to the story?

3. Suppose the story ended with Jackie coming out of the church feeling relieved. What is gained by including that last little exchange with Nora?

Discussing the Story

4. In your opinion, did Mrs. Ryan do a good job of preparing the children to make their first confession? Explain your answer.

5. What are some things the young priest does and says that make Jackie feel better? If Mrs. Ryan had been the priest, how might she have handled the same confession?

6. Jackie's grandmother's presence is felt throughout much of the story. Yet we never meet her. Why does the author do this? If we *were* to meet her, is it possible she would not prove to be the old witch Jackie claims she is? Give reasons for your opinion.

Discussing the Author's Work

7. Frank O'Connor is famous for writing simple stories about simple people. But it is said that with his stories he dealt with important and complicated problems of life. What important and complicated problems of living does the author deal with in this story?

8. Frank O'Connor wanted to write stories that were purely Irish. He wanted to make the Irish people aware and proud of their heritage. How does "First Confession" help to do this?

9. "First Confession" is very Irish. Why do you think people who aren't Irish, and who aren't Catholics, enjoy it just as much as Irish Catholics do?

Writing Exercise

Imagine that you are Nora, Jackie's older sister. Retell, from *her* point of view, that little episode involving the bread-knife.

Here is Jackie's version:

> When Mother was at work and my grandmother made the dinner I wouldn't touch it. Nora once tried to make me, but I hid under the table from her and took the bread-knife with me for protection. Nora let on to be very indignant (she wasn't, of course, but she knew Mother saw through her, so she sided with Gran) and came after me. I lashed out at her with the bread-knife, and after that she left me alone. I stayed there till Mother came in from work and made my dinner, but when Father came in later Nora said in a shocked voice: "Oh, Dadda, do you know what Jackie did at dinnertime?" Then, of course, it all came out; Father gave me a flaking; Mother interfered, and for days after that he didn't speak to me and Mother barely spoke to Nora. And all because of that old woman! God knows, I was heart-scalded.

As you write, it may help to think of your mini-story along these lines:

1. The Beginning: Nora describes the lovely dinner Gran prepared. This should lead into . . .

2. The Conflict: Jackie refuses to eat his supper. Now build up to . . .

3. The Climax: Jackie threatens Nora with the bread-knife from under the table. And, finally . . .

4. The Winding Down: Their parents get home from work.

Remember: You are presenting *Nora's* side of things.

Unit 2   Plot

To Build a Fire
BY JACK LONDON

About the Illustration

What is happening in this picture? Point out some details in the drawing to support your response.

Here are some questions to help you think:

☐ In what kind of a place is this scene set?

☐ What is the man doing?

☐ How do you think the man feels? What makes you think that?

☐ How would you describe the feeling of this entire scene? Is it cheerful? sad? tense? frightening? What details do you think give the scene that feeling?

Unit 2

Introduction   What the Story Is About/What the Lesson Is About

Story   To Build a Fire

Lesson   Plot

Activities   Comprehension Questions/Discussion Guides/Writing Exercise

Introduction

What the Story Is About

The story takes place near the Alaskan border, in Canada's Yukon Territory. It is winter, around the year 1898. For several years, ever since the discovery of gold in this wilderness not far from the Arctic Circle, adventurers have been rushing north to seek their fortunes. These men from the south were called *cheechakos* (chē chä′ kōs), which was the Chinook Indian word for *newcomer*.

Because they were newcomers to this wild country, the cheechakos were not used to its ways and its weather. They could not imagine how cold it could become in winter. And they found it hard to believe that such beautiful country could be so dangerous to travel in.

The newcomer that Jack London tells about in "To Build a Fire" has ventured out alone in the coldest part of the winter. The sun has not shone above the horizon for many days. Daylight is no more than a gray gloom. When we meet the *cheechako*, he is heading for a mining camp, to join his friends. He is traveling with a dog and has taken a roundabout route to camp, in order to check out the bends and turns of the Yukon River. The men are planning to cut timber in the spring and float the logs down the river. It is extremely cold, but the man knows that camp is only a few hours away, and he is sure he will have no trouble getting there.

He has heard stories about the bitter cold, and he has been warned of its dangers by some of the old-timers. But he laughs at the stories and only half believes the warnings. He is strong, clever in the wilderness, for a newcomer, and he is confident of his ability to survive. But, being new to the land, he doesn't understand the fierce treachery of the northern wilderness. His journey becomes a life and death struggle with the forces of nature.

"To Build a Fire" is probably Jack London's finest short story. It is just the kind of story he wrote best, in which a man and a half-wild dog engage in a bitter contest with the forces of the wilderness. From beginning to end, you will find yourself shivering from the bitter cold and the spine-tingling suspense. And when you have finished reading, you will know that you have read a story that is impossible to forget.

Jack London was an adventurer, a self-taught writer and a natural yarn spinner. When he was twenty-one, he went north to seek his fortune in the gold fields of Alaska and the Yukon. He returned a year later sick and penniless but with a head full of stories that were to make him famous. After reading "To Build a Fire," you may want to read one of Jack London's exciting novels: *The Call of the Wild, White Fang* and *The Sea-Wolf*.

If you want to know more about Jack London's life, one of the best-known biographies is *Sailor on Horseback* by Irving Stone.

What the Lesson Is About

The lesson that follows the story is about plot—how an author plans a story so that it moves along well and holds your interest.

You have probably noticed that as you read a story you move from one scene of action to another. This is the movement of the plot. Each action causes something new to happen, which keeps the story going in an orderly way. It is the plot that keeps you reading a story from beginning to end.

The following questions will help you to focus on elements of the plot in Jack London's story "To Build a Fire." Read the story carefully and try to answer these questions as you go along:

1   At the beginning of the story, what do you find out about the weather that could give the man trouble later on?

2   The author tells about bubbling springs of water that are hidden under the snow. How do these springs contribute to the battle, or conflict, between the man and the Arctic wilderness?

3   The man accidentally falls into a hidden spring. Why is this event a turning point in the story?

4 Near the end of the story, the man is seized by fear and panic. This is a high point in the action of the story. After this, what is said in the story that tells you that the action is starting to calm down?

To Build a Fire

Jack London

Day had broken cold and gray, exceedingly cold and gray, when the man turned aside from the main Yukon trail and climbed the high earth-bank, where a dim and little-traveled trail led eastward through the fat spruce timberland. It was a steep bank, and he paused for breath at the top, excusing the act to himself by looking at his watch. It was nine o'clock. There was no sun nor hint of sun, though there was not a cloud in the sky. It was a clear day, and yet there seemed an intangible pall over the face of things, a subtle gloom that made the day dark, and that was due to the absence of sun. This fact did not worry the man. He was used to the lack of sun. It had been days since he had seen the sun, and he knew that a few more days must pass before that cheerful orb, due south, would just peep above the skyline and dip immediately from view.

The man flung a look back along the way he had come. The Yukon lay a mile wide and hidden under three feet of ice. On top of this ice were as many feet of snow. It was all pure white, rolling in gentle undulations where the ice-jams of the freeze-up had formed. North and south, as far as his eye could see, it was unbroken white, save for a dark hair-line that curved and twisted from around the spruce-covered island to the south, and that curved and twisted away into the north, where it disappeared behind another spruce-covered island. This dark hair-line was the trail—the main trail—that led south five hundred miles to the Chilcoot Pass, Dyea, and salt water; and that led north seventy miles to Dawson, and still on to the north a thousand miles to Nulato, and finally to St. Michael on Bering Sea, a thousand miles and half a thousand more.

But all this—the mysterious, far-reaching hair-line trail,

the absence of sun from the sky, the tremendous cold, and the strangeness and weirdness of it all—made no impression on the man. It was not because he was long used to it. He was a newcomer in the land, a *Cheechako*, and this was his first winter. The trouble with him was that he was without imagination. He was quick and alert in the things of life, but only in the things, and not in the significances. Fifty degrees below zero meant eighty-odd degrees of frost. Such fact impressed him as being cold and uncomfortable, and that was all. It did not lead him to meditate upon his frailty as a creature of temperature, and upon man's frailty in general, able only to live within certain narrow limits of heat and cold; and from there on it did not lead him to the conjectural field of immortality and man's place in the universe. Fifty degrees below zero stood for a bite of frost that hurt and that must be guarded against by the use of mittens, ear-flaps, warm moccasins, and thick socks. Fifty degrees below zero was to him just precisely fifty degrees below zero. That there should be anything more to it than that was a thought that never entered his head.

As he turned to go on, he spat speculatively. There was a sharp, explosive crackle that startled him. He spat again. And again, in the air, before it could fall to the snow, the spittle crackled. He knew that at fifty below spittle crackled on the snow, but this spittle had crackled in the air. Undoubtedly it was colder than fifty below—how much colder he did not know. But the temperature did not matter. He was bound for the old claim on the left fork of Henderson Creek, where the boys were already. They had come over across the divide from the Indian Creek country, while he had come the round-about way to take a look at the possibilities of getting out logs in the spring from the islands in the Yukon. He would be in to camp by six o'clock; a bit after dark, it was true, but the boys would be there, a fire would be going, and a hot supper would be ready. As for lunch, he pressed his hand against the protruding bundle under his jacket. It was also under his shirt, wrapped up in a handkerchief and lying against the naked skin. It was the only way to keep the biscuits from freezing. He smiled agreeably to himself as he thought of those biscuits, each cut open and sopped in bacon grease, and each enclosing a generous slice of fried bacon.

He plunged in among the big spruce trees. The trail was faint. A foot of snow had fallen since the last sled had passed over, and he was glad he was without a sled, traveling light. In fact, he carried nothing but the lunch wrapped in the handkerchief. He was surprised, however, at the cold. It certainly was cold, he concluded, as he rubbed his numb nose and cheek-bones with his mittened hand. He was a warm-whiskered man, but the hair on his face did not protect the high cheek-bones and the eager nose that thrust itself aggressively into the frosty air.

At the man's heels trotted a dog, a big native husky, the proper wolf-dog, gray-coated and without any visible or temperamental difference from its brother, the wild wolf. The animal was depressed by the tremendous cold. It knew that it was no time for traveling. Its instinct told it a truer tale than was told to the man by the man's judgment. In reality, it was not merely colder than fifty below zero; it was colder than sixty below, than seventy below. It was seventy-five below zero. Since the freezing point is thirty-two above zero, it meant that one hundred and seven degrees of frost obtained. The dog did not know anything about ther-mometers. Possibly in its brain there was no sharp con-sciousness of a condition of very cold such as was in the man's brain. But the brute had its instinct. It experienced a vague but menacing apprehension that subdued it and made it slink along at the man's heels, and that made it question eagerly every unwonted movement of the man as if expecting him to go into camp or to seek shelter somewhere and build a fire. The dog had learned fire, and it wanted fire, or else to burrow under the snow and cuddle its warmth away from the air.

The frozen moisture of its breathing had settled on its fur

in a fine powder of frost, and especially were its jowls, muzzle, and eyelashes whitened by its crystalled breath. The man's red beard and mustache were likewise frosted, but more solidly, the deposit taking the form of ice and increasing with every warm, moist breath he exhaled. Also, the man was chewing tobacco, and the muzzle of ice held his lips so rigidly that he was unable to clear his chin when he expelled the juice. The result was that a crystal beard of the color and solidity of amber was increasing its length on his chin. If he fell down it would shatter itself, like glass, into brittle fragments. But he did not mind the appendage. It was the penalty all tobacco-chewers paid in that country, and he had been out before in two cold snaps. They had not been so cold as this, he knew, but by the spirit thermometer at Sixty Mile he knew they had been registered at fifty below and at fifty-five.

He held on through the level stretch of woods for several miles, crossed a wide flat of nigger-heads, and dropped down a bank to the frozen bed of a small stream. This was Henderson Creek, and he knew he was ten miles from the forks. He looked at his watch. It was ten o'clock. He was making four miles an hour, and he calculated that he would arrive at the forks at half-past twelve. He decided to celebrate that event by eating his lunch there.

The dog dropped in again at his heels, with a tail drooping discouragement, as the man swung along the creek-bed. The furrow of the old sled-trail was plainly visible, but a dozen inches of snow covered the marks of the last runners. In a month no man had come up or down that silent creek. The man held steadily on. He was not much given to thinking, and just then particularly he had nothing to think about save that he would eat lunch at the forks and that at six o'clock he would be in camp with the boys. There was nobody to talk to; and, had there been, speech would have been impossible because of the ice-muzzle on his mouth. So he continued monotonously to chew tobacco and to increase the length of his amber beard.

Once in a while the thought reiterated itself that it was very cold and that he had never experienced such cold. As he walked along he rubbed his cheek-bones and nose with the back of his mittened hand. He did this automatically, now and again changing hands. But rub as he would, the instant he stopped his cheek-bones went numb, and the following instant the end of his nose went numb. He was sure to frost his cheeks; he knew that, and experienced a pang of regret that he had not devised a nose-strap of the sort Bud wore in cold snaps. Such a strap passed across the cheeks, as well, and saved them. But it didn't matter much, after all. What were frosted cheeks? A bit painful, that was all; they were never serious.

Empty as the man's mind was of thoughts, he was keenly observant, and he noticed the changes in the creek, the curves and bends and timber-jams, and always he sharply noted where he placed his feet. Once, coming around a bend, he shied abruptly, like a startled horse, curved away from the place where he had been walking, and retreated several paces back along the trail. The creek he knew was frozen clear to the bottom,—no creek could contain water in that arctic winter,—but he knew also that there were springs that bubbled out from the hillsides and ran along under the snow and on top the ice of the creek. He knew that the coldest snaps never froze these springs, and he knew likewise their danger. They were traps. They hid pools of water under the snow that might be three inches deep, or three feet. Sometimes a skin of ice half an inch thick covered them, and in turn was covered by the snow. Sometimes there were alternate layers of water and ice-skin, so that when one broke through he kept on breaking through for a while, sometimes wetting himself to the waist.

That was why he had shied in such panic. He had felt the give under his feet and heard the crackle of a snow-hidden ice-skin. And to get his feet wet in such a temperature meant trouble and danger. At the very least it meant delay, for he would be forced to stop and build a fire, and under its protection to bare his feet while he dried his socks and moccasins. He stood and studied the creek-bed and its banks, and decided that the flow of water came from the right. He reflected a while, rubbing his nose and cheeks, then skirted to the left, stepping gingerly and testing the footing for each step. Once clear of the danger, he took a fresh chew of tobacco and swung along at his four-mile gait.

In the course of the next two hours he came upon several similar traps. Usually the snow above the hidden pools had a sunken, candied appearance that advertised the danger. Once again, however, he had a close call; and once, suspecting danger, he compelled the dog to go on in front. The dog did not want to go. It hung back until the man shoved it forward, and then it went quickly across the white, unbroken surface. Suddenly it broke through, floundered to one side, and got away to firmer footing. It had wet its forefeet and legs, and almost immediately the water that clung to it turned to ice. It made quick efforts to lick the ice off its legs, then dropped down in the snow and began to bite out the ice that had formed between the toes. This was a matter of instinct. To permit the ice to remain would mean sore feet. It did not know this, it merely obeyed the mysterious prompting that arose from the deep crypts of its being. But the man knew, having achieved a judgment on the subject, and he removed the mitten from his right hand and helped tear out the ice-particles. He did not expose his fingers more than a minute, and was astonished at the swift numbness that smote them. It certainly was cold. He pulled on the mitten hastily, and beat the hand savagely across his chest.

At twelve o'clock the day was at its brightest. Yet the sun was too far south on its winter journey to clear the horizon. The bulge of the earth intervened between it and Henderson Creek, where the man walked under a clear sky at noon and cast no shadow. At half-past twelve, to the minute, he arrived at the forks of the creek. He was pleased at the speed

To Build a Fire

he had made. If he kept it up, he would certainly be with the boys by six. He unbuttoned his jacket and shirt and drew forth his lunch. The action consumed no more than a quarter of a minute, yet in that brief moment the numbness laid hold of the exposed fingers. He did not put the mitten on, but, instead struck the fingers a dozen sharp smashes against his leg. Then he sat down on a snow-covered log to eat. The sting that followed upon the striking of his fingers against his leg ceased so quickly that he was startled. He had had no chance to take a bite of biscuit. He struck the fingers repeatedly and returned them to the mitten, baring the other hand for the purpose of eating. He tried to take a mouthful, but the ice-muzzle prevented. He had forgotten to build a fire and thaw out. He chuckled at his foolishness, and as he chuckled he noted the numbness creeping into the exposed fingers. Also, he noted that the stinging which had first come to his toes when he sat down was already passing away. He wondered whether the toes were warm or numb. He moved them inside the moccasins and decided that they were numb.

He pulled the mitten on hurriedly and stood up. He was a bit frightened. He stamped up and down until the stinging returned into the feet. It certainly was cold, was his thought. That man from Sulphur Creek had spoken the truth when telling how cold it sometimes got in the country. And he had laughed at him at the time! That showed one must not be too sure of things. There was no mistake about it, it *was* cold. He strode up and down, stamping his feet and threshing his arms, until reassured by the returning warmth. Then he got out matches and proceeded to make a fire. From the undergrowth, where high water of the previous spring had lodged a supply of seasoned twigs, he got his firewood. Working carefully from a small beginning, he soon had a roaring fire, over which he thawed the ice from his face and in the protection of which he ate his biscuits. For the moment the cold of space was outwitted. The dog took satisfaction in the fire, stretching out close enough for warmth and far enough away to escape being singed.

When the man had finished, he filled his pipe and took his comfortable time over a smoke. Then he pulled on his mittens, settled the earflaps of his cap firmly about his ears, and took the creek trail up the left fork. The dog was disappointed and yearned back toward the fire. This man did not know cold. Possibly all the generations of his ancestry had been ignorant of cold, of real cold, of cold one hundred and seven degrees below freezing point. But the dog knew; all its ancestry knew, and it had inherited the knowledge. And it knew that it was not good to walk abroad in such fearful cold. It was the time to lie snug in a hole in the snow and wait for a curtain of cloud to be drawn across the face of outer space whence this cold came. On the other hand, there was no keen intimacy between the dog and the man. The one was the toil-slave of the other, and the only caresses it had ever received were the caresses of the whip-lash and of harsh and menacing throat-sounds that threatened the whiplash. So the dog made no effort to communicate its apprehension to the man. It was not concerned in the welfare of the man; it was for its own sake that it yearned back toward the fire. But the man whistled, and spoke to it with the sound of whiplashes, and the dog swung in at the man's heel and followed after.

The man took a chew of tobacco and proceeded to start a new amber beard. Also, his moist breath quickly powdered with white his mustache, eyebrows, and lashes. There did not seem to be so many springs on the left fork of the Henderson, and for half an hour the man saw no signs of any. And then it happened. At a place where there were no signs, where the soft, unbroken snow seemed to advertise solidity beneath, the man broke through. It was not deep. He wet himself halfway to the knees before he floundered out to the firm crust.

He was angry, and cursed his luck aloud. He had hoped to

To Build a Fire

get into camp with the boys at six o'clock, and this would delay him an hour, for he would have to build a fire and dry out his foot-gear. This was imperative at that low temperature—he knew that much; and he turned aside to the bank, which he climbed. On top, tangled in the underbrush about the trunks of several small spruce trees, was a high-water deposit of dry firewood—sticks and twigs, principally, but also larger portions of seasoned branches and fine, dry, last-year's grasses. He threw down several large pieces on top of the snow. This served for a foundation and prevented the young flame from drowning itself in the snow it otherwise would melt. The flame he got by touching a match to a small shred of birch bark that he took from his pocket. This burned even more readily than paper. Placing it on the foundation, he fed the young flame with wisps of dry grass and with the tiniest dry twigs.

He worked slowly and carefully, keenly aware of his danger. Gradually, as the flame grew stronger, he increased the size of the twigs with which he fed it. He squatted in the snow, pulling the twigs out from their entanglement in the brush and feeding directly to the flame. He knew there must be no failure. When it is seventy-five below zero, a man must not fail in his first attempt to build a fire—that is, if his feet are wet. If his feet are dry, and he fails, he can run along the trail for half a mile and restore his circulation. But the circulation of wet and freezing feet cannot be restored by running when it is seventy-five below. No matter how fast he runs, the wet feet will freeze the harder.

All this the man knew. The old-timer on Sulphur Creek had told him about it the previous fall, and now he was appreciating the advice. Already all sensation had gone out of his feet. To build the fire he had been forced to remove his mittens, and the fingers had quickly gone numb. His pace of four miles an hour had kept his heart pumping blood to the surface of his body and to all the extremities. But the instant he stopped, the action of the pump eased down. The cold of space smote the unprotected tip of the planet, and he, being on that unprotected tip, received the full force of the blow. The blood of his body recoiled before it. The blood was alive, like the dog, and like the dog it wanted to hide away and cover itself up from the fearful cold. So long as he walked four miles an hour, he pumped that blood, will-nilly, to the surface; but now it ebbed away and sank down into the recesses of his body. The extremities were the first to feel its absence. His wet feet froze the faster, and his exposed fingers numbed the faster, though they had not yet begun to freeze. Nose and cheeks were already freezing, while the skin of all his body chilled as it lost its blood.

But he was safe. Toes and nose and cheeks would be only touched by the frost, for the fire was beginning to burn with strength. He was feeding it with twigs the size of his finger. In another minute he would be able to feed it with branches the size of his wrist, and then he could remove his wet foot-gear, and, while it dried, he could keep his naked feet warm by the fire, rubbing them at first, of course, with snow. The fire was a success. He was safe. He remembered the advice of the old-timer on Sulphur Creek, and smiled. The old-timer had been very serious in laying down the law that no man must travel alone in the Klondike after fifty below. Well, here he was; he had had the accident; he was alone; and he had saved himself. Those old-timers were rather womanish, some of them, he thought. All a man had to do was to keep his head; and he was all right. Any man who was a man could travel alone. But it was surprising, the rapidity with which his cheeks and nose were freezing. And he had not thought his fingers could go lifeless in so short a time. Lifeless they were, for he could scarcely make them move together to grip a twig, and they seemed remote from his body and from him. When he touched a twig, he had to look and see whether or not he had hold of it. The wires were pretty well down between him and his finger-ends.

All of which counted for little. There was the fire,

snapping and crackling and promising life with every dancing flame. He started to untie his moccasins. They were coated with ice; the thick German socks were like sheaths of iron halfway to the knees; and the moccasin strings were like rods of steel all twisted and knotted as by some conflagration. For a moment he tugged with his numb fingers, then, realizing the folly of it, he drew his sheath-knife.

But before he could cut the strings, it happened. It was his own fault or, rather, his mistake. He should not have built the fire under the spruce tree. He should have built it in the open. But it had been easier to pull the twigs from the brush and drop them directly on the fire. Now the tree under which he had done this carried a weight of snow on its boughs. No wind had blown for weeks, and each bough was fully freighted. Each time he had pulled a twig he had communicated a slight agitation to the tree—an imperceptible agitation, so far as he was concerned, but an agitation sufficient to bring about the disaster. High up in the tree one bough capsized its load of snow. This fell on the boughs beneath, capsizing them. This process continued, spreading out and involving the whole tree. It grew like an avalanche, and it descended without warning upon the man and the fire, and the fire was blotted out! Where it had burned was a mantle of fresh and disordered snow.

The man was shocked. It was as though he had just heard his own sentence of death. For a moment he sat and stared at the spot where the fire had been. Then he grew very calm. Perhaps the old-timer on Sulphur Creek was right. If he had only had a trail-mate he would have been in no danger now. The trail-mate could have built the fire. Well, it was up to him to build the fire over again, and this second time there must be no failure. Even if he succeeded, he would most likely lose some toes. His feet must be badly frozen by now, and there would be some time before the second fire was ready.

Such were his thoughts, but he did not sit and think them. He was busy all the time they were passing through his mind. He made a new foundation for a fire, this time in the open, where no treacherous tree could blot it out. Next, he gathered dry grasses and tiny twigs from the high-water flotsam. He could not bring his fingers together to pull them out, but he was able to gather them by the handful. In this way he got many rotten twigs and bits of green moss that were undesirable, but it was the best he could do. He worked methodically, even collecting an armful of the larger branches to be used later when the fire gathered strength. And all the while the dog sat and watched him, a certain yearning wistfulness in its eyes, for it looked upon him as the fire-provider, and the fire was slow in coming.

When all was ready, the man reached in his pocket for a second piece of birch bark. He knew the bark was there, and, though he could not feel it with his fingers, he could hear its crisp rustling as he fumbled for it. Try as he would, he could not clutch hold of it. And all the time, in his consciousness, was the knowledge that each instant his feet were freezing. This thought tended to put him in a panic, but he fought against it and kept calm. He pulled on his mittens with his teeth, and threshed his arms back and forth, beating his hands with all his might against his sides. He did this sitting down, and he stood up to do it; and all the while the dog sat in the snow, its wolf-brush of a tail curled around warmly over its forefeet, its sharp wolf-ears pricked forward intently as it watched the man. And the man, as he beat and threshed with his arms and hands, felt a great surge of envy as he regarded the creature that was warm and secure in its natural covering.

After a time he was aware of the first far-away signals of sensation in his beaten fingers. The faint tingling grew stronger till it evolved into a stinging ache that was excruciating, but which the man hailed with satisfaction. He stripped the mitten from his right hand and fetched forth the birch bark. The exposed fingers were quickly going numb again. Next he brought out his bunch of sulphur matches. But the tremendous cold had already driven the life out of his fingers. In his effort to separate one match from the others, the whole bunch fell in the snow. He tried to pick it out of the snow, but failed. The dead fingers could neither touch nor clutch. He was very careful. He drove the thought of his freezing feet, and nose, and cheeks, out of his mind, devoting his whole soul to the matches. He watched, using the sense of vision in place of touch, and when he saw his fingers on each side the bunch, he closed them—that is, he willed to close them, for the wires were down, and the fingers did not obey. He pulled the mitten on the right hand, and beat it fiercely against his knee. Then, with both mittened hands, he scooped the bunch of matches, along with much snow, into his lap. Yet he was no better off.

After some manipulation he managed to get the bunch between the heels of his mittened hands. In this fashion he carried it to his mouth. The ice crackled and snapped when by a violent effort he opened his mouth. He drew the lower jaw in, curled the upper lip out of the way, and scraped the bunch with his upper teeth in order to separate a match. He succeeded in getting one, which he dropped on his lap. He was no better off. He could not pick it up. Then he devised a way. He picked it up in his teeth and scratched it on his leg. Twenty times he scratched before he succeeded in lighting it. As it flamed he held it with his teeth to the birch bark. But the burning brimstone went up his nostrils and into his lungs, causing him to cough spasmodically. The match fell into the snow and went out.

The old-timer on Sulphur Creek was right, he thought in the moment of controlled despair that ensued: after fifty below, a man should travel with a partner. He beat his hands, but failed in exciting any sensation. Suddenly he bared both hands, removing the mittens with his teeth. He caught the whole bunch between the heels of his hands. His arm-muscles not being frozen enabled him to press the hand-heels tightly against the matches. Then he scratched the bunch along his leg. It flared into flame, seventy sulphur matches at once! There was no wind to blow them out. He kept his head to one side to escape the strangling fumes, and held the blazing bunch to the birch bark. As he so held it, he became aware of sensation in his hand. His flesh was burning. He could smell it. Deep down below the surface he could feel it. The sensation developed into pain that grew acute. And still he endured it, holding the flame of the matches clumsily to the bark that would not light readily because his own burning hands were in the way, absorbing most of the flame.

At last, when he could endure no more, he jerked his hands apart. The blazing matches fell sizzling into the snow, but the birch bark was alight. He began laying dry grasses and the tiniest twigs on the flame. He could not pick and choose, for he had to lift the fuel between the heels of his hands. Small pieces of rotten wood and green moss clung to the twigs, and he bit them off as well as he could with his teeth. He cherished the flame carefully and awkwardly. It meant life, and it must not perish. The withdrawal of blood from the surface of his body now made him begin to shiver, and he grew more awkward. A large piece of green moss fell squarely on the little fire. He tried to poke it out with his fingers, but his shivering frame made him poke too far, and he disrupted the nucleus of the little fire, the burning grasses and tiny twigs separating and scattering. He tried to poke them together again, but in spite of the tenseness of the effort, his shivering got away with him, and the twigs were hopelessly scattered. Each twig gushed a puff of smoke and went out. The fire-provider had failed. As he looked apathetically about him, his eyes chanced on the dog, sitting across the ruins of the fire from him, in the snow, making restless, hunching movements, slightly lifting one forefoot and then the other, shifting its weight back and forth on them with wistful eagerness.

To Build a Fire

The sight of the dog put a wild idea into his head. He remembered the tale of the man, caught in a blizzard, who killed a steer and crawled inside the carcass, and so was saved. He would kill the dog and bury his hands in the warm body until the numbness went out of them. Then he could build another fire. He spoke to the dog, calling it to him; but in his voice was a strange note of fear that frightened the animal, who had never known the man to speak in such way before. Something was the matter, and its suspicious nature sensed danger—it knew not what danger, but somewhere, somehow, in its brain arose an apprehension of the man. It flattened its ears down at the sound of the man's voice, and its restless, hunching movements and the liftings and shiftings of its forefeet became more pronounced; but it would not come to the man. He got on his hands and knees and crawled toward the dog. This unusual posture again excited suspicion, and the animal sidled mincingly away.

The man sat up in the snow for a moment and struggled for calmness. Then he pulled on his mittens, by means of his teeth, and got upon his feet. He glanced down at first in order to assure himself that he was really standing up, for the absence of sensation in his feet left him unrelated to the earth. His erect position in itself started to drive the webs of suspicion from the dog's mind; and when he spoke peremptorily, with the sound of whiplashes in his voice, the dog rendered its customary allegiance and came to him. As it came within reaching distance, the man lost his control. His arms flashed out to the dog, and he experienced genuine surprise when he discovered that his hands could not clutch, that there was neither bend nor feeling in the fingers. He had forgotten for the moment that they were frozen and that they were freezing more and more. All this happened quickly, and before the animal could get away, he encircled its body with his arms. He sat down in the snow, and in this fashion held the dog, while it snarled and whined and struggled.

But it was all he could do, hold its body encircled in his

arms and sit there. He realized that he could not kill the dog. There was no way to do it. With his helpless hands he could neither draw nor hold his sheath-knife nor throttle the animal. He released it, and it plunged wildly away, with tail between its legs, and still snarling. It halted forty feet away and surveyed him curiously, with ears sharply pricked forward. The man looked down at his hands in order to locate them, and found them hanging on the ends of his arms. It struck him as curious that one should have to use his eyes in order to find out where his hands were. He began threshing his arms back and forth, beating the mittened hands against his sides. He did this for five minutes, violently, and his heart pumped enough blood up to the surface to put a stop to his shivering. But no sensation was aroused in the hands. He had an impression that they hung like weights on the ends of his arms, but when he tried to run the impression down, he could not find it.

A certain fear of death, dull and oppressive, came to him. This fear quickly became poignant as he realized that it was no longer a mere matter of freezing his fingers and toes, or of losing his hands and feet, but that it was a matter of life and death with the chances against him. This threw him into a panic, and he turned and ran up the creek-bed along the old, dim trail. The dog joined in behind and kept up with him. He ran blindly, without intention, in fear such as he had never known in his life. Slowly, as he plowed and floundered through the snow, he began to see things again,—the banks of the creeks, the old timber-jams, the leafless aspens, and the sky. The running made him feel better. He did not shiver. Maybe, if he ran on, his feet would thaw out; and, anyway, if he ran far enough, he would reach camp and the boys. Without doubt he would lose some fingers and toes and some of his face; but the boys would take care of him, and save the rest of him when he got there. And at the same time there was another thought in his mind that said he would never get to the camp and the boys; that it was too many miles

To Build a Fire

away, that the freezing had too great a start on him, and that he would soon be stiff and dead. This thought he kept in the background and refused to consider. Sometimes it pushed itself forward and demanded to be heard, but he thrust it back and strove to think of other things.

It struck him as curious that he could run at all on feet so frozen that he could not feel them when they struck the earth and took the weight of his body. He seemed to himself to skim along above the surface, and to have no connection with the earth. Somewhere he had once seen a winged Mercury, and he wondered if Mercury felt as he felt when skimming over the earth.

His theory of running until he reached camp and the boys had one flaw in it: he lacked the endurance. Several times he stumbled, and finally he tottered, crumpled up, and fell. When he tried to rise, he failed. He must sit and rest, he decided, and next time he would merely walk and keep on going. As he sat and regained his breath, he noted that he was feeling quite warm and comfortable. He was not shivering, and it even seemed that a warm glow had come to his chest and trunk. And yet, when he touched his nose or cheeks, there was no sensation. Running would not thaw them out. Nor would it thaw out his hands and feet. Then the thought came to him that the frozen portions of his body must be extending. He tried to keep this thought down, to forget it, to think of something else; he was aware of the panicky feeling that it caused, and he was afraid of the panic. But the thought asserted itself, and persisted, until it produced a vision of his body totally frozen. This was too much, and he made another wild run along the trail. Once he slowed down to a walk, but the thought of the freezing extending itself made him run again.

And all the time the dog ran with him, at his heels. When he fell down a second time, it curled its tail over its forefeet and sat in front of him, facing him, curiously eager and intent. The warmth and security of the animal angered him, and he cursed it till it flattened down its ears appeasingly. This time the shivering came more quickly upon the man. He was losing in his battle with the frost. It was creeping into his body from all sides. The thought of it drove him on, but he ran no more than a hundred feet, when he staggered and pitched headlong. It was his last panic. When he had recovered his breath and control, he sat up and entertained in his mind the conception of meeting death with dignity. However, the conception did not come to him in such terms. His idea of it was that he had been making a fool of himself, running around like a chicken with its head cut off—such was the simile that occurred to him. Well, he was bound to freeze anyway, and he might as well take it decently. With this newfound peace of mind came the first glimmerings of drowsiness. A good idea, he thought, to sleep off to death. It was like taking an anaesthetic. Freezing was not so bad as people thought. There were lots worse ways to die.

He pictured the boys finding his body next day. Suddenly he found himself with them, coming along the trail and looking for himself. And, still with them, he came around a turn in the trail and found himself lying in the snow. He did not belong with himself any more, for even then he was out of himself, standing with the boys and looking at himself in the snow. It certainly was cold, was his thought. When he got back to the States he could tell the folks what real cold was. He drifted on from this to a vision of the old-timer on Sulphur Creek. He could see him quite clearly, warm and comfortable, and smoking a pipe.

"You were right, old hoss; you were right," the man mumbled to the old-timer of Sulphur Creek.

Then the man drowsed off into what seemed to him the most comfortable and satisfying sleep he had ever known. The dog sat facing him and waiting. The brief day drew to a close in a long, slow twilight. There were no signs of a fire to be made, and, besides, never in the dog's experience had it known a man to sit like that in the snow and make no fire.

To Build a Fire

As the twilight drew on, its eager yearning for the fire mastered it, and with a great lifting and shifting of forefeet, it whined softly, then flattened its ears down in anticipation of being chidden by the man. But the man remained silent. Later, the dog whined loudly. And still later it crept close to the man and caught the scent of death. This made the animal bristle and back away. A little longer it delayed, howling under the stars that leaped and danced and shone brightly in the cold sky. Then it turned and trotted up the trail in the direction of the camp it knew, where were the other food-providers and fire-providers.

Plot

Think about the situation described in the following scene. It is one you have surely come across before in a number of stories and movies:

> The enemy is closing in on the fort. Surrounded and outnumbered, the gallant defenders have sent a messenger for help. If someone can blow up the bridge that spans the river, the enemy will be slowed down. Then, perhaps, help will arrive in time. Captain Braveheart volunteers for the dangerous job.

At this point you can't wait for the answers to a dozen questions that spring to mind. Can Captain Braveheart succeed? Will help arrive in time? What will happen next?

The built-in question "What will happen next?" is what keeps a story moving and keeps you interested in reading it. When your curiosity is aroused, when you must know what will happen, the author has got you hooked on the plot of the story. You are led from one problem to another and from one kind of action to another, from the beginning of the story to the end.

An author plans or *plots* a story so that one action leads to another. Problems or conflicts arise and must be solved: the fort is surrounded, or the bridge must be blown up, so a character in the story, Captain Braveheart, takes action to deal with the problem. But the action always creates a new problem. Perhaps Captain Braveheart is wounded. What will he do now?

Actions are related by cause and effect. A problem arises—this is a cause for action. The effect of the action causes a new problem. And so the story, the plot, goes from problem to action to a new problem and a new action.

If there are just a series of actions, there is no story: Paul went to the store, came home, watched TV and went to bed. The reason there is no story here is that there are no problems, no conflicts, that lead the story from one action to another.

But if Paul went to the store, witnessed a murder, watched TV to pretend he hadn't been out, and pretended to be asleep when a strange car pulled into the driveway, then you'd have a plot and a story.

Plot is the backbone or framework of a story. Some stories have stronger plots than others. But there must always be some sort of plot to hold a story together and take you from one end of it to the other.

In this lesson, we will look at four ways in which author Jack London develops the plot of "To Build a Fire":

1 The author uses exposition to prepare the reader for the conflicts and actions to come.

2 The author uses conflicts and complications to move the story along.

3 The conflicts and complications are used to lead the plot to a crisis and climax.

4 The author gives the plot a beginning, a middle and an end.

Before you can understand what is going on in a story, there are some things you have to know. You have to know who the characters are and a little bit about them. You have to know the setting of the story—where and when the story takes place. And you

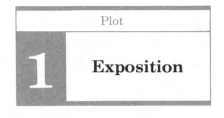

have to know what is going on at the point at which the story begins.

An author reveals, or exposes, all of these facts to the reader in what is called the *exposition*. In addition, the author gives hints in an exposition of problems to come. It is these hints that arouse your curiosity and make you want to see what the problems are and how they are dealt with. In other words, the author uses the exposition to tempt you and lead you into the story.

Jack London provides many important facts in the opening paragraphs of "To Build a Fire." He also hints broadly at the cause of trouble to come.

> Day had broken cold and gray, exceedingly cold and gray, when the man turned aside from the main Yukon trail and climbed the high earth-bank, where a dim and little-traveled trail led eastward through the fat spruce timberland. It was a steep bank, and he paused for breath at the top, excusing the act to himself by looking at his watch. It was nine o'clock. There was no sun nor hint of sun, though there was not a cloud in the sky. It was a clear day, and yet there seemed an intangible pall over the face of things, a subtle gloom that made the day dark, and that was due to the absence of sun. This fact did not worry the man. He was used to the lack of sun. It had been days since he had seen the sun, and he knew that a few more days must pass before that cheerful orb, due south, would just peep above the skyline and dip immediately from view.

The first thing you learn about in the exposition is the cold: "Day had broken cold and gray, exceedingly cold and gray. . . ." The author emphasizes that it is cold to be sure you pay attention to this fact. It is the main fact on which the story turns. It also provides the main conflict, the man's major problem.

The main character of the story is "the man." You never learn his name, but that is not important to the story. What is important is that he is a man, a kind of creature that doesn't get along very well in severe cold.

You find out that he is on a trail in the Yukon. The author goes on to explain that the sun has not shone that day, even though the sky has been clear. This fact emphasizes the cold once again. It is the middle of the Arctic winter, when the sun doesn't rise above the horizon.

The author says that there is a pall and gloom over the face of things. And such talk makes you feel in your bones that something is about to happen. You are instantly curious to know what will happen in such a place, and you read on.

Exercise A

Read the following passage and answer the questions about it using what you have learned in this part of the lesson.

> But all this—the mysterious, far-reaching hair-line trail, the absence of sun from the sky, the tremendous cold, and the strangeness and weirdness of it all—made no impression on the man. It was not because he was long used to it. He was a newcomer in the land, a *cheechako*, and this was his first winter. The trouble with him was that he was without imagination. He was quick and alert in the things of life, but only in the things, and not in the significances. Fifty degrees below zero meant eighty-odd degrees of frost. Such fact impressed him as being cold and uncomfortable, and that was all. It did not lead him to meditate upon his frailty as a creature of temperature, and upon man's frailty in general, able only to live within certain narrow limits of heat and cold . . . .

Put an *x* in the box beside the correct answer.

1. The author makes an important point about the strangeness of the country, the cold and the man. It is a hint of trouble to come. The point is that the cold and the strangeness of the country

   ☐ a. filled the man with fear.

   ☐ b. did not make any impression on the man.

To Build a Fire

☐ c. made the man aware that he was in danger.

☐ d. made the man alert and careful.

2. In this part of the exposition, the author tells the reader something about human beings and temperature, something that the man in the story does not think about. This basic fact that is revealed becomes the main problem for the man—it causes the major crisis of the story. Copy the sentence that tells what the problem is.

_____

_____

_____

_____

_____

Now check your answers using the Answer Key on page 452. Correct any wrong answers and review this part of the lesson if you don't understand why an answer was wrong.

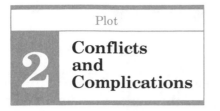

Plot

2 Conflicts and Complications

You probably know from your own experience that one problem can lead to another. Sometimes when you have a problem, what you do to solve the problem only complicates matters. Consider this situation: Myra has a conflict with a teacher in school. She decides to tell her parents about it. But this only complicates matters by creating a new problem: Myra's parents side with the teacher and ground Myra for a week. Feeling she has been treated unfairly, Myra decides that she will teach her parents a lesson. She sneaks out and goes joyriding in the family car. Finding the car gone and thinking it is stolen, Myra's mother calls the police. The police spot Myra in the car and signal her to stop. Myra speeds off in a panic, with the police in pursuit.

As you can see, Myra's small problem at school was complicated by a series of new conflicts and new actions. And the conflicts and actions were all related. Each led to another.

This is the way plots are built. In "To Build a Fire," a man is planning to earn some money by cutting timber and selling it. He wants to float the logs down the Yukon River in the spring. Figuring out how to do this is a small problem. He decides to check out the bends and curves in the river to see how much trouble he can expect with the job. But the man's action—traveling alone—puts him in conflict with the great forces of nature. The severe cold is a complication that calls for another action. The man's new actions cause still more conflicts.

In general, there are four kinds of conflict that a character in a story may face:

1. **Conflict with other characters.** At one point, the man is in conflict with the dog. He tries to kill it.

2. **Conflict with nature.** The man's fight against the cold is clearly a conflict with nature.

3. **Conflict within oneself.** This is often called inner conflict. The man in the story experiences an inner conflict when he feels fear and panic rising within him, but knows he must stay calm if he is to act to save himself.

4. **Conflict with society.** Someone who has been arrested

and is facing a court trial is in conflict with society. Someone who speaks out against, or protests, something that most people think is good is in conflict with society. There is no real conflict with society in this story.

If the man in the story had traveled quietly and safely to camp, there would have been no story. There may have been an interesting description of life in the Arctic wilderness, but no story. It is the conflicts and the actions that they trigger, together with the resulting complications, that make a story. The rule is: conflict creates plot.

Watch for the gradually rising conflict in this passage from the story:

> Empty as the man's mind was of thoughts, he was keenly observant, and he noticed the changes in the creek, the curves and bends and timber-jams, and always he sharply noted where he placed his feet. Once, coming around a bend, he shied abruptly, like a startled horse, curved away from the place where he had been walking, and retreated several paces back along the trail. The creek he knew was frozen clear to the bottom,—no creek could contain water in that arctic winter,—but he knew also that there were springs that bubbled out from the hillsides and ran along under the snow and on top the ice of the creek. He knew that the coldest snaps never froze these springs, and he knew likewise their danger. They were traps. They hid pools of water under the snow that might be three inches deep, or three feet . . . .
>
> That was why he had shied in such panic. He had felt the give under his feet and heard the crackle of a snow-hidden ice-skin.

What Jack London is describing here is the beginning of the man's conflict with nature. The Arctic wilderness has laid "traps" for the man. The traps are springs of water hidden under the snow. To avoid falling into these springs and getting wet, with the accompanying danger of freezing his feet, the man must be alert and observant. He treads across the snow with great care.

At this point in the story, several possible complications have been suggested. It is extremely cold, even for the Arctic. The man is traveling alone, which he shouldn't be doing. And there is danger from hidden springs of water. These things are controlling the man's actions and creating new problems as the story goes along. In this way, the plot is progressing from conflict to action to complication to new problems and new actions.

Exercise B

Read the following passage and answer the questions about it using what you have learned in this part of the lesson.

He unbuttoned his jacket and shirt and drew forth his lunch. The action consumed no more than a quarter of a minute, yet in that brief moment the numbness laid hold of the exposed fingers. He did not put the mitten on, but, instead struck the fingers a dozen sharp smashes against his leg. Then he sat down on a snow-covered log to eat. The sting that followed upon the striking of his fingers against his leg ceased so quickly that he was startled. He had had no chance to take a bite of biscuit. He struck the fingers repeatedly and returned them to the mitten, baring the other hand for the purpose of eating. He tried to take a mouthful, but the ice-muzzle prevented. He had forgotten to build a fire and thaw out. He chuckled at his foolishness, and as he chuckled he noted the numbness creeping into the exposed fingers. Also, he noted that the stinging which had first come to his toes when he sat down was already passing away. He wondered whether the toes were warm or numb. He moved them inside the moccasins and decided that they were numb.

Put an x in the box beside the correct answer.

1. What is the major complication that is told about in the passage?

☐ a. The man doesn't have enough to eat.

☐ b. There is no wood to build a fire.

☐ c. The man's mittens are not warm enough.

☐ d. The man's fingers and toes are freezing.

2. The man forgot to do something when he stopped for lunch. This mistake is causing new problems for him. What was the first thing he should have done when he stopped to eat?

_____

Now check your answers using the Answer Key on page 452. Correct any wrong answers and review this part of the lesson if you don't understand why an answer was wrong.

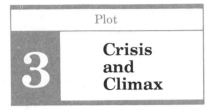

Plot

3 Crisis and Climax

In a tug of war, each team pulls and strains against the other. First one side and then the other seems to be winning, as the conflict continues. Finally, one team makes its greatest effort. All the team members strain, with all the strength and determination they have, against the force of the other team. This is the high point of the action for them. With this effort they will win or lose. This high point is the *climax* of the conflict.

The climax of an action is also a turning point. All the strength of the people, and all their emotional reserves, have been put into their effort. At this point, something has to give. They must either move toward victory or they must be defeated, because they have no more strength or energy for the conflict.

Such a turning point in a conflict is called a *crisis*. For instance, when news reporters speak of a crisis in Europe, they mean a turning point in some event; some sort of conflict that has been going on has reached a point at which an important change will occur.

In a story, as one conflict leads to another, the suspense grows. The emotions of both the characters in the story and of the reader mount to a high point. This is the climax of the story. The climax may occupy several chapters in a novel, or just a few paragraphs in a short story. Then an event, or a series of events, that can be seen as a turning point in the fortunes of the hero or heroine will take place. From that point on things will either improve or move toward some tragic or unhappy conclusion.

As you have seen, "To Build a Fire" tells of a conflict between a man and the forces of nature. The emotional excitement of the story begins to build from the moment you learn that it is seventy-five degrees below zero. Who can imagine such cold! And here is a man struggling against it. The conflict and the fearful excitement grow as the man makes one mistake after another. Each time he tries to build a fire there is hope that he will win the struggle. And each time he fails you catch your breath.

Finally, he makes his final and greatest effort to save himself. The emotions of both the man in the story and the reader are at their highest point. This is the climax of the story. At the end of his effort, when he fails to build a fire, the man gives in to the idea of death. This is the turning point, the crisis, of the story.

The climax of the story takes place over several paragraphs. One of these paragraphs follows.

To Build a Fire

Then the thought came to him that the frozen portions of his body must be extending. He tried to keep this thought down, to forget it, to think of something else; he was aware of the panicky feeling that it caused, and he was afraid of the panic. But the thought asserted itself, and persisted, until it produced a vision of his body totally frozen. This was too much, and he made another wild run along the trail. Once he slowed down to a walk, but the thought of the freezing extending itself made him run again.

The man's first shock (and the reader's, as well) came when he fell into the hidden spring. The man knew this was dangerous, but he did not think it was serious. Then his beautiful fire was smothered by falling snow. The struggle he underwent after that was more frightening, as he tried to start a fire with his frozen fingers.

Now the man is at the end of his rope, and he gives in to panic. This is the highest point of a climax that began some paragraphs before, at the point when the man finally realized that "it was a matter of life and death with the chances against him."

Exercise C

Read the following passage and answer the questions about it using what you have learned in this part of the lesson.

And all the time the dog ran with him, at his heels. When he fell down a second time, it curled its tail over its forefeet and sat in front of him, facing him, curiously eager and intent. The warmth and security of the animal angered him, and he cursed it till it flattened down its ears appeasingly. This time the shivering came more quickly upon the man. He was losing in his battle with the frost. It was creeping into his body from all sides. The thought of it drove him on, but he ran no more than a hundred feet, when he staggered and pitched headlong. It was his last panic. When he had recovered his breath and control, he sat up and entertained in his mind the conception of meeting death with dignity.

Put an *x* in the box beside the correct answer.

1. Since a crisis is a turning point, it is followed by an important change. How do the man's feelings change in this passage?

   ☐ a. He changes from fearing death to deciding to meet it with dignity.

   ☐ b. He changes from loving the dog to hating it.

   ☐ c. He changes from fear to confidence that he can survive.

   ☐ d. He changes from running to just sitting in the snow.

2. The man has been running in panic and fear. A short sentence near the end of the paragraph tells you that this is over now. Things have suddenly changed. Write the sentence here.

   _____

   _____

Now check your answers using the Answer Key on page 452. Correct any wrong answers and review this part of the lesson if you don't understand why an answer was wrong.

In ancient Greece, more than two thousand years ago, drama was the most important form of storytelling. At that time, the great philosopher Aristotle proposed some "rules" for writing plays. One thing that is important, he said, is that the story have a beginning, a middle and an end.

Plot

4 A Beginning, Middle and End

At first glance, this seems like pretty simple stuff for a great philosopher. Everything has a beginning and end, you might say. And somewhere in between there must be a middle.

Indeed, it does *seem* simple, until you try it. Think of some of the compositions you yourself have written. Did you find it easy to start writing? More writers fail because they cannot write beginnings than for any other reason. If you wanted to write about your vacation, for instance, where would you start? Would you begin with the packing, with the auto trip or with your arrival at the lake?

You would have the same questions and problems with what to put in the middle. If you were to try to include everything that happened on your vacation, you'd have the dullest story ever told. How do you pick and choose, then, among all the activities and events? And where do you stop? A story can't go on forever. But *how* to stop can be a problem. Many good stories fall flat at the end, leaving the reader dissatisfied and angry.

So you can see why a story must have a beginning, a middle and an end. But what Aristotle was really getting at was that it is important that the beginning, middle and end of a story work together. They must all be connected.

Let's see how Jack London handled these problems in "To Build a Fire."

The Beginning. You recall that there has to be an exposition at the beginning of a story. This provides the *who, what, when, where* and *why* of the story. But in the exposition the author tells you only what you need to know to get into the story. The only details he provides are those that are necessary in order for you to understand what is about to happen.

The author connects the beginning of a story to the middle by introducing in the beginning things that relate to the conflicts and actions that will take place in the middle.

> . . . the tremendous cold, and the strangeness and weird-
> ness of it all—made no impression on the man.

This information prepares you for the conflict between the man and
the cold that occupies the middle of the story.

> As he turned to go on, he spat speculatively. There was
> a sharp, explosive crackle that startled him.

Of all the things the author can tell you, why does he dwell on the
man spitting? It is to show just how cold it is, of course. And this leads
you to the middle of the story.

The Middle. Conflicts, complications and actions occupy the middle
of the story. And, as you have seen, these things lead you through the
story to the climax, or high point of interest and excitement.

Suppose the story had been written like this: At the beginning,
the man is out checking the bends and turns of a river. After telling
you how cold it is, the author describes plans for cutting and shipping
timber. Suddenly, the man falls in a spring and begins to freeze. The
trouble with this is that there is no connection between the beginning
and the middle. The conflicts don't develop, they are simply dropped
on you. A plot must *develop*. Conflicts and actions must grow out of
the beginning and then proceed to develop from one another.

The End. There is an old joke among writers that says the easiest
way to end a story is to skip a line and write THE END. This does the
trick, but it does leave a reader hanging.

Suppose Jack London had never told you whether the man lived or
died? Did he reach camp or not? Many good stories end just that way.
They leave readers to figure out their own endings. But this kind of
finish leaves most readers a bit uneasy. Some people even get angry
because they feel that an author has wasted their time by giving them
a story without an end.

Suppose London had not connected the end of the story to the
beginning and the middle—if when he was close to death, the man had
been rescued by a member of the Royal Canadian Mounted Police who
happened to be passing by? This would be worse than no ending at all!
While it's nice to have a happy ending, a sudden rescue in *this* story
would have nothing to do with all the conflict that has gone before.

There is usually one other thing that happens in an ending. In most stories, an author will bring the reader down gently from the high point of excitement—the climax. The problems of the story are solved or concluded in some way. This is called the *resolution* of the story. In a detective mystery, for example, this is the place where the author answers all the questions about how the crime was committed and "whodunit."

The following paragraph from "To Build a Fire" comes right after the climax of the story. How does it help bring you down from the climax?

> When he had recovered his breath and control, he sat up and entertained in his mind the conception of meeting death with dignity. However, the conception did not come to him in such terms. His idea of it was that he had been making a fool of himself, running around like a chicken with its head cut off—such was the simile that occurred to him. Well, he was bound to freeze anyway, and he might as well take it decently. With this newfound peace of mind came the first glimmerings of drowsiness. A good idea, he thought, to sleep off to death. It was like taking an anaesthetic. Freezing was not so bad as people thought.

The man has gone from wild panic to quiet control. This in itself relieves the tension. The conflict is over and the man accepts the fact that he has lost, "Well . . . he might as well take it decently . . . . Freezing was not so bad as people thought."

Notice how the ending is related to the middle of the story and to the beginning. The main conflict all along has been between the man and the cold. The action has led the man from what seemed a simple journey at first, to certain death on the trail.

With the conflict between the man and the cold resolved, the author turns to the smaller conflict between the man and the dog. This is resolved in the paragraph you will work with in Exercise D.

Exercise D

Read the following passage and answer the questions about it using what you have learned in this part of the lesson.

The brief day drew to a close in a long, slow twilight. There were no signs of a fire to be made, and, besides, never in the dog's experience had it known a man to sit like that in the snow and make no fire. As the twilight drew on, its eager yearning for the fire mastered it, and with a great lifting and shifting of forefeet, it whined softly, then flattened its ears down in anticipation of being chidden by the man. But the man remained silent. Later, the dog whined loudly. And still later it crept close to the man and caught the scent of death. . . . Then it turned and trotted up the trail in the direction of the camp it knew, where were the other food-providers and fire-providers.

Put an *x* in the box beside the correct answer.

1. The dog has also experienced many conflicts. How does the dog finally resolve its problems?

   ☐ a. The dog remains loyal to its master.

   ☐ b. The dog cries at the loss of its friend.

   ☐ c. The dog goes to find other people to provide for its needs.

   ☐ d. The dog runs away in fear.

2. There are many stories that tell about a day in someone's life. This is one of those stories. It begins with the words, "Day had broken. . . . " The paragraph you just read contains a sentence that tells the reader that the day, as well as the story, is coming to an end. Copy the sentence on the lines below.

   _____

   _____

Now check your answers using the Answer Key on page 452. Correct any wrong answers and review this part of the lesson if you don't understand why an answer was wrong. Now go on to do the Comprehension Questions.

To Build a Fire

Comprehension Questions

Answer these questions without looking back at the story. Choose the best answer to each question and put an *x* in the box beside it.

Recalling
Facts

1. Why was the day dark and gloomy?

   ☐ a. A storm was approaching.

   ☐ b. The sun did not rise above the horizon.

   ☐ c. It was snowing.

   ☐ d. It was late summer.

Making
Inferences

2. The author tells you how far the man is from the nearest town. This fact is important because it lets you know that the man is

   ☐ a. probably lonesome.

   ☐ b. lost.

   ☐ c. very frightened.

   ☐ d. in deep wilderness.

Understanding
Main Ideas

3. The most important point that the author makes about the man is that he

   ☐ a. didn't think enough about the cold.

   ☐ b. was an old hand in the Arctic cold.

   ☐ c. was safe enough as long as he had the dog for company.

   ☐ d. didn't really know where he was going.

Plot

99

4. How cold was it?

☐ a. It was more than seventy degrees below zero.

☐ b. It was about fifty degrees below zero.

☐ c. There were eighty degrees of frost.

☐ d. There was no way of telling how cold it was.

5. The man did not *meditate upon his frailty*. This means he did not

☐ a. fear the danger.

☐ b. think about his weakness.

☐ c. believe the warnings he was given.

☐ d. worry unnecessarily.

6. One reason the man was on the trail alone was that he had

☐ a. become lost.

☐ b. waited for good weather.

☐ c. crossed the mountains.

☐ d. gone a different way from his companions.

7. What did the dog know by instinct that the man did not know by using his judgment?

☐ a. It was too cold to be traveling.

☐ b. It was a longer trip than the man knew.

☐ c. It would soon be snowing very hard.

☐ d. It would be impossible to make a fire.

8. Once, coming around a bend, the man *shied abruptly*. This means that the man

☐ a. embarrassed himself.

☐ b. sprang over a fallen object.

☐ c. jumped back suddenly.

☐ d. almost fell down.

9. What are referred to as "traps" in the story?

☐ a. Snares set by hunters

☐ b. Heavy snow on the trees

☐ c. Pools of water under the snow

☐ d. The Arctic cold and ice

10. When the man stopped for lunch, he took off his mitten and drew his biscuits out from under his shirt. His fingers became numb almost at once. What was the man's mistake?

☐ a. He should have made a fire first.

☐ b. He should not have stopped for lunch.

☐ c. He should have waited for sunrise.

☐ d. He should have waited until he got back to camp.

11. The man built two successful fires. What happened after he built the second one?

☐ a. The dog wouldn't leave it.

☐ b. It was buried by falling snow.

☐ c. The man ate lunch and moved on.

☐ d. The man fell into a spring of water.

12. Why did the man have so much trouble trying to build a fire the third time?

☐ a. He fell into a panic.

☐ b. His matches got buried in the snow.

☐ c. He couldn't find the birch bark.

☐ d. His fingers had become numb.

13. "The match fell into the snow and went out . . . .
The old-timer . . . was right, he thought in the
moment of cold despair that *ensued*." *Ensued*
probably means

☐ a. broke forth.

☐ b. was heard.

☐ c. followed.

☐ d. rushed.

14. When the man tries to kill the dog in order to warm
his hands, you get the feeling that the man is

☐ a. becoming desperate.

☐ b. thinking clearly.

☐ c. getting even with the dog.

☐ d. being cruel and spiteful.

15. What is the most important thing that fire provides
in the Arctic wilderness?

☐ a. Food

☐ b. Warmth

☐ c. Courage

☐ d. Light

Now check your answers using the Answer Key on page 452. Make no mark for right answers. <u>Correct</u> any wrong answers you may have by putting a checkmark (✓) in the box next to the right answer. Count the number of questions you answered correctly and plot the total on the Comprehension Scores graph on page 462.

Next, look at the questions you answered incorrectly. What types of questions were they? Count the number you got wrong of each type and enter the numbers in the spaces below.

Recognizing Words in Context   _____

Recalling Facts   _____

Keeping Events in Order   _____

Making Inferences   _____

Understanding Main Ideas   _____

Now use these numbers to fill in the Comprehension Skills Profile on page 463.

Discussion Guides

The questions below will help you to think about the story and the lesson you have just read. If you don't discuss these questions in class, try to think about them or discuss them with your classmates.

Discussing Plot

1. The author often uses some device in a story to tie the plot together from beginning to end. It is sometimes called a "thread" that runs through the story. Cold and fire are used this way in "To Build a Fire." How are they threads that run through the story?

2. One kind of conflict is conflict between people. The dog in the story isn't a person, but it is a character. What kinds of conflict does the dog experience?

3. In a way, each new problem in a story brings a new turning point or crisis. How was falling in the water a crisis? What about the snow falling on the fire?

Discussing the Story

4. There is an old saying, "Fools rush in where angels fear to tread." Early in the story, Jack London says of the man, "He was without imagination." How are these two statements alike?

5. In many of his short stories and novels, Jack London points out that people are frail creatures. How is the man in the story frail?

6. In the story, the man dies and the dog lives. Does this mean the dog is smarter than the man? Or is there some other reason why the dog survives while the man does not?

Discussing the Author's Work

7. A good storyteller captures your interest at once. Review the first two paragraphs of the story. What do you find there that captures your interest?

8. Many of Jack London's stories end with someone's death. Is the man's death a good ending for this story? Would you have ended the story some other way? Explain your opinions.

To Build a Fire

9. How does Jack London use the old-timer from Sulphur Creek as a character in the story, even though the old-timer never appears on the scene?

Writing Exercise

1. Think of an idea for a story in which the characters are in conflict with nature. (There may, of course, be other kinds of conflict as well.) Here are some suggestions:

   • Two people on a hike become lost in the woods.

   • A man is trapped in his car by a sudden blizzard.

   • A skier, traveling alone, breaks an ankle.

   • Two people in a sailboat are caught in a storm.

2. Write a plot outline for your story by answering the following questions:

A. **Exposition**

   1. Who are the characters and what are they like?

   _____

   _____

   _____

   2. Where and when does the story take place?

   _____

   _____

3. What is going on as the story begins?

_____

_____

_____

B. **Conflict**

1. Make a list of two or three conflicts that the main characters will experience.

_____

_____

_____

2. Tell briefly how one conflict will lead to another.

_____

_____

_____

_____

_____

_____

C. **Climax and Ending**

1. Describe the conflict that will be the highest point of excitement in your story.

_____

_____

_____

To Build a Fire

_____

2. How will the story end?

_____

_____

_____

Unit 3   Character

Raymond's Run

BY TONI CADE BAMBARA

About the Illustration

What can you tell about the characters in this illustration? Point out some details in the drawing to support your response.

Here are some questions to help you think:

☐ What are the two girls doing? What is the boy doing?

☐ Why do you think there is a fence between the girls and the boy?

☐ What is special about the boy's appearance?

☐ How does the girl who is looking over at the boy seem to feel about him?

Unit 3

Introduction   What the Story Is About/What the Lesson Is About

Story   Raymond's Run

Lesson   Character

Activities   Comprehension Questions/Discussion Guides/Writing Exercise

Introduction

What the Story Is About

Hazel Elizabeth Deborah Parker, known as Squeaky, is a young girl growing up in New York City's district of Harlem. She is a runner and proud of it. "The big kids call me Mercury," she says, "because I'm the swiftest thing in the neighborhood."

It is Squeaky's job in the family to look after her brother Raymond when they are outdoors. Raymond is older and bigger than Squeaky, but he is mentally retarded. Because of his handicap, Raymond is often the butt of taunts from neighborhood kids. At least that used to be the case when his brother George was taking care of him. But now that Squeaky is in charge, things are different. If anybody has anything to say to Raymond, "they have to come by me," she says.

Squeaky will stand for no nonsense from anyone. And she has no patience for things she considers stupid, dishonest, phony or disloyal. She is both independent and feisty, that is short-tempered and quarrelsome. No one crosses her without hearing about it, and they had better be ready to fight if they push her too far.

You will undoubtedly admire Squeaky for her self-confidence, for the way she cares for Raymond, and for her fierce independence. But you may wonder if she isn't just a bit too proud of herself. Even her defense of Raymond seems to stem more from the desire to protect her own reputation than from concern for her brother.

The story builds toward a race that Squeaky is sure she will win. The race is the climax of the story, and it brings about a change in Squeaky. You will want to watch for this change. But if the story leads to a race that features Squeaky, why is the title of the story "Raymond's Run"? Try to settle this question in your mind after you have finished reading.

Toni Cade Bambara was born in New York City and attended Queens College there. Before turning to teaching and writing, Ms. Bambara studied drama and dancing in Italy, France and at the well-known Katherine Dunham Dance Studio in New York. She is now writer-in-residence at Spelman College in Atlanta.

After reading "Raymond's Run," you may want to read other stories by Toni Bambara, which are collected in a book titled *The Sea Birds Are Still Alive*. Or you may wish to read her novel *The Salt Eaters*, published by Random House, 1980.

What the Lesson Is About

The lesson following the reading selection is about character. People, as well as animals and other creatures, are the characters you find in stories. But the word *character* has another, more important meaning. Character is the sum total of a person—what that person is like. Character is how a person looks, acts and feels.

In order for a story to be believable, to have a true-to-life ring to it, the characters must be realistic and believable. The technique an author uses to breathe life into the make-believe characters of fiction is called *characterization*. The lesson will point out some of the ways an author accomplishes this very difficult task.

The questions below will help you to focus on character in "Raymond's Run." Read the story carefully and try to answer these questions as you go along:

1 Can you get to know Squeaky, Raymond and other people in the story from things Squeaky tells you?

2 What do you learn about the characters in the story from the way they talk to one another and from the way they behave toward one another?

3 The author tries to make you like Squeaky and dislike the other girls in the story. How does she do this?

4 How does the change that takes place in Squeaky at the end of the story help you to understand her better?

Raymond's Run

Toni Cade Bambara

I don't have much work to do around the house like some girls. My mother does that. And I don't have to earn my pocket money by hustling; George runs errands for the big boys and sells Christmas cards. And anything else that's got to get done, my father does. All I have to do in life is mind my brother Raymond, which is enough.

Sometimes I slip and say my little brother Raymond. But as any fool can see he's much bigger and he's older too. But a lot of people call him my little brother cause he needs looking after cause he's not quite right. And a lot of smart mouths got lots to say about that too, especially when George was minding him. But now, if anybody has anything to say to Raymond, anything to say about his big head, they have to come by me. And I don't play the dozens or believe in standing around with somebody in my face doing a lot of talking. I much rather just knock you down and take my chances even if I am a little girl with skinny arms and a squeaky voice, which is how I got the name Squeaky. And if things get too rough, I run. And as anybody can tell you, I'm the fastest thing on two feet.

There is no track meet that I don't win the first place medal. I use to win the twenty-yard dash when I was a little kid in kindergarten. Nowadays it's the fifty-yard dash. And tomorrow I'm subject to run the quarter-mile relay all by myself and come in first, second, and third. The big kids call me Mercury cause I'm the swiftest thing in the neighborhood. Everybody knows that—except two people who know better, my father and me.

He can beat me to Amsterdam Avenue with me having a two fire-hydrant headstart and him running with his hands in his pockets and whistling. But that's private information.

Cause can you imagine some thirty-five-year-old man stuffing himself into PAL shorts to race little kids? So as far as everyone's concerned, I'm the fastest and that goes for Gretchen, too, who has put out the tale that she is going to win the first place medal this year. Ridiculous. In the second place, she's got short legs. In the third place, she's got freckles. In the first place, no one can beat me and that's all there is to it.

I'm standing on the corner admiring the weather and about to take a stroll down Broadway so I can practice my breathing exercises, and I've got Raymond walking on the inside close to the buildings cause he's subject to fits of fantasy and starts thinking he's a circus performer and that the curb is a tightrope strung high in the air. And sometimes after a rain, he likes to step down off his tightrope right into the gutter and slosh around getting his shoes and cuffs wet. Then I get hit when I get home. Or sometimes if you don't watch him, he'll dash across traffic to the island in the middle of Broadway and give the pigeons a fit. Then I have to go behind him apologizing to all the old people sitting around trying to get some sun and getting all upset with the pigeons fluttering around them, scattering their newspapers and upsetting the waxpaper lunches in their laps. So I keep Raymond on the inside of me, and he plays like he's driving a stage coach which is O.K. by me so long as he doesn't run me over or interrupt my breathing exercises, which I have to do on account of I'm serious about my running and don't care who knows it.

Now some people like to act like things come easy to them, won't let on that they practice. Not me. I'll high prance down 34th Street like a rodeo pony to keep my knees strong even if it does get my mother uptight so that she walks ahead like she's not with me, don't know me, is all by herself on a shopping trip, and I am somebody else's crazy child.

Now you take Cynthia Procter for instance. She's just the opposite. If there's a test tomorrow, she'll say something like, "Oh I guess I'll play handball this afternoon and watch television tonight," just to let you know she ain't thinking about the test. Or like last week when she won the spelling bee for the millionth time, "A good thing you got 'receive,' Squeaky, cause I would have got it wrong. I completely forgot about the spelling bee." And she'll clutch the lace on her blouse like it was a narrow escape. Oh, brother.

But of course when I pass her house on my early morning trots around the block, she is practicing the scales on the piano over and over and over and over. Then in music class, she always lets herself get bumped around so she falls accidently on purpose onto the piano stool and is so surprised to find herself sitting there, and so decides just for fun to try out the ole keys and what do you know—Chopin's waltzes just spring out of her fingertips and she's the most surprised thing in the world. A regular prodigy. I could kill people like that.

I stay up all night studying the words for the spelling bee. And you can see me anytime of day practicing running. I never walk if I can trot and shame on Raymond if he can't keep up. But of course he does, cause if he hangs back someone's liable to walk up to him and get smart, or take his allowance from him, or ask him where he got that great big pumpkin head. People are so stupid sometimes.

So I'm strolling down Broadway breathing out and breathing in on counts of seven, which is my lucky number, and here comes Gretchen and her sidekicks—Mary Louise who used to be a friend of mine when she first moved to Harlem from Baltimore and got beat up by everybody till I took up for her on account of her mother and my mother used to sing in the same choir when they were young girls, but people ain't grateful, so now she hangs out with the new girl Gretchen and talks about me like a dog; and Rosie who is as fat as I am skinny and has a big mouth where Raymond is concerned and is too stupid to know that there is not a big deal of difference between herself and Raymond and that she can't afford to throw stones. So they are steady coming up Broadway and I see right away that it's going to be one of those Dodge City scenes cause the street ain't that big and they're close to the buildings just as we are. First I think I'll step into the candy store and look over the new comics and let them pass. But that's chicken and I've got a reputation to consider. So then I think I'll just walk straight on through them or over them if necessary. But as they get to me, they slow down. I'm ready to fight, cause like I said I don't feature a whole lot of chitchat, I much prefer to just knock you down right from the jump and save everybody a lotta precious time.

"You signing up for the May Day races?" smiles Mary Louise, only it's not a smile at all.

A dumb question like that doesn't deserve an answer. Besides, there's just me and Gretchen standing there really, so no use wasting my breath talking to shadows.

"I don't think you're going to win this time," says Rosie, trying to signify with her hands on her hips all salty, completely forgetting that I have whupped her behind many times for less salt than that.

"I always win cause I'm the best," I say straight at Gretchen who is, as far as I'm concerned, the only one talking in this ventriloquist-dummy routine.

Gretchen smiles but it's not a smile and I'm thinking that girls never really smile at each other because they don't know how and don't want to know how and there's probably no one to teach us how cause grown-up girls don't know either. Then they all look at Raymond who has just brought his mule team to a standstill. And they're about to see what trouble they can get into through him.

"What grade you in now, Raymond?"

"You got anything to say to my brother, you say it to me, Mary Louise Williams of Raggedy Town, Baltimore."

"What are you, his mother?" sasses Rosie.

"That's right, Fatso. And the next word out of anybody

and I'll be their mother too." So they just stand there and Gretchen shifts from one leg to the other and so do they. Then Gretchen puts her hands on her hips and is about to say something with her freckle-face self but doesn't. Then she walks around me looking me up and down but keeps walking up Broadway, and her sidekicks follow her. So me and Raymond smile at each other and he says, "Gidyap" to his team and I continue with my breathing exercises, strolling down Broadway toward the icey man on 145th with not a care in the world cause I am Miss Quicksilver herself.

I take my time getting to the park on May Day because the track meet is the last thing on the program. The biggest thing on the program is the May Pole dancing which I can do without, thank you, even if my mother thinks it's a shame I don't take part and act like a girl for a change. You'd think my mother'd be grateful not to have to make me a white organdy dress with a big satin sash and buy me new white baby-doll shoes that can't be taken out of the box till the big day. You'd think she'd be glad her daughter ain't out there prancing around a May Pole getting the new clothes all dirty and sweaty and trying to act like a fairy or a flower or whatever you're supposed to be when you should be trying to be yourself, whatever that is, which is, as far as I am concerned, a poor Black girl who really can't afford to buy shoes and a new dress you only wear once a lifetime cause it won't fit next year.

I was once a strawberry in a Hansel and Gretel pageant when I was in nursery school and didn't have no better sense than to dance on tiptoe with my arms in a circle over my head doing umbrella steps and being a perfect fool just so my mother and father could come dressed up and clap. You'd think they'd know better than to encourage that kind of nonsense. I am not a strawberry. I do not dance on my toes. I run. That is what I am all about. So I always come late to the May Day program, just in time to get my number pinned on and lay in the grass till they announce the fifty-yard dash.

I put Raymond in the little swings, which is a tight squeeze this year and will be impossible next year. Then I look around for Mr. Pearson who pins the numbers on. I'm really looking for Gretchen if you want to know the truth, but she's not around. The park is jam-packed. Parents in hats and corsages and breast-pocket handkerchiefs peeking up. Kids in white dresses and light blue suits. The parkees unfolding chairs and chasing the rowdy kids from Lenox as if they had no right to be there. The big guys with their caps on backwards, leaning against the fence swirling the basketballs on the tips of their fingers waiting for all these crazy people to clear out the park so they can play. Most of the kids in my class are carrying bass drums and glockenspiels and flutes. You'd think they'd put in a few bongos or something for real like that.

Then here comes Mr. Pearson with his clipboard and his cards and pencils and whistles and safety pins and fifty million other things he's always dropping all over the place with his clumsy self. He sticks out in a crowd cause he's on stilts. We used to call him Jack and the Beanstalk to get him mad. But I'm the only one that can outrun him and get away, and I'm too grown for that silliness now.

"Well, Squeaky," he says checking my name off the list and handing me number seven and two pins. And I'm thinking he's got no right to call me Squeaky, if I can't call him Beanstalk.

"Hazel Elizabeth Deborah Parker," I correct him and tell him to write it down on his board.

"Well, Hazel Elizabeth Deborah Parker, going to give someone else a break this year?" I squint at him real hard to see if he is seriously thinking I should lose the race on purpose just to give someone else a break.

"Only six girls running this time," he continues, shaking his head sadly like it's my fault all of New York didn't turn out in sneakers. "That new girl should give you a run for your money." He looks around the park for Gretchen like a periscope in a submarine movie. "Wouldn't it be a nice gesture if you were . . . to ahhh . . . "

I give him such a look he couldn't finish putting that idea into words. Grownups got a lot of nerve sometimes. I pin number seven to myself and stomp away—I'm so burnt. And I go straight for the track and stretch out on the grass while the band winds up with "Oh the Monkey Wrapped His Tail Around the Flag Pole," which my teacher calls by some other name. The man on the loudspeaker is calling everyone over to the track and I'm on my back looking at the sky trying to pretend I'm in the country, but I can't, because even grass in the city feels hard as sidewalk and there's just no pretending you are anywhere but in a "concrete jungle" as my grandfather says.

The twenty-yard dash takes all of the two minutes cause most of the little kids don't know no better than to run off the track or run the wrong way or run smack into the fence and fall down and cry. One little kid though has got the good sense to run straight for the white ribbon up ahead so he wins. Then the second graders line up for the thirty-yard dash and I don't even bother to turn my head to watch cause Raphael Perez always wins. He wins before he even begins by psyching the runners, telling them they're going to trip on their shoelaces and fall on their faces or lose their shorts or something, which he doesn't really have to do since he is very fast, almost as fast as I am. After that is the forty-yard dash which I use to run when I was in first grade. Raymond is hollering from the swings cause he knows I'm about to do my thing cause the man on the loudspeaker has just announced the fifty-yard dash, although he might just as well be giving a recipe for Angel Food cake cause you can hardly make out what he's saying for the static. I get up and slip off my sweat pants and then I see Gretchen standing at the starting line kicking her legs out like a pro. Then as I get

121

into place I see that ole Raymond is in line on the other side of the fence, bending down with his fingers on the ground just like he knew what he was doing. I was going to yell at him but then I didn't. It burns up your energy to holler.

Every time, just before I take off in a race, I always feel like I'm in a dream, the kind of dream you have when you're sick with fever and feel all hot and weightless. I dream I'm flying over a sandy beach in the early morning sun, kissing the leaves of the trees as I fly by. And there's always the smell of apples, just like in the country when I was little and use to think I was a choo-choo train, running through the fields of corn and chugging up the hill to the orchard. And all the time I'm dreaming this, I get lighter and lighter until I'm flying over the beach again, getting blown through the sky like a feather that weighs nothing at all. But once I spread my fingers in the dirt and crouch over for the Get on Your Mark, the dream goes and I am solid again and am telling myself, Squeaky you must win, you must win, you are the fastest thing in the world, you can even beat your father up Amsterdam if you really try. And then I feel my weight coming back just behind my knees then down to my feet then into the earth and the pistol shot explodes in my blood and I am off and weightless again, flying past the other runners, my arms pumping up and down and the whole world is quiet except for the crunch as I zoom over the gravel in the track. I glance to my left and there is no one. To the right a blurred Gretchen who's got her chin jutting out as if it would win the race all by itself. And on the other side of the fence is Raymond with his arms down to his side and the palms tucked up behind him, running in his very own style and the first time I ever saw that and I almost stop to watch my brother Raymond on his first run. But the white ribbon is bouncing toward me and I tear past it racing into the distance till my feet with a mind of their own start digging up footfuls of dirt and brake me short. Then all the kids standing on the side pile on me, banging me on the back and slapping my head with their May Day programs, for I have won again and everybody on 151st Street can walk tall for another year.

"In first place . . . " the man on the loudspeaker is clear as a bell now. But then he pauses and the loudspeaker starts to whine. Then static. And I lean down to catch my breath and here comes Gretchen walking back for she's overshot the finish line too, huffing and puffing with her hands on her hips taking it slow, breathing in steady time like a real pro and I sort of like her a little for the first time. "In first place . . . " and then three or four voices get all mixed up on the loudspeaker and I dig my sneaker into the grass and stare at Gretchen who's staring back, we both wondering just who did win. I can hear old Beanstalk arguing with the man on the loudspeaker and then a few others running their mouths about what the stop watches say.

Then I hear Raymond yanking at the fence to call me and I wave to shush him, but he keeps rattling the fence like a gorilla in a cage like in them gorilla movies, but then like a dancer or something he starts climbing up nice and easy but very fast. And it occurs to me, watching how smoothly he climbs hand over hand and remembering how he looked running with his arms down to his side and with the wind pulling his mouth back and his teeth showing and all, it occurred to me that Raymond would make a very fine runner. Doesn't he always keep up with me on my trots? And he surely knows how to breathe in counts of seven cause he's always doing it at the dinner table, which drives my brother George up the wall. And I'm smiling to beat the band cause if I've lost this race, or if me and Gretchen tied, or even if I've won, I can always retire as a runner and begin a whole new career as a coach with Raymond as my champion. After all, with a little more study I can beat Cynthia and her phony self at the spelling bee. And if I bugged my mother, I could get piano lessons and become a star. And I have a big rep as the baddest thing around. And I've got a roomful of ribbons and medals and awards. But what has Raymond got to call his own?

So I stand there with my new plan, laughing out loud by this time as Raymond jumps down from the fence and runs over with his teeth showing and his arms down to the side which no one before him has quite mastered as a running style. And by the time he comes over I'm jumping up and down so glad to see him—my brother Raymond, a great runner in the family tradition. But of course everyone thinks I'm jumping up and down because the men on the loudspeaker have finally gotten themselves together and compared notes and are announcing "In first place—Miss Hazel Elizabeth Deborah Parker." (Dig that.) "In second place—Miss Gretchen P. Lewis." And I look over at Gretchen wondering what the P stands for. And I smile. Cause she's good, no doubt about it. Maybe she'd like to help me coach Raymond; she obviously is serious about running, as any fool can see. And she nods to congratulate me and then she smiles. And I smile. We stand there with this big smile of respect between us. It's about as real a smile as girls can do for each other, considering we don't practice real smiling every day you know, cause maybe we too busy being flowers or fairies or strawberries instead of something honest and worthy of respect . . . you know . . . like being people.

Character

The best authors are those who create characters you can believe in. Characters in stories are not real, of course. But when an author's imagination and a reader's imagination work together, characters *seem* to be alive in the world of the story. When this happens, we say the author has made the characters *believable*.

In "Raymond's Run," Toni Cade Bambara has given life to Hazel Elizabeth Deborah Parker—Squeaky—who lives at some uncertain address in the vicinity of Broadway and 145th Street in the district of Harlem in New York City. You are led to believe that Squeaky is a real person because you are told what she looks like, and you are told what she thinks and how she feels. While you are reading the story, you come to see Squeaky's world and the characters in it as she sees them. And you come to feel much the same way about them as she does. When this happens you are *identifying* with Squeaky. And because you can identify with Squeaky, you also believe in her brother Raymond and all the other characters that you see through her eyes.

Getting to know the characters in a story is one of the great joys of reading. Seldom, in real life, do you get to know as much about the personal thoughts and feelings of a person as you do about the characters from the stories and novels you read. Characters in a story are presented, described and explained to you by the author. This kind of in-depth introduction is a service you don't have when you meet a new person at school. This "service" that a writer provides is the process known as *characterization*.

Characterization is very much in the control of the author. It is like a paintbrush in the hands of an artist. By adding a line here and there, an artist can make a person look beautiful or ugly. A subtle shading around the eyes can make a person appear mean or kind, sad or cheerful. In the same way, with a word or two, a description or an action, an author can make you like or dislike a character. Depending on how the author wants you to feel, you may sympathize with one character and wish the worst for another. As you will see in the lesson, understanding the characters in a story is not something you have to work very hard at. In the hands of a good author, characters clearly identify and explain themselves.

In this lesson we will look at four ways in which author Toni Bambara creates characters whom you can understand and believe in:

1 The characters are described by the author.

2 The author shows you the characters in action.

3 The author explains how the characters feel.

4 By showing you different aspects of the personalities of the characters, the author helps you to analyze and understand them.

There are many parts to a person's character. The most obvious part of any person, of course, is what he or she looks like. Is he tall or short? Is she dark or fair? Age, dress, facial expression and many other details go into the first impression you have of any new person you meet.

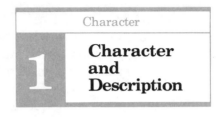

Character

1 **Character and Description**

After you have known someone awhile, you know a lot more about that person's character. You know whether the person is clever or dull, friendly or distant, nervous and self-conscious, or cool and self-possessed. Now you are getting at the person's inner nature.

When you meet a character in a story, the more you learn about the character the more interesting the character becomes. Authors realize this and go to great lengths to acquaint you with their characters. This is especially true of the main characters in a story.

The easiest way to present a character is with a description. Because the author has planned her characters very carefully, she is able to describe both their outer and inner characters any time she wishes. Sometimes an author will do this straightaway. Other times, though, an author will describe a character little by little as a story goes along. Author Toni Bambara gets right to it in the following early paragraph from "Raymond's Run." Notice how much you learn about both the "outer" and the "inner" Squeaky from the author's description. And you learn a good bit about Raymond, too.

(Like Frank O'Connor's story "First Confession," this story is told in the *first person*. This means the story is told as if one of the characters is speaking directly to you. In this case, Squeaky is speaking to the reader. Keep in mind, however, that it is really the *author* speaking to you *through* the character Squeaky.)

Sometimes I slip and say my little brother Raymond. But as any fool can see he's much bigger and he's older too. But a lot of people call him my little brother cause he needs looking after cause he's not quite right. And a lot of smart mouths got lots to say about that too, especially when George was minding him. But now, if anybody has anything to say to Raymond, anything to say about his big head, they have to come by me. And I don't play the dozens or believe in standing around with somebody in my face doing a lot of talking. I much rather just knock you down and take my chances even if I am a little girl with skinny arms and a squeaky voice, which is how I got the name Squeaky. And if things get too rough, I run. And as anybody can tell you, I'm the fastest thing on two feet.

First the author has Squeaky describe Raymond for you. Plainly, he is mentally retarded. Moreover, he is not very attractive. His head is too large. But Squeaky is fiercely loyal to her brother.

As she describes herself, you learn a great deal about both the outer and the inner Squeaky. She is little and skinny and has a squeaky voice. But what she lacks in size she makes up for in courage and "street smarts." Not one to waste words on people who cross her, she prefers to get on with a fight rather than stand around trading insults (playing "the dozens"). She is smart enough to know, however, when it's time to run. This brings us to a most important point about Squeaky's character, as far as the progress of the story is concerned. She describes herself as "the fastest thing on two feet."

In the passage in exercise A, see how much you can learn about the girls Squeaky meets on Broadway from the author's (Squeaky's) description.

Exercise A

Read the following passage and answer the questions about it using what you have learned in this part of the lesson.

So I'm strolling down Broadway . . . and here comes Gretchen and her sidekicks—Mary Louise who used to be a friend of mine when she first moved to Harlem from Baltimore and got beat up by everybody till I took up for her . . . , but people ain't grateful, so now she hangs out with the new girl Gretchen and talks about me like a dog; and Rosie who is as fat as I am skinny and has a big mouth where Raymond is concerned and is too stupid to know that there is not a big deal of difference between herself and Raymond. . . .

Put an *x* in the box beside the correct answer.

1. From the description of Mary Louise, the author wants you to know that she is the kind of person who

   ☐ a. will stand up for a friend.

   ☐ b. moves around a lot from place to place.

   ☐ c. betrays a friendship.

   ☐ d. is grateful for favors done her.

2. On the lines provided, write the expression from the passage that describes what a character *looks* like. Also, write one expression that describes what Squeaky thinks about one of the other characters.

   _____

   _____

   _____

Now check your answers using the Answer Key on page 453. Correct any wrong answers and review this part of the lesson if you don't understand why an answer was wrong.

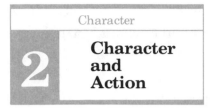

Character

2 Character and Action

We judge people not only by their appearance but by how they behave, as well. A person may be beautifully dressed and act nasty and cruel. Another person may look plain or unattractive and have the soul of a saint. A complete picture of character emerges only after you get to know someone well.

An author, then, in addition to describing characters to you, develops them through their actions. Developing a character through description is called *exposition*. The author *exposes* the character to you. Developing a character through his or her actions is called *characterization by dramatic action*.

The action in plays, in movies or on television is dramatic action. It may consist of anything from a wild fist fight to a quiet conversation. Most dramatic action, in fact, is conversation—usually called *dialogue*. In the following passage you get a very good idea of what Cynthia Procter is like, both from what she says and from what she does:

> Now you take Cynthia Procter for instance. She's just the opposite [of me]. If there's a test tomorrow, she'll say something like, "Oh I guess I'll play handball this afternoon and watch television tonight," just to let you know she ain't thinking about the test. Or like last week when she won the spelling bee for the millionth time, "A good thing you got 'receive,' Squeaky, cause I would have got it wrong. I completely forgot about the spelling bee." And she'll clutch the lace on her blouse like it was a narrow escape. Oh, brother.

From her words and actions, Cynthia shows herself to be a bit of a phony. She would like you to think she doesn't work hard for her accomplishments when, in fact, she has to work very hard. In the next paragraph Squeaky describes how Cynthia practices the piano for hours on end. Then in music class she sits down to play and acts as if the music just springs from her fingertips through sheer genius.

Cynthia Procter's actions in the story have another purpose that you should be aware of. She is used to help you get to know Squeaky better. Cynthia is the *opposite* of Squeaky. Squeaky is straightforward. She has to work hard for the things she does well, and she doesn't care who knows it. Cynthia's phoniness and Squeaky's feelings about Cynthia serve to emphasize Squeaky's directness.

Exercise B

Read the following passage and answer the questions about it using what you have learned in this part of the lesson.

[Mary Louise asks Raymond a question and Squeaky answers for him.]

"What grade you in now, Raymond?"

"You got anything to say to my brother, you say it to me, Mary Louise Williams of Raggedy Town, Baltimore."

"What are you, his mother?" sasses Rosie.

"That's right, Fatso. And the next word out of anybody and I'll be their mother too." So they just stand there and Gretchen shifts from one leg to the other and so do they. Then Gretchen puts her hands on her hips and is about to say something with her freckle-face self but doesn't. Then she walks around me looking me up and down but keeps walking up Broadway, and her sidekicks follow her. So me and Raymond smile at each other and he says, "Gidyap" to his team and I continue with my breathing exercises, strolling down Broadway toward the icey man on 145th with not a care in the world cause I am Miss Quicksilver herself.

Put an x in the box beside the correct answer.

1. By their actions, Mary Louise, Rosie and Gretchen show themselves to be

☐ a. determined.

☐ b. clever.

☐ c. unhappy.

☐ d. cowardly.

2. Squeaky has a lot of confidence in herself. Which sentence in the passage most clearly shows (and tells) how Squeaky feels about herself? Write the sentence here.

_____

_____

_____

_____

_____

Now check your answers using the Answer Key on page 453. Correct any wrong answers and review this part of the lesson if you don't understand why an answer was wrong.

Each person you know affects you differently. You *feel* differently about different people. You love members of your family, but you may love a boy-friend or girlfriend in a very different way. Some people are annoying to you, others are downright scary.

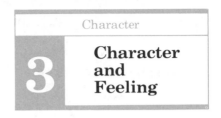

3 **Character and Feeling**

There are still others whom you admire, and some who make you uneasy for reasons you can't explain. There is no limit to the range of feelings you can have toward people.

Authors see to it that you develop feelings about the characters you meet in their stories. They do this with the *tone* they use, as you will see in a lesson further on in this book. You can tell, for instance, by the way the author has Squeaky talk about Mary Louise and Rosie, that she doesn't like them. The author passes this tone or attitude on to you, and you come to feel the same way as Squeaky does about the girls—you sympathize with her.

> "You signing up for the May Day races?" smiles Mary Louise, only it's not a smile at all. . . .
>
> "I don't think you're going to win this time," says Rosie, trying to signify with her hands on her hips all salty, completely forgetting that I have whupped her behind many times for less salt than that.
>
> "I always win cause I'm the best," I say straight at Gretchen who is, as far as I'm concerned, the only one talking in this ventriloquist-dummy routine.
>
> Gretchen smiles but it's not a smile and I'm thinking that girls never really smile at each other because they don't know how. . . .

From the very beginning of the story, the author has put you on Squeaky's side. This is the feeling of sympathy you are expected to have for the main character. If you stop to think about it, though, you might not be especially fond of Squeaky if you were to know her in real life. She thinks an awful lot of herself—she's very proud—and doesn't seem to get along very well with other people. She has a chip on her shoulder. And she is a little too unforgiving of common faults in others.

The author destroyed any sympathetic feelings you might have had for Mary Louise and Rosie a few paragraphs back. You know just how to feel about them. Now the author adds to your feelings of dislike. Mary

Louise asks a "dumb question" and Squeaky ignores her. Rosie, who has been described as fat and stupid, is now pictured as sassy and prissy. And at this point you would just love to see Squeaky whup her as she says she has done before.

Exercise C

Read the following passage and answer the questions about it using what you have learned in this part of the lesson.

> Then here comes Mr. Pearson with his clipboard and his cards and pencils and whistles and safety pins and fifty million other things he's always dropping all over the place with his clumsy self. He sticks out in a crowd cause he's on stilts. We used to call him Jack and the Beanstalk to get him mad. . . .
>
> "Well, Hazel Elizabeth Deborah Parker, going to give someone else a break this year?" I squint at him real hard to see if he is seriously thinking I should lose the race on purpose just to give someone else a break. . . .
>
> . . . "That new girl should give you a run for your money. . . . Wouldn't it be a nice gesture if you were . . . to ahhh . . . "
>
> I give him such a look he couldn't finish putting that idea into words. Grownups got a lot of nerve sometimes. I pin number seven to myself and stomp away—I'm so burnt.

Put an *x* in the box beside the correct answer.

1. How does Squeaky feel toward Mr. Pearson after he hints that she should lose the race on purpose?

   ☐ a. Hostile and angry

   ☐ b. Jaunty and amused

   ☐ c. Understanding and sympathetic

   ☐ d. Awestruck and fearful

2. Briefly, in your own words, tell what it is in the passage that gives you the feeling that Mr. Pearson is (a) a bit silly, and (b) somewhat dishonest.

a. _____

_____

_____

b. _____

_____

Now check your answers using the Answer Key on page 453. Correct any wrong answers and review this part of the lesson if you don't understand why an answer was wrong.

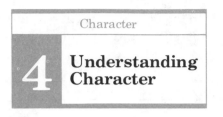

Character

4 Understanding Character

One of the great practical benefits of reading is that it helps develop your ability to understand people. This is one of the most important skills in life. People who don't understand others, who can't figure out their natures and true intentions, are doomed to make very serious mistakes in their human relationships.

Reading stories and novels brings you in contact with all sorts of people you might not otherwise meet. Readers in California, for example, might never have known a girl from Harlem if they hadn't met Squeaky. But, most importantly, authors provide readers with opportunities to think very carefully about various types of characters. You don't often get a chance to focus as closely on a person in real life as you do on a character in a story. You especially don't get the chance to look *inside* a person, at their very thoughts, as you do with Squeaky.

Thinking about characters and discussing them with other people is called *character analysis*. Character analysis is an effort to understand a character by putting together the facts and feelings about them that an author provides. Once you feel you understand a character, you usually make judgments about him or her.

We will analyze Squeaky's character a bit in the passage that follows. Then you can do your own analysis in Exercise D.

> . . . It occurred to me that Raymond would make a very fine runner. Doesn't he always keep up with me on my trots? And he surely knows how to breathe in counts of seven. . . . And I'm smiling to beat the band cause if I've lost this race, or if me and Gretchen tied, or even if I've won, I can always retire as a runner and begin a whole new career as a coach with Raymond as my champion. After all, with a little more study I can beat Cynthia and her phony self at the spelling bee. And if I bugged my mother, I could get piano lessons and become a star. . . . And I've got a roomful of ribbons and medals and awards. But what has Raymond got to call his own? . . .
>
> . . . And by the time he comes over I'm jumping up and down so glad to see him—my brother Raymond, a great runner in the family tradition.

This passage should cause you to stop and take a new look at Squeaky. A change has come over her. Not only do you see her in a new light, you are forced to stop and think about her actions and feelings up to this point.

This is the first time you've seen Squeaky really happy. Oh, she's been proud of herself, but not simply happy about something. This is also the first time she has thought about someone else being a winner besides herself. And the thought doesn't upset her.

You have to feel sympathetic toward the old Squeaky who hates phonies and is always ready for a fight. Good old self-confident Squeaky. But now, in doing your analysis of her, you can probably see that Squeaky was something of a stinker. She didn't get along very well with people. She demanded too much. Her thoughts were almost entirely related to herself.

Now, for the first time, Squeaky is thinking about others. And she finds she is happier for it.

Exercise D

Read the following passage and answer the questions about it using what you have learned in this part of the lesson.

"In first place—Miss Hazel Elizabeth Deborah Parker." (Dig that.) "In second place—Miss Gretchen P. Lewis." And I look over at Gretchen wondering what the P stands for. And I smile. Cause she's good, no doubt about it. Maybe she'd like to help me coach Raymond; she obviously is serious about running, as any fool can see. And she nods to congratulate me and then she smiles. And I smile. We stand there with this big smile of respect between us. It's about as real a smile as girls can do for each other. . . .

Put an x in the box beside the correct answer.

1. Throughout most of the story Squeaky speaks against people. Which one of the following phrases spoken by Squeaky in the passage you just read tells you that you are seeing a new Squeaky?

   ☐ a. "respect between us"

   ☐ b. "I look over at Gretchen"

   ☐ c. "as any fool can see"

   ☐ d. "she nods to congratulate me"

2. Squeaky does something here she hasn't done before for other girls. As you think about it, it makes you certain that there has been a change in Squeaky. It is one word that appears five times in the passage. The word also appeared earlier in the story with a very different feeling attached to it. Write the word here.

   _____

Use the Answer Key on page 453 to check your answers. Correct any wrong answers and review this part of the lesson if you don't understand why an answer was wrong. Now go on to do the Comprehension Questions.

Comprehension Questions

Recalling
Facts

1. Squeaky says that she has only one family chore to do. What is it?

   ☐ a. Running

   ☐ b. Making money

   ☐ c. Doing the dishes

   ☐ d. Minding Raymond

Making
Inferences

2. Squeaky seems to depend on two things to win her battles. What are they?

   ☐ a. Her fists and her feet

   ☐ b. Her head and her heart

   ☐ c. Her mouth and her breathing exercises

   ☐ d. Her friends and her foes

Recalling
Facts

3. What does Squeaky do most of the time when she is out with Raymond?

   ☐ a. She plays stagecoach with Raymond.

   ☐ b. She fights with Cynthia or Rosie.

   ☐ c. She practices breathing and running.

   ☐ d. She hangs around and plays the dozens.

Character

4. People tease Raymond about his appearance. What, especially, do they tease him about?

☐ a. His running

☐ b. His large head

☐ c. His fat body

☐ d. His big mouth

5. Cynthia Procter sits down at the piano and acts as though the waltzes she plays just spring from her fingertips. She seems like a regular *prodigy*. A *prodigy* is a

☐ a. person of great talent.

☐ b. show-off.

☐ c. great nuisance.

☐ d. female musician.

6. "Here comes Gretchen and her *sidekicks*." *Sidekicks* are

☐ a. family members or relatives.

☐ b. enemies or tormentors.

☐ c. friends or partners.

☐ d. weapons or side arms.

7. Squeaky says she doesn't want to act chicken because she has her *reputation* to consider. Her *reputation* is her

☐ a. brother's physical condition.

☐ b. recognized standing in the neighborhood.

☐ c. ability to run faster than anyone else.

☐ d. feeling for her family.

8. During Squeaky's run, another event occurs that is important in the story. What is that event?

☐ a. Raymond runs too, and does very well.

☐ b. The Maypole dancing is going on.

☐ c. Mr. Pearson tries to get Squeaky to lose the race.

☐ d. Raymond climbs over the fence.

9. Throughout the story Squeaky works hard to be the best, the baddest thing around—Miss Quicksilver herself. But at the end of the story, she plans to do something that is very different. What does Squeaky plan to do?

☐ a. She wants to help someone else to be the best.

☐ b. She wants to work to become even better herself.

☐ c. She wants to finally get even with Mary Louise and Rosie.

☐ d. She wants to beat Gretchen again next year.

10. After the race Squeaky asks herself, "But what has Raymond got to call his own?" The answer isn't given in the story. But you may infer that the answer is

☐ a. "more than Squeaky."

☐ b. "his brother George."

☐ c. "everyone's love."

☐ d. "nothing."

11. What causes Squeaky and Gretchen to respect one another?

☐ a. Their meeting on Broadway

☐ b. The spelling bee

☐ c. The May Day celebration

☐ d. The race

Keeping
Events in
Order

12. Three of the events listed below are talked about in the story, but they do not take place at the time when the story takes place. Choose the event that *did* occur during the time of the story.

☐ a. Raymond chased the pigeons.

☐ b. Cynthia won the spelling bee.

☐ c. Mary Louise asked Raymond what grade he was in.

☐ d. Squeaky was a strawberry in the school play.

Making
Inferences

13. Which one of the following words best describes Squeaky's attitude toward her family?

☐ a. Anger

☐ b. Ambition

☐ c. Doubt

☐ d. Loyalty

Understanding
Main Ideas

14. Which one of the following statements best describes Squeaky's attitude during most of the story?

☐ a. She is jealous of Gretchen.

☐ b. She resents her brother George.

☐ c. She is quarrelsome.

☐ d. She is open and generous.

Understanding
Main Ideas

15. There is one thing that seems to bother Squeaky more than anything else. What is it?

☐ a. Serious people

☐ b. People who are false, or phony

☐ c. Other runners

☐ d. People who practice too much

Now check your answers using the Answer Key on page 453. Make no mark for right answers. <u>Correct</u> any wrong answers you may have by putting a checkmark (✓) in the box next to the right answer. Count the number of questions you answered correctly and plot the total on the Comprehension Scores graph on page 462.

Next, look at the questions you answered incorrectly. What types of questions were they? Count the number you got wrong of each type and enter the numbers in the spaces below.

Recognizing Words in Context   _____

Recalling Facts   _____

Keeping Events in Order   _____

Making Inferences   _____

Understanding Main Ideas   _____

Now use these numbers to fill in the Comprehension Skills Profile on page 463.

Discussion Guides

The questions below will help you to think about the story and the lesson you have just read. If you don't discuss these questions in class, try to think about them or discuss them with your classmates.

Discussing Characterization

1. Sqeaky is the main character (sometimes called the *protagonist*) of the story. Of all the characters in a story, readers are usually made to feel the most sympathy for the protagonist. This is pretty much true for Squeaky. But how would you feel about Squeaky if she were in your class at school? Give reasons for the way you feel.

2. Some characters in a story are not very important. They are used as background or setting. Which people described in the story are used this way?

3. When you only see one side of a character in a story—only a good side, or only a bad side—the character is said to be a *flat* character. If you can see many different traits in a character—good *and* bad—the character is a *round* character. Who are flat characters and who are round characters in this story? Try to give reasons for your choices.

Discussing the Story

4. Why do you think the story is called "Raymond's Run" instead of "Squeaky's Run"?

5. If you belonged to a group whose job it was to defend the rights of mentally retarded children, how would you judge the story "Raymond's Run"?

6. One of the great things about reading short stories and novels is that you can learn important lessons about life and living from the experiences of the characters. What did you learn about life and living from this story?

Discussing the Author's Work

7. Toni Cade Bambara is a black author writing about black people in "Raymond's Run." Frank O'Connor was Irish and wrote about Irish people in "First Confession." Most authors of short stories and novels

establish this kind of relationship between their stories and their lives. Why do you think this is so?

8. If you don't live in New York City, some things in the story may not mean much to you. For example, "I continue . . . strolling down Broadway toward the icey man on 145th. . . . " Here's another: " . . . can you imagine some thirty-five-year-old man stuffing himself into PAL shorts . . . ?" (PAL stands for Police Athletic League, an athletic association.) Do things like this add anything to the story, or do they make the story less interesting? Give examples and reasons for your opinion.

9. In addition to being a writer, Toni Bambara has a background in acting and dancing. At one time she was director of recreation for a New York City mental hospital. What evidence of these experiences can you find in the story?

Writing Exercise

Try one of the following exercises.

1. Rosie is described in the story as fat, stupid and sassy. The author doesn't want you to like her. But no one is all bad. Write a description of Rosie that will influence readers to like her, or at least sympathize with her.

2. Imagine a character named Grunt Bearclaws. Grunt is the meanest, dirtiest man alive. Write an account of a meeting or run-in you have with Grunt.

   • Tell what is said between you and what happens.

   • Write in such a way that readers will dislike Grunt, but feel sorry for him at the same time.

Unit 4   Setting

Chocolate Pudding

BY NORMA FOX MAZER

About the Illustration

How would you describe the setting in which this scene is taking place? Point out some details in the drawing to support your response.

Here are some questions to help you think:

☐ What kind of a place are these two people in? Is it large or small? Rich or poor? What details about the place lead you to those conclusions?

☐ What are the boy and the girl doing?

☐ What kind of mood do the boy and the girl seem to be in? How do they seem to feel about each other?

Unit 4

Introduction

What the Story Is About

A lot of chocolate pudding is eaten in the course of this story. It's Chrissy's favorite dessert. In fact, when she was small, the first words she learned to read were the ingredients on a box of chocolate pudding mix: sugar, cornstarch, cocoa. When it comes to chocolate pudding, she is what you might call a *connoisseur*—a real expert.

Chocolate pudding is not, however, what the story is about. The story is about feelings of loneliness. Chrissy is sixteen and lives in a trailer with her father and uncle. Her mother died when she was a baby, so the two men are all the family she has. Unfortunately, they are alcoholics. They work hard to accumulate money, and then they blow it all in wild drinking sprees.

Although Chrissy, her father and uncle are fond of one another, it is a poor and lonely life that they lead. The men drink to dull their feelings. Chrissy eats chocolate pudding to soothe hers.

At sixteen, Chrissy has long since given up expecting that things will change much. What, then, should she make of the strange feeling of expectation that sweeps over her one morning on her way to school? "Something will happen today," she says to herself. "Something will happen."

Something *does* happen that day. In fact, two things happen. One makes her feel wintry and frozen, as though she were encased in ice. But the other kindles a "curious, stifling heat" inside her, which leaves her breathless. And there's more than chocolate pudding involved here.

Author Norma Fox Mazer is part of a "writing family." She is married to another author, Harry Mazer, and they have four children— three daughters and a son. She likes to write about "the ordinary, the everyday, the real. . . . " She has said, "In my books and stories, I want people to eat chocolate pudding, break a dish, yawn, look in a store window, wear socks with holes in them. . . . " And you will agree that these are just the kinds of people you meet in this story.

After reading "Chocolate Pudding" you may want to meet some of Norma Mazer's other real, everyday characters. You can find them in the collection from which this story was taken, titled *Dear Bill,*

Remember Me? Another good choice is a book she wrote with her husband called *The Solid Gold Kid.*

What the Lesson Is About

The lesson that follows the story is about setting. The setting of a story is the backdrop for the events that take place. It includes many things—the time, the place, the scenery and even the people themselves. Sights, sounds and smells can all be part of the setting for a story.

The setting helps readers keep track of where a story is taking place and of what is going on in a story. But the best settings take you one step further. They help you to understand how the characters feel about the places in which they find themselves. And a good setting helps you share more fully in the experience of the story.

The questions below will help you to see how Norma Fox Mazer developed the setting in "Chocolate Pudding." Read the story carefully and try to answer these questions as you go along:

1. In the first part of the story you will read about the trailer in which Chrissy lives with her father and uncle. How do you think this setting affects Chrissy's life?

2. The wintry weather plays a part in the setting of the story. How does the bitter cold outside make the trailer seem inside?

3. A little further along in the story there is a scene in the school cafeteria. What are some details of the setting that give you a sense of really being there?

4. Toward the end of the story you see the trailer through another person's eyes. What ideas does the author present by doing this?

Chocolate Pudding

Norma Fox Mazer

Chocolate pudding is my favorite dessert. When it's on the menu in the school cafeteria, I order four or five puddings in those little brown cups, and eat nothing else for lunch. At home, I cook my own chocolate pudding, and when it's cooled enough for that lovely silky skin to come over the top—chocolate skin, I call it—I often eat it straight from the pot. I eat the soft puddingish part first, saving the chocolate skin for last.

I always offer Dad and Uncle some pudding, but neither one is ever interested. They don't eat much, anyway. When they're drinking, I don't believe they eat at all; betweentimes, they'll eat a hunk of cheese, some bread, a few boiled potatoes, sometimes a piece of fruit. Although they're brothers, they haven't the same interests (except for the drinking), nor the same sort of disposition, nor do they look alike. Uncle hasn't Dad's wild mop of red hair, or Dad's white, freckled skin, or Dad's blue eyes, either. (I often think of Dad years ago, when he met my mother and they loved each other—his eyes really blue then, not glaring and watery, and his red hair, and that beautiful jaunty smile. Uncle says girls always liked Dad.) Uncle is shorter and stouter than Dad, brown hair, brown eyes, even his skin is a sort of neutral, light-tannish color. Uncle looks as he is: calm; I've never seen him lose his temper.

Uncle's mad for oranges the way I am for chocolate pudding. When I was a little girl, whenever Uncle took out the curved paring knife from the silverware pitcher and sat down at the table with an orange, I'd come in as close as I could, leaning on his leg to watch, fascinated, as he slowly took off the peel in a perfect spiral.

"Let me have it, please, Uncle," I'd plead, hopping up and down.

"You want a bite of my orange, Chrissy?" he'd say, dividing the orange perfectly in half with the flat of his thumb poked through the center.

"No, Uncle, no! No orange. The peel! Please, Uncle."

"The peel?" he'd say, as if sincerely astonished at such a bizarre request.

When Uncle gave me the peel, and he always did after only a moment of teasing, I'd go under the table with it, near Uncle's feet, and play Eskimo House. There was snow all around, but the Eskimo people inside their orange igloo were cozy and eating spaghetti out of a can the way Uncle, Dad, and I did in winter when the snow plastered itself in little bunches and clumps against the windows, and the wind shrieked across the flat fields outside our wooden trailer.

Our trailer is one long, narrow room. We do our cooking on a two-burner hotplate, we have a refrigerator, table, three chairs, an electric heater, a sink. No more, no less than we need, as Uncle says. Our privy is out back, fifteen feet from the well, as required by state law. Uncle and Dad sleep on the pullout couch, while I used to have a cot with chairs shoved against it to keep me from falling out. But now Uncle and Dad have built a wall across the back of the trailer, making a room for me. They built in a bed, desk, a few shelves. There's a window over my bed. Sometimes when Uncle and Dad are away, I sit on my bed eating chocolate pudding from the pot and looking out the window into the fields.

One afternoon some years ago (I must have been about ten), I came off the school bus, my stomach hollow with hunger, and rushed down our dirt road. My coat was half on, my shoes were untied. I banged on the trailer as I ran alongside it. "Dad? Uncle? Are you there?" The trailer was empty; I went to the cupboard where we kept the chocolate pudding, always Migh-T-Fine in the little white cardboard box with red letters. There was no chocolate pudding. Disbelievingly, I pulled out everything, flinging around

Chocolate Pudding

boxes and tins. Rage bubbled up in me, thickened, spilled over.

"Damn it, Dad, you did the shopping last week," I shouted. "Damn you. Damn you, damn you, you forgot my chocolate pudding!" I threw myself down on my bed and as I did I thought of the ingredients of chocolate pudding, which were the first words I'd learned to read: *sugar, cornstarch, cocoa* . . . each word carrying a magical, mysterious weight as fine, powdery, and sweet as the granules themselves.

Revived, alert, excited, I got up and dumped cups of cornstarch, cocoa, and sugar together in a pot. I made a terrible mess, bitter and gluey, which I threw out in disgust. Then I started again. And gradually, over the next weeks, I learned to make chocolate pudding properly.

Now I make my own pudding all the time. I vary it, depending on my mood, thin and creamy, or very sweet, or thick, or dark as night. My only regret is that neither Dad nor Uncle shares my pleasure in chocolate pudding. "We've no taste for chocolate," Uncle says. "Though your mother liked it very well."

When my mother was alive, which wasn't even till I was two years old, she and Dad and I lived in an apartment over the drugstore in Middle Square. In my room, tacked up on the wall next to my bed, I have a few snapshots from that time. Often I lie on my stomach across my bed, staring at those pictures, trying to know the people in them. One is of my father sitting on a couch, holding a baby—me—rather stiffly on his knee. He is wearing glasses and his hair falls down over his forehead. He has a serious, almost desperate, look of intensity on his face as he stares straight into the camera that my mother held. Then there is another picture of him and my mother, standing in front of their new car. My mother is shading her eyes from the sun, bending a little, smiling and squinting. She is wearing a long, full skirt, shoes with pointed toes, a blouse with buttons down the front. Her hair is flying out to one side, as is her skirt. My father is grinning, he's got his arm around her, he looks jaunty, arrogant, a stranger to me, as strange as my mother.

It was after my mother died that Dad and I moved in with Uncle in the trailer. The two of them cared for me and brought me up. "You look just like your mother," Uncle told me so many times. "Very much like. Except for the hair," he always added. My hair is quite long, reddish; in this way I take after Dad.

How calm Uncle is. I've never heard him raise his voice. One hot summer night when the cicadas were screaming a car drove fast up our road, billowing dust behind it, and a bag of rotting garbage flew straight at the trailer.

"The world is a very ignorant place," was all Uncle said as we cleaned up the slimy mess. "That's a fact, Chrissy." Another time some boys shot out our windows with BB guns, and Uncle called in the State Troopers. Two of them came, very big men in gray uniforms with broad hats and guns holstered at their waists. They walked around the trailer, looking at the windows. They seemed to know Uncle and called him Jack in serious voices, behind which I heard something else that I couldn't identify, but which made me pace angrily behind them.

"Jack," they said, "sure you didn't do this yourself one night, Jack? When you were soaked? You sure, Jack?"

Even then, Uncle didn't get angry.

But I did. I went all cold and shaking. "I was here, right here, in the trailer," I said, "when they drove past and shot at us. Are you going to accuse me of doing it? Are you? *Are you?*"

"Chrissy," Uncle said, putting his hand on my shoulders. "Chrissy, now, Chrissy." His voice, even, calm, soothing, went around my rage, enclosed it, kept it from bursting beyond control. I believe Uncle has the same effect on Dad.

Even if someone cheats them out of their rightful pay, Uncle won't get angry. He says it's not worth it. He and Dad hire out to work as a team, doing odd jobs for the people hereabouts. They'll clean out cellars, tear down old buildings, mix cement, repair roofs, or do the milking for a farmer called away from the farm. They never leave any job before it's finished, and they give good work for their pay. At the end of a working day, they come home, take out the bills and coins they've earned and put them into the tomato juice can we keep on the top shelf of the cupboard.

In January the weather was bitter. Morning after morning, I woke to see my window opaque with frost flowers. Still, Dad and Uncle went out to work often and the tomato juice can was stuffed to the brim with bills and coins. The last day of January was so cold that as I ran down our frozen rutted lane for the school bus the inside of my nose felt fragile as glass. But that night in our trailer it was cozy, the electric heater humming, as I did my homework and Dad listened to Radio Australia on short wave. Uncle was in a mood to talk. "Your mother loved cold weather like this, Chrissy. There was nothing she liked so much as a walk in the cold or a snowball fight."

"My mother was fun to be with?"

"Oh, yes, Ellen was a lovely girl, cheerful and laughing. Nothing got her down. Isn't that right?" he asked Dad. But Dad was lost in some other thought.

"The day I see you take a drink, Chrissy," Dad said, "is the day I'm through with living."

Tears came to his eyes. He put his head down on the table. (Once Dad was very strong—Uncle has told me so.) I've seen him cry many times, drinking does it to him. When I was younger I'd shake his arm, pleading with him not to cry. Crying myself.

But now I'm sixteen, and something hardened in me. "Quit that crying, Dad, just quit it."

Uncle tossed his orange peel into the garbage bag near the door.

Dad lifted his head. He's half blind in one eye, from what I don't know as he refuses to go to a doctor. He wears very thick glasses behind which his eyes, red-veined, seem to glare, but it's only that he's trying to see.

"Get me the cigarettes, Chrissy," He lit up.

"Let me have a puff," I said.

In school, girls are always collecting in the lav or standing around outside the building to sneak a smoke behind their hands. "Chrissy, got a ciggy?" they'll say, because they know I always carry half a pack or so with me. We bend our heads together, lighting up, then pass the cigarette around. It's very easy and friendly, and once in a while I'll wonder if it might go beyond this to a real friendship. It never has.

"I'm sorry," I said after a bit to Dad. "For yelling."

"Oh, it's a good thing you did. I cry too easily these days. I need someone to yell at me."

"Well, don't expect me to make a habit of it." I mashed out the cigarette in the sink. "Uncle can yell at you."

"Oh, not me," Uncle said hastily, "not me," and then, for some reason, we all three laughed.

Toward the end of February, the cold eased, and as March came in I saw the restlessness coming over Dad and Uncle. Dad listening to his broadcasts for only a few moments, then standing up, scratching his arms and his neck, whispering to himself. And Uncle putting down his book, picking it up, putting it down again. After a while, not picking it up at all.

There were chunks of dirty ice piled at the sides of the road where I waited for the school bus, while the sun, thin as a slice of cucumber, still threw enough warmth to burn into my scalp. I felt the restlessness myself, and longed for something. But what?

One night the wind blew with such force, such screaming and wailing through the trees and around the corners of the trailer, such rattling of the windows and shaking of the boards that I couldn't sleep. I sat up in bed and pressed my face to the cold window, trembling and thrilled. I stayed that way for hours before finally falling asleep.

In the morning I felt stupid with tiredness. The wind had died. The sky was blue and calm. Sheets of light poured from the sky, and the sight of a tree, white against the sun, its branches swollen with buds, agitated me in a strange and painful way. Something will happen today, I thought, as I climbed on the bus. Something will happen. The bus jolted forward. The smell of wet mittens and peanuts came to me. Diane Lucas sat down next to me and told me about the wind blowing the roof off her cousin Eddy's barn last night. "They came banging on our door at three o'clock in the morning," she said happily. I nodded, looking at her little pointed chin and delicate white teeth.

In school, the morning passed slowly. The classrooms were all too hot. I leaned my head on my hand. I couldn't remember why I had been so agitated, so feverish with excitement. I drew rows of little cups across a piece of paper and wrote CHOCOLATE PUDDING, shading the letters carefully.

In the cafeteria at lunch time the menu featured sloppy joes and chocolate pudding. I ordered four chocolate puddings and took the cups on a tray to a table in the corner of the lunchroom. I said hello to the others at the table and skinned the top off my first pudding. Slowly I ate the soft insides, cleaning out the little brown dish thoroughly. The kids were talking about Mrs. Fannon, the Latin teacher. "God, she's fierce," Melissa Maguire said. "You have her, don't you, Chrissy?"

"Doesn't everyone?" I said. They laughed. It was a saying in Peter V. Newsome High that you hadn't been educated till Margaret Fannon had called you a nincompoop, a mental incompetent, and utterly beyond redemption.

Saving the chocolate skins in my empty dish, I continued working on the puddings. I had gone through a phase a few years before when I had knocked myself out smiling at Melissa and Debby Pearce, joining their conversations and finding clever things to say about teachers and other kids.

I walked in the halls with them, and played on their teams in gym. Once or twice Melissa—or was it Debby?—said something about calling me up. But of course we had no phone. After a while, without anything being said, without anything having happened, one way or the other, I again went my own way.

"I hear Fannon never gives anything over a B," Debby said. "I don't see why anyone takes her classes. A *B!* That would ruin my average."

"Oh, you only have to know how to get around her," Neil Rosencranz said, winking at me. "It's a challenge."

I went on eating my chocolate pudding. Far back in my mind, behind the chatter, the scrape of dishes, the crinkling of sandwich wrappers, I heard the fierce moaning of the wind as it gnawed at the trailer, and I thought of Dad and Uncle sleeping on the pullout coach, their boots tumbled together, safe in the trailer, enclosed, protected. But at the same moment, perhaps for the first time, I thought how frail the trailer was, how weather-beaten the boards, how flimsy the putty that held the windows in place, and I imagined the trailer crumpling in on itself like a deflated paper bag.

Carefully I took the chocolate skin off the last pudding and added it to the others. Two more boys sat down at the table. One of them, Teddy Finkel, had six chocolate puddings on his tray. "Look at that," Debby Pearce said. "Everyone! Look at Teddy Finkel's tray!" Everyone did. "Now look at Chrissy's tray. Isn't that unbelievable?"

"Weird," Melissa said. "It's a convention of chocolate pudding freaks."

Teddy Finkel looked over at me with interest. He had a long bony face and dark hair parted in the middle. "Are you that way about chocolate pudding, too?" We had gone to the same schools for years, but rarely spoken to each other.

"Yes, I like chocolate pudding," I said. I still hadn't eaten the chocolate skins.

"We chocolate pudding freaks don't *like* chocolate

pudding, we *revere* it," Teddy Finkel said, digging into a pudding with gusto. In two seconds he'd cleaned it up and started on another. I kept my head down. When I glanced up, his eyes were on me. His expression was mild, playful, curious. He seemed to be asking me a question, or was that my imagination? I felt stifled, breathless. I wanted to throw off my sweater and push away the tray. I ate the last of the chocolate skins and left the cafeteria.

Later that afternoon I saw Teddy Finkel coming toward me in the hall near the science room. He raised his hand and, as he passed, said, "The secret word is chocolate pudding."

I thought of him as the bus jogged me homeward. Again that curious, stifling heat rose behind my ribs. When I got off the bus I cut across the fields toward the trailer. The sun had warmed our road and turned it to muck. The fields were soggy on top, still frozen beneath.

In the trailer I kicked off my drenched shoes and sang one of the old World War II songs Dad and Uncle liked. "When the lights go on again all over the world, when the boys come home again all over the world . . ." I looked out the window for Dad and Uncle, wondering if they were working today.

It grew dark and still they hadn't come home. I had a pot of coffee ready for them on the stove. I did my homework. The clock ticked louder than necessary. Finally I thought of checking the tomato juice can. It was empty, except for a five-dollar bill. So they were gone. Drinking. For a moment my face felt encased in ice, like a spring puddle covered with a skin of ice that wrinkles and crackles at the touch of a foot. The touch of Uncle's voice calling "Chrissy," the sound of Dad's terrible cough outside in the wet darkness, and my ice, too, would crack.

There now, Chrissy, the world is a foolish place. Don't try to figure it out.

Yes, Uncle.

I thought of the wind last night, the frozen fields, that pale burning sun, the tense anticipation that had gripped me like a fever. How sure I'd been that something was going to happen! Yes, and this was it. I poured a cup of coffee and drank it down.

The next day, as I was leaving school and heading for the bus, Teddy Finkel caught me by the arm and said in my ear, "Chocolate pudding." I looked at him, unsmiling. I felt wintry, frozen.

On the school bus I heard the laughter and jokes of the other kids as if from a distance. I thought of nothing, as if I were half asleep. Perhaps I was. I had slept poorly the night before, jerking awake many times, listening, listening, listening to the darkness and the night. When I got off the bus I walked slowly down the muddy road, my booksack slung over one shoulder. Suddenly I started running, and I banged on the side of the trailer the way I used to do, calling "Dad? Uncle?" I knew, however, that the trailer would be empty.

Several days passed. Each afternoon when I returned from school I felt first sick with disappointment, then fiercely glad they hadn't come back. They would be weepy with remorse, ill, weak, bruised, smelling of vomit. All the money would be gone. I would have to make them food, heat water for them to wash, and take their stinking clothes to the laundromat. Dad would cry day and night, tears would leak from his very pores. *Forgive me Chrissy forgive your old father he's no good no good do you forgive me Chrissy Chrissy I've hurt you . . .*

Oh, I knew it all. I knew just how it would be. How they would smell. How they would look. How the sight of them would make it difficult for me to breathe.

"Stay away," I raged aloud one night, pacing up and down the trailer, reaching out to bang my fists against the walls. "Stay away, both of you! Do you think I want you back, smelling of vomit? Stay away, I tell you," I screamed. "Do you hear me, you two?"

I slept well that night. I woke up once and listened to the

quiet of the trailer, the quiet outside. Quite near, an owl hooted, the one that sounds like a horse whinnying. I breathed easily, in and out, in and out, and stetched my legs till my toes touched the bottom of the bed. My head was muzzy with dreams and I fell asleep again, at once.

In the morning, rain drummed lightly on the tin roof of the trailer and smeared the windows. Crows cawed far away.

When I arrived at school, Teddy Finkel was at the water fountain on the first floor. Straightening, he saw me and said, "Chocolate!" Later, we passed each other again in the hall near the gym. Almost simultaneously, we both said, "Pudding."

He reversed himself to walk with me. "I guess we've worn that joke out," he said.

"Why do we keep bumping into each other?" I said. He followed me into the library and sat down where I did, at one of the long tables under a window. I took out my biology notebook.

"You going to work?" he said.

"That was the general idea."

"A better idea is to talk to me. Tell me what you like besides chocolate pudding."

"Oh—" I shrugged. I didn't know what to say. Did he mean what other foods I liked, or what else I liked to do besides eat chocolate pudding? I flipped open my notebook.

"Nice neat work," he said, leaning over to look. "You like bio?"

"Yes." I started drawing an amoeba in pencil, just lightly, till I felt I had it right.

He pulled a book off a shelf behind him, opened it, and stared staight into it. "You're not really very friendly, are you?" he said.

"Because I don't flirt?"

"I don't think smiling is exactly flirting," he said. "I mean, we had a little joke going, a little thing between us, the chocolate pudding, and you never once smiled."

I bent my head over my notebook. I felt something fasten itself, like a bone, or a hook, in my throat. I made another little squiggly line on my amoeba.

"Listen, you know what my whole name is?" he said. "Theodore Roosevelt Finkel. My mother named me after him. She really did. Listen, I don't tell that to everyone. It's an offering, a friendship offering."

I turned my head a fraction and looked into his eyes. They were the color of prunes, that shiny soft black of stewed prunes, an amazing color.

"What are you thinking about now?" he said.

"I'm thinking that I promised myself to get this bio notebook caught up, and with you bothering me I never will. And I'm thinking that your eyes are really strange, and how long is it going to take for you to get sick of sitting around getting nowhere with me?"

"But I don't want to get somewhere with you," he said. "I just want to get to know you."

"Why?"

"Why?" he repeated.

"Yes. Why?" I really wanted to know.

"You're not like other girls, are you? I mean, you really aren't like other girls at all, are you?"

I felt suddenly depressed. It was true. I'd known it for a long time. I wasn't like other girls, like Melissa or Debby, who knew how to talk to boys easily, how to laugh and say amusing things. "I'm sorry." I flipped senselessly through my bio book.

"Sorry! Don't say that. Don't be *sorry*, Chrissy." He put his hand into my biology book, flattening it out. "You're not a phony, that's all I meant. God, some of the hypocritical types around here—they make me want to puke." Two red spots of excitement appeared high on his cheekbones. Then the bell rang, and I started pushing my papers together. I hadn't done a bit of work, but it didn't matter, the trailer would be quiet again tonight without Dad and Uncle.

Chocolate Pudding

"Well, are we friends?" Teddy said, walking out of the library with me.

"I don't know." I hurried up the stairs.

"You mean that, don't you?"

"Yes," I said impatiently. "Why would I say it, otherwise?"

"God, I like you," he said. "I really like you! We're going to be friends. Definitely." He grabbed my arm. "What are you doing after school?"

"Going home."

"I'll come with you."

"I go on the bus, school bus."

"I know."

"I live fifteen miles out."

"Okay."

I stopped in front of Mrs. Fannon's classroom. "How will you get back?"

He raised his thumb and jerked it across his shoulder.

A shiver crossed my neck. I shifted my books from one arm to the other. At last I said, "I don't know if I want you to come home with me. I don't know, I just don't know!"

"Listen," he said. "Listen—" He touched my shoulder. "It's all right. Really." He peered into my face seriously and reassuringly. Then he walked down the corridor.

After school he was waiting outside where the buses were lined up at the curb. "Hi," he said. It was still raining. I felt the other kids looking at us. I climbed on the bus.

"He's with me," I said to the driver, tilting my head back at Teddy. We took two seats toward the rear of the bus.

"Hi, Chrissy!" Diane Lucas called in an excited voice, as she stared at Teddy. "Got company?"

"It must be a drag taking the bus every day," Teddy said. He leaned back in the seat, folding his arms across his chest.

"I don't mind. I'm used to it."

The bus filled up. Kids were yelling to each other. Someone blew up a lunch bag and popped it. "All right, you kids, settle down," Mrs. Johnson, the bus driver, yelled. Nobody paid any attention.

The bus left the school grounds, drove through Middle Square, past the bank with its fluted columns, the supermarket, a dress shop, the laundromat. A few people hurried through the rain, shoulders hunched. I stared at everything through the rain-smeared windows as if seeing it all for the first time, conscious of Teddy looking across my shoulder. On the outskirts of Middle Square, we drove by a set of stone gates with a white arch over them lettered STONY ACRES. Behind the arch I caught a glimpse of big houses, wet clean road, and clipped lawns, soggy and glistening.

"That's where I live," Teddy said. "Did you ever hear such a phony name? Stony Acres. Ha!" The bus swept past. "Are you at the end of the line?"

"Not quite. A few kids live farther out than me."

"Do you usually do homework or something on the ride?"

"Usually."

"Well, don't let me stop you. Just do what you usually do, you know?"

I shook my head. I was looking at his eyes again, that strange dark soft color. "It's okay. I don't have that much."

He started telling me about the piano lessons his folks had given him years ago. "It was like I was playing with my feet, I drove my piano teacher crazy. My parents wanted me to have a certain basic musical education. I kept at it for five years. Five years! My parents don't give up easily. Five years of torture for my piano teacher."

I laughed. I forgot to look out the window. I forgot how disastrous this afternoon would turn if Uncle and Dad were home, needing me to help them sober up. It was only when Teddy followed me off the bus and walked beside me down our road that I remembered. I dodged puddles and approached the trailer slowly. The pickup truck was parked, as always, to one side. That meant nothing. They never took the pickup when they went off.

"What are those TV's doing outside?" Teddy said, pointing to the two TV sets stacked one atop the other at one end of the trailer. Uncle had thrown a short piece of canvas over the top of them and forgotten them.

"Some people gave them to Uncle and Dad in part payment for work they did. We have no place for them inside." I opened the door and stood there, listening. The trailer was silent. Everything as I had left it in the morning.

"Can I come in out of the rain?" Teddy said from behind me, and I moved out of the doorway.

"Come in—please." I put my books down on the table. I saw how shabby everything was. How bare and worn.

"Is this it?" Teddy prowled the length of the trailer in four strides. He reached up and touched the ceiling, then stretched out his arms, almost touching the walls. "This is it?"

"Yes."

"You do everything right here—cook, eat, sleep, your homework, everything?"

"Yes." I folded my arms across my chest.

"God!" His eyes were shining. "It's wonderful. It's so honest. So essential." He indicated the door to my room. "What's that? A bathroom?"

"My room."

"Can I see?"

"All right." As soon as I said it, I felt very scared in a way I couldn't understand.

Teddy put his head inside the door, then stepped in. For a moment there was silence. I felt chilled.

"Chrissy," he said. "This is great. This is fantastic. You know what, this is exactly like a room I've dreamed of having."

"Don't—" I said.

"My God, for years I've had this dream of a perfect room, just plain, a bed or cot, maybe even just a mattress on the floor, a plain desk, some shelves, a couple drawers." His hand sliced the air, as if cutting his dream room off before it got too big.

I sat down on my bed, staring around at everything, as if seeing it for the first time. The same thing that happened on the bus. Teddy sat down next to me. "I've always liked my room," I said.

Our faces were very close. He had a faint mustache growing across his upper lip and he smelled soapy. "Would it be all right—you wouldn't be mad if I kissed you?"

Our lips touched. I had never known such sweetness. I leaped up, frightened, filled with a crazy happiness. It seemed it might once have felt this way, but when? When? I laughed out loud and pulled Teddy up. "Let's have some chocolate pudding!"

I got out the cocoa tin, the sack of sugar, the box of cornstarch, and measured the ingredients into a pan. I poured in milk and stirred the mixture over the hotplate. Teddy hovered at my shoulder, watching. As the pudding thickened and came to a boil, I reached into the cupboard over the hotplate for two dessert cups. "Sometimes I eat it straight out of the pot," I said.

"Why not now?"

"You're company."

He put his hand to his chest, pretended to stagger back, knocking against the broom closet. "Ooow! You know how to hurt a man. Company!"

I took the pot off the stove and set it down in the middle of the table. I took two spoons from the pitcher and we sat down across from each other. The chocolate pudding was thick and shiny. Teddy dipped in his spoon and took a taste. He closed his eyes and hummed. "I've never had chocolate pudding like this."

"We should have taken off the chocolate skin," I said, a bit regretfully.

He dipped up spoonful after spoonful. "You're a genius, a chocolate-pudding genius. Chrissy, I swear it, after this, never again chocolate pudding in a tin."

"A tin?" I said. I felt extraordinarily happy.

"My mother the tennis player buys chocolate pudding in little tins," Teddy said. "You know. They're in the market. Little tins about so big. Puddin'-In-A-Tin, it's called. Evil people somewhere have plotted this conspiracy against chocolate pudding lovers of the world. They squeeze something thick, gluey, and brown into little tins and label it chocolate pudding. And to think that, till this moment, I had no idea of the extent of their evil conspiracy! True, I knew tinned chocolate pudding tasted different than school-cafeteria chocolate pudding, but their diabolical cleverness succeeded in making me believe it *was* chocolate pudding, even if of an inferior grade. But this—" He shook his head and dipped again into the pot.

"Now that I have tasted true chocolate pudding, I've seen the light. Praise the Lord, I've seen the light! And it's clear now that what has been packed into chocolate pudding tins and passed off on the world as chocolate pudding is really—" He paused, looked at me seriously, said, "Are you ready for this shocking revelation?"

"Ready," I said.

"Then listen closely. That stuff in those tins is really hippopotamus mud."

"Hippopotamus mud?"

"Absolutely. Mud in which hippos have been rolling and playing for days to get it to the proper consistency. I see it all now!" He picked up the pot and scraped the inside.

I tipped back on my chair, watching Teddy. He was wearing a soft, clean, denim shirt, and worn-looking jeans. His jacket, which he had tossed over the other chair, was fur-lined. An image of his house suddenly sprang into my mind. It would have eight or ten rooms, each one larger than our whole trailer, a fireplace, wall oven, a garage for two cars, and two cars in the garage. It would have a patio in back, and big double glass doors that slid open. His mother played tennis and his father was, perhaps, a doctor.

"Is your father a doctor, and do you have a fireplace in your house?"

"No and qualified yes. He's a lawyer and there are two fireplaces. One in the parents' bedroom, one in the living room."

"Two," I said.

"Yes. And more rooms than we need. And furniture, and all kinds of garbage. Conspicuous, wasteful, disgusting consumption. Let's not talk about my house or my family."

"Don't you like them?"

"Actually, I do. But the way we live—" He drew his thin shoulders together. "You people have the right idea. Everything basic. Where's the john?" He stood up.

"Privy outside. Go right around the side of the trailer. You can't miss it."

"My God!" His face glowed as he rushed outside. I let my chair down onto the floor, took the pot to the sink and filled it with water to soak. Teddy came back in, shutting the trailer door carefully behind him, shaking rain off his shoulders and his head. "Do you use that in winter, too?"

"Yes," I said, "but at night I use a pot if I have to."

"It's what we all have to come back to." He leaned against the table. "We Americans use too much of everything. Too much gas, too much electricity, too much food, too much of all the natural resources. The figures per capita compared to the rest of the world are really gross. Wait a second, I'll show you an article—" He dug into his pockets, taking out a handful of change, a few bills, keys, scraps of paper, throwing it all down on the table, talking about the world food crisis and how it could be solved. "Well, I can't find it, but you know what I mean." He pushed his hair back behind his ears. "You're doing things right. Basic. Down to the bone. It's terrific."

We went on talking. I made him laugh by telling him how I learned to read from chocolate pudding boxes when I was about four years old. It got dark outside. We drank milk, and ate bread with peanut butter. I turned on a light. It was warm in the trailer. That strange feeling of happiness crept over me again. It was an amnesiac feeling, as if happiness had made me forget all sorts of important things. After a few moments it came to me that I had forgotten to think about Uncle and Dad. I sat straighter, alert, listening for them in the rainy darkness outside.

Teddy stood up. "I really have to go." I gave him directions for getting out to the highway. He didn't think he'd have any trouble getting a ride back to the Square. "If I get stuck, I can always call my mother from a gas station and she'll come pick me up. She's a good kid, my mother." He took my hand. "Anyway. Right?"

"Basic," I said.

"Chocolate pudding," he said.

"Okay. Chocolate pudding."

"Remember that. The two most important words in the world. Choc-o-late pud-ding." In the midst of our silliness, we kissed again.

Teddy left. I sat down at the table and opened my notebook. I found myself listening, as I had every night lately, for sounds which might be Uncle and Dad returning. I was chilly and got a sweater. How lonely the rain sounded tapping on our tin roof. Suddenly, I ran to the door and pulled it open.

"Theodore Roosevelt Finkel," I called. He was gone. I ran into the road. It was dark. Rain fell heavily all around. "Teddy," I called. "Teddy!"

"Over here!" His voice came from a distance. "Chrissy— you okay?"

"Okay," I replied. "See you tomorrow." The rain seemed to wash away my voice. I put my hands around my mouth, and called as loud as I could, "Chocolate pudding!" And from a distance, Teddy's voice came singing out of the darkness, *"Choc-o-late pud-ding."*

Setting

Every story has three major elements: plot, character and setting. Of the three, setting is the least obvious. Unlike vivid characters and exciting plots, settings tend to slip into the background. This, actually, is where they belong. Settings are not meant to play an active role in stories.

But you would miss them sorely if they were left out. This is because setting works hand-in-hand with the other elements of a story. Characters are shaped by their surroundings. Plots spring naturally out of a certain setting, and move forward with changes of scene. Important ideas are reinforced by the settings. And, last but not least, feelings—yours and the characters'—are influenced by the many details of an author's carefully prepared setting.

Setting consists of many things, including the place and the time of the story, sights, sounds, smells, clothing, transportation and the weather. Even minor characters, when they are just buzzing around in the background, can be thought of as part of the setting.

Authors do not spell out every last detail of every setting. If they did, the story would become bogged down in endless description. Instead, they pick and choose, presenting the reader with only those details that are important to the story.

In the hands of a skillful writer like Norma Fox Mazer, settings enhance the story in four important ways:

1 They suggest the kind of action that might take place.

2 They influence the way characters feel and, in turn, the way you feel.

3 They help you picture the story in your mind, so that you feel you are really there.

4 They reinforce important ideas, or themes, that the author wants to get across.

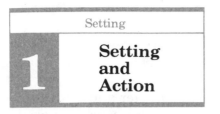

1 Setting and Action

The action of a story—the events that unfold—tends to suit the setting. To put it another way, settings are created to match, or go with, the story being told. In many cases, settings actually help create the actions that occur.

For example, the setting of "First Confession," the first story in this book, is a town in Ireland in which most of the people are Catholics. The story is about an Irish boy taking part in a Catholic ceremony. "To Build a Fire" is set in Alaska. The action consists of a man's trek across lonely terrain in sub-zero weather. The brutal cold, which is part of the setting, actually controls the man's adventures. The setting of "Raymond's Run" is Harlem, a black district in New York City, and the story is about a black girl growing up there. Each of these stories could only have happened, in the way they happened, in the settings the authors prepared for them.

You find the same relationship between setting and action in "Chocolate Pudding." Early in the story, Norma Fox Mazer describes the trailer in which Chrissy lives. How does the whole story seem to flow from this setting?

> Our trailer is one long, narrow room. We do our cooking on a two-burner hotplate, we have a refrigerator, table, three chairs, an electric heater, a sink. No more, no less than we need, as Uncle says. Our privy is out back, fifteen feet from the well, as required by state law. Uncle and Dad sleep on the pullout couch, while I used to have a cot with chairs shoved against it to keep me from falling out. But now Uncle and Dad have built a wall across the back of the trailer, making a room for me. They built in a bed, desk, a few shelves. There's a window over my bed. Sometimes when Uncle and Dad are away, I sit on my bed eating chocolate pudding from the pot and looking out the window into the fields.

Clearly, Chrissy and her father and uncle are poor. Many details in the setting suggest this. They cook on a hotplate instead of a stove. They have no bathroom, just an outdoor privy. And, we learn later, they are isolated fifteen miles from town without a telephone. Their trailer is small, and there is room for only the barest necessities.

In one way or another, all of the events that unfold have their roots in this setting: Chrissy's need for the comfort that comes from eating chocolate pudding, the men's refuge in drinking, the long rides to and from school and Teddy's visit. These actions and events spring naturally out of the setting the author has prepared for us.

The setting described in Exercise A also prepares us for what happens next. Try to see how it does this.

Exercise A

Read the following passage and answer the questions about it using what you have learned in this part of the lesson.

Carefully I took the chocolate skin off the last pudding and added it to the others. Two more boys sat down at the table. One of them, Teddy Finkel, had six chocolate puddings on his tray. "Look at that," Debby Pearce said. "Everyone! Look at Teddy Finkel's tray!" Everyone did. "Now look at Chrissy's tray. Isn't that unbelievable?"

"Weird," Melissa said. "It's a convention of chocolate pudding freaks."

Put an *x* in the box beside the correct answer.

1. What action that is important to the story develops from this scene?

   □ a. Chrissy learns to make chocolate pudding

   □ b. Debbie and Melissa's conversation

   □ c. The meeting between Teddy and Chrissy

   □ d. Dad and Uncle's drunken spree

2. We said that people and things can be part of a setting. What item that can be considered part of the setting here helps develop the action? Write your answer here.

_____

Now check your answers using the Answer Key on page 454. Correct any wrong answers and review this part of the lesson if you don't understand why an answer was wrong.

Settings have a powerful effect on human feelings. For instance, we tend to feel peaceful in a rose garden, reverent in a church and frazzled in a traffic jam.

Setting

Setting and Feelings

2

On the other hand, our feelings can affect the way we view a setting. Your own home might, at times, make you feel stifled, cooped up and confined. But if you have been away for a while and felt homesick, the same setting could make you feel safe and secure.

Settings and feelings interact in stories, as well. Authors create settings that have a certain effect on characters. The settings affect readers in much the same way they affect the characters. Readers sense the atmosphere, or mood, of the setting and share the characters' feelings for it.

In "Chocolate Pudding," Norma Fox Mazer makes the small, simple trailer where Chrissy lives seem downright cozy. See how she uses setting in the following passage to create this feeling:

> The last day of January was so cold that as I ran down our frozen rutted lane for the school bus the inside of my nose felt fragile as glass. But that night in our trailer it was cozy, the electric heater humming, as I did my homework and Dad listened to Radio Australia on short wave. Uncle was in a mood to talk.

How warm and friendly this setting makes you feel. Outside it's bitterly cold. But inside, the electric heater is humming on a happy family scene. Chrissy is doing her homework, Dad is fiddling with his radio, and Uncle is in a mood to chat. At such times, the trailer seems a warm, safe place to be.

But the trailer doesn't always feel like such a peaceful haven. When Dad and Uncle are away, Chrissy feels lonely in the trailer. The setting is the same, but Chrissy's feelings have changed.

In Exercise B, we get another view of the trailer. How do Chrissy's feelings affect the setting this time?

Exercise B

Read the following passage and answer the questions about it using what you have learned in this part of the lesson.

> . . . I heard the fierce moaning of the wind as it gnawed at the trailer, and I thought of Dad and Uncle sleeping on the pullout couch, their boots tumbled together, safe in the trailer, enclosed, protected. But at the same moment, perhaps for the first time, I thought how frail the trailer was, how weather-beaten the boards, how flimsy the putty that held the windows in place, and I imagined the trailer crumpling in on itself like a deflated paper bag.

Put an *x* in the box beside the correct answer.

1. As Chrissy's feelings change, so does the setting. One moment the trailer feels

   ☐ a. lonely, the next moment it seems festive.

   ☐ b. strange, the next moment it seems familiar.

   ☐ c. uncomfortable, the next moment it seems comfortable.

   ☐ d. safe, the next moment it seems fragile and unsafe.

2. Find three words that are used in the first half of the passage to describe one view Chrissy has of the trailer. Then find three words in the second half of the passage that describe the other view she has of the trailer. Write the words on the lines below.

   View 1 _____

   _____

   View 2 _____

   _____

Now check your answers using the Answer Key on page 454. Correct any wrong answers and review this part of the lesson if you don't understand why an answer was wrong.

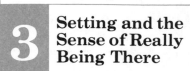

Setting

3 Setting and the Sense of Really Being There

In theater, the large canvases on which scenery is painted are called "flats." When you stop to think about it, that's a good name for them. They provide only one dimension of the play's setting. But there is more to setting than just scenery. The actors who portray the characters, their costumes, the sound effects and the lighting all contribute to the total effect, or setting. Together, they give the audience the sense of really being at the scene of the play.

Authors strive to create the same complete effects for the settings in their stories. They want to provide readers with more than just flat pictures. They try to place readers in the midst of scenes. They do this by describing sights, sounds, smells, textures—the little things that make a setting come alive.

Pay attention to how Norma Fox Mazer places you in the midst of a school cafeteria in the passage below:

> In the cafeteria at lunch time the menu featured sloppy joes and chocolate pudding. I ordered four chocolate puddings and took the cups on a tray to a table in the corner of the lunchroom. I said hello to the others at the table and skinned the top off my first pudding. Slowly I ate the soft insides, cleaning out the little brown dish thoroughly. The kids were talking about Mrs. Fannon, the Latin teacher. "God, she's fierce," Melissa Maguire said. "You have her, don't you, Chrissy?"
>
> "Doesn't everyone?" I said. They laughed. . . .
>
> "I hear Fannon never gives anything over a B," Debby said. . . .
>
> "Oh, you only have to know how to get around her," Neil Rosencranz said, winking at me. "It's a challenge."
>
> I went on eating my chocolate pudding. Far back in my mind [I heard] the chatter, the scrape of dishes, the crinkling of sandwich wrappers. . . .

Notice the different kinds of details you get in this setting. You follow Chrissy through the cafeteria line to a corner table of the lunchroom. You eat a chocolate pudding with her. You take part in the chitchat that bounces back and forth across the table. You hear the everyday sounds of a lunchroom at lunchtime—"the scrape of dishes, the crinkling of sandwich wrappers."

These are details that appeal to all your senses. As a result, you don't just "see" this setting, you feel it. You have a sense of really being there.

Now look at the school bus scene in Exercise C, and try to decide how the author makes you a part of this setting.

Exercise C

Read the following passage and answer the questions about it using what you have learned in this part of the lesson.

The bus filled up. Kids were yelling to each other. Someone blew up a lunch bag and popped it. "All right, you kids, settle down," Mrs. Johnson, the bus driver, yelled. Nobody paid any attention.

The bus left the school grounds, drove through Middle Square, past the bank with its fluted columns, the supermarket, a dress shop, the laundromat. A few people hurried through the rain, shoulders hunched. I stared at everything through the rain-smeared windows as if seeing it all for the first time, conscious of Teddy looking across my shoulder. On the outskirts of Middle Square, we drove by a set of stone gates with a white arch over them lettered STONY ACRES. Behind the arch I caught a glimpse of big houses, wet clean road, and clipped lawns, soggy and glistening.

"That's where I live," Teddy said.

Put an x in the box beside the correct answer.

1. What element of setting does the author describe in the first paragraph?

☐ a. Tastes and smells

☐ b. Background noises

☐ c. The weather

☐ d. Scenery and feelings

2. Like a real bus ride, this one gives the reader a sense of movement—of going from one place to another. The second paragraph describes three settings that Chrissy and Teddy ride through. List the three settings on the lines below.

_____

_____

_____

Now check your answers using the Answer Key on page 454. Correct any wrong answers and review this part of the lesson if you don't understand why an answer was wrong.

It's hard to talk about a story without discussing the ideas it presents. There are several ideas that are presented in "Chocolate Pudding." One concerns alcoholism—what it is like when a member of your family drinks too much. Another idea is about poverty—what it is like to be poor.

Setting

4 | **Setting and Ideas**

The ideas in a story are also called its *themes*. When authors choose settings for their stories, they look for settings that can help them express the story's themes. Each setting should be an appropriate place for these ideas to develop.

As Chrissy and Teddy become friendly with each other, both realize how different their backgrounds are. She comes from a poor background, he comes from a wealthy one. This contrast becomes an important idea in the story, and Norma Fox Mazer uses settings to help get it across.

In the passage below, Teddy visits Chrissy's home for the first time. How does this setting remind us of the difference in their backgrounds?

> "Come in—please." I [Chrissy] put my books down on the table. I saw how shabby everything was. How bare and worn.
> "Is this it?" Teddy prowled the length of the trailer in four strides. He reached up and touched the ceiling, then stretched out his arms, almost touching the walls. "This is it?"

Here we see the trailer through another pair of eyes—Teddy's—and what a different impression we get of it. To Chrissy, the trailer is home. It is filled with memories, with things that are familiar, comforting and dear to her. To Teddy, however, the trailer represents a very different lifestyle from the one he is familiar with. But though his first impression is that the trailer is small, he thinks it is a wonderful place to live because it doesn't contain any unnecessary things. "It's so honest. So essential," he says. He respects the way she lives, even though it's very different from the way he lives.

Chrissy, too, is seeing the trailer through new eyes. As if for the first time, she sees "how shabby everything is. How bare and worn." She knows now what kind of a house Teddy lives in, and she's seeing the trailer as she imagines it must look to him. The author could hardly have chosen a better setting to illustrate the difference between Teddy's background and Chrissy's.

In Exercise D we get a chance to compare Chrissy's home with Teddy's. See how this setting completes our understanding of this important theme.

Exercise D

Read the following passage and answer the questions about it using what you have learned in this part of the lesson.

I tipped back on my chair, watching Teddy. He was wearing a soft, clean, denim shirt, and worn-looking jeans. His jacket, which he had tossed over the other chair, was fur-lined. An image of his house suddenly sprang into my mind. It would have eight or ten rooms, each one larger than our whole trailer, a fireplace, wall oven, a garage for two cars, and two cars in the garage. It would have a patio in back, and big double glass doors that slid open. His mother played tennis and his father was, perhaps, a doctor.

Put an *x* in the box beside the correct answer.

1. This is the kind of setting that

□ a. you might find in the pages of a home magazine.

□ b. really doesn't exist.

□ c. everyone needs in order to be happy.

□ d. Chrissy finds distasteful.

2. One small detail mentioned early in the passage triggers this image of Teddy's house in Chrissy's mind. Find this detail and write it on the line below.

_____

Use the Answer Key on page 454 to check your answers. Correct any wrong answers and review this part of the lesson if you don't understand why an answer was wrong. Now go on to do the Comprehension Questions.

Comprehension Questions

Answer these questions without looking back at the story. Choose the best answer to each question and put an *x* in the box beside it.

Recognizing Words in Context

1. Chrissy used to ask Uncle for his orange peel. " 'The peel?' he'd say, as if sincerely astonished at such a *bizarre* request." Something that is *bizarre* is

   ☐ a. commonplace.

   ☐ b. greedy.

   ☐ c. strange.

   ☐ d. rude.

Recalling Facts

2. Where is Chrissy's mother?

   ☐ a. She and Chrissy's father are divorced.

   ☐ b. She is in a hospital.

   ☐ c. No one knows for sure.

   ☐ d. She died when Chrissy was small.

Understanding Main Ideas

3. Except for when Dad and Uncle are drinking, how would you describe Chrissy's home life?

   ☐ a. Harsh and cruel

   ☐ b. Homey and peaceful

   ☐ c. Lonely and cheerless

   ☐ d. Lively and gay

Making Inferences

4. When the State Troopers came about the windows that had been shot out, there was something in their attitude that made Chrissy angry. What do you think she heard, or sensed, behind their words?

   ☐ a. Anger

    ☐ b. Hatred

    ☐ c. Disbelief

    ☐ d. Pity

Making Inferences

5. What was most likely on Dad and Uncle's minds the evening they were so restless?

    ☐ a. Drinking

    ☐ b. Chrissy's mother

    ☐ c. Money problems

    ☐ d. Chrissy's future

Keeping Events in Order

6. "Something will happen today," Chrissy said to herself one morning. That was the day Dad and Uncle left on one of their drinking sprees. But what else happened that day?

    ☐ a. The windows of the trailer were shot out.

    ☐ b. Someone threw garbage at their trailer.

    ☐ c. Chrissy took a drink.

    ☐ d. Chrissy met Teddy Finkel.

Recognizing Words in Context

7. "It was a saying in Peter V. Newsome High that you hadn't been educated till Margaret Fannon had called you a nincompoop, a mental incompetent, and utterly beyond *redemption*." Someone who is *beyond redemption* is probably

    ☐ a. beyond saving or helping.

    ☐ b. too old.

    ☐ c. out of control.

    ☐ d. beyond reproach.

8. "We chocolate pudding freaks don't *like* chocolate pudding," says Teddy Finkel, "we *revere* it." To *revere* something is to

☐ a. have mixed feelings about it.

☐ b. be afraid of it.

☐ c. adore it.

☐ d. hate it.

9. "There now, Chrissy, the world is a foolish place. Don't try to figure it out." Which of the characters in the story would be likely to speak these words?

☐ a. Dad

☐ b. Uncle

☐ c. Teddy Finkel

☐ d. Diane Lucas

10. What is Teddy Finkel's middle name?

☐ a. Washington

☐ b. Benjamin

☐ c. Roosevelt

☐ d. Fannon

11. What does Teddy Finkel seem to like most about Chrissy?

☐ a. Her looks

☐ b. Her intelligence

☐ c. Her courage

☐ d. Her honesty

12. How much time goes by between the time Teddy and
    Chrissy first meet in the cafeteria and the time Teddy
    visits Chrissy after school?

    ☐ a. A day

    ☐ b. Several days

    ☐ c. A couple of weeks

    ☐ d. A month or more

13. What word does Teddy use to describe the way in
    which Chrissy, her father and her uncle live?

    ☐ a. Basic

    ☐ b. Cool

    ☐ c. Wasteful

    ☐ d. Pitiful

14. At one point in the story Chrissy says, "That strange
    feeling of happiness crept over me again." When in
    the story does she feel like this?

    ☐ a. While talking with Teddy in the trailer

    ☐ b. While riding the bus to school

    ☐ c. While eating chocolate pudding

    ☐ d. While talking with Dad and Uncle

15. How does Chrissy seem to feel about Teddy Finkel by
    the end of the story?

    ☐ a. She is madly in love with him.

    ☐ b. She wishes he would leave her alone.

    ☐ c. She looks forward to seeing more of him.

    ☐ d. She envies his family's wealth.

Now check your answers using the Answer Key on page 454. Make no mark for right answers. <u>Correct</u> any wrong answers you may have by putting a checkmark (✓) in the box next to the right answer. Count the number of questions you answered correctly and plot the total on the Comprehension Scores graph on page 462.

Next, look at the questions you answered incorrectly. What types of questions were they? Count the number you got wrong of each type and enter the numbers in the spaces below.

Recognizing Words in Context   _____

Recalling Facts   _____

Keeping Events in Order   _____

Making Inferences   _____

Understanding Main Ideas   _____

Now use these numbers to fill in the Comprehension Skills Profile on page 463.

Discussion Guides

The questions below will help you to think about the story and the lesson you have just read. If you don't discuss these questions in class, try to think about them or discuss them with your classmates.

Discussing Setting

1. When the author describes the trailer she tells us exactly how it looks—its size, its furnishings, its surroundings. But when she describes the school cafeteria, she describes the students, their conversations and the everyday lunchroom sounds—not a word about what the cafeteria looks like. Why does she provide this detailed information in one case and not the other?

2. Before the story is over, we see the trailer through two pairs of eyes— Chrissy's and Teddy's. How did you feel about the trailer before Teddy's visit and then during his visit?

3. It is dark and raining outside when Chrissy says good-bye to Teddy at the end of the story. Why is this a good setting for this scene? How does it make Chrissy feel?

Discussing the Story

4. At one time Chrissy had hoped that Melissa Maguire or Debby Pearce might become her close friends. One of them said something about calling her up. "But of course we had no phone," says Chrissy, "and nothing came of it." Why do you think these friendships failed to blossom?

5. Dad says, "The day I see you take a drink, Chrissy, is the day I'm through with living." Do you think Chrissy will follow in her dad's footsteps, or has she learned something from living with Dad and Uncle? Give reasons for your answer.

6. What do you think will come of the budding friendship between Chrissy and Teddy? What difference, if any, will their different backgrounds make?

Discussing the Author's Work

7. Norma Fox Mazer spends her summers in Canada in a cottage "without electricity, telephone, newspaper, radio, indoor plumbing, stove, refrigerator, lights, etc., etc., etc." How is this background reflected in her story "Chocolate Pudding"?

8. How does the author present something of a lesson about alcohol abuse in this story? Does she preach, argue, or use some other method?

9. The story collection from which "Chocolate Pudding" was taken won many awards for young adult literature. What do you think makes Norma Mazer's stories so popular with young adults?

Writing Exercise

One setting you have probably had a hand in creating is your own room at home. You may have posters on the walls, souvenirs and photos on shelves and bureaus, trophies and collections of one kind or another. Perhaps you chose the color scheme, or picked out the wallpaper or the bedspread. Write a few paragraphs describing this setting. Organize your thoughts in the following way:

1. Describe your room. Include not only how it looks but also its sounds, odors, textures and other details that make up a complete, well-rounded setting and give the reader a sense of really being there.

2. Next, describe how this setting makes you feel. (You probably feel different ways at different times.)

3. Finally, describe one thing that this setting says about you—something a person could learn about you by looking at your room. [Hint: This might be a special interest, a personal style, a goal in life, etc.]

Chocolate Pudding

Unit 5   Theme

The Moustache
BY ROBERT CORMIER

About the Illustration

How would you describe the feelings between these two people? Point out some details in the drawing to support your response.

Here are some questions to help you think:

☐ How can you tell that these two people know each other very well? What do you think their relationship might be?

☐ What do you think the old woman's feelings are? What makes you think that?

☐ What do you think the young man's feelings are? What makes you think that?

Unit 5

Introduction	What the Story Is About/What the Lesson Is About
Story	The Moustache
Lesson	Theme
Activities	Comprehension Questions/Discussion Guides/Writing Exercise

Introduction

What the Story Is About

The moustache in the title of the story belongs to Mike. Mike is seventeen years old. It is his first moustache, and he is secretly proud of it.

His mother thinks it makes him look too old. His girlfriend isn't exactly crazy about it either. But the moustache has a very different effect on Mike's grandmother. It reminds her of someone else.

Family resemblances are funny things. Rarely are they obvious. A son is seldom really the "spitting image" of his father, and a daughter is not a carbon copy of her mother. In fact, likenesses are apt to skip a generation and pop up in a grandchild. Even then, the resemblance is usually subtle—a certain smile, a way of walking, a crinkling of the eyes. Photographs rarely capture such traits. But an older relative who knows both the older and the younger person may see the similarity right off. This is especially true when the relative hasn't seen the young person for a while.

That is the situation in "The Moustache." Mike's grandmother is in a nursing home. She suffers from a disease of the arteries that sometimes comes with aging. It causes her to become confused. Sometimes she doesn't recognize people she knows. Or she forgets what day or even what year it is. She recalls events of fifty years ago as if they happened yesterday. But the things that really did happen yesterday, she often can't remember at all.

Lately, Mike's grandmother has been dwelling on events that happened forty years ago. They are not happy memories, but she cannot let go of them. When Mike walks into her room wearing his new moustache and a spiffy raincoat, she is taken aback. It is not her grandson she sees, but someone else. Mike doesn't realize it at first, but he has become a bit player in the final act of a very tragic drama.

Author Robert Cormier says that he wrote this and other stories about young people at a time when he and his wife were bringing up three teenagers. "The house sang in those days," he says, "with the vibrant songs of youth—tender, hectic, tragic, and ecstatic. Hearts were broken on Sunday afternoon and repaired by the following Thursday evening, but how desperate it all was in the interim. The telephone never stopped ringing, the shower seemed to be constantly running, the

Beatles became a presence in our lives." Clearly, he loved having a house full of teenagers. And it shows in his stories.

One of his best-known works is a hard-hitting novel for young adults called *The Chocolate War*. It's about a high school freshman who refuses to sell candy for a school fund-raising event. This and other novels by Cormier have been called brutally real. To this Cormier replies, "As long as what I write is true and believable, why should I have to create happy endings?"

What the Lesson Is About

The lesson that follows this story is about themes. In music, especially in longer pieces of music, a theme is a melody that is repeated in various places throughout the composition. In a song, the theme might be the chorus, or refrain, that is repeated after each verse. The idea expressed in the refrain ties together the various verses.

In a story, a theme is an idea or a feeling that connects the reader to the story. Stories never exactly describe people's lives. But a good story is about a feeling, an experience or an idea with which everyone can identify—one that occurs in every person and every generation. The details that are described in a story may be unique, but the ideas and feelings are familiar. These are a story's themes. They are part of the message an author offers readers through the story.

Several ideas are offered to readers as themes in "The Moustache." One idea is about aging. Another deals with guilt feelings. And there are others, as you will see.

The questions below will help you to focus on themes in "The Moustache." Read the story carefully and try to answer these questions as you go along:

1   How has Mike's grandmother changed from the way she was before she became ill? How does this make you feel about aging?

2   What kind of thoughts are running through Mike's mind as he nears the nursing home?

3   In the course of his visit with his grandmother, what does Mike learn that changes his image of old people in general?

4   What feeling prompts Mike to kiss his grandmother?

The Moustache

Robert Cormier

At the last minute Annie couldn't go. She was invaded by one of those twenty-four-hour flu bugs that sent her to bed with a fever, moaning about the fact that she'd also have to break her date with Handsome Harry Arnold that night. We call him Handsome Harry because he's actually handsome, but he's also a nice guy, cool, and he doesn't treat me like Annie's kid brother, which I am, but like a regular person. Anyway, I had to go to Lawnrest alone that afternoon. But first of all I had to stand inspection. My mother lined me up against the wall. She stood there like a one-man firing squad, which is kind of funny because she's not like a man at all, she's very feminine, and we have this great relationship—I mean, I feel as if she really likes me. I realize that sounds strange, but I know guys whose mothers love them and cook special stuff for them and worry about them and all but there's something missing in their relationship.

Anyway. She frowned and started the routine.

"That hair," she said. Then admitted: "Well, at least you combed it."

I sighed. I have discovered that it's better to sigh than argue.

"And that moustache." She shook her head. "I still say a seventeen-year-old has no business wearing a moustache."

"It's an experiment," I said. "I just wanted to see if I could grow one." To tell the truth, I had proved my point about being able to grow a decent moustache, but I also had learned to like it.

"It's costing you money, Mike," she said.

"I know, I know."

The money was a reference to the movies. The Downtown Cinema has a special Friday night offer—half-price admission for high school couples, seventeen or younger. But the woman in the box office took one look at my moustache and charged me full price. Even when I showed her my driver's license. She charged full admission for Cindy's ticket, too, which left me practically broke and unable to take Cindy out for a hamburger with the crowd afterward. That didn't help matters, because Cindy has been getting impatient recently about things like the fact that I don't own my own car and have to concentrate on my studies if I want to win that college scholarship, for instance. Cindy wasn't exactly crazy about the moustache, either.

Now it was my mother's turn to sigh.

"Look," I said, to cheer her up. "I'm thinking about shaving it off." Even though I wasn't. Another discovery: You can build a way of life on postponement.

"Your grandmother probably won't even recognize you," she said. And I saw the shadow fall across her face.

Let me tell you what the visit to Lawnrest was all about. My grandmother is seventy-three years old. She is a resident—which is supposed to be a better word than *patient*—at the Lawnrest Nursing Home. She used to make the greatest turkey dressing in the world and was a nut about baseball and could even quote batting averages, for crying out loud. She always rooted for the losers. She was in love with the Mets until they started to win. Now she has arteriosclerosis, which the dictionary says is "a chronic disease characterized by abnormal thickening and hardening of the arterial walls." Which really means that she can't live at home anymore or even with us, and her memory has betrayed her as well as her body. She used to wander off and sometimes didn't recognize people. My mother visits her all the time, driving the thirty miles to Lawnrest almost every day. Because Annie was home for a semester break from college, we had decided to make a special Saturday visit. Now Annie was in bed, groaning theatrically—she's a drama major—but I told my mother I'd go, anyway. I hadn't seen my grandmother since she'd been admitted to Lawnrest. Besides, the place is located on the Southwest Turnpike, which meant I could barrel along in my father's new Le Mans. My ambition was to see the speedometer hit seventy-five. Ordinarily, I used the old station wagon, which can barely stagger up to fifty.

Frankly, I wasn't too crazy about visiting a nursing home. They reminded me of hospitals and hospitals turn me off. I mean, the smell of ether makes me nauseous, and I feel faint at the sight of blood. And as I approached Lawnrest—which is a terrible cemetery kind of name, to begin with—I was sorry I hadn't avoided the trip. Then I felt guilty about it. I'm loaded with guilt complexes. Like driving like a madman after promising my father to be careful. Like sitting in the parking lot, looking at the nursing home with dread and thinking how I'd rather be with Cindy. Then I thought of all the Christmas and birthday gifts my grandmother had given me and I got out of the car, guilty, as usual.

Inside, I was surprised by the lack of hospital smell, although there was another odor or maybe the absence of an odor. The air was antiseptic, sterile. As if there was no atmosphere at all or I'd caught a cold suddenly and couldn't taste or smell.

A nurse at the reception desk gave me directions—my grandmother was in East Three. I made my way down the tiled corridor and was glad to see that the walls were painted with cheerful colors like yellow and pink. A wheelchair suddenly shot around the corner, self-propelled by an old man, white-haired and toothless, who cackled merrily as he barely missed me. I jumped aside—here I was, almost getting wiped out by a two-mile-an-hour wheelchair after doing seventy-five on the pike. As I walked through the corridor seeking East Three, I couldn't help glancing into the rooms, and it was like some kind of wax museum—all these figures in various stances and attitudes, sitting in beds or chairs, standing at windows, as if they were frozen forever in these postures. To tell the truth, I began to hurry because I was getting depressed. Finally, I saw a beautiful girl approaching, dressed in white, a nurse or an attendant, and I was so happy to see someone young, someone walking and acting normally, that I gave her a wide smile and a big hello and I must have looked like a kind of nut. Anyway, she looked right through me as if I were a window, which is about par for the course whenever I meet beautiful girls.

I finally found the room and saw my grandmother in bed. My grandmother looks like Ethel Barrymore. I never knew who Ethel Barrymore was until I saw a terrific movie, *None But the Lonely Heart*, on TV, starring Ethel Barrymore and Cary Grant. Both my grandmother and Ethel Barrymore have these great craggy faces like the side of a mountain and wonderful voices like syrup being poured. Slowly. She was propped up in bed, pillows puffed behind her. Her hair had been combed out and fell upon her shoulders. For some reason, this flowing hair gave her an almost girlish appearance, despite its whiteness.

She saw me and smiled. Her eyes lit up and her eyebrows arched and she reached out her hands to me in greeting. "Mike, Mike," she said. And I breathed a sigh of relief. This was one of her good days. My mother had warned me that she might not know who I was at first.

I took her hands in mine. They were fragile. I could actually feel her bones, and it seemed as if they would break if I pressed too hard. Her skin was smooth, almost slippery, as if the years had worn away all the roughness the way the wind wears away the surfaces of stones.

"Mike, Mike, I didn't think you'd come," she said, so happy, and she was still Ethel Barrymore, that voice like a caress. "I've been waiting all this time." Before I could reply, she looked away, out the window. "See the birds? I've been watching them at the feeder. I love to see them come. Even the blue jays. The blue jays are like hawks—they take the food that the small birds should have. But the small birds, the chickadees, watch the blue jays and at least learn where the feeder is."

She lapsed into silence, and I looked out the window. There was no feeder. No birds. There was only the parking lot and the sun glinting on car windshields.

She turned to me again, eyes bright. Radiant, really. Or was it a medicine brightness? "Ah, Mike. You look so grand, so grand. Is that a new coat?"

"Not really," I said. I'd been wearing my Uncle Jerry's old army-fatigue jacket for months, practically living in it, my mother said. But she insisted that I wear my raincoat for the visit. It was about a year old but looked new because I didn't wear it much. Nobody was wearing raincoats lately.

"You always loved clothes, didn't you, Mike?" she said.

I was beginning to feel uneasy because she regarded me with such intensity. Those bright eyes. I wondered—are old people in places like this so lonesome, so abandoned that they go wild when someone visits? Or was she so happy because she was suddenly lucid and everything was sharp and clear? My mother had described those moments when my grandmother suddenly emerged from the fog that so often obscured her mind. I didn't know the answers, but it felt kind of spooky, getting such an emotional welcome from her.

"I remember the time you bought the new coat—the Chesterfield," she said, looking away again, as if watching the birds that weren't there. "That lovely coat with the velvet collar. Black, it was. Stylish. Remember that, Mike? It was hard times, but you could never resist the glitter."

I was about to protest—I had never heard of a Chesterfield, for crying out loud. But I stopped. Be patient with her, my mother had said. Humor her. Be gentle.

We were interrupted by an attendant who pushed a wheeled cart into the room. "Time for juices, dear," the woman said. She was the standard forty- or fifty-year-old woman: glasses, nothing hair, plump cheeks. Her manner was cheerful but a businesslike kind of cheerfulness. I'd hate to be called "dear" by someone getting paid to do it. "Orange or grape or cranberry, dear? Cranberry is good for the bones, you know."

My grandmother ignored the interruption. She didn't even bother to answer, having turned away at the woman's arrival, as if angry about her appearance.

The woman looked at me and winked. A conspiratorial kind of wink. It was kind of horrible. I didn't think people winked like that anymore. In fact, I hadn't seen a wink in years.

"She doesn't care much for juices," the woman said, talking to me as if my grandmother weren't even there. "But she loves her coffee. With lots of cream and two lumps of sugar. But this is juice time, not coffee time." Addressing my grandmother again, she said, "Orange or grape or cranberry, dear?"

"Tell her I want no juices, Mike," my grandmother commanded regally, her eyes still watching invisible birds.

The woman smiled, patience like a label on her face. "That's all right, dear. I'll just leave some cranberry for you. Drink it at your leisure. It's good for the bones."

She wheeled herself out of the room. My grandmother was still absorbed in the view. Somewhere a toilet flushed. A wheelchair passed the doorway—probably that same old driver fleeing a hit-run accident. A television set exploded with sound somewhere, soap-opera voices filling the air. You can always tell soap-opera voices.

I turned back to find my grandmother staring at me. Her hands cupped her face, her index fingers curled around her cheeks like parenthesis marks.

"But you know, Mike, looking back, I think you were right," she said, continuing our conversation as if there had been no interruption. "You always said, 'It's the things of the spirit that count, Meg.' The spirit! And so you bought the baby-grand piano—a baby grand in the middle of the

Depression. A knock came on the door and it was the deliveryman. It took five of them to get it into the house." She leaned back, closing her eyes. "How I loved that piano, Mike. I was never that fine a player, but you loved to sit there in the parlor, on Sunday evenings, Ellie on your lap, listening to me play and sing." She hummed a bit, a fragment of melody I didn't recognize. Then she drifted into silence. Maybe she'd fallen asleep. My mother's name is Ellen, but everyone always calls her Ellie. "Take my hand, Mike," my grandmother said suddenly. Then I remembered—my grandfather's name was Michael. I had been named for him.

"Ah, Mike," she said, pressing my hands with all her feeble strength. "I thought I'd lost you forever. And here you are, back with me again . . . ."

Her expression scared me. I don't mean scared as if I were in danger but scared because of what could happen to her when she realized the mistake she had made. My mother always said I favored her side of the family. Thinking back to the pictures in the old family albums, I recalled my grandfather as tall and thin. Like me. But the resemblance ended there. He was thirty-five when he died, almost forty years ago. And he wore a moustache. I brought my hand to my face. I also wore a moustache now, of course.

"I sit here these day, Mike," she said, her voice a lullaby, her hand still holding mine, "and I drift and dream. The days are fuzzy sometimes, merging together. Sometimes it's like I'm not here at all but somewhere else altogether. And I always think of you. Those years we had. Not enough years, Mike, not enough . . . ."

Her voice was so sad, so mournful that I made sounds of sympathy, not words exactly but the kind of soothings that mothers murmur to their children when they awaken from bad dreams.

"And I think of that terrible night, Mike, that terrible night. Have you ever really forgiven me for that night?"

"Listen . . . " I began. I wanted to say: "Nana, this is Mike your grandson, not Mike your husband."

"Sh . . . sh . . . " she whispered, placing a finger as long and cold as a candle against my lips. "Don't say anything. I've waited so long for this moment. To be here. With you. I wondered what I would say if suddenly you walked in that door like other people have done. I've thought and thought about it. And I finally made up my mind—I'd ask you to forgive me. I was too proud to ask before." Her fingers tried to mask her face. "But I'm not proud anymore, Mike." That great voice quivered and then grew strong again. "I hate you to see me this way—you always said I was beautiful. I didn't believe it. The Charity Ball when we led the grand march and you said I was the most beautiful girl there . . . "

"Nana," I said. I couldn't keep up the pretense any longer, adding one more burden to my load of guilt, leading her on this way, playing a pathetic game of make-believe with an old woman clinging to memories. She didn't seem to hear me.

"But that other night, Mike. The terrible one. The terrible accusations I made. Even Ellie woke up and began to cry. I went to her and rocked her in my arms and you came into the room and said I was wrong. You were whispering, an awful whisper, not wanting to upset little Ellie but wanting to make me see the truth. And I didn't answer you, Mike. I was too proud. I've even forgotten the name of the girl. I sit here, wondering now—was it Laura or Evelyn? I can't remember. Later, I learned that you were telling the truth all the time, Mike. That I'd been wrong . . . " Her eyes were brighter than ever as she looked at me now, but tear-bright, the tears gathering. "It was never the same after that night, was it, Mike? The glitter was gone. From you. From us. And then the accident . . . and I never had the chance to ask you to forgive me . . . "

My grandmother. My poor, poor grandmother. Old people aren't supposed to have those kinds of memories. You see their pictures in the family albums and that's what they are: pictures. They're not supposed to come to life. You drive out in your father's Le Mans doing seventy-five on the pike and all you're doing is visiting an old lady in a nursing home. A duty call. And then you find out that she's a person. She's *somebody*. She's my grandmother, all right, but she's also herself. Like my own mother and father. They exist outside of their relationship to me. I was scared again. I wanted to get out of there.

"Mike, Mike," my grandmother said. "Say it, Mike."

I felt as if my cheeks would crack if I uttered a word.

"Say you forgive me, Mike. I've waited all these years . . . "

I was surprised at how strong her fingers were.

"Say, '*I forgive you, Meg.*' "

I said it. My voice sounded funny, as if I were talking in a huge tunnel. "I forgive you, Meg."

Her eyes studied me. Her hands pressed mine. For the first time in my life, I saw love at work. Not movie love. Not Cindy's sparkling eyes when I tell her that we're going to the beach on a Sunday afternoon. But love like something alive and tender, asking nothing in return. She raised her face, and I knew what she wanted me to do. I bent and brushed my lips against her cheek. Her flesh was like a leaf in autumn, crisp and dry.

She closed her eyes and I stood up. The sun wasn't glinting on the cars any longer. Somebody had turned on another television set, and the voices were the show-off voices of the panel shows. At the same time you could still hear the soap-opera dialogue on the other television set.

I waited awhile. She seemed to be sleeping, her breathing serene and regular. I buttoned my raincoat. Suddenly she opened her eyes again and looked at me. Her eyes were still bright, but they merely stared at me. Without recognition or curiosity. Empty eyes. I smiled at her, but she didn't smile back. She made a kind of moaning sound and turned away on the bed, pulling the blankets around her.

I counted to twenty-five and then to fifty and did it all over again. I cleared my throat and coughed tentatively. She didn't move; she didn't respond. I wanted to say, "Nana, it's me." But I didn't. I thought of saying, "Meg, it's me." But I couldn't.

Finally I left. Just like that. I didn't say goodbye or anything. I stalked through the corridors, looking neither to the right nor the left, nor caring whether that wild old man with the wheelchair ran me down or not.

On the Southwest Turnpike I did seventy-five—no, eighty—most of the way. I turned the radio up as loud as it could go. Rock music—anything to fill the air. When I got home, my mother was vacuuming the living-room rug. She shut off the cleaner, and the silence was deafening. "Well, how was your grandmother?" she asked.

I told her she was fine. I told her a lot of things. How great Nana looked and how she seemed happy and had called me Mike. I wanted to ask her—hey, Mom, you and Dad really love each other, don't you? I mean—there's nothing to forgive between you, is there? But I didn't.

Instead I went upstairs and took out the electric razor Annie had given me for Christmas and shaved off my moustache.

The Moustache

Theme

It's often hard to retell a story to a friend. For example, read the conversation below, in which someone is trying to tell a friend about a story she read.

> "Gee, I just finished this great story. You ought to read it."
> "Oh, yeah? What's it about?"
> "Well, this guy goes to visit his grandmother in a nursing home. Oh—and he grew this moustache first. Well, *she* thinks *he's* her dead husband, and she starts apologizing for a fight they had forty years ago. . . ."

The story sounds flat. Something has been lost in the retelling. That something is the essence of the story, the point of it all—in short, the themes. Themes are the main ideas contained in a story. It is a story's themes that speak to us directly. The details of a story might concern only a particular character in a particular situation. But the themes of a story apply to us all.

The attempt, above, to give a blow-by-blow account of the story was uninteresting because it failed to get across the story's themes. Suppose, instead, the story were told this way:

> "Gee, I just finished this great story. You ought to read it."
> "Oh, yeah? What's it about?"
> "Well, it's about this guy who visits his grandmother in a nursing home. He feels guilty because he hasn't seen her for a while. Then he finds out *she* feels guilty about something too. And he realizes she's not just a grandmother, or just an old person, but a *real* person with a flesh-and-blood past."

The difference between the two versions is that the second one hints at some of the story's themes: guilt, aging and the relationship between a boy and his grandmother. These are good reasons for someone to want to read this story. Everyone has feelings of guilt. Everyone thinks about growing old and knows people who are old. That's why the story about Mike and his grandmother is worth reading. And that's what you were trying to get across to your friend.

Themes may be major or minor. A major theme is an idea the author returns to time and again. It becomes one of the most important ideas in the story. Minor themes are ideas that may appear from time to time. Together, the major and minor themes of a story can transform a small tale of little importance into a story that touches the lives of all who read it.

Themes in stories are expressed in several ways. In this lesson we'll look at four ways in which author Robert Cormier expresses themes:

1 Themes are expressed and emphasized by the way the author makes us feel.

2 Themes are presented in thoughts and conversations.

3 Themes are suggested through the characters.

4 The actions, or events, in the story are used to suggest themes.

You have seen in earlier lessons that the way you feel as you read a story is no accident. Authors take great pains to make you feel a certain way. They use these feelings to express themes.

Theme

Themes and Feelings

1

In "The Moustache," author Robert Cormier has something to say about aging. It is a major theme of the story. So he shows you Mike's feelings about his grandmother, who is in failing health. Because Mike is the main character in the story, you come to *identify* with him—you share his feelings. By sharing his feelings you also share the ideas that go through his mind.

In the following passage, Mike introduces his grandmother. How does the author make you feel about Mike's grandmother? How does he want you to feel about aging?

> Let me tell you what the visit to Lawnrest was all about. My grandmother is seventy-three years old. She is a resident—which is supposed to be a better word than *patient*—at the Lawnrest Nursing Home. She used to make the greatest turkey dressing in the world and was a nut about baseball and could even quote batting averages, for crying out loud. She always rooted for the losers. She was in love with the Mets until they started to win. Now she has arteriosclerosis, which the dictionary says is "a chronic disease characterized by abnormal thickening and hardening of the arterial walls." Which really means that she can't live at home anymore or even with us, and her memory has betrayed her as well as her body. She used to wander off and sometimes didn't recognize people.

Mike's grandmother is an old lady whose mind is failing. Her memory betrays her. Sometimes she doesn't recognize people. Because of these problems, she can't live at home anymore, or even with her daughter.

It is possible for different people to have different feelings about something like this. In real life, some people feel disgusted by someone like Mike's grandmother. Others may react with cruel humor. But chances are good that you felt neither amused nor disgusted by Nana in the story. You probably felt sympathetic, because that's how the author wants you to feel.

Notice how he guides your feelings. He wants you to see Nana as a person, not just an old lady. So he tells you what she was like before she was sick. She made great turkey stuffing. She liked baseball. She always rooted for the losers. She was the kind of person you probably would have liked. And you can't help sharing Mike's grief over his grandmother's present condition.

This is one of the ideas or themes that Robert Cormier wants to leave with you. Old people in failing health were once active, caring persons. Like Nana, they have been "betrayed" by old age. If you now feel more sympathetic towards such people, then you have grasped one of the themes of "The Moustache."

The author also guides your feelings to make a point about nursing homes. Read the passage in Exercise A and try to decide what idea the author wants to get across.

Exercise A

Read the following passage and answer the questions about it using what you have learned in this part of the lesson.

Inside [the nursing home], I was surprised by the lack of hospital smell, although there was another odor or maybe the absence of an odor. The air was antiseptic, sterile. As if there was no atmosphere at all or I'd caught a cold suddenly and couldn't taste or smell.

. . . As I walked through the corridor seeking East Three, I couldn't help glancing into the rooms, and it was like some kind of wax museum—all these figures in various stances and attitudes, sitting in beds or chairs, standing at windows, as if they were frozen forever in these postures.

Put an *x* in the box beside the correct answer.

1. One idea, also tied to the theme of aging, is about nursing homes. What feeling does the author give to the nursing home through his description?

   ☐ a. It seems stifling, without air.

   ☐ b. It seems just like a hospital.

□ c. It seems homey and comfortable.

□ d. It seems like a hospital pretending to be a real home.

2. In the second part of the passage, Mike compares the nursing home to something else. This is one way the author shapes the reader's feelings about nursing homes. On the line below, write the thing to which Mike compares the nursing home.

_____

Now check your answers using the Answer Key on page 455. Correct any wrong answers and review this part of the lesson if you don't understand why an answer was wrong.

	Theme
2	**Themes, Thoughts and Conversations**

There is no such thing as idle talk in a story. Authors put words in their characters' mouths only for good reasons. One of these is to develop a story's themes.

Imagine, for example, that someone you love is very ill. You try to go about your daily routine. But you can't help thinking about this person's illness. The topics of illness and death crop up in your conversations. From the things you say, friends might conclude that death and dying are much on your mind. If you were a character in a story, then death and dying would be themes of the story.

In "The Moustache," two ways you learn what is on Mike's mind are from his thoughts and from his conversations. You know what Mike is thinking because he tells you. When he is not talking to another character, you could say he is talking directly to the reader.

His thoughts and conversations provide clues to an important theme. Read the following thoughts that run through Mike's mind as he nears the nursing home. See if you can find the important idea they contain.

> . . . As I approached Lawnrest—which is a terrible cemetery kind of name, to begin with—I was sorry I hadn't avoided the trip. Then I felt guilty about it. I'm loaded with guilt complexes. Like driving like a madman after promising my father to be careful. Like sitting in the parking lot, looking at the nursing home with dread and thinking how I'd rather be with Cindy. Then I thought of all the Christmas and birthday gifts my grandmother had given me and I got out of the car, guilty, as usual.

One idea in this passage stands out—the idea of guilt. Mike feels guilty about many things. Like not visiting his grandmother more often. Like driving too fast. And like wishing he were with his girlfriend instead of his grandmother. "I'm loaded with guilt complexes," he says.

This is not the last we hear about guilt, either. Later in the story, Mike feels guilty for letting his grandmother go on thinking he is her husband.

Clearly, guilt is a major theme of "The Moustache." It appears time and again. It is a part of Mike's life. And, like aging, it is a part of readers' lives too. We can all identify with Mike's feelings of guilt, because all of us have things that we feel guilty about. The idea of guilt, like the idea of aging, hits home to readers.

In Exercise B, we find that something has been bothering Mike's grandmother for almost forty years. This is revealed in her conversation with Mike, whom she thinks is her husband. Look for the theme behind her words.

Exercise B

Read the following passage and answer the questions about it using what you have learned in this part of the lesson.

"But that other night, Mike. The terrible one. The terrible accusations I made. Even Ellie woke up and began to cry. I went to her and rocked her in my arms and you came into the room and said I was wrong. You were whispering, an awful whisper, not wanting to upset little Ellie but wanting to make me see the truth. And I didn't answer you, Mike. I was too proud. . . . Later, I learned that you were telling the truth all the time, Mike. That I'd been wrong . . . " Her eyes were brighter than ever as she looked at me now, but tear-bright, the tears gathering. "It was never the same after that night, was it, Mike? The glitter was gone. From you. From us. And then the accident . . . and I never had the chance to ask you to forgive me . . . "

Put an *x* in the box beside the correct answer.

1. What theme is raised in this passage?

   ☐ a. Old age—Grandmother mourns her lost youth.

   ☐ b. Motherhood—Grandmother worries that she wasn't a good mother to Ellie.

   ☐ c. Death—Grandmother is afraid of dying.

   ☐ d. Guilt—Grandmother feels guilty about never having asked her husband to forgive her.

2. Looking back, Grandmother sees a flaw in her own character. It is a fault that all of us must guard against in ourselves. Find the short sentence that reveals this flaw. Copy the sentence on the line below.

_____

Now check your answers using the Answer Key on page 455. Correct any wrong answers and review this part of the lesson if you don't understand why an answer was wrong.

The characters in a story are also used to express themes. This is always the case with the main character, who usually illustrates the most important theme of the story. A good way to get at this theme is to ask yourself the question, What does the main

character learn in the course of the story? If you can answer this question, then you have probably found the most important theme of the story.

Ask yourself what Mike learned in the course of this story. Then read the following passage from "The Moustache." What has Mike just learned? What theme does this suggest?

> My grandmother. My poor, poor grandmother. Old people aren't supposed to have those kinds of memories. You see their pictures in the family albums and that's what they are: pictures. They're not supposed to come to life. You drive out in your father's Le Mans doing seventy-five on the pike and all you're doing is visiting an old lady in a nursing home. A duty call. And then you find out that she's a person. She's *somebody*. She's my grandmother, all right, but she's also herself.

Mike has just learned to see beyond a stereotype. He thought grandmothers were just little old ladies who made great turkey stuffing and gave lavish presents to their grandchildren. Now he sees that grandmothers are real people. They carry all the emotional baggage that he does—the terrible mistakes, the pangs of remorse, the bitter memories as well as the sweet.

This is quite a discovery for Mike. He simply hadn't thought about grandmothers in those terms. He has learned an important lesson. He has learned that other people—even old people—have complicated feelings just as he does.

Now that you have answered the question, What has Mike learned? you have uncovered an important theme. We must all realize that other people are just as complicated as we are. Everyone must be given credit for having deep and sometimes troubled feelings.

Minor characters as well as main characters may also be used to develop a theme. This is the case with the attendant who brings fruit juices to Mike's grandmother. She isn't part of the story line. In fact, she interrupts it. The part she plays doesn't reveal anything about Mike that we don't already know. But she *does* help develop one of the themes of the story. Go on to Exercise C and try to decide what ideas this character develops.

Exercise C

Read the following passage and answer the questions about it using what you have learned in this part of the lesson.

We were interrupted by an attendant who pushed a wheeled cart into the room. "Time for juices, dear," the woman said. She was the standard forty- or fifty-year-old woman: glasses, nothing hair, plump cheeks. Her manner was cheerful but a businesslike kind of cheerfulness. I'd hate to be called "dear" by someone getting paid to do it. "Orange or grape or cranberry, dear? Cranberry is good for the bones, you know." . . .

The woman looked at me and winked. A conspiratorial kind of wink. It was kind of horrible. I didn't think people winked like that anymore. In fact, I hadn't seen a wink in years.

"She doesn't care much for juices," the woman said, talking to me as if my grandmother weren't even there. . . . Addressing my grandmother again, she said, "Orange or grape or cranberry, dear?"

"Tell her I want no juices, Mike," my grandmother commanded regally, her eyes still watching invisible birds.

The woman smiled, patience like a label on her face. "That's all right, dear. I'll just leave some cranberry for you. Drink it at your leisure. It's good for the bones."

Put an *x* in the box beside the correct answer.

1. The way this attendant treats Mike's grandmother helps develop the theme of aging. It shows that old people are sometimes treated as

   ☐ a. slaves.

   ☐ b. animals.

   ☐ c. children.

   ☐ d. royalty.

2. Find at least three things Mike doesn't like about the way this attendant treats his grandmother. Write them on the lines below.

   _____

   _____

   _____

   _____

Now check your answers using the Answer Key on page 455. Correct any wrong answers and review this part of the lesson if you don't understand why an answer was wrong.

Theme

4 **Theme and Action**

People naturally express ideas and feelings through their actions. For instance, a person who is speechless with anger might kick something. This is an action that expresses fury and rage. When someone is overjoyed, he might toss his hat into the air—an action showing high spirits. On Memorial Day, a person might lay a wreath on a grave. This action expresses respect for the person buried there. Actions, then, are not just empty gestures. They are full of meaning.

Authors give a lot of thought to the actions they include in their stories. One thing they think about is what an action will "say" in the story. In other words, how will the action express an idea or theme?

There are many actions in "The Moustache" that express themes of the story. One such action comes toward the end of Mike's visit. Look for it at the end of the following passage:

> "Say you forgive me, Mike. I've waited all these years . . ."
> I was surprised at how strong her fingers were.
> "Say, *'I forgive you, Meg.'* "
> I said it. . . . "I forgive you, Meg."
> Her eyes studied me. Her hands pressed mine. For the first time in my life, I saw love at work. Not movie love. Not Cindy's sparkling eyes when I tell her that we're going to the beach on a Sunday afternoon. But love like something alive and tender, asking nothing in return. She raised her face, and I knew what she wanted me to do. I bent and brushed my lips against her cheek.

The meaningful action here is the kiss. It completes the act of forgiveness that Mike's grandmother sought from her husband. (Remember, she thinks Mike is her husband.)

The kiss helps express an important theme in the story. That theme is love. Mike has just learned something new about love. Before, he thought of love only as it was presented in the movies—as romantic or passionate. But now he sees that real love goes deeper than that. The kind of love he sees in his grandmother's eyes is unselfish—"love like something alive and tender, asking nothing in return." So Mike responds with an equally unselfish act of love, and kisses his grandmother.

Another action that expresses a theme comes at the very end of the story. Review the ending by reading the passage in Exercise D. Try to decide how the final action helps to get across an important theme.

Exercise D

Read the following passage and answer the questions about it using what you have learned in this part of the lesson.

When I got home, my mother was vacuuming the living-room rug. She shut off the cleaner, and the silence was deafening. "Well, how was your grandmother?" she asked.

I told her she was fine. I told her a lot of things. How great Nana looked and how she seemed happy and had called me Mike. I wanted to ask her—hey, Mom, you and Dad really love each other, don't you? I mean—there's nothing to forgive between you, is there? But I didn't.

Instead I went upstairs and took out the electric razor Annie had given me for Christmas and shaved off my moustache.

Put an x in the box beside the correct answer.

1. The author doesn't tell us why Mike shaves off his moustache. But this action is probably related to the theme of

☐ a. vanity—Mike thinks he will look better without a moustache.

☐ b. growing up—Mike realizes that there's more to being mature than sporting a moustache.

☐ c. aging—Mike is worried that the moustache makes him look like an old man.

☐ d. grief—it shows how upset he is over his grandmother's condition.

2. Two questions are on the tip of Mike's tongue. They have to do with the themes of love and forgiveness. What does Mike almost say to his mother that shows he is thinking hard about these ideas?

_____

_____

_____

Use the Answer Key on page 455 to check your answers. Correct any wrong answers and review this part of the lesson if you don't understand why an answer was wrong. Now go on to do the Comprehension Questions.

Comprehension Questions

Answer these questions without looking back at the story. Choose the best answer to each question and put an *x* in the box beside it.

Keeping
Events in
Order

1. How long has Mike's grandmother been "confused" in her mind?

   ☐ a. Since Mike's mother was born

   ☐ b. Since her husband died

   ☐ c. For as long as Mike has known her

   ☐ d. Just in the past year or two

Recognizing
Words in
Context

2. Mike glances into some of the rooms in the nursing home. He sees "all these figures in various *stances* and *attitudes*, sitting in beds or chairs, standing at windows, as if they were frozen forever in these *postures*." The words *stances, attitudes* and *postures* all seem to

   ☐ a. relate to poses or positions.

   ☐ b. be different and unrelated.

   ☐ c. mean freezing in cold rooms.

   ☐ d. suggest noise and activity.

Recognizing
Words in
Context

3. Mike says, "My mother had described those moments when my grandmother suddenly emerged from the fog that so often *obscured* her mind." Instead of *obscured*, the author could have used the word

   ☐ a. destroyed.

   ☐ b. cased.

   ☐ c. clouded.

   ☐ d. penetrated.

4. A person whose behavior is *condescending* tends to look down on other people. Who in the story has a condescending air?

☐ a. The juice lady

☐ b. Cindy

☐ c. Mike

☐ d. Nana

5. At what point in the story does Mike realize that his grandmother thinks he is someone else?

☐ a. As soon as she greets him

☐ b. When she admires his coat

☐ c. When she recalls playing the piano for him and Ellie

☐ d. Not until after he has left

6. Who is Meg?

☐ a. Mike's older sister

☐ b. The young nurse

☐ c. Mike's mother

☐ d. Mike's grandmother

7. What feeling does Mike often have that his grandmother also seems to have?

☐ a. He feels guilty.

☐ b. He feels confused.

☐ c. He feels alone.

☐ d. He feels bored.

8. Whom does Mike resemble?

☐ a. His father

☐ b. His sister

☐ c. His grandmother

☐ d. His mother's father

Recalling
Facts

9. How old was Mike's grandfather when he died?

☐ a. Thirty-five

☐ b. Seventeen

☐ c. Almost forty

☐ d. Around Mike's mother's age

Recognizing
Words in
Context

10. Grandma said, "The days are fuzzy sometimes, merging together." In other words, in her mind

☐ a. one day combines with another.

☐ b. each day stands alone.

☐ c. the days come and go.

☐ d. the days are sad and weary.

Making
Inferences

11. What happened between Mike's grandmother and grandfather when they were young?

☐ a. They couldn't agree on how to raise Ellie.

☐ b. He thought she was seeing another man.

☐ c. She thought he was seeing another woman.

☐ d. They had a big argument over money.

Understanding
Main Ideas

12. What does Mike's grandmother wish she had done before her husband died?

☐ a. Demanded an apology

☐ b. Asked him to forgive her

☐ c. Learned to play the piano better

☐ d. Earned a better salary

13. Which one of the following quotations from the story signals a great discovery that Mike makes?

☐ a. "She made a kind of moaning sound and turned away. . . ."

☐ b. "I was beginning to feel uneasy because she regarded me with such intensity."

☐ c. "She lapsed into silence, and I looked out the window."

☐ d. "She's *somebody*. She's my grandmother, all right, but she's also herself."

14. What was the last thing Mike said to his grandmother?

☐ a. "Goodbye, Nana."

☐ b. "I forgive you, Meg."

☐ c. "Nana, it's me."

☐ d. "Meg, it's me."

15. How does Mike feel as he drives home?

☐ a. Relieved and free

☐ b. Sullen and sulky

☐ c. Troubled and shaken

☐ d. Peaceful and serene

Now check your answers using the Answer Key on page 455. Make no mark for right answers. <u>Correct</u> any wrong answers you may have by putting a checkmark (✓) in the box next to the right answer. Count the number of questions you answered correctly and plot the total on the Comprehension Scores graph on page 462.

Next, look at the questions you answered incorrectly. What types of questions were they? Count the number you got wrong of each type and enter the numbers in the spaces below.

Recognizing Words in Content   _____

Recalling Facts   _____

Keeping Events in Order   _____

Making Inferences   _____

Understanding Main Ideas   _____

Now use these numbers to fill in the Comprehension Skills Profile on page 463.

Discussion Guides

The questions below will help you to think about the story and the lesson you have just read. If you don't discuss these questions in class, try to think about them or discuss them with your classmates.

Discussing Theme

1. Relationships between family members is a theme of the collection from which this story was taken. What kind of relationship does Mike seem to have with his family?

2. Minor characters are sometimes used to comment on a theme (see part 3 of the lesson). Think about the old man in the wheelchair who almost runs Mike down in the corridor. What does he add to the theme of aging?

3. Guilt is a theme in the story. How do the characters Mike and Nana both illustrate this theme?

Discussing the Story

4. Do you think Mike should have made his grandmother understand that he wasn't her husband? Why or why not?

5. Mike drives home from the nursing home at eighty miles an hour with the radio blaring. Why do you think he behaves this way?

6. Why do you think Mike shaves off his moustache at the end of the story?

Discussing the Author's Work

7. What are some of the little touches, or details, that the author uses to make Mike seem like a real teenager?

8. Sometimes Mike's grandmother seems to be living in the distant past, sometimes in the real present, and sometimes in a confused present in which she doesn't see things as they really are. Find places in the story where each of these happens. What does her changing view of reality add to the story?

9. Author Robert Cormier once said that "fashions change along with slang and pop tunes and fads, but emotions remain the same." What are some emotions in "The Moustache" that never go out of style?

Writing Exercise

1. In the story, Mike learns something about people from his experience with his grandmother. Think of something you learned from an experience you had. Describe the experience <u>briefly</u>, and tell what you learned from it. Use no more than two sentences. *This is your theme statement.*

2. Write a more detailed account of the experience. Explain in more detail what you learned from the experience. In your account, include at least two of the following elements to illustrate *what* you learned, *how* you learned it, and how you *felt.*

   • Something that was said (conversation)

   • Something you did (action)

   • A description of the other person (character)

   • A description of your feelings

Unit 6 Use of Language

Another April

BY JESSE STUART

About the Illustration

What can you learn about the old man in this picture from the details in the drawing?

Here are some questions to help you think:

☐ What does the expression on the old man's face tell you about the kind of person he is?

☐ How do the people in the house seem to feel about the old man?

☐ It's obviously springtime in the picture. What is unusual about the way the man is dressed? Why do you think he is dressed this way?

☐ What can you tell about the man from the way he is touching the turtle?

Unit 6

Introduction

What the Story Is About

"Another April" is about an old man who has been cooped up in the house all winter and is going outside for his first walk of the spring.

Grandpa is 91 years old. Up until the age of 80, he used to farm and cut timber in the hills of eastern Kentucky. He was a powerful man, recalls his daughter. "No man could cut more timber, . . . no man in the timber woods could sink an ax deeper into a log . . . . And no man could lift the end of a bigger saw log than Pop could." Now the old man lives on his daughter's farm and submits to being cared for like a hothouse petunia. "Mom . . . wanted him to live a long time," the boy observes.

Even the boy, though, can see that Grandpa is showing his age. His hearing is poor, for one thing. And his walks about their farm get shorter and shorter each year. This year the boy watches from inside the house as Grandpa makes his familiar circuit of the farm. A pine cone, a butterfly, a branch of blossoms, the hog pen—all engage his attention along the way.

But the boy is unprepared for Grandpa's last stop: the smokehouse. There, beneath the smokehouse floor, lives an old terrapin. A terrapin is a land turtle, about as big as a man's hand, with a high, domed shell. This terrapin, however, is no ordinary terrapin. For carved into its shell is the date 1847. That would make the terrapin at least 95 years old—older, even, than Grandpa.

It is this terrapin that Grandpa has gone looking for. In fact, it is a visit with the terrapin that is the whole point of his walk. "I'm a-goin' to see my old friend," Grandpa says. "I know he'll still be there."

Why does Grandpa want to see an old terrapin, and what has he got to say to it? That is what the boy, as well as the reader, seeks to understand.

Like the boy in the story, author and poet Jesse Stuart, born in 1907, was a Kentucky farmboy. "I live on a farm," he once said. "I have lived here all my life. I am interested in farming and, until the year I had a heart attack (1954) I did considerable farm work." This background plays an important role in his writing, yet it never outweighs the deeper appeal of his stories. As one critic put it, they "all have a heart."

If "Another April" makes a Jesse Stuart fan out of you, then there's a wealth of good reading ahead for you. You'll want to read *Tales from the*

Plum Grove Hills, the collection of stories from which "Another April" was chosen, and *Mongrel Mettle: The Autobiography of a Dog*. Also look for *The Thread That Runs So True*, an account of the author's teaching experiences.

What the Lesson Is About

The lesson following this story is about how authors use language. As they put words to paper, authors make many choices. Their big concern, their reason for writing stories at all, is, How can I share this experience with a total stranger?

Within this larger question are countless smaller ones. How do I reproduce, on paper, the way people talk in the region in which I've set my story? What words pack the most punch for the idea I'm trying to get across? How can I make readers see a familiar thing through new eyes? How can I draw their attention to certain things that I especially want them to notice?

Jesse Stuart deals with all these concerns in "Another April."

The questions below will help you to focus on how he uses language to do this. Read the story carefully, and try to answer these questions as you go along:

1 What do you learn about the characters—their education, their background, where they live—simply from the way they talk?

2 The author has a way of describing things that is almost like painting a picture. Which passages would you call vivid or colorful, and why?

3 Good writers use unexpected comparisons to describe things. One example in the story compares the old man's laugh with the March wind. What are some other comparisons the author uses?

4 Grandpa exaggerates when he tells the boy, "Yer Ma's a-puttin' enough clothes on me to kill a man." What is the purpose of this exaggeration?

Another April

Jesse Stuart

Now, Pap, you won't get cold," Mom said as she put a heavy wool cap over his head.

"Huh, what did ye say?" Grandpa asked, holding his big hand cupped over his ear to catch the sound.

"Wait until I get your gloves," Mom said, hollering real loud in Grandpa's ear. Mom had forgotten about his gloves until he raised his big bare hand above his ear to catch the sound of Mom's voice.

"Don't get 'em," Grandpa said, "I won't ketch cold."

Mom didn't pay any attention to what Grandpa said. She went on to get the gloves anyway. Grandpa turned toward me. He saw that I was looking at him.

"Yer Ma's a-puttin' enough clothes on me to kill a man," Grandpa said, then he laughed a coarse laugh like March wind among the pine tops at his own words. I started laughing but not at Grandpa's words. He thought I was laughing at them and we both laughed together. It pleased Grandpa to think that I had laughed with him over something funny that he had said. But I was laughing at the way he was dressed. He looked like a picture of Santa Claus. But Grandpa's cheeks were not cherry-red like Santa Claus' cheeks. They were covered with white thin beard— and above his eyes were long white eyebrows almost as white as percoon petals and very much longer.

Grandpa was wearing a heavy wool suit that hung loosely about his big body but fitted him tightly round the waist where he was as big and as round as a flour barrel. His pant legs were as big 'round his pipestem legs as emptied meal sacks. And his big shoes, with his heavy wool socks dropping down over their tops, looked like sled runners. Grandpa wore a heavy wool shirt and over his wool shirt he wore a heavy wool sweater and then his coat over the top of all this. Over his coat he wore a heavy overcoat and about his neck he wore a wool scarf.

The way Mom had dressed Grandpa you'd think there was a heavy snow on the ground but there wasn't. April was here instead and the sun was shining on the green hills where the wild plums and the wild crab apples were in bloom enough to make you think there were big snowdrifts sprinkled over the green hills. When I looked at Grandpa and then looked out at the window at the sunshine and the green grass I laughed more. Grandpa laughed with me.

"I'm a-goin' to see my old friend," Grandpa said just as Mom came down the stairs with his gloves.

"Who is he, Grandpa?" I asked, but Grandpa just looked at my mouth working. He didn't know what I was saying. And he hated to ask me the second time.

Mom put the big wool gloves on Grandpa's hands. He stood there just like I had to do years ago, and let Mom put his gloves on. If Mom didn't get his fingers back in the glove-fingers exactly right Grandpa quarreled at Mom. And when Mom fixed his fingers exactly right in his gloves the way he wanted them Grandpa was pleased.

"I'll be a-goin' to see 'im," Grandpa said to Mom. "I know he'll still be there."

Mom opened our front door for Grandpa and he stepped out slowly, supporting himself with his big cane in one hand. With the other hand he held to the door facing. Mom let him out of the house just like she used to let me out in the spring. And when Grandpa left the house I wanted to go with him, but Mom wouldn't let me go. I wondered if he would get away from the house—get out of Mom's sight—and pull off his shoes and go barefooted and wade the creeks like I used to do when Mom let me out. Since Mom wouldn't let me go with Grandpa, I watched him as he walked slowly down the path in front of our house. Mom stood there watching Grandpa too. I think she was afraid that he would fall. But Mom was fooled; Grandpa toddled along the path better than my baby brother could.

"He used to be a powerful man," Mom said more to herself than she did to me. "He was a timber cutter. No man could cut more timber than my father; no man in the timber woods could sink an ax deeper into a log than my father. And no man could lift the end of a bigger saw log than Pop could."

"Who is Grandpa goin' to see, Mom?" I asked.

"He's not goin' to see anybody," Mom said.

"I heard 'im say that he was goin' to see an old friend," I told her.

"Oh, he was just a-talkin'," Mom said.

I watched Grandpa stop under the pine tree in our front yard. He set his cane against the pine tree trunk, pulled off his gloves and put them in his pocket. Then Grandpa stooped over slowly, as slowly as the wind bends down a sapling, and picked up a pine cone in his big soft fingers. Grandpa stood fondling the pine cone in his hand. Then, one by one, he pulled the little chips from the pine cone—tearing it to pieces like he was hunting for something in it—and after he had torn it to pieces he threw the pine-cone stem on the ground. Then he pulled pine needles from a low-hanging pine bough and he felt of each pine needle between his fingers. He played with them a long time before he started down the path.

"What's Grandpa doin'?" I asked Mom.

But Mom didn't answer me.

"How long has Grandpa been with us?" I asked Mom.

"Before you's born," she said. "Pap has been with us eleven years. He was eighty when he quit cuttin' timber and farmin'; now he's ninety-one."

I had heard her say that when she was a girl he'd walk out on the snow and ice barefooted and carry wood in the house and put it on the fire. He had shoes but he wouldn't bother to put them on. And I heard her say that he would cut timber on the coldest days without socks on his feet but with his feet stuck down in cold brogan shoes and he worked stripped above the waist so his arms would have freedom when he swung his double-bitted ax. I had heard her tell how he'd sweat and how the sweat in his beard would be icicles by the time he got home from work on the cold winter days. Now Mom wouldn't let him get out of the house for she wanted him to live a long time.

As I watched Grandpa go down the path toward the hog pen he stopped to examine every little thing along his path. Once he waved his cane at a butterfly as it zigzagged over his head, its polka-dot wings fanning the blue April air. Grandpa would stand when a puff of wind came along, and hold his face against the wind and let the wind play with his white whiskers. I thought maybe his face was hot under his beard and he was letting the wind cool his face. When he reached the hog pen he called the hogs down to the fence. They came running and grunting to Grandpa just like they were talking to him. I knew that Grandpa couldn't hear them trying to talk to him but he could see their mouths working and he knew they were trying to say something. He leaned his cane against the hog pen, reached over the fence, and patted the hogs' heads. Grandpa didn't miss patting one of our seven hogs.

As he toddled up the little path alongside the hog pen he stopped under a blooming dogwood. He pulled a white blossom from a bough that swayed over the path above his head, and he leaned his big bundled body against the dogwood while he tore each petal from the blossom and examined it carefully. There wasn't anything his dim blue eyes missed. He stopped under a redbud tree before he reached the garden to break a tiny spray of redbud blossoms. He took each blossom from the spray and examined it carefully.

"Gee, it's funny to watch Grandpa," I said to Mom, then I laughed.

"Poor Pap," Mom said. "He's seen a lot of Aprils come and

go. He's seen more Aprils than he will ever see again."

I don't think Grandpa missed a thing on the little circle he took before he reached the house. He played with a bumblebee that was bending a windflower blossom that grew near our corncrib beside a big bluff. But Grandpa didn't try to catch the bumblebee in his big bare hand. I wondered if he would and if the bumblebee would sting him, and if he would holler. Grandpa even pulled a butterfly cocoon from a blackberry briar that grew beside his path. I saw him try to tear it into shreds but he couldn't. There wasn't any butterfly in it, for I'd seen it before. I wondered if the butterfly with the polka-dot wings, that Grandpa waved his cane at when he first left the house, had come from this cocoon. I laughed when Grandpa couldn't tear the cocoon apart.

"I'll bet I can tear that cocoon apart for Grandpa if you'd let me go help him," I said to Mom.

"You leave your Grandpa alone," Mom said. "Let 'im enjoy April."

Then I knew that this was the first time Mom had let Grandpa out of the house all winter. I knew that Grandpa loved the sunshine and the fresh April air that blew from the redbud and dogwood blossoms. He loved the bumble-bees, the hogs, the pine cones, and pine needles. Grandpa didn't miss a thing along his walk. And every day from now on until just before frost Grandpa would take this little walk. He'd stop along and look at everything as he had done summers before. But each year he didn't take as long a walk as he had taken the year before. Now this spring he didn't go down to the lower end of the hog pen as he had done last year. And when I could first remember Grandpa going on his walks he used to go out of sight. He'd go all over the farm. And he'd come to the house and take me on his knee and tell me about all what he had seen. Now Grandpa wasn't getting out of sight. I could see him from the window along all of his walk.

Grandpa didn't come back into the house at the front door. He tottled around back of the house toward the smokehouse and I ran through the living room to the dining room so I could look out the window and watch him.

"Where's Grandpa goin?" I asked Mom.

"Now never mind," Mom said. "Leave Grandpa alone. Don't go out there and disturb him."

"I won't bother 'im, Mom," I said. "I just want to watch 'im."

"All right," Mom said.

But Mom wanted to be sure that I didn't bother him so she followed me into the dining room. Maybe she wanted to see what Grandpa was going to do. She stood by the window and we watched Grandpa as he walked down beside our smokehouse where a tall sassafras tree's thin leaves fluttered in the blue April wind. Above the smokehouse and the tall sassafras was a blue April sky—so high you couldn't see the sky-roof. It was just blue space and little white clouds floated upon this blue.

When Grandpa reached the smokehouse he leaned his cane against the sassafras tree. He let himself down slowly to his knees as he looked carefully at the ground. Grandpa was looking at something and I wondered what it was. I just didn't think or I would have known.

"There you are, my good old friend," Grandpa said.

"Who is his friend, Mom?" I asked.

Mom didn't say anything. Then I saw.

"He's playin' with that old terrapin, Mom," I said.

"I know he is," Mom said.

"The terrapin doesn't mind if Grandpa strokes his head with his hand," I said.

"I know it," Mom said.

"But the old terrapin won't let me do it," I said. "Why does he let Grandpa?"

"The terrapin knows your Grandpa."

"He ought to know me," I said, "but when I try to stroke

his head with my hand, he closes up in his shell."

Mom didn't say anything. She stood by the window watching Grandpa and listening to Grandpa talk to the terrapin.

"My old friend, how do you like the sunshine?" Grandpa asked the terrapin.

The terrapin turned his fleshless face to one side like a hen does when she looks at you in the sunlight. He was trying to talk to Grandpa; maybe the terrapin could understand what Grandpa was saying.

"Old fellow, it's been a hard winter," Grandpa said. "How have you fared under the smokehouse floor?"

"Does the terrapin know what Grandpa is sayin'?" I asked Mom.

"I don't know," she said.

"I'm awfully glad to see you, old fellow," Grandpa said.

He didn't offer to bite Grandpa's big soft hand as he stroked his head.

"Looks like the terrapin would bite Grandpa," I said.

"That terrapin has spent the winters under that smokehouse for fifteen years," Mom said. "Pap has been acquainted with him for eleven years. He's been talkin' to that terrapin every spring."

"How does Grandpa know the terrapin is old?" I asked Mom.

"It's got 1847 cut on its shell," Mom said. "We know he's ninety-five years old. He's older than that. We don't know how old he was when that date was cut on his back."

"Who cut 1847 on his back, Mom?"

"I don't know, child," she said, "but I'd say whoever cut that date on his back has long been under the ground."

Then I wondered how a terrapin could get that old and what kind of a looking person he was who cut the date on the terrapin's back. I wondered where it happened—if it happened near where our house stood. I wondered who lived here on this land then, what kind of a house they lived in, and if they had a sassafras with tiny thin April leaves on its top growing in their yard, and if the person that cut the date on the terrapin's back was buried at Plum Grove, if he had farmed these hills where we lived today and cut timber like Grandpa had—and if he had seen the Aprils pass like Grandpa had seen them and if he enjoyed them like Grandpa was enjoying this April. I wondered if he had looked at the dogwood blossoms, the redbud blossoms, and talked to this same terrapin.

"Are you well, old fellow?" Grandpa asked the terrapin.

The terrapin just looked at Grandpa.

"I'm well as common for a man of my age," Grandpa said.

"Did the terrapin ask Grandpa if he was well?" I asked Mom.

"I don't know," Mom said. "I can't talk to a terrapin."

"But Grandpa can."

"Yes."

"Wait until tomatoes get ripe and we'll go to the garden together," Grandpa said.

"Does the terrapin eat tomatoes?" I asked Mom.

"Yes, that terrapin has been eatin' tomatoes from our garden for fifteen years," Mom said. "When Mick was tossin' the terrapins out of the tomato patch, he picked up this one and found the date cut on his back. He put him back in the patch and told him to help himself. He lives from our garden every year. We don't bother him and don't allow anybody else to bother him. He spends his winters under our smokehouse floor buried in the dry ground."

"Gee, Grandpa looks like the terrapin," I said.

Mom didn't say anything; tears came to her eyes. She wiped them from her eyes with the corner of her apron.

"I'll be back to see you," Grandpa said. "I'm a-gettin' a little chilly; I'll be gettin' back to the house."

The terrapin twisted his wrinkled neck without moving his big body, poking his head deeper into the April wind as

Another April

Grandpa pulled his bundled body up by holding to the sassafras tree trunk.

"Good-by, old friend!"

The terrapin poked his head deeper into the wind, holding one eye on Grandpa, for I could see his eye shining in the sinking sunlight.

Grandpa got his cane that was leaned against the sassafras tree trunk and hobbled slowly toward the house. The terrapin looked at him with first one eye and then the other.

Use of Language

Suppose your best friend has gone away for the summer. You vowed to keep in touch, so you sit down to write a letter. You talk about the weather, mutual friends, what you have been doing lately, and how you have been feeling. Sound like a lot to cover?

Now stop and consider what you *do not* have to convey to your friend. Because you know each other so well, and because you share a similar background, you don't have to describe your neighborhood and your section of the country, introduce the people who live there—how they talk and how they live, or express how it feels to live in this place and this time. You and your best friend are on the same wavelength, so to speak.

Authors, on the other hand, write stories that will be read by strangers. This simple fact explains why authors are so choosy about words. They don't know who the reader is, where he or she comes from, or when he is reading their stories. Yet, they have something to share and only one way to reach their readers—through language. So they choose their words carefully and use them to create special effects. These special effects help you to see, feel, hear and even smell the stories you read.

In writing "Another April," author Jesse Stuart had to convey what it was like to be an old man welcoming another April—perhaps his last—in the hill country of Kentucky. In this lesson we will look at four ways in which the author uses language to do this:

1 The author uses dialect—the local speech of the people.

2 The author uses colorful language to convey shades of meaning.

3 The author uses comparisons to create vivid pictures in the reader's mind.

4 The author uses figures of speech for emphasis.

Use of Language

1 Using Dialect

Authors develop what you might call an "ear for speech." They pay more than the usual attention to conversations that go on around them. They listen not only to what is said, but also to how it is worded. Their ears perk up at words or expressions that are a little bit different. They are alert to unusual pronunciations. They make special note of any slang that people use. All of these elements make up *dialect*. Dialect is a way of speaking that has developed over time among certain people living in a certain area. It is one of those special effects that authors strive to create with words.

Most people think of dialect as something that sounds foreign and is hard to understand, like this Irish brogue from the lips of Mr. Dooley, a character created by Finley Peter Dunne:

> "I know a man be th' name iv Clancy wanst, Jawn. He was fr'm th' County May-o, but a good man f'r all that. . . ."

Some people think that dialect is filled with slang, like this example of the faddish babble of the "Valley Girl" of the early 1980s:

> "You don't want to wear stuff that people don't wear. People'd look at you and just go, 'Ew, she's a zod, like get away.'"

But dialect does not have to be either foreign sounding or hard to understand. Sometimes just a word or two, a different way of saying something, an unusual word order, or a different pronunciation is enough to bring to mind a person of a certain time or place.

Jesse Stuart uses dialect with a light but sure touch. Take Grandpa's way of speaking, for instance:

> "Huh, what did ye say?" Grandpa asked. . . .
> "Wait until I get your gloves," Mom said. . . .
> "Don't get 'em," Grandpa said. "I won't ketch cold."

Grandpa says "ye" instead of "you"—a quaint speech habit that lingers only in isolated areas. His speech is not precise; he drops sounds here and there, like the *th* in *them* ("Don't get 'em"). Grandpa says "ketch," which is a regional pronunciation of the word *catch*. And later we find a lilting quality in his speech: "I'm a-goin' to see my old friend. . . ." "I'll be a-goin' to see 'im. . . ."

These little touches fill out the reader's mental picture of this character. He is an unschooled man of another generation; not a rich man or a powerful man, but a simple man whose dialect reflects the hill country where he has spent his life.

The boy's speech also reveals his background. He says, "If Mom didn't get his fingers back in the glove-fingers exactly right Grandpa *quarreled at* Mom." Further on he says, "[Grandpa would] take me on his knee and tell me about *all what* he had seen." It's not good grammar to say "quarreled *at*" instead of "quarreled *with*," or "all *what* he had seen" instead of "all *that* he had seen." Yet these expressions lend a flavor to the boy's speech. When you read his words, you realize that he has grown up in an area where old ways linger, and where school learning takes a back seat to making one's living off the land.

Now go on to Exercise A, and try to notice the effect that dialect has elsewhere in the story.

Exercise A

Read the following passage and answer the questions about it using what you have learned in this part of the lesson.

"Who is Grandpa goin' to see, Mom?" I asked.

"He's not goin' to see anybody," Mom said.

"I heard 'im say that he was goin' to see an old friend," I told her.

"Oh, he was just a-talkin'," Mom said.

. . . .

"He's playin' with that old terrapin, Mom," I said.

. . . .

"Looks like the terrapin would bite Grandpa," I said.

"That terrapin has spent the winters under that smokehouse for fifteen years," Mom said. "Pap has been acquainted with him for eleven years. He's been talkin' to that terrapin every spring."

"How does Grandpa know the terrapin is old?" I asked Mom.

"It's got 1847 cut on its shell," Mom said. "We know he's ninety-five years old. He's older than that. We don't know how old he was when that date was cut on his back."

. . . .

Then I wondered how a terrapin could get that old and what kind of a looking person he was who cut the date on the terrapin's back.

Put an x in the box beside the correct answer.

1. The boy and his mother's way of speaking might best be described as

☐ a. rough and coarse.

☐ b. precise and fussy.

☐ c. foreign and strange.

☐ d. "down-home" and countrified.

2. The boy wonders "how a terrapin could get that old and what kind of a looking person he was who cut the date on the terrapin's back." Find the phrase that is not grammatically correct in this sentence, yet lends an interesting flavor to the boy's speech. Write it here.

_____

Now check your answers using the Answer Key on page 456. Correct any wrong answers and review this part of the lesson if you don't understand why an answer was wrong.

Another April

Artists, fashion designers and other people who work with color know how important it is to select just the right shades. They combine lights with darks to achieve contrast. They create highlights with a single dab of an arresting color. There may be twenty

possible shades of pink, but only one that is the right shade for the apple blossoms a painter has in mind.

An author's palette consists of words rather than colors. Yet it is every bit as varied as the artist's paint palette. Just as there can be twenty different shades of pink, there can be twenty different words that mean close to the same thing. Nevertheless, there are different shades of meaning even among words that are synonyms.

Look at the words Jesse Stuart chose to describe Grandpa's way of walking: "Grandpa *toddled* along the path better than my baby brother could."

The author had many words from which to choose to describe how Grandpa walked. He could have said, "Grandpa *trudged* along the path." Or he could have used the verb tiptoed, sauntered, swaggered, strutted, skipped, ambled or shuffled. Yet, the author chose to say that Grandpa toddled, and for good reason. The word *toddle* has a shade of meaning that calls to mind a very small child. A child just learning to walk moves with a flat-footed, unsteady gait called toddling. Grandpa's walk is something like a toddler's walk. But the word does even more than this; it carries the feeling that Grandpa himself has become, in his very old age, something of a child again. His thoughts and his pleasures are the very simple thoughts and very simple pleasures of a small child. All in all, no word other than *toddle* is quite as right for describing Grandpa's walk.

Colorful language involves more than isolated words, however. Color also results from the way an author puts words *together*. Carefully chosen words are combined to create a story whose *total effect* is pleasing. You don't usually stop and admire each individual word in a story any more than you do the individual patches of color in a painting. Yet each is important, because when they are carefully put together, these elements create a whole that is well balanced. A story will have a sound and a clarity to it that hold your interest. Carefully chosen language allows you to understand exactly what is going on and just how the characters feel.

Jesse Stuart uses colorful language to convey the special feeling that the month of April brings:

> The way Mom had dressed Grandpa you'd think there was a heavy snow on the ground but there wasn't. April was here instead and the sun was shining on the green hills where the wild plums and the wild crab apples were in bloom enough to make you think there were big snowdrifts sprinkled over the green hills. When I looked at Grandpa and then looked out at the window at the sunshine and the green grass I laughed more. Grandpa laughed with me.

Notice the contrasts: Grandpa is dressed for winter, but outside it is spring; white blossoms against green hills; a young boy and an old man; and a new year. The paragraph sparkles with the kind of language that makes you *feel* the month of April—a month when laughter is very near the surface. The author has arranged his picture and colored it exactly right, so that you share the infectious high spirits of a brilliant spring day with Grandpa and the boy.

Exercise B

Read the following passage and answer the questions about it using what you have learned in this part of the lesson.

> I watched Grandpa stop under the pine tree in our front yard. He set his cane against the pine tree trunk, pulled off his gloves and put them in his pocket. Then Grandpa stooped over slowly, as slowly as the wind bends down a sapling, and picked up a pine cone in his big soft fingers. Grandpa stood fondling the pine cone in his hand. Then, one by one, he pulled the little chips from the pine cone—tearing it to pieces like he was hunting for something in it—and after he had torn it to pieces he threw the pine-cone stem on the ground. . . .
> Grandpa didn't come back into the house at the front door. He tottled around back of the house toward the smokehouse and I ran through the living room to the dining room so I

could look out the window and watch him.

"Where's Grandpa goin?" I asked Mom.

"Now never mind," Mom said. "Leave Grandpa alone. Don't go out there and disturb him."

"I won't bother 'im, Mom," I said. "I just want to watch 'im." . . .

. . . We watched Grandpa as he walked down beside our smokehouse where a tall sassafras tree's thin leaves fluttered in the blue April wind. Above the smokehouse and the tall sassafras was a blue April sky—so high you couldn't see the sky-roof. It was just blue space and little white clouds floated upon this blue.

Put an *x* in the box beside the correct answer.

1. The boy watched as "Grandpa stood *fondling* the pine cone in his hand." The word *fondle* means to stroke or caress. Someone might fondle a baby or a puppy, for example. What does the word *fondle* tell you about Grandpa's feelings toward the pine cone?

   ☐ a. That the pine cone is somehow precious to Grandpa

   ☐ b. That the pine cone is like a baby

   ☐ c. That the pine cone is ordinary and unimportant

   ☐ d. That the pine cone feels hard and jagged

2. In the last paragraph, the author uses words to paint a picture of April in which two colors stand out. On the lines below, write the words, phrases or sentences that contribute to this picture.

   _____

   _____

   _____

Now check your answers using the Answer Key on page 456. Correct any wrong answers and review this part of the lesson if you don't understand why an answer was wrong.

Use of Language

3 Using Comparisons

Sometimes the best way to describe a thing is to compare it to something else. Take Grandpa's laugh, for example. The author wants to tell the reader not just how it *sounds*, but how it makes the boy *feel* to hear it. To do this, the author draws an unusual comparison. He refers to Grandpa's laugh as "a coarse laugh like March wind among the pine tops. . . ."

Now, strictly speaking, you might argue that a laugh could never be mistaken for the sound of the wind. But it is not simply the sound of the laugh that the author wants to describe. It is its effect on the boy.

So, looking at the comparison in this light, we not only hear Grandpa's laugh—"a coarse laugh," probably rough or hoarse—we feel it "like the March wind among the pine tops." To a small boy sitting at the foot of a tall pine, the wind above is a mighty, uncontrollable force of nature that he does not fully understand. Grandpa is something like that too. The boy cannot quite grasp what it means to be ninety-one years old. In spite of Grandpa's childlike ways, he is not a playmate. He's more a force of nature, distant and elemental, like the rough March wind.

All of this, and more, is suggested by comparing Grandpa's laugh to the March wind. You may not have thought of all this as you read. You often have to stop and think about an unusual comparison to grasp its full meaning. But you probably sensed that Grandpa somehow stood apart from the boy, as if he lived high up and far away.

Comparisons that start with the word *like* or *as* are called *similes* (sim'-uh-lees). Jesse Stuart sprinkles similes throughout "Another April." Wherever they are used, they offer the reader both an image and a feeling for the thing the author is describing. For instance, in another part of the story the author writes, "Grandpa stooped over slowly, as slowly as the wind bends down a sapling. . . ." The phrase "as slowly as the wind bends down a sapling" is a simile. It not only tells you how slowly Grandpa stooped over, but also links him once again with nature—the sapling.

Toward the end of the story, the author uses a simile to describe the terrapin's actions when Grandpa is talking to it: "The terrapin turned his fleshless face to one side *like a hen does when she looks at you in the sunlight.*" The simile is "like a hen does when she looks at you in the sunlight." Anyone who knows chickens will at once picture the sharp turn of the turtle's head and the way it cocks it to one side. And what is the feeling here? It's one of curiosity. The author is suggesting that the

Another April

terrapin is curious to hear what Grandpa has to say. Perhaps it is intent on trying to understand Grandpa's words.

Now read the passage in Exercise C, in which the author describes how Grandpa is dressed for his walk.

Exercise C

Read the following passage and answer the questions about it using what you have learned in this part of the lesson.

Grandpa was wearing a heavy wool suit that hung loosely about his big body but fitted him tightly round the waist where he was as big and as round as a flour barrel. His pant legs were as big 'round his pipestem legs as emptied meal sacks. And his big shoes, with his heavy wool socks dropping down over their tops, looked like sled runners.

Put an *x* in the box beside the correct answer.

1. The similes used in this description do more than just tell what Grandpa was wearing. They lend a feeling that might best be described as

   ☐ a. sad.

   ☐ b. frightening.

   ☐ c. comical.

   ☐ d. puzzling.

2. There are three similes in the passage above. Two are introduced by the word *as*, and the third by the word *like*. Find these similes and copy them on the lines below.

   _____

   _____

   _____

Now check your answers using the Answer Key on page 456. Correct any wrong answers and review this part of the lesson if you don't understand why an answer was wrong.

A figure of speech is an unusual way of saying something. It is not a statement of fact. It's more a kind of word play that stands out and draws the reader's attention.

There are many kinds of figures of speech, and each has its own name. You've already met one of the most common—the simile. A simile is never a straightforward statement of fact; it is a fanciful comparison. It calls your attention to the thing being described by comparing it to something else.

Other figures of speech make their point in different ways. One you probably use yourself is exaggeration. *Exaggeration* is the intentional overstatement of a point for the purpose of emphasizing it; for example, "That test was so hard my brain blew a fuse!" No one hearing this would accept it as fact. But they would know that you thought the test was very difficult.

Grandpa exaggerates when he tells the boy, "Yer Ma's a-puttin' enough clothes on me to kill a man." This is a humorous exaggeration that draws attention to the way Grandpa is bundled up.

You could also add emphasis by doing just the opposite—by *understating*, rather than *overstating*, the facts. This figure of speech is called *understatement*. For instance, Jesse Stuart says that Grandpa wore "a heavy wool shirt and over his wool shirt he wore a heavy wool sweater and then his coat over the top of all this. Over his coat he wore a heavy overcoat and about his neck he wore a wool scarf." If you were to remark that Grandpa had on "a stitch or two," you would be using understatement to make the point that Grandpa was wearing an awful lot of clothes.

If, as a way of teasing Grandpa about all the clothes he is wearing, you were to say, "Sure you got enough clothes on, Gramp?" you would be using a figure of speech called irony. *Irony* is saying the opposite of what you really mean.

Another way authors call your attention to a thing is by giving it human qualities. This figure of speech is called *personification*. If you said, "The branches of the old pine lovingly caressed the small cottage," you would be giving the pine tree human feelings that a tree doesn't actually have. A tree cannot caress, nor can it love. But by using this figure of speech, you would communicate your feelings about the tree.

One last figure of speech we'll talk about here is alliteration. *Alliteration* is the use of the same letter sound at the beginnings of two or more words that are close to one another, as in the following sentence: Grandpa "leaned his big bundled body against the dogwood." The phrase "*big bundled body*" is an example of alliteration. Each word starts with the *b* sound. You must slow down just a bit in order to pronounce the phrase. This makes you linger over the words and savor the sounds.

There are many other figures of speech that authors use. Sometimes these expressions are funny. Sometimes they are dramatic, angry, sad or just thought-provoking. They are always used for emphasis—to call attention to something that is being said.

Exercise D

Read the following passage and answer the questions about it using what you have learned in this part of the lesson.

Grandpa would stand when a puff of wind came along, and hold his face against the wind and let the wind play with his white whiskers.

Put an *x* in the box beside the correct answer.

1. Jesse Stuart uses personification to describe how the wind feels to Grandpa. The human quality that he gives to the wind makes it seem

   ☐ a. mournful.

   ☐ b. jealous.

   ☐ c. mean.

   ☐ d. playful.

2. We usually talk about the wind *wh*ispering, *wh*istling, or *wh*ining. We use words that begin with the *w* sound to describe it. Find a part of a sentence in the passage that uses the sound to create alliteration. Copy it on the lines below.

_____

Use the Answer Key on page 456 to check your answers. Correct any wrong answers and review this part of the lesson if you don't understand why an answer was wrong. Now go on to do the Comprehension Questions.

Comprehension Questions

Answer these questions without looking back at the story. Choose the best answer to each question and put an *x* in the box beside it.

Recalling
Facts

1. Grandpa says, "I'm a-goin' to see my old friend." What old friend does he mean?

   ☐ a. A neighbor

   ☐ b. An ancient pine

   ☐ c. One of the hogs

   ☐ d. A terrapin

Making
Inferences

2. As she helps him get dressed to go outside, mother seems to treat Grandpa like a

   ☐ a. child.

   ☐ b. stranger.

   ☐ c. brother.

   ☐ d. father.

Understanding
Main Ideas

3. What kind of a man was Grandpa in his prime?

   ☐ a. Fearful and timid

   ☐ b. Shy and bookish

   ☐ c. Powerful and vigorous

   ☐ d. Sickly and frail

Recalling
Facts

4. How old is the boy?

   ☐ a. Five years old

   ☐ b. About ten years old

   ☐ c. About fourteen years old

   ☐ d. Sixteen years old

5. Grandpa's first stop on his walk is the

☐ a. hog pen.

☐ b. mailbox.

☐ c. smokehouse.

☐ d. pine tree.

6. Grandpa picks apart a pine cone, pulls the petals off some blossoms, and plucks a cocoon from a briar bush. What can you infer from these actions?

☐ a. He is destructive.

☐ b. He probably doesn't realize what he is doing.

☐ c. He is trying to observe and appreciate as much of nature as he can.

☐ d. He is angry about something.

7. Grandpa used to "cut timber on the coldest days without socks on his feet but with his feet stuck down in cold *brogan* shoes. . . ." From the meaning of this sentence, you can understand that *brogans* are a kind of

☐ a. lightweight sneaker.

☐ b. open sandal.

☐ c. flexible running shoe.

☐ d. sturdy work shoe.

8. The boy has noticed that over the years Grandpa's walks have been getting

☐ a. fewer in number.

☐ b. shorter in length.

☐ c. longer.

☐ d. less enjoyable.

9. How does Mom seem to feel about her father?

☐ a. She hates what he has become.

☐ b. She loves him very much.

☐ c. She feels that he is a burden.

☐ d. She is ashamed of him.

10. Mother says, "whoever cut that date on his [the terrapin's] back *has long been under the ground.*" This is another way of saying that that person

☐ a. has moved away.

☐ b. has long been forgotten.

☐ *c.* is in hiding.

☐ d. is dead and buried.

11. What does the terrapin do that shows it knows Grandpa?

☐ a. It lets Grandpa stroke its head.

☐ b. It comes when Grandpa calls.

☐ c. It makes sounds as if trying to speak.

☐ d. It moves its tail, as if wagging it.

12. Grandpa tells the terrapin, "I'm *well as common for a man of my age.*" Grandpa means that he is

☐ a. feeling about as well as can be expected.

☐ b. feeling better than a common person.

☐ c. enjoying better health than others his age.

☐ d. feeling worse than usual.

13. Both Grandpa and the terrapin

   ☐ a. wish they were young again.

   ☐ b. have lost interest in life.

   ☐ c. enjoy simple pleasures like sunshine and tomatoes from the garden.

   ☐ d. are unhappy.

14. At what point in the story do tears come to mother's eyes?

   ☐ a. When she recalls the kind of man Grandpa used to be

   ☐ b. When Grandpa pets the hogs

   ☐ c. When Grandpa smells the redbud and dogwood blossoms

   ☐ d. When the boy says that Grandpa looks like the terrapin

15. How does this family seem to feel about old age?

   ☐ a. It deserves great respect.

   ☐ b. It is a time of pain and sorrow.

   ☐ c. It is degrading and embarrassing.

   ☐ d. It is something to make fun of.

Now check your answers using the Answer Key on page 456. Make no mark for right answers. <u>Correct</u> any wrong answers you may have by putting a checkmark (✓) in the box next to the right answer. Count the number of questions you answered correctly and plot the total on the Comprehension Scores graph on page 462.

Next, look at the questions you answered incorrectly. What types of questions were they? Count the number you got wrong of each type and enter the numbers in the spaces below.

Recognizing Words in Content _____

Recalling Facts _____

Keeping Events in Order _____

Making Inferences _____

Understanding Main Ideas _____

Now use these numbers to fill in the Comprehension Skills Profile on page 463.

Another April

Discussion Guides

The questions below will help you to think about the story and the lesson you have just read. If you don't discuss these questions in class, try to think about them or discuss them with your classmates.

Discussing Use of Language

1. A number of different terms are used by the characters in the story to show their relationships: Mom, Ma, Pap, Grandpa, Pop. Which of these might be called dialect? What terms do *you* use to refer to your parents and grandparents?

2. Twice in the story the author describes Grandpa's walk as "toddling." Yet, in the very last paragraph the author says, "Grandpa got his cane that was leaned against the sassafras tree trunk and *hobbled* slowly toward the house." What is the small difference between "toddled" and "hobbled"? Why do you think Jesse Stuart changed to the word *hobble* at the end of the story?

3. Personification is the giving of human qualities to a thing or animal. Does Jesse Stuart personify the terrapin? Explain your answer.

Discussing the Story

4. Why doesn't the mother allow the boy to join his grandfather on his first walk of the spring?

5. Why do you think Grandpa wants to visit the terrapin? What are some things they have in common?

6. Is Grandpa just an old man with the mind of a child? Or is he a wise old man who has sorted out the important from the unimportant things in life? Give examples that support both views.

Discussing the Author's Work

7. Find some things in the story that are strictly regional—that are found only in the region of the country where the story is set. Then point out some things about this story that people everywhere would recognize and understand. (For example, terrapins are common in the South, but not up North. The mother's concern for her elderly father is universal—similar feelings exist everywhere.)

8. None of the characters in this story have names. They are referred to by their place in the family—mother, Grandpa, the boy. What do you think the author wants to emphasize by doing this?

9. How does the author seem to feel about the countryside he describes in this story? How does he seem to feel about the people—the small farmers and the lumberjacks—who make their living here?

Writing Exercise

The boy says: "I wondered how a terrapin could get that old and what kind of a looking person he was who cut the date on the terrapin's back. I wondered where it happened—if it happened near where our house stood. I wondered who lived here on this land then, what kind of a house they lived in, and if they had a sassafras with tiny thin April leaves on its top growing in their yard, and if the person that cut the date on the terrapin's back was buried at Plum Grove, if he had farmed these hills where we lived today and cut timber like Grandpa had—and if he had seen the Aprils pass like Grandpa had seen them and if he enjoyed them like Grandpa was enjoying this April. I wondered if he had looked at the dogwood blossoms, the redbud blossoms, and talked to this same terrapin."

Try to imagine how the turtle *did* get the year 1847 carved on its shell, and write a few paragraphs answering the boy's questions about the terrapin and the person who put the date on its back.

In telling your story, do the following things:

1. Use dialect to show how the person who carved the date spoke. You might have him talking to the terrapin while carving the date. (Review part 1 of the lesson.)

2. Use colorful language to describe the countryside as it might have looked in 1847. (Look back at part 2 of the lesson.)

3. Use at least one simile. (Look back at part 3 of the lesson.)

4. Include an example of alliteration, and one other figure of speech mentioned in part 4 of the lesson.

Unit 7 Tone and Mood

Sucker

BY CARSON McCULLERS

About the Illustration

How would you describe the feelings of the boy who is sitting up in the bed? What do you think might have made him feel that way? Point out some details in the drawing to support your response.

Here are some questions to help you think:

☐ How would you describe the expression on the young boy's face?

☐ Who do you think the older boy in the drawing might be? How do you think he feels? What details about him make you think that?

☐ What do you think might be happening in this scene?

Unit 7

Introduction   What the Story Is About/What the Lesson Is About

Story   Sucker

Lesson   Tone and Mood

Activities   Comprehension Questions/Discussion Guides/Writing Exercise

Introduction

What the Story Is About

In households where there are many people but not many rooms, the children are usually expected to share a bedroom. This often means two to a bed. Such is the case with Pete and Richard, two boys growing up in the depression years of the 1930s. At the time of the story, Pete is sixteen and Richard is twelve.

If you have ever had to share a room with someone, you probably know that roommates often bicker with each other. But this is not the case with Pete and Richard. As Pete tells it:

> It was always like I had a room to myself. Sucker [Richard] slept in my bed with me but that didn't interfere with anything. The room was mine and I used it as I wanted to.

It almost seems that Richard doesn't exist for Pete, except for those times when Pete feels like playing tricks on him. And when Pete *does* notice him, he calls him by the very uncomplimentary name of "Sucker." But Sucker worships Pete. He would do anything to have Pete pay attention to him and like him.

Pete is having a similar problem with Maybelle Watts. He has a crush on Maybelle, but she ignores him. It's as if Pete doesn't exist as far as she is concerned—except for the times when she chooses to embarrass him in public.

So, here we have two boys who live about as close together as people can and yet who are miles apart. Each boy is looking for attention and love. Each is made miserable by the person whose affection he craves. Where this all leads is what the story is about.

Author Carson McCullers is best remembered for her novel *The Heart Is a Lonely Hunter*. This book was made into a movie in 1968 and it is still shown on TV from time to time. She also wrote *Member of the Wedding,* which was a popular movie in 1952 and remained popular for many years after. If you enjoy "Sucker," you will probably enjoy reading both of these fine books.

Carson McCullers is one of the great examples of what a person can accomplish in the face of a severe physical handicap. A series of strokes left her paralyzed on the left side of her body for most of her adult life. She finished one of her novels by typing steadily, at the rate of one page a day, with only one hand. She is recognized as one of the outstanding writers of stories set in the southern United States, where she was born and grew up.

What the Lesson Is About

The lesson that follows the story is about tone and mood. Every piece of writing has a tone, just as your voice has a tone when you speak. And the tone of a story changes constantly, just as your manner of speaking changes according to how you feel. The way you feel is called your mood.

How the author feels is the author's mood. And the author develops the moods of the characters. You can tell from the tone of the story how the author feels about the characters, the actions, and the ideas that are being presented. Tone, therefore, is sometimes called the author's *attitude*. And tone and mood, as you will see in the lesson, work very closely together.

The questions below will help you to focus on tone and mood as they develop in the story "Sucker." Read the story carefully and try to answer these questions as you go along:

1 How does the tone change with each new turn in the story? What are some of the different feelings (moods) that the characters experience?

2 How does the author let you know how she feels, and how she wants *you* to feel, about Maybelle Watts by the way she describes Maybelle?

3 What does Maybelle contribute to the tone and mood of the scenes in which she appears? What feeling do you get from the scenes set in the boys' bedroom?

4 The only dialogue—conversation—in the story is between Pete and Sucker. How do these conversations make you feel?

Sucker

Carson McCullers

It was always like I had a room to myself. Sucker slept in my bed with me but that didn't interfere with anything. The room was mine and I used it as I wanted to. Once I remember sawing a trap door in the floor. Last year when I was a sophomore in high school I tacked on my wall some pictures of girls from magazines and one of them was just in her underwear. My mother never bothered me because she had the younger kids to look after. And Sucker thought anything I did was always swell.

Whenever I would bring any of my friends back to my room all I had to do was just glance once at Sucker and he would get up from whatever he was busy with and maybe half smile at me, and leave without saying a word. He never brought kids back there. He's twelve, four years younger than I am, and he always knew without me even telling him that I didn't want kids that age meddling with my things.

Half the time I used to forget that Sucker isn't my brother. He's my first cousin but practically ever since I remember he's been in our family. You see his folks were killed in a wreck when he was a baby. To me and my kid sisters he was like our brother.

Sucker used to always remember and believe every word I said. That's how he got his nick-name. Once a couple of years ago I told him that if he'd jump off our garage with an umbrella it would act as a parachute and he wouldn't fall hard. He did it and busted his knee. That's just one instance. And the funny thing was that no matter how many times he got fooled he would still believe me. Not that he was dumb in other ways—it was just the way he acted with me. He would look at everything I did and quietly take it in.

There is one thing I have learned, but it makes me feel

guilty and hard to figure out. If a person admires you a lot you despise him and don't care—and it is the person who doesn't notice you that you are apt to admire. This is not easy to realize. Maybelle Watts, this senior at school, acted like she was the Queen of Sheba and even humiliated me. Yet at this same time I would have done anything in the world to get her attentions. All I could think about day and night was Maybelle until I was nearly crazy. When Sucker was a little kid and on up until the time he was twelve I guess I treated him as bad as Maybelle did me.

Now that Sucker has changed so much it is a little hard to remember him as he used to be. I never imagined anything would suddenly happen that would make us both very different. I never knew that in order to get what has happened straight in my mind I would want to think back on him as he used to be and compare and try to get things settled. If I could have seen ahead maybe I would have acted different.

I never noticed him much or thought about him and when you consider how long we have had the same room together it is funny the few things I remember. He used to talk to himself a lot when he'd think he was alone—all about him fighting gangsters and being on ranches and that sort of kids' stuff. He'd get in the bathroom and stay as long as an hour and sometimes his voice would go up high and excited and you could hear him all over the house. Usually, though, he was very quiet. He didn't have many boys in the neighborhood to buddy with and his face had the look of a kid who is watching a game and waiting to be asked to play. He didn't mind wearing the sweaters and coats that I outgrew, even if the sleeves did flop down too big and make his wrists look as thin and white as a little girl's. That is how I remember him—getting a little bigger every year but still being the same. That was Sucker up until a few months ago when all this trouble began.

Maybelle was somehow mixed up in what happened so I guess I ought to start with her. Until I knew her I hadn't given much time to girls. Last fall she sat next to me in General Science class and that was when I first began to notice her. Her hair is the brightest yellow I ever saw and occasionally she will wear it set into curls with some sort of gluey stuff. Her fingernails are pointed and manicured and painted a shiny red. All during class I used to watch Maybelle, nearly all the time except when I thought she was going to look my way or when the teacher called on me. I couldn't keep my eyes off her hands, for one thing. They are very little and white except for that red stuff, and when she would turn the pages of her book she always licked her thumb and held out her little finger and turned very slowly. It is impossible to describe Maybelle. All the boys are crazy about her but she didn't even notice me. All I could do was sit and look at her in class—and sometimes it was like the whole room could hear my heart beating and I wanted to holler or light out and run for Hell.

At night, in bed, I would imagine about Maybelle. Often this would keep me from sleeping until as late as one or two o'clock. Sometimes Sucker would wake up and ask me why I couldn't get settled and I'd tell him hush his mouth. I suppose I was mean to him lots of times. I guess I wanted to ignore somebody like Maybelle did me. You could always tell by Sucker's face when his feelings were hurt. I don't remember all the ugly remarks I must have made because even when I was saying them my mind was on Maybelle.

That went on for nearly three months and then somehow she began to change. In the halls she would speak to me and every morning she copied my homework. At lunch time once I danced with her in the gym. One afternoon I got up nerve and went around to her house with a carton of cigarettes. I knew she smoked in the girls' basement and sometimes outside of school—and I didn't want to take her candy because I think that's been run into the ground. She was very nice and it seemed to me everything was going to change.

It was that night when this trouble really started. I had come into my room late and Sucker was already asleep. I felt too happy and keyed up to get in a comfortable position and I was awake thinking about Maybelle a long time. Then I dreamed about her and it seemed I kissed her. It was a surprise to wake up and see the dark. I lay still and a little while passed before I could come to and understand where I was. The house was quiet and it was a very dark night.

Sucker's voice was a shock to me. "Pete? . . . "

I didn't answer anything or even move.

"You do like me as much as if I was your own brother, don't you, Pete?"

I couldn't get over the surprise of everything and it was like this was the real dream instead of the other.

"You have liked me all the time like I was your own brother, haven't you?"

"Sure," I said.

Then I got up for a few minutes. It was cold and I was glad to come back to bed. Sucker hung on to my back. He felt little and warm and I could feel his warm breathing on my shoulder.

"No matter what you did I always knew you liked me."

I was wide awake and my mind seemed mixed up in a strange way. There was this happiness about Maybelle and all that—but at the same time something about Sucker and his voice when he said these things made me take notice. Anyway I guess you understand people better when you are happy than when something is worrying you. It was like I had never really thought about Sucker until then. I felt I had always been mean to him. One night a few weeks before I had heard him crying in the dark. He said he had lost a boy's beebee gun and was scared to let anybody know. He wanted me to tell him what to do. I was sleepy and tried to make him hush and when he wouldn't I kicked at him. That was just one of the things I remembered. It seemed to me he had always been a lonesome kid. I felt bad.

There is something about a dark cold night that makes you feel close to someone you're sleeping with. When you talk together it is like you are the only people awake in the town.

"You're a swell kid, Sucker," I said.

It seemed to me suddenly that I did like him more than anybody else I knew—more than any other boy, more than my sisters, more in a certain way even than Maybelle. I felt good all over and it was like when they play sad music in the movies. I wanted to show Sucker how much I really thought of him and make up for the way I had always treated him.

We talked for a good while that night. His voice was fast and it was like he had been saving up these things to tell me for a long time. He mentioned that he was going to try to build a canoe and that the kids down the block wouldn't let him in on their football team and I don't know what all. I talked some too and it was a good feeling to think of him taking in everything I said so seriously. I even spoke of Maybelle a little, only I made out like it was her who had been running after me all this time. He asked questions about high school and so forth. His voice was excited and he kept on talking fast like he could never get the words out in time. When I went to sleep he was still talking and I could feel his breathing on my shoulder, warm and close.

During the next couple of weeks I saw a lot of Maybelle. She acted as though she really cared for me a little. Half the time I felt so good I hardly knew what to do with myself.

But I didn't forget about Sucker. There were a lot of old things in my bureau drawer I'd been saving—boxing gloves and Tom Swift books and second rate fishing tackle. All this I turned over to him. We had some more talks together and it was really like I was knowing him for the first time.

When there was a long cut on his cheek I knew he had been monkeying around with this new first razor set of mine, but I didn't say anything. His face seemed different now. He used to look timid and sort of like he was afraid of a whack over the head. That expression was gone. His face, with those wide-open eyes and his ears sticking out and his mouth never quite shut, had the look of a person who is surprised and expecting something swell.

Once I started to point him out to Maybelle and tell her he was my kid brother. It was an afternoon when a murder mystery was on at the movie. I had earned a dollar working for my Dad and I gave Sucker a quarter to go and get candy and so forth. With the rest I took Maybelle. We were sitting near the back and I saw Sucker come in. He began to stare at the screen the minute he stepped past the ticket man and he stumbled down the aisle without noticing where he was going. I started to punch Maybelle but couldn't quite make up my mind. Sucker looked a little silly—walking like a drunk with his eyes glued to the movie. He was wiping his reading glasses on his shirt tail and his knickers flopped down. He went on until he got to the first few rows where the kids usually sit. I never did punch Maybelle. But I got to thinking it was good to have both of them at the movie with the money I earned.

I guess things went on like this for about a month or six weeks. I felt so good I couldn't settle down to study or put my mind on anything. I wanted to be friendly with everybody. There were times when I just had to talk to some person. And usually that would be Sucker. He felt as good as I did. Once he said: "Pete, I am gladder that you are like my brother than anything else in the world."

Then something happened between Maybelle and me. I never have figured out just what it was. Girls like her are hard to understand. She began to act different toward me. At first I wouldn't let myself believe this and tried to think it was just my imagination. She didn't act glad to see me any more. Often she went out riding with this fellow on the football team who owns this yellow roadster. The car was the color of her hair and after school she would ride off with him, laughing and looking into his face. I couldn't think of anything to do about it and she was on my mind all day and night. When I did get a chance to go out with her she was snippy and didn't seem to notice me. This made me feel like something was the matter—I would worry about my shoes clopping too loud on the floor, or the fly of my pants, or the bumps on my chin. Sometimes when Maybelle was around, a devil would get into me and I'd hold my face stiff and call grown men by their last names without the Mister and say rough things. In the night I would wonder what made me do all this until I was too tired for sleep.

At first I was so worried I just forgot about Sucker. Then later he began to get on my nerves. He was always hanging around until I would get back from high school, always looking like he had something to say to me or wanted me to tell him. He made me a magazine rack in his Manual Training class and one week he saved his lunch money and bought me three packs of cigarettes. He couldn't seem to take it in that I had things on my mind and didn't want to fool with him. Every afternoon it would be the same—him in my room with this waiting expression on his face. Then I wouldn't say anything or I'd maybe answer him rough-like and he would finally go on out.

I can't divide that time up and say this happened one day and that the next. For one thing I was so mixed up the weeks just slid along into each other and I felt like Hell and didn't care. Nothing definite was said or done. Maybelle still rode around with this fellow in his yellow roadster and sometimes she would smile at me and sometimes not. Every afternoon I went from one place to another where I thought she would be. Either she would act almost nice and I would begin thinking how things would finally clear up and she would care for me—or else she'd behave so that if she hadn't been a girl I'd have wanted to grab her by that white little neck and choke her. The more ashamed I felt for making a fool of myself the more I ran after her.

Sucker kept getting on my nerves more and more. He would look at me as though he sort of blamed me for something, but at the same time knew that it wouldn't last long. He was growing fast and for some reason began to stutter when he talked. Sometimes he had nightmares or would throw up his breakfast. Mom got him a bottle of cod liver oil.

Then the finish came between Maybelle and me. I met her going to the drug store and asked for a date. When she said no I remarked something sarcastic. She told me she was sick and tired of my being around and that she had never cared a rap about me. She said all that. I just stood there and didn't answer anything. I walked home very slowly.

For several afternoons I stayed in my room by myself. I didn't want to go anywhere or talk to anyone. When Sucker would come in and look at me sort of funny I'd yell at him to get out. I didn't want to think of Maybelle and I sat at my desk reading *Popular Mechanics* or whittling at a toothbrush rack I was making. It seemed to me I was putting that girl out of my mind pretty well.

But you can't help what happens to you at night. That is what made things how they are now.

You see a few nights after Maybelle said those words to me I dreamed about her again. It was like that first time and I was squeezing Sucker's arm so tight I woke him up. He reached for my hand.

"Pete, what's the matter with you?"

All of a sudden I felt so mad my throat choked—at myself and the dream and Maybelle and Sucker and every single person I knew. I remembered all the times Maybelle had humiliated me and everything bad that had ever happened. It seemed to me for a second that nobody would ever like me but a sap like Sucker.

Sucker

"Why is it we aren't buddies like we were before? Why—?"

"Shut your damn trap!" I threw off the cover and got up and turned on the light. He sat in the middle of the bed, his eyes blinking and scared.

There was something in me and I couldn't help myself. I don't think anybody ever gets that mad but once. Words came without me knowing what they would be. It was only afterward that I could remember each thing I said and see it all in a clear way.

"Why aren't we buddies? Because you're the dumbest slob I ever saw! Nobody cares anything about you! And just because I felt sorry for you sometimes and tried to act decent don't think I give a damn about a dumb-bunny like you!"

If I'd talked loud or hit him it wouldn't have been so bad. But my voice was slow and like I was very calm. Sucker's mouth was part way open and he looked as though he'd knocked his funny bone. His face was white and sweat came out on his forehead. He wiped it away with the back of his hand and for a minute his arm stayed raised that way as though he was holding something away from him.

"Don't you know a single thing? Haven't you ever been around at all? Why don't you get a girl friend instead of me? What kind of a sissy do you want to grow up to be anyway?"

I didn't know what was coming next. I couldn't help myself or think.

Sucker didn't move. He had on one of my pajama jackets and his neck stuck out skinny and small. His hair was damp on his forehead.

"Why do you always hang around me? Don't you know when you're not wanted?"

Afterward I could remember the change in Sucker's face. Slowly that blank look went away and he closed his mouth. His eyes got narrow and his fists shut. There had never been such a look on him before. It was like every second he was getting older. There was a hard look to his eyes you don't see usually in a kid. A drop of sweat rolled down his chin and he didn't notice. He just sat there with those eyes on me and he didn't speak and his face was hard and didn't move.

"No, you don't know when you're not wanted. You're too dumb. Just like your name—a dumb Sucker."

It was like something had busted inside me. I turned off the light and sat down in the chair by the window. My legs were shaking and I was so tired I could have bawled. The room was cold and dark. I sat there for a long time and smoked a squashed cigarette I had saved. Outside the yard was black and quiet. After a while I heard Sucker lie down.

I wasn't mad any more, only tired. It seemed awful to me that I had talked like that to a kid only twelve. I couldn't take it all in. I told myself I would go over to him and try to make it up. But I just sat there in the cold until a long time had passed. I planned how I could straighten it out in the morning. Then, trying not to squeak the springs, I got back in bed.

Sucker was gone when I woke up the next day. And later when I wanted to apologize as I had planned he looked at me in this new hard way so that I couldn't say a word.

All of that was two or three months ago. Since then Sucker has grown faster than any boy I ever saw. He's almost as tall as I am and his bones have gotten heavier and bigger. He won't wear any of my old clothes any more and has bought his first pair of long pants—with some leather suspenders to hold them up. Those are just the changes that are easy to see and put into words.

Our room isn't mine at all any more. He's gotten up this gang of kids and they have a club. When they aren't digging trenches in some vacant lot and fighting they are always in my room. On the door there is some foolishness written in Mercurochrome saying "Woe to the Outsider who Enters" and signed with crossed bones and their secret initials. They have rigged up a radio and every afternoon it blares out music. Once as I was coming in I heard a boy telling something in a low voice about what he saw in the back of his big brother's automobile. I could guess what I didn't hear. *That's what her and my brother do. It's the truth—parked in the car.* For a minute Sucker looked surprised and his face was almost like it used to be. Then he got hard and tough again. "Sure, dumbell. We know all that." They didn't notice me. Sucker began telling them how in two years he was planning to be a trapper in Alaska.

But most of the time Sucker stays by himself. It is worse when we are alone together in the room. He sprawls across the bed in those long corduroy pants with the suspenders and just stares at me with that hard, half sneering look. I fiddle around my desk and can't get settled because of those eyes of his. And the thing is I just have to study because I've gotten three bad cards this term already. If I flunk English I can't graduate next year. I don't want to be a bum and I just have to get my mind on it. I don't care a flip for Maybelle or any particular girl any more and it's only this thing between Sucker and me that is the trouble now. We never speak except when we have to before the family. I don't even want to call him Sucker any more and unless I forget I call him by his real name, Richard. At night I can't study with him in the room and I have to hang around the drug store, smoking and doing nothing, with the fellows who loaf there.

More than anything I want to be easy in my mind again. And I miss the way Sucker and I were for a while in a funny, sad way that before this I never would have believed. But everything is so different that there seems to be nothing I can do to get it right. I've sometimes thought if we could have it out in a big fight that would help. But I can't fight him because he's four years younger. And another thing—sometimes this look in his eyes makes me almost believe that if Sucker could he would kill me.

Tone and Mood

When you stop to think about it, it's amazing how much you can do with the tone of your voice. For example, read these two words aloud: *Oh, Mother.* Now see how many different ways you can say these words—just these two words—to give them a different feeling and a different meaning each time.

Raise your voice a little at the end and it means that you are about to ask a question. Say it sharply and it sounds as though you are peeved about something. Say it slowly, with a sob in your voice, and you express sympathy or sorrow. You can express fear, anger, joy, disgust—all with the way you adjust your tone. The way you say the words—your tone—often provides more meaning for a listener than the words themselves.

Other things besides your voice can have tone as well. Music has tone. Places have tone. Think of the atmospheres or tones that you connect with a church, a school, a ball park and your home. People also have tone. A person in authority often projects an assertive, capable tone, while a clown projects a humorous tone.

Stories, or any writing, for that matter, must have tone, too. If an author fails to provide a variety of tones in a story, you soon become extremely bored with it. What is worse, you will have a very difficult time trying to figure out what the author wants you to know, feel or understand about the story.

Tone carries with it a *mood.* Mood is a feeling or an emotion. A person may have a blue mood or a happy mood, a carefree mood or a troubled mood. He may be suspicious, angry, satisfied, eager or disappointed. There is virtually no limit to the kinds of moods or feelings that a person may experience.

The tone of a march may put you in a patriotic mood. A love song may make you feel a bit dreamy. The tone of a church may inspire feelings of awe or reverence. The tone of a ball park may make you feel bubbly and excited.

Tone and mood are very similar because they both involve feelings. They are so similar, in fact, that many people say there is no difference at all between them. For our purposes, however, we will say that the difference is this: Tone is a manner, atmosphere, or attitude that carries, or conveys, a feeling. Mood is the feeling itself.

Here is how tone and mood work together in a story: As an author writes, he or she is in a particular mood, just as you are when you speak. The author feels a certain way about an idea or a character and expresses this mood or feeling through the tone of the story. You sense the tone as you read, you notice that the story has a certain mood. And if the author has successfully fashioned the tone and mood of the story, you begin to feel just the way he or she wants you to feel.

When you speak, there are several things that contribute to the tone you use to express your feelings. Your choice of words, the level of your voice, the expression on your face and your movements all help to provide the tone that conveys your mood. An author, however, as we say many times in the lessons in this book, has only words to work with. As you have surely seen in the story you have just read, a good author provides exactly the tone needed to control the mood of the story and your mood as a reader, as well.

In this lesson we will look at four things that help develop true-to-life tones and moods in Carson McCuller's story.

1 The author changes tones and moods to reflect the kinds of changes in tone and mood that occur in real life.

2 The author chooses words carefully to create the tones and moods she wants.

3 Characters and settings are used to create tone and mood.

4 Dialogue—conversation between characters—is used to create tone and mood.

People's moods are like the weather—always changing. You may feel happy upon awakening, bored in a dull class, excited at a pep rally, nervous taking a test, thoughtful on your way home from school, and warm in the company of a favorite friend.

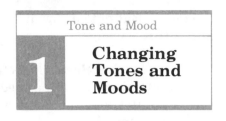

Tone and Mood

1 Changing Tones and Moods

Tones change too—tones of places, people and voices. Classrooms, gyms, auditoriums—all have their own sights, sounds and smells that provide each with a special and different tone. The people whom you meet in your life all bring their own special tones with them. There is a difference between a severe principal and your favorite teacher. You sense a different tone in each, and each puts you in a different mood.

People and places are *dynamic*. This means they are always changing. And as they change, tones and moods change with them. In order for a story to be convincing, its tone and mood must change continually, just as happens in real life. These changes are what keep your interest alive. The changing tones and moods are used to pass along information that the author wants you to have about the characters and ideas in the story.

In the story "Sucker," Carson McCullers begins with a rather light tone. As a reader, you respond with a light mood. You are even somewhat amused at the way Pete keeps his room. But five paragraphs later, the tone has made a definite change. You begin to feel that something has gone wrong between Pete and Sucker. You feel a bit uneasy, just as Pete is worried and uneasy. Watch for the change in tone and mood between these two passages:

> It was always like I had a room to myself. Sucker slept in my bed with me but that didn't interfere with anything. The room was mine and I used it as I wanted to. Once I remember sawing a trap door in the floor. Last year . . . I tacked on my wall some pictures of girls from magazines and one of them was just in her underwear. My mother never bothered me because she had the younger kids to look after. And Sucker thought anything I did was always swell.

The passage above has a light, amusing tone. Both boys seem comfortable and satisfied with the way things are at this point. This is the mood. But notice how different the tone and its corresponding mood are in this passage:

> Now that Sucker has changed so much it is a little hard to remember him as he used to be. I never imagined anything would suddenly happen that would make us both very different. I never knew that in order to get what has happened straight in my mind I would want to think back on him as he used to be and compare and try to get things settled. If I could have seen ahead maybe I would have acted different.

Pete has become thoughtful and a bit sad. The author uses the change of tone between the two passages to do two things. She communicates Pete's new feeling to you to let you know that things are not as they should be between the two boys, and she makes you worry about this a bit, just as Pete is worried. What this does, of course, is draw you into the story as you become anxious to know what has caused the tone of the story, and Pete's mood, to go from light to heavy or threatening.

Exercise A

Read the following passages and answer the questions about them using what you have learned in this part of the lesson.

Passage A

> We talked for a good while that night. His voice was fast and it was like he had been saving up these things to tell me for a long time. . . . I talked some too and it was a good feeling to think of him taking in everything I said so seriously. . . . His voice was excited and he kept on talking fast like he could never get the words out in time. When I went to sleep he was still talking and I could still feel his breathing on my shoulder, warm and close.

Passage B

> At first I was so worried I just forgot about Sucker. Then later he began to get on my nerves. . . . He couldn't seem to take it in that I had things on my mind and didn't want to fool with him. Every afternoon it would be the same—him in my room with this waiting expression on his face. Then I wouldn't say anything or I'd maybe answer him rough-like and he would finally go on out.

Put an *x* in the box beside the correct answer.

1. Between passage A and passage B, the mood changes from

   ☐ a. happy excitement to annoyance and disappointment.

   ☐ b. easy humor to fond thoughtfulness.

   ☐ c. unhappiness to hopeless despair.

   ☐ d. nervousness to peaceful calmness.

2. In each passage, find (1) a phrase that describes the expression on a person's face or a person's way of speaking (these things create the tone of the passage), and (2) a phrase that describes a feeling (the mood of the passage).

   Passage A

   (1) An expression or way of speaking: _____

   _____

   (2) A feeling: _____

   _____

   Passage B

   (1) An expression or way of speaking: _____

   _____

(2) A feeling: _____

_____

Now check your answers using the Answer Key on page 457. Correct any wrong answers and review this part of the lesson if you don't understand why an answer was wrong.

If you were to receive a gift of striped socks for your birthday, you might say, "Gee, thanks. That was very thoughtful of you. I do like striped socks."

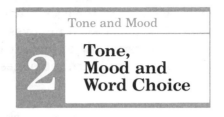

Tone and Mood

2 Tone, Mood and Word Choice

But if you were given a new pet, a puppy that you'd wanted for years, you would probably explode with, "A dog! Just what I've always wanted! Oh, thank you!"

In both cases, you would have expressed your appreciation for a gift. But it wouldn't have been hard to tell from your tone of voice how you felt about a new puppy as compared to a pair of socks. Your choice of words and the way you said the words would have created a tone that gave away your feelings—your mood.

In much the same way, an author might describe a sunrise in a story in a number of different ways:

A sudden burst of gold announced a glorious new day.

The merciless ball of fire crept over the barren hills.

Dawn broke on another day.

All of these sentences express the same idea—morning has come. But, in each case, the choice of words creates a tone that would clearly show how the author and the characters in a story felt about the arrival of a new day.

When Maybelle is described in "Sucker," you can tell at once, from the tone of the description, how the author feels about Maybelle and how she wants *you* to feel about her. And of course you can tell how poor Pete feels. All of this information is conveyed by just the right choice of words.

Maybelle was somehow mixed up in what happened so I guess I ought to start with her. Until I knew her I hadn't given much time to girls. Last fall she sat next to me in General Science class and that was when I first began to notice her. Her hair is the brightest yellow I ever saw and occasionally she will wear it set into curls with some sort of gluey stuff. Her fingernails are pointed and manicured and painted a shiny red. All during class I used to watch Maybelle, nearly all the time except when I thought she was going to look my way or when the teacher called on me. I couldn't keep my eyes off her hands, for one thing. They are very little and white except for that red stuff, and when she would turn the pages of her book she always licked her thumb. . . .

Poor Pete seems to be struck dumb by Maybelle's "great beauty." But, from the tone the author creates with a few choice words in just the right place, readers know just how to feel about Maybelle. Maybelle's hair is bright yellow and "set into curls *with some sort of gluey stuff.*" Her hands, which Pete loves to watch, are very small and white "*except for that red stuff.*" And Maybelle has the sloppy habit of licking her thumb every time she turns a page. Through her choice of words, Carson McCullers creates a tone that says, in effect, "I think Maybelle is a pretty little slob. And I'm sure, dear reader, that you will feel the same way when I get through with her."

Exercise B

Read the following passage and answer the questions about it using what you have learned in this part of the lesson.

Afterward I could remember the change in Sucker's face. Slowly that blank look went away and he closed his mouth. His eyes got narrow and his fists shut. There had never been such a look on him before. It was like every second he was getting older. There was a hard look to his eyes you don't see usually in a kid. A drop of sweat rolled down his chin and he didn't notice. He just sat there with those eyes on me and he didn't speak and his face was hard and didn't move.

Put an *x* in the box beside the correct answer.

1. From the way the author describes Sucker, you can tell that Sucker's feelings toward Pete have

☐ a. become more like those of a brother.

☐ b. not changed, even though Pete has changed.

☐ c. changed to pity because Pete is so upset.

☐ d. changed from admiration to hatred.

2. Many expressions in the passage set a tone that creates a tense mood. Write at least two of the expressions that make you feel this tense mood.

_____

_____

_____

Now check your answers using the Answer Key on page 457. Correct any wrong answers and review this part of the lesson if you don't understand why an answer was wrong.

	Tone and Mood
3	**Tone and Mood— Characters and Setting**

In earlier lessons you learned how authors use setting and characters to provide just the right atmosphere for the action in their stories. The same sort of thing is done all the time in TV commercials. If a sponsor wants to create a macho image for a product, the scene might be set in the wide open spaces of the outdoors. The action might include cowboys doing chores that require strength and endurance. On the other hand, in a commercial for a luxury item, the scene may be the front of a fine theater or a mansion, and the actors might be dressed in expensive formal attire. Characters and setting are used to create any tone the sponsor wants to project. It is hoped, of course, that the tone will influence your mood and make you want to buy the products that you see advertised.

There are three characters in "Sucker." Each creates a special feeling. There are two settings. Most of the story is set in the bedroom that the boys share. But there is one scene in which the three characters appear together in a movie theater. Let's look at this scene first. Then in Exercise C you can examine one of the scenes in the boys' room. Each setting and the characters involved create a different tone and mood.

> Once I started to point him out to Maybelle and tell her he was my kid brother. It was an afternoon when a murder mystery was on at the movie. . . . We were sitting near the back and I saw Sucker come in. He began to stare at the screen the minute he stepped past the ticket man and he stumbled down the aisle without noticing where he was going. I started to punch Maybelle but couldn't quite make up my mind. Sucker looked a little silly—walking like a drunk with his eyes glued to the movie. He was wiping his reading glasses on his shirt tail and his knickers flopped down. He went on until he got to the first few rows where the kids usually sit. I never did punch Maybelle. But I got to thinking it was good to have both of them at the movie with the money I earned.

Notice that whenever Sucker appears you tend to feel sympathetic toward him. Pete is always a bit edgy. In this scene he feels warm and good about having done something nice for Sucker, but he also feels embarrassed by Sucker in Maybelle's presence. Maybelle has a chilling effect on this scene, as she does on other parts of the story.

The movie theater is used in much the same way the boys' room is used. It brings the characters together in a close, quiet atmosphere.

Exercise C

Read the following passage and answer the questions about it using what you have learned in this part of the lesson.

It was that night when this trouble really started. I had come into my room late and Sucker was already asleep. I felt too happy and keyed up to get in a comfortable position and I was awake thinking about Maybelle a long time. Then I dreamed about her and it seemed I kissed her. It was a surprise to wake up and see the dark. I lay still and a little while passed before I could come to and understand where I was. The house was quiet and it was a very dark night. . . .

[Sucker talks with Pete]

Then I got up for a few minutes. It was cold and I was glad to come back to bed. Sucker hung on to my back. He felt little and warm and I could feel his warm breathing on my shoulder. . . .

There is something about a dark cold night that makes you feel close to someone you're sleeping with. When you talk together it is like you are the only people awake in the town.

Put an x in the box beside the correct answer.

1. How would you best describe the feeling (mood) between the two boys in this scene?

   ☐ a. Warm and close

   ☐ b. Strange and scary

   ☐ c. Strained and tense

   ☐ d. Angry and unhappy

2. The author uses three small words to describe the house and the night. These words help set the tone of the scene. Find these three words and write them here.

_____

Now check your answers using the Answer Key on page 457. Correct any wrong answers and review this part of the lesson if you don't understand why an answer was wrong.

Authors often set the tones and express the moods of stories in much the same way you set the tone and mood of situations when you speak. They use dialogue—conversation between characters. There are only two examples of dialogue in "Sucker," but, between them, they sum up the two major moods of the story. We will look at the first below, and you can deal with the second yourself in Exercise D.

Tone and Mood

4 Tone, Mood and Dialogue

> The house was quiet and it was a very dark night.
>
> Sucker's voice was a shock to me. "Pete? . . ."
>
> I didn't answer anything or even move.
>
> "You do like me as much as if I was your own brother, don't you Pete?"
>
> I couldn't get over the surprise of everything and it was like this was the real dream instead of the other.
>
> "You have liked me all the time like I was your own brother, haven't you?"
>
> "Sure," I said. . . .
>
> "No matter what you did I always knew you liked me."
>
> I was wide awake and my mind seemed mixed up in a strange way. There was this happiness about Maybelle and all that—but at the same time something about Sucker and his voice when he said these things made me take notice.

Pete is in a happy mood because Maybelle has finally noticed him. It is at this point that Sucker makes his very moving appeal for love. Sucker is an orphan, remember, and has probably always felt like an outsider in this family. Pete's habit of ignoring Sucker certainly hasn't helped matters.

In order to set the tone for this moment, Carson McCullers did two things. First, she established a feeling of closeness between the boys on a cold, dark night. (You saw this in the passage used in Exercise C.) Then she made the dialogue very simple. That is how conversation usually is when people are expressing very deep feelings.

"You do like me . . . You have liked me . . ." is Sucker's simple appeal. "Sure," Pete says. And that's all Sucker wants to hear. This simple dialogue sets the tone and mood of the scene.

Exercise D

Read the following passage and answer the questions about it using what you have learned in this part of the lesson.

"Pete, what's the matter with you?"

All of a sudden I felt so mad my throat choked—at myself and the dream and Maybelle and Sucker and every single person I knew. I remembered all the times Maybelle had humiliated me and everything bad that had ever happened. It seemed to me for a second that nobody would ever like me but a sap like Sucker.

"Why is it we aren't buddies like we were before? Why—?"

"Shut your damn trap!" I threw off the cover and got up and turned on the light. He sat in the middle of the bed, his eyes blinking and scared.

There was something in me and I couldn't help myself. I don't think anybody ever gets that mad but once. Words came without me knowing what they would be. . . .

"Why aren't we buddies? Because you're the dumbest slob I ever saw! Nobody cares anything about you! And just because I felt sorry for you sometimes and tried to act decent don't think I give a damn about a dumb-bunny like you!"

If I'd talked loud or hit him it wouldn't have been so bad. But my voice was slow and like I was very calm.

Put an x in the box beside the correct answer.

1. The author describes Pete's tone of voice. It was low, slow and calm. If you were Sucker, which one of the following words would best describe your feelings?

   ☐ a. Puzzlement

   ☐ b. Relief

   ☐ c. Shock

   ☐ d. Sorrow

2. Pete's words seem to be out of his control. This is how words usually come out when a person feels deep anger and disappointment. Find two sentences in the passage that tell you that Pete's words are out of control. Write them here.

_____

_____

_____

Now check your answers using the Answer Key on page 457. Correct any wrong answers and review this part of the lesson if you don't understand why an answer was wrong. Now go on to do the Comprehension Questions.

Comprehension Questions

Answer these questions without looking back at the story. Choose the best answer to each question and put an *x* in the box beside it.

Recalling
Facts

1. Pete and Sucker are
   ☐ a. brothers.
   ☐ b. cousins.
   ☐ c. friends.
   ☐ d. unrelated.

Recognizing
Words in
Context

2. "Maybelle Watts . . . acted like she was the Queen of Sheba and even *humiliated* me." The word *humiliated* means
   ☐ a. uplifted.
   ☐ b. amazed.
   ☐ c. horrified.
   ☐ d. embarrassed.

Keeping
Events in
Order

3. When did Pete begin to act kindly toward Sucker?
   ☐ a. When Maybelle began to pay attention to Pete
   ☐ b. When Sucker entered the movie theater
   ☐ c. When Maybelle became tired of Pete
   ☐ d. When Sucker jumped off the garage and broke his knee

Sucker

4. "I didn't want to take her candy because I think that's been *run into the ground*." The expression *run into the ground* means

☐ a. made dirty.

☐ b. too expensive.

☐ c. done too much.

☐ d. made to seem foolish.

5. Which one of the following quotations from the story sums up a very important idea in the story?

☐ a. "If a person admires you a lot you despise him and don't care—and it is the person who doesn't notice you that you are apt to admire."

☐ b. "Whenever I would bring any of my friends back to my room all I had to do was just glance once at Sucker and he would get up . . . and leave. . . ."

☐ c. "Maybelle was somehow mixed up in what happened so I guess I ought to start with her."

☐ d. "Once I started to point him out to Maybelle and tell her he was my kid brother."

6. Which one of these ideas is suggested by the story?

☐ a. Maybelle and Pete were plotting against Sucker.

☐ b. Maybelle treated Pete much the same as Pete treated Sucker.

☐ c. It was Sucker's fault that Pete and Maybelle broke up.

☐ d. It is better for young people not to have strong feelings about other people.

7. Which one of the following statements best describes Sucker's feelings early in the story?

☐ a. He is jealous of Maybelle.

☐ b. He is lonesome.

☐ c. He misses his mother.

☐ d. He is afraid of Pete.

8. Which one of the following statements is true?

☐ a. Pete never liked Sucker. He only pretended to from time to time.

☐ b. Pete was not really mean to Sucker. He would just tease him a bit.

☐ c. Pete could not stop loving Maybelle even after he had told Sucker that he didn't like him.

☐ d. At one point in the story, Pete felt that he liked Sucker more than anyone else.

9. "He used to look *timid* and sort of like he was afraid of a whack over the head." The word *timid* means

☐ a. shy or afraid.

☐ b. ignorant or stupid.

☐ c. funny or laughable.

☐ d. confused or muddled.

10. In the movies, Pete started to point Sucker out to Maybelle. But he decided not to. Why do you think Pete didn't tell Maybelle about Sucker?

☐ a. He was embarrassed by Sucker's appearance.

☐ b. He was too much in love with Maybelle to think of Sucker.

☐ c. Maybelle didn't give him a chance to talk.

☐ d. Sucker was too timid to meet Maybelle.

11. Which of the events below happened first?

□ a. Pete told Sucker that he was a dumb slob.

□ b. Pete saw Sucker at the movies.

□ c. Pete told Sucker that he liked him.

□ d. Pete visited Maybelle at her home.

12. After breaking up with Maybelle, Pete said something that showed he had the same kind of fear that Sucker had. Which one of the following sentences contains this idea?

□ a. "Afterward I could remember the change in Sucker's face."

□ b. "If I'd talked loud or hit him it wouldn't have been so bad."

□ c. "It seemed to me for a second that nobody would ever like me. . . ."

□ d. "I don't think anybody ever gets that mad but once."

13. Which one of these events marks the turning point in Sucker's feelings toward Pete?

□ a. "It was that night when this trouble really started. I had come into my room late and Sucker was already asleep."

□ b. "During the next couple of weeks I saw a lot of Maybelle. She acted as though she really cared for me a little."

□ c. "Slowly that blank look went away and he closed his mouth. His eyes got narrow and his fists shut."

□ d. "Then something happened between Maybelle and me. I never have figured out just what it was."

14. At the beginning of the story Pete says: "The room was mine. . . ." Near the end of the story he says: "Our room isn't mine at all any more." This change suggests that Sucker

☐ a. is not timid anymore where Pete is concerned.

☐ b. seems pleased that Pete is doing poorly in school.

☐ c. and Pete finally learned to share with each other.

☐ d. has changed because he is old enough for long pants.

15. By the end of the story, Sucker has changed. One major change is that he

☐ a. stays alone more than ever.

☐ b. finally has friends who come to his room.

☐ c. makes up with Pete, and they become close friends.

☐ d. finds himself a girlfriend, just as Pete did.

Now check your answers using the Answer Key on page 457. Make no mark for right answers. <u>Correct</u> any wrong answers you may have by putting a checkmark (✓) in the box next to the right answer. Count the number of questions you answered correctly and plot the total on the Comprehension Scores graph on page 462.

Next, look at the questions you answered incorrectly. What types of questions were they? Count the number you got wrong of each type and enter the numbers in the spaces below.

Recognizing Words in Context   _____

Recalling Facts   _____

Keeping Events in Order   _____

Making Inferences   _____

Understanding Main Ideas   _____

Now use these numbers to fill in the Comprehension Skills Profile on page 463.

Discussion Guides

The questions below will help you to think about the story and the lesson you have just read. If you don't discuss these questions in class, try to think about them or discuss them with your classmates.

Discussing Tone and Mood

1. One explanation of tone is that it is the author's attitude toward a character, a situation, or an idea in a story. It is a reflection of the author's mood—how she feels. It is clear that the author is sympathetic toward Sucker and that she doesn't like Maybelle. How does the author feel about Pete? And how is her attitude reflected in the tone of the story?

2. Early in the story, Pete feels close to Sucker in their cold, dark, quiet room. Later, after Pete's cruel outburst at Sucker, he says, "My legs were shaking and I was so tired I could have bawled. The room was cold and dark. . . . Outside the yard was black and quiet." What makes the tone of these two scenes, which take place in the very same setting, so entirely different?

3. In the last part of the story, the author emphasizes the look in Sucker's eyes. How do Sucker's eyes affect tone and mood in the story? Drawing on your own experience, describe how people's eyes can affect tones and moods in real life.

Discussing the Story

4. Sucker wanted Pete to like him. Pete wanted Maybelle to like him. Maybelle wanted many boys to like her. And it seemed that no one was happy. Why do you think this is so?

5. Pete presents a puzzle at the beginning of the story. He says, "There is one thing . . . makes me feel guilty and hard to figure out. If a person admires you a lot you despise him and don't care—and it is the person who doesn't notice you that you are apt to admire." This is true in many relationships. Describe a situation like this from your own experience.

6. People change in this story. Pete tells you at the beginning of the story that people have changed. He says "Sucker has changed so much . . . . I never imagined anything would suddenly happen that would

make us both very different." Make a list of the ways in which Sucker was different at the end of the story. How was Pete different?

Discussing the Author's Work

7. It has been said that in nearly all her stories Carson McCullers wrote about loneliness. Is this story about loneliness? Explain your answer.

8. It has also been said that once you know that Carson McCullers suffered from a severe physical handicap, you can find many characters in her stories who also suffer handicaps. What handicaps do you think the characters in this story have?

9. Carson McCullers' best-known book is titled *The Heart Is a Lonely Hunter*. Why might this also be a good title for the story you have just read? (The title comes from a poem by William Sharp that begins, "My heart is a lonely hunter that hunts on a lonely hill.")

Writing Exercise

You have seen that in the story "Sucker" Carson McCullers used a cold, dark, quiet house to create two entirely different tones and two very different moods.

Try this exercise. Write three paragraphs, following the directions below:

1. In each paragraph, describe a place. You may use the same in each paragraph or a different place in each. You might describe a house, a room, a cemetery, woods, a cave—anything you wish.

2. Use the words *cold, dark*, and *quiet* in each paragraph. You may use the words together or scatter them about in the paragraph.

3. Provide a different tone and mood in each paragraph. One scene might be mysterious and frightening, another chilling and angry, and the third calm and peaceful. Choose any tones and moods you like.

4. It may help to reread those parts of the story in which Carson McCullers uses the words *cold, dark* and *quiet* in describing the boys' room.

Unit 8   Science Fiction

A Sound of Thunder

BY RAY BRADBURY

About the Illustration

What is fantastic about the scene depicted in this drawing? What details lead you to suspect that this is a story that could only happen in someone's imagination?

Here are some questions to help you think:

☐ What kind of animal is in this picture? When would you guess the story takes place?

☐ What things in the picture are out of place with the setting? Where would you guess they came from?

☐ What do you think the men in the picture are doing? Support your response.

Unit 8

Introduction

What the Story Is About

"A Sound of Thunder" is about time travel. As the story opens, a man named Eckels hands over a check for ten thousand dollars, the price of a ride in a time machine. What great moment in history does he wish to visit? you wonder. Some important battle, no doubt; a famous leader, maybe; or perhaps some distant ancestor.

Well, not exactly. Ten thousand dollars buys this man a place in a safari, a safari back in time to hunt the biggest game of all: *Tyrannosaurus rex*, the "thunder lizard"![1] That is why Mr. Eckels has come to the small office of Time Safari, Inc. "Safaris to any year in the past," they advertise. "You name the animal. We take you there. You shoot it."

The year is 2055. The place is the United States. It is one day after a presidential election that marked the end of a bitterly fought campaign. Eckels and the others are glad that Keith won, and not Deutscher. "If Deutscher had gotten in," says the man behind the desk, "we'd have the worst kind of dictatorship. . . . Anyway, Keith's President now. All you got to worry about is —"

" 'Shooting my dinosaur,' Eckels finished it for him."

Actually, there are a few other things to worry about too. Staying alive, for one. Hunting dinosaurs is risky business. Equally risky is the danger of tampering with the past. You don't want to do anything that would change the course of history.

The leaders of Time Safari, Inc. take great pains not to disturb the past. They hunt only creatures that would have died a natural death a minute or two later. And they erect an "anti-gravity path" that floats just above the ground, so that no one will tread on prehistoric plants or insects. "Stay on the Path," repeats Travis, the safari leader, to the hunters.

So Eckels sets out on his time safari like a small boy setting out on an innocent adventure. But the world he leaves is not the world he returns to, because along the way, trouble develops. The past is violated. And the consequences of one false step echo through eons of time.

---

[1] Even great writers sometimes make mistakes. If you haven't already spotted the mistake that Ray Bradbury made in this story, get a good dictionary and look up "thunder lizard" or "brontosaurus."

The author, Ray Bradbury, has been called "the world's greatest living science fiction writer." Some admirers, however, insist that he writes not about science so much as about people. Probably the truth lies somewhere in between. Bradbury's special brand of science fiction explores the impact of scientific development on human life. Far from being a cheerleader for science, Bradbury feels that scientific knowledge, if improperly used, can do humankind more harm than good. His stories, he has said, "are intended as much to instruct how to prevent dooms, as to predict them."

About his writing he says, "I write for fun. . . . I have fun with ideas. I play with them. I approach my craft with enthusiasm and respect. If my work sparks serious thought, fine. But I don't write with that in mind."

If you enjoy "A Sound of Thunder," you'll probably want to go on to some other Bradbury favorites such as *The Martian Chronicles* and *Something Wicked This Way Comes* (both novels), and *The Illustrated Man, The Small Assassin* and *Dandelion Wine*, which are short story collections.

What the Lesson Is About

The lesson that follows "A Sound of Thunder" is about science fiction. Science fiction has been criticized by a lot of people who mistake it for the Buck Rogers/Flash Gordon variety of space adventure that is no more than a display of special effects. The kind of science fiction we will talk about in this lesson is much more than that.

Good science fiction is both good science and good fiction. You learn something about science from reading it, and you learn something about people—maybe even about yourself. You also get a glimpse of the future—at least one person's vision of the future. And some of the visions that science fiction writers have had have been uncannily accurate!

Science fiction writers, however, never claim to predict the future. Rather, they try to present a variety of possible tomorrows for us to think about today. Some of these are positively chilling. Others are very beautiful. What really happens in the future will depend upon the choices we make today. All science fiction writers ask is that we think about these choices before we make them.

The questions below will help you to focus on some of the characteristics of science fiction that you will find in "A Sound of Thunder." Read the story and try to answer these questions as you go along:

1 Through this story, you will enter a world of the future, where some things are familiar while other things are strange and hard to believe. What are some strange and unbelievable things about this world? What are some things that are familiar to you?

2 You will learn something about evolution—how things evolve, or develop, over long periods of time. How does this touch of science help make the rest of the story more believable?

3 You will see how one man acts under great stress. Why is this scene a good picture of human nature?

4 How does the story draw you into its fantasy world?

A Sound of Thunder

Ray Bradbury

The sign on the wall seemed to quaver under a film of sliding warm water. Eckels felt his eyelids blink over his stare, and the sign burned in this momentary darkness:

TIME SAFARI, INC.
SAFARIS TO ANY YEAR IN THE PAST.
YOU NAME THE ANIMAL.
WE TAKE YOU THERE.
YOU SHOOT IT.

A warm phlegm gathered in Eckels' throat; he swallowed and pushed it down. The muscles around his mouth formed a smile as he put his hand slowly out upon the air, and in that hand waved a check for ten thousand dollars to the man behind the desk.

"Does this safari guarantee I come back alive?"

"We guarantee nothing," said the official, "except the dinosaurs." He turned. "This is Mr. Travis, your Safari Guide in the Past. He'll tell you what and where to shoot. If he says no shooting, no shooting. If you disobey instructions, there's a stiff penalty of another ten thousand dollars, plus possible government action, on your return."

Eckels glanced across the vast office at a mass and tangle, a snaking and humming of wires and steel boxes, at an aurora that flickered now orange, now silver, now blue. There was a sound like a gigantic bonfire burning all of Time, all the years and all the parchment calendars, all the hours piled high and set aflame.

A touch of the hand and this burning would, on the instant, beautifully reverse itself. Eckels remembered the wording in the advertisements to the letter. Out of chars and ashes, out of dust and coals, like golden salamanders, the old years, the green years, might leap; roses sweeten the air, white hair turn Irish-black, wrinkles vanish; all, everything fly back to seed, flee death, rush down to their beginnings, suns rise in western skies and set in glorious easts, moons eat themselves opposite to the custom, all and everything cupping one in another like Chinese boxes, rabbits into hats, all and everything returning to the fresh death, the seed death, the green death, to the time before the beginning. A touch of a hand might do it, the merest touch of a hand.

"Hell and damn," Eckels breathed, the light of the Machine on his thin face. "A real Time Machine." He shook his head. "Makes you think. If the election had gone badly yesterday, I might be here now running away from the results. Thank God Keith won. He'll make a fine President of the United States."

"Yes," said the man behind the desk. "We're lucky. If Deutscher had gotten in, we'd have the worst kind of dictatorship. There's an anti-everything man for you, a militarist, anti-Christ, anti-human, anti-intellectual. People called us up, you know, joking but not joking. Said if Deutscher became President they wanted to go live in 1492. Of course it's not our business to conduct Escapes, but to form Safaris. Anyway, Keith's President now. All you got to worry about is—"

"Shooting my dinosaur," Eckels finished it for him.

"A *Tyrannosaurus rex*. The Thunder Lizard, the damnedest monster in history. Sign this release. Anything happens to you, we're not responsible. Those dinosaurs are hungry."

Eckels flushed angrily. "Trying to scare me!"

"Frankly, yes. We don't want anyone going who'll panic at the first shot. Six Safari leaders were killed last year, and a dozen hunters. We're here to give you the damnedest thrill a *real* hunter ever asked for. Traveling you back sixty million years to bag the biggest damned game in all Time. Your personal check's still there. Tear it up."

Mr. Eckels looked at the check for a long time. His fingers twitched.

"Good luck," said the man behind the desk. "Mr. Travis, he's all yours."

They moved silently across the room, taking their guns with them, toward the Machine, toward the silver metal and the roaring light.

First a day and then a night and then a day and then a night, then it was day-night-day-night-day. A week, a month, a year, a decade! A.D. 2055. A.D. 2019. 1999! 1957! Gone! The Machine roared.

They put on their oxygen helmets and tested the intercoms.

Eckels swayed on the padded seat, his face pale, his jaw stiff. He felt the trembling in his arms and he looked down and found his hands tight on the new rifle. There were four other men in the Machine. Travis, the Safari Leader, his assistant, Lesperance, and two other hunters, Billings and Kramer. They sat looking at each other, and the years blazed around them.

"Can these guns get a dinosaur cold?" Eckels felt his mouth saying.

"If you hit them right," said Travis on the helmet radio. "Some dinosaurs have two brains, one in the head, another far down the spinal column. We stay away from those. That's stretching luck. Put your first two shots into the eyes, if you can, blind them, and go back into the brain."

The Machine howled. Time was a film run backward. Suns fled and ten million moons fled after them. "Good God," said Eckels. "Every hunter that ever lived would envy us today. This makes Africa seem like Illinois."

The Machine slowed; its scream fell to a murmur. The Machine stopped.

The sun stopped in the sky.

The fog that had enveloped the Machine blew away and

they were in an old time, a very old time indeed, three hunters and two Safari Heads with their blue metal guns across their knees.

"Christ isn't born yet," said Travis. "Moses has not gone to the mountain to talk with God. The Pyramids are still in the earth, waiting to be cut out and put up. *Remember* that. Alexander, Caesar, Napoleon, Hitler—none of them exists."

The men nodded.

"That"—Mr. Travis pointed—"is the jungle of sixty million two thousand and fifty-five years before President Keith."

He indicated a metal path that struck off into green wilderness, over steaming swamp, among giant ferns and palms.

"And that," he said, "is the Path, laid by Time Safari for your use. It floats six inches above the earth. Doesn't touch so much as one grass blade, flower, or tree. It's an anti-gravity metal. It's purpose is to keep you from touching this world of the past in any way. Stay on the Path. Don't go off it. I repeat. *Don't go off.* For *any* reason! If you fall off, there's a penalty. And don't shoot any animal we don't okay."

"Why?" asked Eckels.

They sat in the ancient wilderness. Far birds' cries blew on a wind, and the smell of tar and an old salt sea, moist grasses, and flowers the color of blood.

"We don't want to change the Future. We don't belong here in the Past. The government doesn't *like* us here. We have to pay big graft to keep our franchise. A Time Machine is damn finicky business. Not knowing it, we might kill an important animal, a small bird, a roach, a flower even, thus destroying an important link in a growing species."

"That's not clear," said Eckels.

"All right," Travis continued, "say we accidently kill one mouse here. That means all the future families of this one particular mouse are destroyed, right?"

"Right."

"And all the families of the families of the families of that one mouse! With a stamp of your foot, you annihilate first one, then a dozen, then a thousand, a million, a *billion* possible mice!"

"So they're dead," said Eckels. "So what?"

"So what?" Travis snorted quietly. "Well, what about the foxes that'll need those mice to survive? For want of ten mice, a fox dies. For want of ten foxes, a lion starves. For want of a lion, all manner of insects, vultures, infinite billions of life forms are thrown into chaos and destruction. Eventually it all boils down to this: fifty-nine million years later, a cave man, one of a dozen on the *entire world*, goes hunting wild boar or saber-tooth tiger for food. But you, friend, have *stepped* on all the tigers in that region. By stepping on *one* single mouse. So the cave man starves. And the cave man, please note, is not just *any* expendable man, no! He is an *entire future nation*. From his loins would have sprung ten sons. From *their* loins one hundred sons, and thus onward to a civilization. Destroy this one man, and you destroy a race, a people, an entire history of life. It is comparable to slaying some of Adam's grandchildren. The stomp of your foot, on one mouse, could start an earthquake, the effects of which could shake our earth and destinies down through Time, to their very foundations. With the death of that one cave man, a billion others yet unborn are throttled in the womb. Perhaps Rome never rises on its seven hills. Perhaps Europe is forever a dark forest, and only Asia waxes healthy and teeming. Step on a mouse and you crush the Pyramids. Step on a mouse and you leave your print, like a Grand Canyon, across Eternity. Queen Elizabeth might never be born, Washington might not cross the Delaware, there might never be a United States at all. So be careful. Stay on the Path. *Never* step off!"

"I see," said Eckels. "Then it wouldn't pay for us even to touch the *grass*?"

"Correct. Crushing certain plants could add up infinitesimally. A little error here would multiply in sixty million years, all out of proportion. Of course maybe our theory is wrong. Maybe Time *can't* be changed by us. Or maybe it can be changed only in little subtle ways. A dead mouse here makes an insect imbalance there, a population disproportion later, a bad harvest further on, a depression, mass starvation, and, finally, a change in *social* temperament in far-flung countries. Something much more subtle, like that. Perhaps only a soft breath, a whisper, a hair, pollen on the air, such a slight, slight change that unless you looked close you wouldn't see it. Who knows? Who really can say he knows? We don't know. We're guessing. But until we do know for certain whether our messing around in Time *can* make a big roar or a little rustle in history, we're being damned careful. This Machine, this Path, your clothing and bodies, were sterilized, as you know, before the journey. We wear these oxygen helments so we can't introduce our bacteria into an ancient atmosphere."

"How do we know which animals to shoot?"

"They're marked with red paint," said Travis. "Today, before our journey, we sent Lesperance here back with the Machine. He came to this particular era and followed certain animals."

"Studying them?"

"Right," said Lesperance. "I track them through their entire existence, noting which of them lives longest. Very few. How many times they mate. Not often. Life's short. When I find one that's going to die when a tree falls on him, or one that drowns in a tar pit, I note the exact hour, minute, and second. I shoot a paint bomb. It leaves a red patch on his hide. We can't miss it. Then I correlate our arrival in the Past so that we meet the Monster not more than two minutes before he would have died anyway. This

A Sound of Thunder

way, we kill only animals with no future, that are never going to mate again. You see how *careful* we are?"

"But if you came back this morning in Time," said Eckels eagerly, "you must've bumped into *us*, our Safari! How did it turn out? Was it successful? Did all of us get through—alive?"

Travis and Lesperance gave each other a look.

"That'd be a paradox," said the latter. "Time doesn't permit that sort of mess—a man meeting himself. When such occasions threaten, Time steps aside. Like an airplane hitting an air pocket. You felt the Machine jump just before we stopped? That was us passing ourselves on the way back to the Future. We saw nothing. There's no way of telling *if* this expedition was a success, *if* we got our monster, or whether all of us—meaning *you*, Mr. Eckels—got out alive."

Eckels smiled palely.

"Cut that," said Travis sharply. "Everyone on his feet!"

They were ready to leave the Machine.

The jungle was high and the jungle was broad and the jungle was the entire world forever and forever. Sounds like music and sounds like flying tents filled the sky, and those were pterodactyls soaring with cavernous gray wings, gigantic bats out of a delirium and a night fever. Eckels, balanced on the narrow Path, aimed his rifle playfully.

"Stop that!" said Travis. "Don't even aim for fun, damn it! If your gun should go off—"

Eckels flushed. "Where's our *Tyrannosaurus*?"

Lesperance checked his wrist watch. "Up ahead. We'll bisect his trail in sixty seconds. Look for the red paint, for Christ's sake. Don't shoot till we give the word. Stay on the Path. *Stay on the Path!*"

They moved forward in the wind of morning.

"Strange," murmured Eckels. "Up ahead, sixty million years, Election Day over. Keith made President. Everyone celebrating. And here we are, a million years lost, and they don't exist. The things we worried about for months, a lifetime, not even born or thought about yet."

"Safety catches off, everyone!" ordered Travis. "You, first shot, Eckels. Second, Billings. Third, Kramer."

"I've hunted tiger, wild boar, buffalo, elephant, but Jesus, this is *it*," said Eckels. "I'm shaking like a kid."

"Ah," said Travis.

Everyone stopped.

Travis raised his hand. "Ahead," he whispered. "In the mist. There he is. There's His Royal Majesty now."

The jungle was wide and full of twitterings, rustlings, mumurs, and sighs.

Suddenly it all ceased, as if someone had shut a door.

Silence.

A sound of thunder.

Out of the mist, one hundred yards away, came *Tyrannosaurus rex*.

"Jesus God," whispered Eckels.

"Sh!"

It came on great oiled, resilient, striding legs. It towered thirty feet above half of the trees, a great evil god, folding its delicate watchmaker's claws close to its oily reptilian chest. Each lower leg was a piston, a thousand pounds of white bone, sunk in thick ropes of muscle, sheathed over in a gleam of pebbled skin like the mail of a terrible warrior. Each thigh was a ton of meat, ivory, and steel mesh. And from the great breathing cage of the upper body those two delicate arms dangled out front, arms with hands which might pick up and examine men like toys, while the snake neck coiled. And the head itself, a ton of sculptured stone, lifted easily upon the sky. Its mouth gaped, exposing a fence of teeth like daggers. Its eyes rolled, ostrich eggs, empty of all expression save hunger. It closed its mouth in a death grin. It ran, its pelvic bones crushing aside trees and bushes, its taloned feet clawing damp earth, leaving prints six inches deep wherever it settled its weight. It ran with a gliding ballet step, far too poised and balanced for its ten tons. It moved into a sunlit arena warily, its beautifully reptile hands feeling the air.

"My God!" Eckels twitched his mouth. "It could reach up and grab the moon."

"Sh!" Travis jerked angrily. "He hasn't seen us yet."

"It can't be killed." Eckels pronounced this verdict quietly, as if there could be no argument. He had weighed the evidence and this was his considered opinion. The rifle in his hands seemed a cap gun. "We were fools to come. This is impossible."

"Shut up!" hissed Travis.

"Nightmare."

"Turn around," commanded Travis. "Walk quietly to the Machine. We'll remit one half your fee."

"I didn't realize it would be this *big*," said Eckels. "I miscalculated, that's all. And now I want out."

"It *sees* us!"

"There's the red paint on its chest!"

The Thunder Lizard raised itself. Its armored flesh glittered like a thousand green coins. The coins, crusted with slime, steamed. In the slime, tiny insects wriggled, so that the entire body seemed to twitch and undulate, even while the monster itself did not move. It exhaled. The stink of raw flesh blew down the wilderness.

"Get me out of here," said Eckels. "It was never like this before. I was always sure I'd come through alive. I had good guides, good safaris, and safety. This time, I figured wrong. I've met my match and admit it. This is too much for me to get hold of."

"Don't run," said Lesperance. "Turn around. Hide in the Machine."

"Yes." Eckels seemed to be numb. He looked at his feet as if trying to make them move. He gave a grunt of helplessness.

"Eckels!"

He took a few steps, blinking, shuffling.

"Not *that* way!"

The Monster, at the first motion, lunged forward with a terrible scream. It covered one hundred yards in four seconds. The rifles jerked up and blazed fire. A windstorm from the beast's mouth engulfed them in the stench of slime and old blood. The Monster roared, teeth glittering with sun.

Eckels, not looking back, walked blindly to the edge of the Path, his gun limp in his arms, stepped off the Path, and walked, not knowing it, in the jungle. His feet sank into green moss. His legs moved him, and he felt alone and remote from the events behind.

The rifles cracked again. Their sound was lost in shriek and lizard thunder. The great lever of the reptile's tail swung up, lashed sideways. Trees exploded in clouds of leaf and branch. The Monster twitched its jeweler's hands down to fondle at the men, to twist them in half, to crush them like berries, to cram them into its teeth and its screaming throat. Its boulder-stone eyes leveled with the men. They saw themselves mirrored. They fired at the metallic eyelids and the blazing black iris.

Like a stone idol, like a mountain avalanche, *Tyrannosaurus* fell. Thundering, it clutched trees, pulled them with it. It wrenched and tore the metal Path. The men flung themselves back and away. The body hit, ten tons of cold flesh and stone. The guns fired. The Monster lashed its armored tail, twitched its snake jaws, and lay still. A fount of blood spurted from its throat. Somewhere inside, a sac of fluids burst. Sickening gushes drenched the hunters. They stood, red and glistening.

The thunder faded.

The jungle was silent. After the avalanche, a green peace. After the nightmare, morning.

Billings and Kramer sat on the pathway and threw up. Travis and Lesperance stood with smoking rifles, cursing steadily.

A Sound of Thunder

In the Time Machine, on his face, Eckels lay shivering. He had found his way back to the Path, climbed into the Machine.

Travis came walking, glanced at Eckels, took cotton gauze from a metal box, and returned to the others, who were sitting on the Path.

"Clean up."

They wiped the blood from their helmets. They began to curse too. The Monster lay, a hill of solid flesh. Within, you could hear the sighs and murmurs as the furthest chambers of it died, the organs malfunctioning, liquids running a final instant from pocket to sac to spleen, everything shutting off, closing up forever. It was like standing by a wrecked locomotive or a steam shovel at quitting time, all valves being released or levered tight. Bones cracked; the tonnage of its own flesh, off balance, dead weight, snapped the delicate forearms, caught underneath. The meat settled, quivering.

Another cracking sound. Overhead, a gigantic tree branch broke from its heavy mooring, fell. It crashed upon the dead beast with finality.

"There," Lesperance checked his watch. "Right on time. That's the giant tree that was scheduled to fall and kill this animal originally." He glanced at the two hunters. "You want the trophy picture?"

"What?"

"We can't take a trophy back to the Future. The body has to stay right here where it would have died originally, so the insects, birds, and bacteria can get at it, as they were intended to. Everything in balance. The body stays. But we *can* take a picture of you standing near it."

The two men tried to think, but gave up, shaking their heads.

They let themselves be led along the metal Path. They sank wearily into the Machine cushions. They gazed back at the ruined Monster, the stagnating mound, where already strange reptilian birds and golden insects were busy at the steaming armor.

A sound on the floor of the Time Machine stiffened them. Eckels sat there, shivering.

"I'm sorry," he said at last.

"Get up!" cried Travis.

Eckels got up.

"Go out on that Path alone," said Travis. He had his rifle pointed. "You're not coming back in the Machine. We're leaving you here!"

Lesperance seized Travis' arm. "Wait—"

"Stay out of this!" Travis shook his hand away. "This son of a bitch nearly killed us. But it isn't *that* so much. Hell, no. It's his *shoes*! Look at them! He ran off the Path. My God, that *ruins* us! Christ knows how much we'll forfeit! Tens of thousands of dollars of insurance! We guarantee no one leaves the Path. He left it. Oh, the damn fool! I'll have to report to the government. They might revoke our license to travel. God knows *what* he's done to Time, to History!"

"Take it easy, all he did was kick up some dirt."

"How do we *know*?" cried Travis. "We don't know anything! It's all a damn mystery! Get out there, Eckels!"

Eckels fumbled his shirt. "I'll pay anything. A hundred thousand dollars!"

Travis glared at Eckels' checkbook and spat. "Go out there. The Monster's next to the Path. Stick your arms up to your elbows in his mouth. Then you can come back with us."

"That's unreasonable!"

"The Monster's dead, you yellow bastard. The bullets! The bullets can't be left behind. They don't belong in the Past; they might change something. Here's my knife. Dig them out!"

The jungle was alive again, full of the old tremorings and bird cries. Eckels turned slowly to regard that primeval garbage dump, that hill of nightmares and terror. After a long time, like a sleepwalker, he shuffled out along the Path.

He returned, shuddering, five minutes later, his arms soaked and red to the elbows. He held out his hands. Each held a number of steel bullets. Then he fell. He lay where he fell, not moving.

"You didn't have to make him do that," said Lesperance.

"Didn't I? It's too early to tell." Travis nudged the still body. "He'll live. Next time he won't go hunting game like this. Okay." He jerked his thumb wearily at Lesperance. "Switch on. Let's go home."

1492.   1776.   1812.

They cleaned their hands and faces. They changed their caking shirts and pants. Eckels was up and around again, not speaking. Travis glared at him for a full ten minutes.

"Don't look at me," cried Eckels. "I haven't done anything."

"Who can tell?"

"Just ran off the Path, that's all, a little mud on my shoes—what do you want me to do—get down and pray?"

"We might need it. I'm warning you, Eckels, I might kill you yet. I've got my gun ready."

"I'm innocent. I've done nothing!"

1999.   2000.   2055.

The Machine stopped.

"Get out," said Travis.

The room was there as they had left it. But not the same as they had left it. The same man sat behind the same desk. But the same man did not quite sit behind the same desk.

Travis looked around swiftly. "Everything okay here?" he snapped.

"Fine. Welcome home!"

Travis did not relax. He seemed to be looking at the very atoms of the air itself, at the way the sun poured through the one high window.

"Okay, Eckels, get out. Don't ever come back."

Eckels could not move.

"You heard me," said Travis. "What're you *staring* at?"

Eckels stood smelling of the air, and there was a thing to the air, a chemical taint so subtle, so slight, that only a faint cry of his subliminal senses warned him it was there. The colors, white, gray, blue, orange, in the wall, in the furniture, in the sky beyond the window, were . . . were . . . And there was a *feel*. His flesh twitched. His hands twitched. He stood drinking the oddness with the pores of his body. Somewhere, someone must have been screaming one of those whistles that only a dog can hear. His body screamed silence in return. Beyond this room, beyond this wall, beyond this man who was not quite the same man seated at this desk that was not quite the same desk . . . lay an entire world of streets and people. What sort of world it was now, there was no telling. He could feel them moving there, beyond the walls, almost, like so many chess pieces blown in a dry wind . . . .

But the immediate thing was the sign painted on the office wall, the same sign he had read earlier today on first entering.

Somehow, the sign had changed:

TYME SEFARI INC.
SEFARIS TU ANY YEER EN THE PAST.
YU NAIM THE ANIMALL.
WEE TAEK YU THAIR.
YU SHOOT ITT.

Eckels felt himself fall into a chair. He fumbled crazily at the thick slime on his boots. He held up a clod of dirt, trembling. "No, it *can't* be. Not a *little* thing like that. No!"

Embedded in the mud, glistening green and gold and black, was a butterfly, very beautiful and very dead.

"Not a little thing like *that*! Not a butterfly!" cried Eckels.

It fell to the floor, an exquisite thing, a small thing that could upset balances and knock down a line of small dominoes and then big dominoes and then gigantic dominoes, all down the years across Time. Eckels' mind whirled. It *couldn't* change things. Killing one butterfly couldn't be *that* important! Could it?

His face was cold. His mouth trembled, asking: "Who—who won the presidential election yesterday?"

The man behind the desk laughed. "You joking? You know damn well. Deutscher, of course! Who else? Not that damned weakling Keith. We got an iron man now, a man with guts, by God!" The official stopped. "What's wrong?"

Eckels moaned. He dropped to his knees. He scrabbled at the golden butterfly with shaking fingers. "Can't we," he pleaded to the world, to himself, to the officials, to the Machine, "can't we take it *back*, can't we *make* it alive again? Can't we start over? Can't we—"

He did not move. Eyes shut, he waited, shivering. He heard Travis breathe loud in the room; he heard Travis shift his rifle, click the safety catch, and raise the weapon.

There was a sound of thunder.

Science Fiction

To most people, science is a mystery and scientists seem to be super sleuths. They peer into microscopes at a universe measured in microns. They gaze through telescopes across distances reckoned in light years. They wrestle with invisible foes. They announce theories that we are hard put to wrap our minds around. They might as well be speaking a different language and living in a different world, as far as the rest of us are concerned.

What is needed is an interpreter. Someone who can help us to understand the effects that science has, or can have, on our lives. Enter the science fiction writer.

Isaac Asimov, one of the foremost writers of science fiction, defined science fiction as "that branch of literature which is concerned with the impact of scientific advance upon human beings." In other words, it is concerned with what science might mean to you and me.

For example, scientists predict that people will one day live in outer space, and science fiction writers wonder what kind of a society we will establish once we're there. Scientists invent robots, and science fiction writers try to imagine a society run by robots. Scientists may one day create life; science fiction writers ask what kind of life we will choose to create, and what the results of our decision will be.

You have probably guessed by now that science fiction is more than just galactic adventures and bug-eyed monsters. It is a way of looking into the future and examining choices.

Of course, it is also entertainment. People enjoy science fiction not because it is science, but because it is good reading.

Good science fiction, then, does four things:

1 It presents things that are strange and unusual. Outer space, alien creatures, and future worlds are standard fare in science fiction.

2 It has an element of science. A sound scientific principle or a believable scientific theory forms the basis of a story.

3 It deals with human nature or society. Even if the characters are little green creatures from Mars, they display human qualities.

4 It tells a good story. The science fiction writer must hold your interest as any other good storyteller must.

Science fiction can always be counted on to contain the unusual—new life forms, other planets, future eras. Sci fi fans always enjoy reading and thinking about such strange, scary or wonderful things.

Science fiction stories are never set in the familiar world of the here and now. By setting a story in some other place or time, the author can create a different kind of society from any that presently exists. It might be totally different, or different in only one small way. It allows the author to step back from the world we live in and look at it as an outsider might. And that, of course, is what science fiction authors hope readers will do as well. It is called *distancing*. This means escaping your own narrow world and looking at things from a new viewpoint.

Readers are encouraged to compare the science fiction world of the story with the world we actually live in and see the similarities, as well as the differences. Is the author's imaginary world better than our own? If so, how might we make our own world better? Is the author's imaginary world a barren wasteland? If it is, what can we do to make sure our own world doesn't end up the same way?

Take a look at the world of the future that Ray Bradbury has created in "A Sound of Thunder." What is unusual about it? What comparisons with our own world might this story lead you to make?

> Eckels glanced across the vast office at a mass and tangle . . . of wires and steel boxes, at an aurora that flickered now orange, now silver, now blue. . . .
>
> "A real Time Machine." He shook his head. "Makes you think. If the election had gone badly yesterday, I might be here now running away from the results. Thank God Keith won. He'll make a fine President of the United States."

The most unusual element of the world that Bradbury has created is the Time Machine. There is no such thing, of course, as a machine that takes people back in time. Yet it is fascinating to think about. What might one find? What might happen if a time traveler stepped back into the past?

A familiar element of this imaginary world is the presidential election. Apparently, in the year 2055 the country still elects its leaders by popular vote. But this election contained a danger that we haven't faced yet.

One of the candidates was a tyrant, a possible dictator.

Right at the outset, then, the author has put readers at a distance from the world of the story. It is not the world we know—it is an imaginary world of the future. Later in the story, Bradbury leads readers to make a comparison between the real world and the world of the story. This comparison makes you realize how easily a country may end up with the wrong kind of leader.

Exercise A

Read the following passage and answer the questions about it using what you have learned in this part of the lesson.

> The Machine slowed; its scream fell to a murmur. The Machine stopped.
>
> The sun stopped in the sky.
>
> The fog that had enveloped the Machine blew away and they were in an old time, a very old time indeed, three hunters and two Safari Heads with their blue metal guns across their knees.
>
> "Christ isn't born yet," said Travis. "Moses has not gone to the mountain to talk with God. The Pyramids are still in the earth, waiting to be cut out and put up. *Remember* that. Alexander, Caesar, Napoleon, Hitler—none of them exists."
>
> The men nodded.
>
> "That"—Mr. Travis pointed—"is the jungle of sixty million two thousand and fifty-five years before President Keith."

Put an *x* in the box beside the correct answer.

1. The author refers to Christ, Moses, Alexander, Caesar, Napoleon and Hitler. What do these men have in common?

   ☐ a. They were all great religious leaders.

   ☐ b. They were all great military leaders.

   ☐ c. They all helped shape the world.

   ☐ d. They all traveled back in time.

A Sound of Thunder

2. The author "distances" the reader from the world of the story by placing the story in another time. On the lines below, copy at least two sentences from the passage that remind readers that the story is not set in the present.

_____

_____

_____

Now check your answers using the Answer Key on page 458. Correct any wrong answers and review this part of the lesson if you don't understand why an answer was wrong.

Science Fiction

2 Science Fiction and Science

Every good science fiction story contains a kernel of science. The story itself may be wildly improbable, but it must be backed up by a reasonable scientific theory.

There are two reasons for this "rule." The most obvious one, of course, is that without an element of science it can't be science fiction. But there's an even better reason: If the author presents something that you know to be true, then you are more willing to go along with the rest of the story.

For example, the average reader would be insulted by a story in which a monster rises out of the sea and devours a city. But suppose the reader is first reminded that radiation can cause animal cells to mutate, or change. Then suppose that in the story a nuclear bomb has been exploded underwater, something we know has actually occurred. With these two facts in mind, you might just be inclined to stretch a point and concede that it is just barely possible that a monster was created as a result of atomic radiation, and that it could rise out of the sea and eat San Francisco. So you put aside the belief that the occurrence is next to impossible, and you just enjoy the story.

Science fiction writers must be careful about the accuracy of the scientific facts they include in their stories. If there is a glaring error in the scientific information, then it is impossible to believe the rest of the story. For instance, take the idea of time travel that is presented in "A Sound of Thunder." If the characters in the story had traveled back in time sixty million years and met Abraham Lincoln, you would have closed the book with a bang. No stretch of the imagination could accept *that*. But to go back sixty million years and meet a dinosaur, you might say to yourself, "Sure, why not?" and continue reading.

Another element of science can be found in the following passage from the story. What do you find here that is generally believed to be true? What effect does it have on the rest of the story?

> "A Time Machine is damn finicky business. Not knowing it, we might kill an important animal, a small bird, a roach, a flower even, thus destroying an important link in a growing species."

Most people accept the scientific theory of evolution. This theory says that life on earth evolved, or developed, slowly over millions of years, with each small change leading to other changes. That is what Travis is talking about in this passage. Interrupt this chain of life, and the link you have removed could cause a whole different sequence of events. And that, of course, is exactly what happens when Eckels steps off the path and crushes a butterfly. The butterfly was a link in the evolutionary chain. If you accept the idea of evolution, you will not find it hard to believe that this one small act could have major consequences.

Exercise B

Read the passages below and answer the questions about them using what you have learned in this part of the lesson.

Passage A

[Travis instructs the hunters before they leave the time machine.]

"This Machine, this Path, your clothing and bodies, were sterilized, as you know, before the journey. We wear these oxygen helmets so we can't introduce our bacteria into an ancient atmosphere."

Passage B

"Can these guns get a dinosaur cold?" Eckels felt his mouth saying.

"If you hit them right," said Travis on the helmet radio. "Some dinosaurs have two brains, one in the head, another far down the spinal column. We stay away from those. That's stretching luck. Put your first two shots into the eyes, if you can, blind them, and go back into the brain."

Put an *x* in the box beside the correct answer.

1. What familiar, present-day scientific procedure does the author refer to in the first passage?

   ☐ a. Preparation for a space launch

   ☐ b. An operation in a hospital

   ☐ c. A demonstration of physics

   ☐ d. An experiment in chemistry

2. One sentence in Passage B presents a scientific fact about the anatomy of dinosaurs. Copy this sentence on the lines below.

   _____

   _____

Now check your answers using the Answer Key on page 458. Correct any wrong answers and review this part of the lesson if you don't understand why an answer was wrong.

Science fiction stories usually contain a lesson or an opinion about the kind of people we are and the kind of society we live in. This sort of "statement" is usually implied, not stated outright. It is *suggested* by the story. That is why when science fiction authors in-

vent new places or new creatures they always give them some familiar qualities. When you think about them, chances are they will remind you of someone or some place you know of.

In "A Sound of Thunder" Ray Bradbury comments on the kind of leaders a society chooses. You can best understand his message if you know something about history. The story was written in 1952, not long after World War II. The brutal reign of Adolf Hitler in Germany was still fresh in people's minds.

In the following passage, a minor character in the story describes two candidates for president of the United States in the year 2055. What kind of leader would each make? Which of these candidates do you think the author would have voted for?

> "Thank God Keith won," [said Eckels.] "He'll make a fine President of the United States."
>
> "Yes," said the man behind the desk. "We're lucky. If Deutscher had gotten in, we'd have the worst kind of dictatorship. There's an anti-everything man for you, a militarist, anti-Christ, anti-human, anti-intellectual. People called us up, you know, joking but not joking. Said if Deutscher became President they wanted to go live in 1492."

The candidate named Keith seems to be a decent sort. He's undoubted-ly the one the author would have voted for. But the other, Deutscher, is described as "anti-everything," the kind who would set himself up as a dictator and wage war on civilization. It's no coincidence that this candidate has a German-sounding name—Deutscher. The author wants you to connect Deutscher with Hitler.

The author's attitude is clear. Leaders like Deutscher and Hitler are a threat to peace and progress. And, through this story, the author suggests that if very small changes were made in society we might have very different kinds of leaders. This is the statement about society that Bradbury makes in "A Sound of Thunder."

Science fiction stories may convey other kinds of statements besides social ones. Often, an author will comment on a new scientific discovery by predicting problems related to the discovery that may arise in the future. In Exercise C, Bradbury issues a sober warning. See if you can figure out what kind of statement he is making in this passage.

Exercise C

Read the following passage and answer the questions about it using what you have learned in this part of the lesson.

> [Travis says,] "Maybe Time *can't* be changed by us. Or maybe it can be changed only in little subtle ways. . . . Who knows? Who really can say he knows? We don't know. We're guessing. But until we do know for certain whether our messing around in Time *can* make a big roar or a little rustle in history, we're being damned careful."

Put an *x* in the box beside the correct answer.

1. Which one of the following expresses a statement that the author makes indirectly about scientific progress?

   ☐ a. Scientific discoveries always benefit humankind.

   ☐ b. Science should be controlled by the government.

   ☐ c. Science will one day be the end of us all.

   ☐ d. Scientists cannot always predict where their work may lead them.

2. Two questions in the passage sum up the author's concern regarding the mysteries of science. Copy these questions on the lines below.

   _____

   _____

Now check your answers using the Answer Key on page 458. Correct any wrong answers and review this part of the lesson if you don't understand why an answer was wrong.

Science Fiction

4 Science Fiction and Storytelling

The incredible creatures presented in science fiction are entertaining. The scientific facts used as a basis for the stories are informative. And the statements about people and society are food for thought. But when you come right down to it, the real reason people read science fiction is to enjoy a good story. Above all, then, a science fiction writer must be a good storyteller.

Like any other teller of tales, the science fiction writer must be able to create characters a reader can believe in. Plots must be exciting and suspenseful. Language should be vivid and precise.

Without a doubt, Ray Bradbury is a master storyteller. That is why his science fiction is so enduringly popular. As an example, take a look at this description of *Tyrannosaurus rex*. How does this passage add suspense, excitement and interest to the story?

> Out of the mist, one hundred yards away, came *Tyrannosaurus rex.* . . .
>
> It came on great oiled, resilient, striding legs. It towered thirty feet above half of the trees, a great evil god, folding its delicate watchmaker's claws close to its oily reptilian chest. Each lower leg was a piston, a thousand pounds of white bone, sunk in thick ropes of muscle, sheathed over in a gleam of pebbled skin like the mail of a terrible warrior. Each thigh was a ton of meat, ivory, and steel mesh. And from the great breathing cage of the upper body those two delicate arms dangled out front, arms with hands which might pick up and examine men like toys, while the snake neck coiled. And the head itself, a ton of sculptured stone, lifted easily upon the sky. Its mouth gaped, exposing a fence of teeth like daggers. Its eyes rolled, ostrich eggs, empty of all expression save hunger. It closed its mouth in a death grin.

Notice how menacing and dangerous the creature is made to appear. It is huge, towering above the treetops. It is strong, with "thick ropes of muscle." It is evil, with hands "which might pick up and examine men like toys." Above all, it is hungry, with "a fence of teeth like daggers."

Can such a creature be stopped by mere bullets? you wonder. Or will the hunters wind up as the dinosaur's mid-morning snack? The author

A Sound of Thunder

has created a tense drama in this scene. What will happen next? Who will win? This kind of suspense, which keeps readers turning pages, is the mark of a good storyteller.

Another equally important skill for a writer is the ability to write a vivid description. Read the passage in Exercise D. How does the author make you "see" this dying prehistoric creature and think about dinosaurs in a way you have never thought about them before?

Exercise D

Read the following passage and answer the questions about it using what you have learned in this part of the lesson.

> The Monster lay, a hill of solid flesh. Within, you could hear the sighs and murmurs as the furthest chambers of it died, the organs malfunctioning, liquids running a final instant from pocket to sac to spleen, everything shutting off, closing up forever. It was like standing by a wrecked locomotive or a steam shovel at quitting time, all valves being released or levered tight. Bones cracked; the tonnage of its own flesh, off balance, dead weight, snapped the delicate forearms, caught underneath. The meat settled, quivering.

Put an *x* in the box beside the correct answer.

1. Think about the terms the author uses to describe this creature: a hill of flesh; chambers; malfunctioning organs; liquids; tonnage; meat. The author wants you to think of "the Monster" as

   ☐ a. a creature with a soul.

   ☐ b. a primitive machine.

   ☐ c. an innocent victim.

   ☐ d. a thinking, rational being.

2. Authors use comparisons to help readers clearly visualize things in stories. In the passage, Ray Bradbury compares the dinosaur to something in the twentieth century. Find the sentence that contains this comparison and write it on the lines below.

_____

_____

_____

Now check your answers using the Answer Key on page 458. Correct any wrong answers and review this part of the lesson if you don't understand why an answer was wrong. Now go on to do the Comprehension Questions.

Comprehension Questions

Answer these questions without looking back at the story. Choose the best answer to each question and put an *x* in the box beside it.

Recalling Facts

1. Why does Eckels want to travel back in time?
   - ☐ a. To escape the police
   - ☐ b. To live in a simpler time
   - ☐ c. To do scientific research
   - ☐ d. To hunt big game

Recognizing Words in Context

2. "Out of *chars* and ashes, . . . " read the ad for Time Safari, "the old years . . . might leap." The word *chars* probably means
   - ☐ a. sackcloth.
   - ☐ b. the earth.
   - ☐ c. burnt wood.
   - ☐ d. dust.

Making Inferences

3. What kind of a leader does President Keith seem to be?
   - ☐ a. Peace-loving and democratic
   - ☐ b. Harsh and cruel
   - ☐ c. A puppet of the rich and powerful
   - ☐ d. A mental and physical weakling

Understanding
Main Ideas

4. Travis asks the time travelers to obey several rules. By far the most important of these rules is to

☐ a. wear oxygen masks.

☐ b. stay on the Path.

☐ c. aim for the dinosaur's eyes.

☐ d. take turns shooting.

Recognizing
Words in
Context

5. Travis says, "The cave man. . . . is not just any *expendable* man, no! He is an entire future nation." Which one of the following words is closest in meaning to *expendable*?

☐ a. Dependable

☐ b. Spendable

☐ c. Commendable

☐ d. Defendable

Understanding
Main Ideas

6. Why, according to Travis, must the time travelers be very careful not to kill any plants or creatures from the past?

☐ a. Because by changing anything in the past they might greatly alter the future

☐ b. Because there is a government fine for illegal hunting in the past

☐ c. Because some of the living things are important to human beings

☐ d. Because they might hurt themselves

Recognizing
Words in
Context

7. Travis says, "With the death of that one cave man, a billion others yet unborn are *throttled* in the womb." Another word for *throttled* is

☐ a. created.

☐ b. nourished.

☐ c. enslaved.

☐ d. strangled.

8. At what point in the story does Eckels first become frightened?

☐ a. When he hands his check to the man behind the desk

☐ b. When the Time Machine starts its journey

☐ c. When he gets his first glimpse of *Tyrannosaurus rex*

☐ d. When they arrive home again in the year 2055

9. When the dinosaur begins to attack, Eckels

☐ a. shoots it in the brain.

☐ b. shoots and misses.

☐ c. becomes frightened and runs.

☐ d. takes its picture.

10. Just before returning home, Travis orders Eckels to

☐ a. retrieve the bullets.

☐ b. bury the monster.

☐ c. pay a fine.

☐ d. sign a release.

11. What is the first thing Eckels notices when he returns from the time safari?

☐ a. The sign on the office door

☐ b. The mud on his boots

☐ c. The crushed butterfly

☐ d. That Deutscher has been elected president

Recalling
Facts

12. What is different about the sign on the office wall when Eckels returns?

☐ a. It has been replaced by a portrait of the new president.

☐ b. It has been turned upside down.

☐ c. The words are spelled differently.

☐ d. It is in a foreign language.

Making
Inferences

13. How does Eckels seem to feel about Deutscher's election as president at the end of the story?

☐ a. He is happy at this turn of events.

☐ b. He feels despair at this change.

☐ c. He thinks Deutscher will be good for the country.

☐ d. He doesn't care who is president.

Understanding
Main Ideas

14. What had Eckels done to change the course of time?

☐ a. He left a bullet in the dinosaur.

☐ b. He removed his oxygen mask.

☐ c. He killed a butterfly.

☐ d. He stepped on the jungle grass.

Making
Inferences

15. The "sound of thunder" referred to in the last line of the story is actually the sound of

☐ a. a dinosaur falling.

☐ b. a violent storm.

☐ c. an angry voice.

☐ d. a rifle shot.

Now check your answers using the Answer Key on page 458. Make no mark for right answers. <u>Correct</u> any wrong answers you may have by putting a checkmark (✓) in the box next to the right answer. Count the number of questions you answered correctly and plot the total on the Comprehension Scores graph on page 462.

Next, look at the questions you answered incorrectly. What types of questions were they? Count the number you got wrong of each type and enter the numbers in the spaces below.

Recognizing Words in Context _____

Recalling Facts _____

Keeping Events in Order _____

Making Inferences _____

Understanding Main Ideas _____

Now use these numbers to fill in the Comprehension Skills Profile on page 463.

Discussion Guides

The questions below will help you to think about the story and the lesson you have just read. If you don't discuss these questions in class, try to think about them or discuss them with your classmates.

Discussing Science Fiction

1. In what ways are the people and the society of the year 2055 a lot like people and society today?

2. What are some of the incredible elements of the vision of the future presented in "A Sound of Thunder"? How do the familiar elements of the story help make the incredible elements more believable?

3. What scientific facts or theories are included in this story?

Discussing the Story

4. Eckels, the big game hunter, learns something about himself in the course of the story. What does he learn?

5. The man behind the desk is a little bit different at the end of the story from how he was at the beginning. In what way has he changed?

6. Author Ray Bradbury suggests that killing a butterfly could change the world millions of years later. How, then, might all the killing that took place during World War II in 1940 through 1945 affect the world of 2045?

Discussing the Author's Work

7. Ray Bradbury was careful to do *none* of the following:

   - make the dinosaur cute and lovable
   - make the world of the future a place of total peace and happiness
   - place the dinosaur in a desert or arctic setting

   Why would it have been *bad* science fiction if the author had done any of these things?

8. Reread the paragraph about time travel that begins, "A touch of the hand . . . " on page 319. In what way is the language of this paragraph poetic? What feelings does it express about time travel—

A Sound of Thunder

fear? disinterest? fascination? awe? Point out some figures of speech and discuss what they add to the passage.

9. Bradbury hints that scientists don't know for sure where their work may lead them. What are some fields of science today that may possibly have harmful effects on the world? Does this possibility mean that we should not investigate these areas? Explain your opinion.

Writing Exercise

Science fiction writers look at scientific advances being made today and think about where they might lead us in the future.

Below are some of the latest areas of scientific research. Choose one and try to imagine where it might one day lead us.

Biological Engineering. "Designing" living things. For example, creating special kinds of bacteria that "eat" oil slicks.

Space Colonies. Sending large groups of people from earth to live in huge space stations.

Longevity. Extending the human life span, perhaps to as long as 150 or 200 years.

Test-tube Babies. New ways for people to conceive and bear children.

Plan your writing exercise this way:

In your opening paragraphs, describe what scientists are actually doing today in the area you chose. This is where you present the facts. (You may want to do some research first. Ask the librarian to help you.)

Then explain what these developments might mean for an average person of the future. This is where you use your imagination. Be specific. Give your average person a name, tell something about this person, and use him or her as an example of how the scientific discovery you chose has affected a particular human being, for better or for worse.

Unit 9   The Folk Story

Naftali the Storyteller and His Horse, Sus

BY ISAAC BASHEVIS SINGER

About the Illustration

How would you describe this scene? Point out some details in the drawing to support your response.

Here are some questions to help you think:

☐ What does the man's style of dress tell you about him and about where he lives?

☐ What elements in the picture tell you that the story is set in another place and time?

☐ What do you think the man and his horse are doing?

Unit 9

Introduction	What the Story Is About/What the Lesson Is About
Story	Naftali the Storyteller and His Horse, Sus
Lesson	The Folk Story
Activities	Comprehension Questions/Discussion Guides/Writing Exercise

Introduction

What the Story Is About

"Naftali the Storyteller and His Horse, Sus" is set in Poland, around a hundred years ago. At that time Poland had a large Jewish population. Many of the Jews lived in small rural villages called *shtetls* (shtet' els). They had their own language (Yiddish), customs and traditions. Learning played an important part in their lives, especially as it applied to their religion and to their role in life as Jews.

Naftali grew up in a Polish shtetl. His father was a coachman and it was expected that, like other boys, Naftali would follow his father's trade. But Naftali had other ideas. He had become interested in stories and storytelling. He could not live without stories, he said. So, in order to be close to what he loved best, he decided to become a traveling bookseller. He bought some books and built a wagon, which he trained his horse to pull. The horse was his beloved Sus.

You will find this story to be a very easy one. It has no conflict and therefore very little plot. It simply tells about Naftali and how he spent his life as a bookseller. What makes the story interesting is the ideas it contains and the pictures it creates in your mind. It gives you a view of a kind of life you probably aren't familiar with. And it stirs your imagination. If you could do anything you wanted to do for a living, what would you do? Would you bring good to the world? Or would you be interested only in money?

"Naftali the Storyteller and His Horse, Sus" is written as a folk story. Among other things, this means it is designed to teach a lesson. What it teaches is the value of reading. In a very simple way, it discusses many of the ideas you have been dealing with throughout this book. But don't be fooled by the simplicity of the story. The ideas run deep and the lessons are very important, as you will see.

Isaac Singer was born in Poland in 1904. He was the son and grandson of rabbis and knew the shtetl life very well. He came to America in 1933 and has lived in New York City most of his life. Though he speaks and writes English perfectly well, he prefers to write his stories in Yiddish. They are then translated into English and many other languages. "I had to stay with my language," he said, "and with the people whom I know best. If you write about the things and the people you know best, you discover your roots."

In more than fifty years as a writer, Isaac Singer has written a huge number of stories that have been published in many places—newspapers, magazines and books, all around the world. He has won many awards for his work. In 1978 he won his highest award, the Nobel Prize for Literature. Some people collect Isaac Singer stories, trying to see if they can find all of them. You may want to do the same. Start with his short stories. *Gimpel the Fool and Other Stories* is one of his most famous collections. Some of his novels are *The Family Moskat*, *The Magician of Lublin*, *The Manor*, and *The Slave*.

Because this story takes place in another country, among a group of people who have a language and customs that are probably foreign to you, it contains some words and expressions that you may not be familiar with. Some of these words and expressions are listed here, in the order in which they appear in the story. The definitions and explanations will help you to understand their importance to the characters in the story.

Yiddish. A language that evolved from German during the Middle Ages. Jews carried the language with them when they went to Poland and Russia.

Reb. A title of respect, as in Reb Zebulun and Reb Falik—two characters in the story. It is usually reserved for learned, prominent or wealthy people.

groshen. A coin that is worth very little.

Pentateuch. The Pentateuch consists of the first five books of the Bible, the books given by Moses. It is the most important part of the Bible for Jews—often called the Law.

Yeshiva. A school that teaches general subjects but emphasizes religious studies.

Cossack. A Russian cavalryman. Cossacks were famous for their horsemanship, and also for their brutality—especially toward the Jews of Russia and Poland.

cabalists. A special sect of Jews who lead simple, religious lives and believe that they have certain knowledge—some of it mystical and magical—that brings them closer to God.

Succoth. A Jewish harvest festival that occurs in the fall, like Thanksgiving.

Western Wall. The last remains of the Temple at Jerusalem, destroyed by the Romans. A very holy place for Jews.

Cave of Machpelah. The place where Abraham was buried. Abraham is considered the founder of the Jewish people.

Rachel's Tomb. Rachel was the wife of Jacob, an important figure in the Old Testament of the Bible. She is considered an ancestor of some of the tribes of Israel.

Hasidim. Hasids or Hasidic Jews—members of a very religious sect.

Passover. One of the major Jewish holidays, which celebrates the Jews' exodus from slavery in Egypt.

Scriptures. The Bible.

What the Lesson Is About

The lesson that follows the story is about folk stories. Stories are as old as the human race itself. In fact, being able to imagine stories and tell them is one of the things that separate people from the beasts. Isaac Singer makes this important point in the story about Naftali.

Simple stories that have been told and retold for so long that their authors have been lost or forgotten are called folk stories. Long before they were written down and put into books, they were preserved by word of mouth among the people, or the folk, from which they came. Such stories have special characteristics that mark them as folk tales, or folk stories. You will learn about these characteristics in the lesson.

Some authors, such as Isaac Singer, like to write stories in a *folk style*. These stories are not real folk tales, because they were not passed down through generations by word of mouth, but they do contain the characteristics of such stories. "Naftali the Storyteller" illustrates many of the elements of true folk stories.

The questions below will help you to focus on the special features of a folk story as you read. Read the story carefully and try to answer these questions as you go along:

1 How would you describe the style of the story? Is it difficult or easy? Is the language elaborate or plain and simple?

2 Magic and fantasy occur in two places in the story. Can you find these two places? Make a note of them when you find them.

3 What do you learn about the Jews of old-time Poland from reading the story?

4 What lessons do you learn from the story about living a good and useful life?

Naftali the Storyteller and His Horse, Sus

Isaac Bashevis Singer

I

The father, Zelig, and the mother, Bryna, both complained that their son, Naftali, loved stories too much. He could never go to sleep unless his mother first told him a story. At times she had to tell him two or three stories before he would close his eyes. He always demanded: "Mama, more, more! . . . "

Fortunately, Bryna had heard many stories from her mother and grandmother. Zelig himself, a coachman, had many things to tell—about spirits who posed as passengers and imps who stole into stables at night and wove braids into the horses' tails and elflocks into their manes. The nicest story was about when Zelig had still been a young coachman.

One summer night Zelig was coming home from Lublin with an empty wagon. It just so happened that he hadn't picked up any passengers from Lublin to his hometown, Janów. He drove along a road that ran through a forest. There was a full moon. It cast silvery nets over the pine branches and strings of pearls over the bark of the tree trunks. Night birds cried. From time to time a wolf's howl was heard. In those days the Polish woods still swarmed with bears, wolves, foxes, martens, and many other wild beasts. That night Zelig was despondent. When his wagon was empty of passengers, his wallet was empty of money, and there wouldn't be enough for Bryna to prepare for the Sabbath.

Suddenly Zelig saw lying in the road a sack that appeared to be full of flour or ground sugar. Zelig stopped his horse and got down to take a look. A sack of flour or sugar would come in handy in a household.

Zelig untied the sack, opened it, took a lick, and decided

that it was ground sugar. He lifted the sack, which was unusually heavy. Zelig was accustomed to carrying his passengers' baggage and he wondered why a sack of sugar should feel so heavy.

"It seems I didn't have enough to eat at the inn," Zelig thought. "And when you don't eat enough, you lose your strength."

He loaded the sack into the wagon. It was so heavy that he nearly strained himself.

He sat down on the driver's box and pulled on the reins, but the horse didn't move.

Zelig tugged harder and cried out, *"Wyszta!"* which in Polish means "Giddap!"

But even though the horse pulled with all his might, the wagon still wouldn't move forward.

"What's going on here?" Zelig wondered. "Can the sack be so heavy that the horse cannot pull it?"

This made no sense, for the horse had often drawn a wagonful of passengers along with their baggage.

"There is something here that's not as it should be," Zelig said to himself. He got down again, untied the sack, and took another lick. God in heaven, the sack was full of salt, not sugar!

Zelig stood there dumfounded. How could he have made such a mistake? He licked again, and again, and it was salt.

"Well, it's one of those nights!" Zelig mumbled to himself.

He decided to heave the sack off the wagon, since it was clear that evil spirits were toying with him. But by now the sack had become as heavy as if it were filled with lead. The horse turned his head backward and stared, as if curious to what was going on.

Suddenly Zelig heard laughter coming from inside the sack. Soon afterward the sack crumbled and out popped a creature with the eyes of a calf, the horns of a goat, and the wings of a bat. The creature said in a human voice, "You didn't lick sugar or salt but an imp's tail."

And with these words the imp burst into wild laughter and flew away.

Dozens of times Zelig the coachman told this same story to Naftali but Naftali never grew tired of hearing it. He could picture it all—the forest, the night, the silver moon, the curious eye of the horse, the imp. Naftali asked all kinds of questions: Did the imp have a beard? Did it have feet? How did its tail look? Where did it fly off to?

Zelig couldn't answer all the questions. He had been too frightened at the time to notice the details. But to the last question Zelig replied, "He probably flew to beyond the Dark Regions, where people don't go and cattle don't stray, where the sky is copper, the earth iron, and where the evil forces live under roofs of petrified toadstools and in tunnels abandoned by moles."

II

Like all the children in town, Naftali rose early to go to cheder. He studied more diligently than the other children. Why? Because Naftali was eager to learn to read. He had seen older boys reading storybooks and he had been envious of them. How happy was one who could read a story from a book!

At six, Naftali was already able to read a book in Yiddish, and from then on he read every storybook he could get his hands on. Twice a year a bookseller named Reb Zebulun visited Janów, and among the other books in the sack he carried over his shoulder were some storybooks. They cost two groshen a copy, and although Naftali got only two groshen a week allowance from his father, he saved up enough to buy a number of storybooks each season. He also read the stories in his mother's Yiddish Pentateuch and in her books of morals.

When Naftali grew older, his father began to teach him

how to handle horses. It was the custom in those days for a son to take over his father's livelihood. Naftali loved horses very much but he wasn't anxious to become a coachman driving passengers from Janów to Lublin and from Lublin to Janów. He wanted to become a bookseller with a sackful of storybooks.

His mother said to him, "What's so good about being a bookseller? From toting the sack day in day out, your back becomes bent, and from all the walking, your legs swell."

Naftali knew that his mother was right and he thought a lot about what he would do when he grew up. Suddenly he came up with a plan that seemed to him both wise and simple. He would get himself a horse and wagon, and instead of carrying the books on his back, he would carry them in the wagon.

His father, Zelig, said, "A bookseller doesn't make enough to support himself, his family, and a horse besides."

"For me it will be enough."

One time when Reb Zebulun the bookseller came to town, Naftali had a talk with him. He asked him where he got the storybooks and who wrote them. The bookseller told him that in Lublin there was a printer who printed these books, and in Warsaw and Vilna there were writers who wrote them. Reb Zebulun said that he could sell many more storybooks, but he lacked the strength to walk to all the towns and villages, and it didn't pay him to do so.

Reb Zebulun said, "I'm liable to come to a town where there are only two or three children who want to read storybooks. It doesn't pay me to walk there for the few groshen I might earn nor does it pay me to keep a horse or hire a wagon."

"What do these children do without storybooks?" Naftali asked. And Reb Zebulun replied, "They have to make do. Storybooks aren't bread. You can live without them."

"I couldn't live without them," Naftali said.

During this conversation Naftali also asked where the

writers got all these stories and Reb Zebulun said, "First of all, many unusual things happen in the world. A day doesn't go by without some rare event happening. Besides, there are writers who make up such stories."

"They make them up?" Naftali asked in amazement. "If that is so, then they are liars."

"They are not liars," Reb Zebulun replied. "The human brain really can't make up a thing. At times I read a story that seems to me completely unbelievable, but I come to some place and I hear that such a thing actually happened. The brain is created by God, and human thoughts and fantasies are also God's works. Even dreams come from God. If a thing doesn't happen today, it might easily happen tomorrow. If not in one country, then in another. There are endless worlds and what doesn't happen on earth can happen in another world. Whoever has eyes that see and ears that hear absorbs enough stories to last a lifetime and to tell to his children and grandchildren."

That's what old Reb Zebulun said, and Naftali listened to his words agape.

Finally, Naftali said, "When I grow up, I'll travel to all the cities, towns, and villages, and I'll sell storybooks everywhere, whether it pays me or not."

Naftali had decided on something else too—to become a writer of storybooks. He knew full well that for this you had to study, and with all his heart he determined to learn. He also began to listen more closely to what people said, to what stories they told, and to how they told them. Each person had his or her own manner of speaking. Reb Zebulun told Naftali, "When a day passes, it is no longer there. What remains of it? Nothing more than a story. If stories weren't told or books weren't written, man would live like the beasts, only for the day."

Reb Zebulun said, "Today we live, but by tomorrow today will be a story. The whole world, all human life, is one long story."

III

Ten years went by. Naftali was now a young man. He grew up tall, slim, fair-skinned, with black hair and blue eyes. He had learned a lot at the studyhouse and in the yeshiva and he was also an expert horseman. Zelig's mare had borne a colt and Naftali pastured and raised it. He called him Sus. Sus was a playful colt. In the summer he liked to roll in the grass. He whinnied like the tinkling sound of a bell. Sometimes, when Naftali washed and curried him and tickled his neck, Sus burst out in a sound that resembled laughter. Naftali rode him bareback like a Cossack. When Naftali passed the marketplace astride Sus, the town girls ran to the windows to look out.

After a while Naftali built himself a wagon. He ordered the wheels from Leib the blacksmith. Naftali loaded the wagon with all the storybooks he had collected during the years and he rode with his horse and his goods to the nearby towns. Naftali bought a whip, but he swore solemnly to himself that he would never use it. Sus didn't need to be whipped or even to have the whip waved at him. He pulled the light wagonful of books eagerly and easily. Naftali seldom sat on the box but walked alongside his horse and told him stories. Sus cocked his ears when Naftali spoke to him and Naftali was sure that Sus understood him. At times, when Naftali asked Sus whether he had liked a story, Sus whinnied, stomped his foot on the ground, or licked Naftali's ear with his tongue as if he meant to say, "Yes, I understand . . . "

Reb Zebulun had told him that animals live only for the day, but Naftali was convinced that animals have a memory too. Sus often remembered the road better than he, Naftali, did. Naftali had heard the story of a dog whose masters had lost him on a distant journey and months after they had come home without their beloved pet, he showed up. The dog crossed half of Poland to come back to his owners. Naftali had heard a similar story about a cat. The fact that pigeons fly back to their coops from very far away was known throughout the world. In those days, they were often used to deliver letters. Some people said this was memory, others called it instinct. But what did it matter what it was called? Animals didn't live for the day only.

Naftali rode from town to town; he often stopped in villages and sold his storybooks. The children everywhere loved Naftali and his horse, Sus. They brought all kinds of good things from home for Sus—potato peels, turnips, and pieces of sugar—and each time Sus got something to eat he waved his tail and shook his head, which meant "Thank you."

Not all the children were able to study and learn to read, and Naftali would gather a number of young children, seat them in the wagon, and tell them a story, sometimes a real one and sometimes a made-up one.

Wherever he went, Naftali heard all kinds of tales— of demons, hobgoblins, windmills, giants, dwarfs, kings, princes, and princesses. He would tell a story nicely, with all the details, and the children never grew tired of listening to him. Even grownups came to listen. Often the grownups invited Naftali home for a meal or a place to sleep. They also liked to feed Sus.

When a person does his work not only for money but out of love, he brings out the love in others. When a child couldn't afford a book, Naftali gave it to him free. Soon Naftali became well known throughout the region. Eventually, he came to Lublin.

In Lublin, Naftali heard many astonishing stories. He met a giant seven feet tall who traveled with a circus and a troupe of midgets. At the circus Naftali saw horses who danced to music, as well as dancing bears. One trickster swallowed a knife and spat it out again, another did a somersault on a high wire, a third flew in the air from one trapeze to another. A girl stood on a horse's back while it raced round and round the circus ring. Naftali struck up an easy friendship with the circus people and he listened to their many interesting stories. They told of fakirs in India who could walk barefoot over burning coals. Others let themselves be buried alive, and after they were dug out several days later, they were healthy and well. Naftali heard astounding stories about sorcerers and miracle workers who could read minds and predict the future. He met an old man who had walked from Lublin to the Land of Israel, then back again. The old man told Naftali about cabalists who lived in caves behind Jerusalem, fasted from one Sabbath to the next, and learned the secrets of God, the angels, the seraphim, the cherubim, and the holy beasts.

The world was full of wonders and Naftali had the urge to write them down and spread them far and wide over all the cities, towns, and villages.

In Lublin, Naftali went to the bookstores and bought storybooks, but he soon saw that there weren't enough storybooks to be had. The storekeepers said that it didn't pay the printers to print them since they brought in so little money. But could everything be measured by money? There were children and even grownups everywhere who yearned to hear stories and Naftali decided to tell all that he had heard. He himself hungered for stories and could never get enough of them.

IV

More years passed, Naftali's parents were no longer living. Many girls had fallen in love with Naftali and wanted to marry him, but he knew that from telling stories and selling storybooks he could not support a family. Besides, he had become used to wandering. How many stories could he hear or tell living in one town? He therefore decided to stay on the road. Horses normally live some twenty-odd years, but Sus was one of those rare horses who live a long time. However, no one lives forever. At forty Sus began to show signs of old age. He seldom galloped now, nor were his eyes as good as they once were. Naftali was already gray himself and the children called him Grandpa.

One time Naftali was told that on the road between Lublin and Warsaw lay an estate where all booksellers came, since the owner was very fond of reading and hearing stories. Naftali asked the way and he was given directions to get there. One spring day he came to the estate. Everything that had been said turned out to be true. The owner of the estate, Reb Falik, gave him a warm welcome and bought many books from him. The children in the nearby town had already heard about Naftali the storyteller and they snatched up all the storybooks he had brought with him. Reb Falik had many horses grazing and when they saw Sus they accepted him as one of their own. Sus promptly began to chew the grass where many yellow flowers grew and Naftali told Reb Falik one story after another. The weather was warm, birds sang, twittered, and trilled, each in its own voice.

The estate contained a tract of forest where old oaks grew. Some of the oaks were so thick they had to be hundreds of years old. Naftali was particularly taken by one oak standing in the center of a meadow. It was the thickest oak Naftali had ever seen in his life. Its roots were spread over a wide area and you could tell that they ran deep. The crown of the oak spread far and wide, and it cast a huge shadow. When Naftali saw this giant oak, which had to be older than all the oaks in the region, it occurred to him: "What a shame an oak hasn't a mouth to tell stories with!"

This oak had lived through many generations. It may have gone back to the times when idol worshippers still lived in Poland. It surely knew the time when the Jews had come to Poland from the German states where they had been persecuted and the Polish king, Kazimierz I, had opened the gates of the land to them. Naftali suddenly realized that he was tired of wandering. He now envied the oak for standing so long in one place, deeply rooted in God's earth. For the first time in his life Naftali got the urge to settle down in one place. He also thought of his horse. Sus was undoubtedly tired of trekking over the roads. It would do him good to get some rest in the few years left him.

Just as Naftali stood there thinking these thoughts, the owner of the estate, Reb Falik, came along in a buggy. He stopped the buggy near Naftali and said, "I see you're completely lost in thought. Tell me what you're thinking."

At first Naftali wanted to tell Reb Falik that many kinds of foolish notions ran through the human mind and that not all of them could be described. But after a while he thought, "Why not tell him the truth?"

Reb Falik seemed a goodhearted man. He had a silver-white beard and eyes that expressed the wisdom and goodness that sometimes come with age. Naftali said, "If you have the patience, I'll tell you."

"Yes, I have the patience. Take a seat in the buggy. I'm going for a drive and I want to hear what a man who is famous for his storytelling thinks about."

Naftali sat down in the buggy. The horses hitched to the buggy walked slowly and Naftali told Reb Falik the story of his life, as well as what his thoughts were when he saw the giant oak. He told him everything, kept nothing back.

When Naftali finished, Reb Falik said, "My dear Naftali, I can easily fulfill all your wishes and fantasies. I am, as you know, an old man. My wife died some time ago. My children live in the big cities. I love to hear stories and I also have lots of stories to tell. If you like, I'll let you build a house in the shade of the oak and you can stay there as long as I live and as long as you live. I'll have a stable built for your horse near the house and you'll both live out your lives in peace. Yes, you are right. You cannot wander forever. There comes a time when every person wants to settle in one place and drink in all the charms that the place has to offer."

When Naftali heard these words, a great joy came over him. He thanked Reb Falik again and again, but Reb Falik said, "You need not thank me so much. I have many peasants and servants here, but I don't have a single person I can talk to. We'll be friends and we'll tell each other lots of stories. What's life, after all? The future isn't here yet and you cannot foresee what it will bring. The present is only a moment and the past is one long story. Those who don't tell stories and don't hear stories live only for that moment, and that isn't enough."

V

Reb Falik's promise wasn't merely words. The very next day he ordered his people to build a house for Naftali the storyteller. There was no shortage of lumber or of craftsmen on the estate. When Naftali saw the plans for the house, he grew disturbed. He needed only a small house for himself and a stable for Sus. But the plans called for a big house with many rooms. Naftali asked Reb Falik why such a big house was being built for him, and Reb Falik replied, "You will need it."

"What for?" Naftali asked.

Gradually, the secret came out. During his lifetime Reb Falik had accumulated many books, so many that he couldn't find room for them in his own big house and many books had to be stored in the cellar and in the attic. Besides, in his talks with Reb Falik, Naftali had said that he had many of his own stories and stories told him by others written down on paper and that he had collected a chestful of manuscripts, but he hadn't been able to have these stories printed, for the printers in Lublin and in the other big cities demanded a lot of money to print them and the number of buyers of storybooks in Poland wasn't large enough to cover such expenses.

Alongside Naftali's house, Reb Falik had a print shop built. He ordered crates of type from Lublin (in those days there was no such thing as a typesetting machine) as well as a hand press. From now on Naftali would have the opportunity to set and print his own storybooks. When he learned what Reb Falik was doing for him, Naftali couldn't believe his ears. He said, "Of all the stories I have ever heard or told, for me this will be by far the nicest."

That very summer everything was ready—the house, the library, the print shop. Winter came early. Right after Succoth the rains began, followed by snow. In winter there is little to do on an estate. The peasants sat in their huts and warmed themselves by their stoves or they went to the tavern. Reb Falik and Naftali spent lots of time together. Reb Falik himself was a treasure trove of stories. He had met many famous squires. In his time he had visited the fairs in Danzig, Leipzig, and Amsterdam. He had even made a trip to the Holy Land and had seen the Western Wall, the Cave of Machpelah, and Rachel's Tomb. Reb Falik told many tales and Naftali wrote them down.

Sus's stable was too big for one horse. Reb Falik had a number of old horses on his estate that could no longer work so Sus wasn't alone. At times, when Naftali came into the stable to visit his beloved Sus, he saw him bowing his head against the horse on his left or his right, and it seemed to Naftali that Sus was listening to stories told him by the other horses or silently telling his own horsy story. It's true that horses cannot speak, but God's creatures can make themselves understood without words.

That winter Naftali wrote many stories—his own and those he heard from Reb Falik. He set them in type and printed them on his hand press. At times, when the sun shone over the silvery snow, Naftali hitched Sus and another horse to a sleigh and made a trip through the nearby towns to sell his storybooks or give them away to those who couldn't afford to buy them. Sometimes Reb Falik went along with him. They slept at inns and spent time with merchants, landowners, and Hasidim on their way to visit their rabbis' courts. Each one had a story to tell and Naftali either wrote them down or fixed them in his memory.

The winter passed and Naftali couldn't remember how. On Passover, Reb Falik's sons, daughters, and grandchildren came to celebrate the holiday at the estate, and again Naftali heard wondrous tales of Warsaw, Cracow, and even of Berlin, Paris, and London. The kings waged wars, but scientists made all kinds of discoveries and inventions. Astronomers discovered stars, planets, comets. Archaeologists dug out ruins of ancient cities. Chemists found new elements. In all the countries, tracks were being laid for railroad trains. Museums, libraries, and theaters were being built. Historians uncovered writings from generations past. The writers in every land described the life and the people among whom they dwelled. Mankind could not and would not forget its past. The history of the world grew ever richer in detail.

That spring something happened that Naftali had been expecting and, therefore, dreading. Sus became sick and stopped grazing. The sun shone outside, and Naftali led Sus out to pasture where the fresh green grass and many flowers sprouted. Sus sat down in the sunshine, looked at the grass and the flowers, but no longer grazed. A stillness shone out from his eyes, the tranquillity of a creature that has lived out its years and is ready to end its story on earth.

One afternoon, when Naftali went out to check on his beloved Sus, he saw that Sus was dead. Naftali couldn't hold back his tears. Sus had been a part of his life.

Naftali dug a grave for Sus not far from the old oak

where Sus had died, and he buried him there. As a marker over the grave, he thrust into the ground the whip that he had never used. Its handle was made of oak.

Oddly enough, several weeks later Naftali noticed that the whip had turned into a sapling. The handle had put down roots into the earth where Sus lay and it began to sprout leaves. A tree grew over Sus, a new oak which drew sustenance from Sus's body. In time young branches grew out of the tree and birds sang upon them and built their nests there. Naftali could hardly bring himself to believe that this old dried-out stick had possessed enough life within it to grow and blossom. Naftali considered it a miracle. When the tree grew thicker, Naftali carved Sus's name into the bark along with the dates of his birth and death.

Yes, individual creatures die, but this doesn't end the story of the world. The whole earth, all the stars, all the planets, all the comets represent within them one divine history, one source of life, one endless and wondrous story that only God knows in its entirety.

A few years afterward, Reb Falik died, and years later, Naftali the storyteller died. By then he was famous for his storybooks not only throughout Poland but in other countries as well. Before his death Naftali asked that he be buried beneath the young oak that had grown over Sus's grave and whose branches touched the old oak. On Naftali's tombstone were carved these words from the Scriptures:

> LOVELY AND PLEASANT IN THEIR LIVES,
> AND IN THEIR DEATH
> THEY WERE NOT DIVIDED

The Folk Story

The best place to start talking about folk stories is with the word *folk* itself. *Folk* is a very old word in the English language. It comes from the German *volk*, meaning people. So a folk story is a people's story. But since we are all people, how are folk stories different from any other stories that people might read or tell?

You will recall that in another lesson we said that words that have similar meanings—synonyms—usually have different shades of meaning. For example, *skinny* means almost the same thing as *slim*—but not quite. A *leap* is somewhat greater than a *jump*, and a *risk* seems more uncertain than a *chance*.

Though *folk* is a synonym for *people*, it more accurately suggests plain, or simple, people. Most, but not all, people are folk. Rulers are not thought of as folk. Rich people are not folk. Folks are you and me and our families. We have the folks over for dinner.

Volkswagen means folk car. It's not a car that is usually driven by the president of a bank, it's driven by the everyday working person who doesn't have a whole lot of money. Folk *lore* is learning or knowledge that comes from among the people. It is not knowledge that is acquired by scientists. Folk lore, or folk learning, deals with natural medicines, ways to make clothes, and many other useful arts.

The first stories you were told as a small child were probably folk stories, or folk tales as they are also called. "Jack and the Beanstalk" is a folk tale. So are "Goldilocks and the Three Bears" and "Little Red Riding Hood." The stories of Paul Bunyan and Pecos Bill are folk stories that grew up among the people of the American frontier during the nineteenth century.

The identities of the authors of folk stories have usually been lost in time. But this is not always the case. Some modern authors have chosen to write in the *style* of the folk story, as Isaac Singer has done. Many of Washington Irving's stories, such as "The Legend of Sleepy Hollow," are very much like folk stories. The Uncle Remus tales by Joel Changler Harris are considered American folk stories. Perhaps you can add some of your own favorites to the list.

Folk stories have certain identifying features. These are the four that we will discuss in the lesson:

1 **Simplicity.** Folk stories are simple tales about simple people.

2 **Fantasy, magic and the supernatural.** Folk stories usually have one or more of these elements.

3 **Customs, traditions and beliefs.** Folk stories are important for reminding people who they are and where they come from.

4 **A lesson.** Folk stories always contain a moral, or teach a lesson.

Everything about a folk story is simple. The language is easy to understand. The ideas are clear and straightforward. The characters are either good or bad, strong or weak, rich or poor, wise or foolish. There are no in-betweens. Consider this passage in which Naftali learns how stories are written.

Folk Story

1 Simplicity

> During this conversation Naftali also asked where the writers got all these stories and Reb Zebulun said, "First of all, many unusual things happen in the world. A day doesn't go by without some rare event happening. Besides, there are writers who make up such stories."
>
> "They make them up?" Naftali asked in amazement. "If that is so, then they are liars."
>
> "They are not liars," Reb Zebulun replied. "The human brain really can't make up a thing. . . . The brain is created by God, and human thoughts and fantasies are also God's works. Even dreams come from God. If a thing doesn't happen today, it might easily happen tomorrow. If not in one country, then in another. There are endless worlds and what doesn't happen on earth can happen in another world. Whoever has eyes that see and ears that hear absorbs enough stories to last a lifetime and to tell to his children and grandchildren."

The language is so simple here that a five-year-old child could understand what is going on. And yet you don't get the feeling that the author is talking down to you.

Notice, too, how simply Isaac Singer has explained some very complicated ideas. He has explained where a writer's ideas come from. He has said in a very few words that all things are possible—somewhere, somehow. Scholars have filled whole libraries writing about these two ideas. By expressing them in about a dozen lines in this story, Singer has said just enough, simply enough, so that anyone—the folk—can understand.

Naftali, his parents and Zebulun the bookseller are poor, simple people. Reb Falik, who enters the story later, is a very rich man. This is the way it is in folk stories. There are no in-betweens. Each character stands out simply and clearly, with no uncertainties, no questions about what kind of a person he is.

Exercise A

Read the following passage and answer the questions about it using what you have learned in this part of the lesson.

Naftali had decided on something else too—to become a writer of storybooks. He knew full well that for this you had to study, and with all his heart he determined to learn. He also began to listen more closely to what people said, to what stories they told, and to how they told them. Each person had his or her own manner of speaking. Reb Zebulun told Naftali, "When a day passes, it is no longer there. What remains of it? Nothing more than a story. If stories weren't told or books weren't written, man would live like the beasts, only for the day."

Reb Zebulun said, "Today we live, but by tomorrow today will be a story. The whole world, all human life, is one long story."

Put an x in the box beside the correct answer.

1. The story tells in very simple terms how to become a writer. Which of the following expressions best sums up the simple but sound advice?

   ☐ a. Excel in all you do.

   ☐ b. Be sure to go to college.

   ☐ c. Study, listen and learn.

   ☐ d. Get the best teachers.

2. Here is a very deep idea that is contained in the story: What makes us human is that we have a past, a history. The study of history, therefore, is the study of humanity. On the lines below, copy the portion of the passage that states this idea clearly and simply.

_____

_____

_____

Now check your answers using the Answer Key on page 459. Correct any wrong answers and review this part of the lesson if you don't understand why an answer was wrong.

Folk Story

2 Fantasy, Magic and the Supernatural

In almost every folk story, something very unusual happens. Trees and animals speak. Gods descend from heaven and change things around in magical ways. There are wizards, witches, fairies, imps and goblins. All have their mischief to make or their wonders to perform.

Fantasy, magic and things supernatural make a good story. People love a good scare. And they like to dream that someone or something magical will come along to solve all their problems and maybe make them rich. In other words, people like to *fantasize*. Most stories, especially folk stories, help us to do this.

But fantasy serves another purpose in folk stories. We said in part one of the lesson that folk stories present ideas in simple ways. Well, very often magic and fantasy are used for this purpose. It's not easy, for example, to explain how the world began or how the first person came to be, so every culture has folk stories that explain these things as magic or as wonderful deeds of the gods. Parents have always had to teach their children to be cautious in the world, to watch out for evil things, and it's not easy to teach about evil. So stories were made up about imps and demons who are always waiting to trip you up. "Naftali the Storyteller and His Horse, Sus" begins with a story about an imp. It is a story within a story. Zelig tells the story often, and young Naftali never tires of hearing it.

Dozens of times Zelig the coachman told this same story to Naftali but Naftali never grew tired of hearing it. He could picture it all—the forest, the night, the silver moon, the curious eye of the horse, the imp. Naftali asked all kinds of questions: Did the imp have a beard? Did it have feet? How did its tail look? Where did it fly off to?

Zelig couldn't answer all the questions. He had been too frightened at the time to notice the details. But to the last question Zelig replied, "He probably flew to beyond the Dark Regions, where people don't go and cattle don't stray, where the sky is copper, the earth iron, and where the evil forces live under roofs of petrified toadstools and in tunnels abandoned by moles."

Surely this must have been an exciting story to listen to. The forest, the night, the moon and the imp must have sent chills up and down young Naftali's spine. The story also undoubtedly excited Naftali's imagination. This is the beginning of his desire to be a writer and storyteller himself. So it is part of his education.

The story also teaches a lesson, as all folk stories do. In answer to Naftali's question about where the imp flew off to, Zelig said that there is a Dark Region where evil forces live. He described it as a horrible place where people and even animals are afraid to go. The lesson is that the evil in life is to be avoided.

Exercise B

Read the following passage and answer the questions about it using what you have learned in this part of the lesson.

Naftali dug a grave for Sus not far from the old oak where Sus had died, and he buried him there. As a marker over the grave, he thrust into the ground the whip that he had never used. Its handle was made of oak.

Oddly enough, several weeks later Naftali noticed that the whip had turned into a sapling. The handle had put down roots into the earth where Sus lay and it began to sprout leaves. A tree grew over Sus, a new oak which drew sustenance from Sus's body .... When the tree grew thicker, Naftali carved Sus's name into the bark along with the dates of his birth and death.

Yes, individual creatures die, but this doesn't end the story of the world. The whole earth, all the stars, all the planets, all the comets represent within them one divine history, one source of life, one endless and wondrous story that only God knows in its entirety.

Put an *x* in the box beside the correct answer.

1. Which one of the following is a lesson that can be learned from the magical sprouting of the whip?

   ☐ a. The death of one thing provides life for another. So, life is eternal.

   ☐ b. Death causes such sorrow that the tears that are shed can make a tree grow.

   ☐ c. Death is the end of all things. Nothing can survive death.

   ☐ d. Death is the greatest story of life.

2. An important Jewish prayer goes, "Hear, O Israel, the Lord our God . . . is One." In a way, Sus's death and the magical sprouting of the whip are used to explain one meaning of this prayer. Which sentence in the passage teaches about the "oneness" of God? Write the sentence on the lines below.

   _____

   _____

   _____

   _____

Now check your answers using the Answer Key on page 459. Correct any wrong answers and review this part of the lesson if you don't understand why an answer was wrong.

Customs, traditions and beliefs are part of our history. And, as Singer points out, history is important to people. Without a past, without history, he says, we would be like the beasts.

Folk Story

3 Customs, Traditions and Beliefs

Our customs and traditions give us roots. They make us feel that we are a part, a continuation, of all that has come before us. They are our link with history. We learn from the past, and we pass our knowledge on to future generations. Animals live simply for each day as it comes, but we live by building on the past and planning for the future.

Many countries, for example, have an Independence Day. In the United States it is July 4, in Mexico it is September 16. Canada has Dominion Day, July 1, and France celebrates Bastille Day on July 14. Each of these holidays celebrates a time when the common people, the folk, broke away from the tyranny of the powerful ruling class. Knowing that our ancestors could accomplish such a thing makes us feel that we are a part of these great events. So they have become part of our traditions. Stories and customs have grown up around them.

Religious traditions and beliefs provide people with moral values. They help to teach the difference between good and bad, right and wrong. And they help people to deal with forces in the world that are beyond understanding. Customs that people follow in the practice of their religions help them maintain their beliefs.

Because customs, traditions and beliefs are part of our folk lore, they are frequently included in folk stories. Notice how Isaac Singer works traditional Jewish experiences into his story.

> Naftali heard astounding stories about sorcerers and miracle workers who could read minds and predict the future. He met an old man who had walked from Lublin to the Land of Israel, then back again. The old man told Naftali about cabalists who lived in caves behind Jerusalem, fasted from one Sabbath to the next, and learned the secrets of God, the angels, the seraphim, the cherubim, and the holy beasts.

[Later in the story:]

This oak had lived through many generations. It may have gone back to the times when idol worshippers still lived in Poland. It surely knew the time when the Jews had come to Poland from the German states where they had been persecuted and the Polish king, Kazimierz I, had opened the gates of the land to them.

The first of these passages tells of a man who had made a pilgrimage to the Holy Land on foot, and who saw and learned wonderful things. This passage is an example of people's devotion to religion. It also mentions the cabalists. They are a sect of very religious Jews who feel that they have special knowledge that brings them very close to God and to the other inhabitants of heaven.

In the second passage, Singer has included a bit of Jewish history. The Jews were driven from Germany in the Middle Ages and were welcomed into Poland by Kazimierz, or Casimir, I. Not long before that, he tells us, the Poles were idol worshippers.

Exercise C

Read the following passage and answer the questions about it using what you have learned in this part of the lesson.

Like all the children in town, Naftali rose early to go to cheder (kay′ der). He studied more diligently than the other children. Why? Because Naftali was eager to learn to read. He had seen older boys reading storybooks and he had been envious of them. How happy was one who could read a story from a book!

At six, Naftali was already able to read a book in Yiddish, and from then on he read every storybook he could get his hands on ... He also read the stories in his mother's Yiddish Pentateuch (Bible) and in her books of morals.

Put an *x* in the box beside the correct answer.

1. You can tell from the meaning of the passage what a *cheder* is and what language is spoken there. Which one of the following is correct?

   ☐ a. A cheder is a church in which Latin is spoken.

   ☐ b. A cheder is a school in which Yiddish is spoken.

   ☐ c. A cheder is a public school in which Polish is spoken.

   ☐ d. A cheder is a synagogue in which Hebrew is spoken.

2. The passage (and, in fact, the whole story) deals with the importance of learning a particular skill. It is a skill that has traditionally been important to Jewish people, and to many other people as well. What is the skill that is emphasized here?

   _____

Now check your answers using the Answer Key on page 459. Correct any wrong answers and review this part of the lesson if you don't understand why an answer was wrong.

4 Teaching Morals and Other Lessons

When you were a small child, someone probably told you at least one of Aesop's fables. They are very famous little stories, and they have been told for many generations. Aesop's fables always involve animals, and they always teach a moral lesson. They are simple folk stories.

Aesop himself is a folk legend. No one is sure if he was a real person or not. Some say that he was a slave on the Greek island of Samos. Others say that he was a crippled storyteller who told stories to ancient Greek kings. Whoever he was, his simple stories have survived for more than 2,000 years. It is the moral lessons that they teach that make them so lasting. Parents often use them to teach their children the lessons of life. Consider this one, from which we get the expression "sour grapes."

A hungry fox saw some luscious clusters of grapes hanging high on a vine. He tried all the tricks he knew to get at them, but try as he would he could not reach them. At last he gave up. To mask his disappointment he announced, "The grapes are very likely sour and not worth my attention."

The moral is: We often despise what we cannot have.

Notice that the moral is stated at the end of the fable. Aesop always ended his tales this way to be sure that the reader wouldn't miss the lesson. Not all folk stories are as blunt about pointing out the moral lessons as Aesop's fables are. But all folk stories do contain lessons that are rather obvious.

Earlier in the lesson you saw how Naftali's father used the story of the imp to teach his son about the forces of evil in the world. Later, Singer told of the sprouting whip to teach that life continues after death, that through death comes new life, in a continuous cycle. There are also many lessons about the value of reading. What lesson is the author trying to teach in this passage.

Wherever he went, Naftali heard all kinds of tales—of demons, hobgoblins, windmills, giants, dwarfs, kings, princes and princesses. He would tell a story nicely, with all the details, and the children never grew tired of listening to him. Even grownups came to listen. Often the grownups invited Naftali home for a meal or a place to sleep. They also liked to feed Sus.

When a person does his work not only for money but out of love, he brings out the love in others. When a child couldn't afford a book, Naftali gave it to him free. Soon Naftali became well known throughout the region.

The lesson in this passage is stated for you, almost as Aesop would have done, except the statement is buried in the middle of the passage instead of being placed at the end. The moral is this: When a person does his work not only for money but out of love, he brings out the love in others.

It is quite true that people are happiest when they are working at something that they like to do. If you work only for money, chances are that you will be quite miserable at your job. The happiest people are those who work for others. If you can perform a service for others, and make a good living too, you have the best of both worlds.

Sometimes in folk stories the moral lesson is found in a *quest* that the main character sets out on. A quest is an adventure in which the hero is searching for something. A quest could be a search for riches that are to be used for some good purpose, or could be a search for the answer to an important question. (Notice that the word *quest* forms the beginning of the word *question*. Both words come from the Latin word meaning to ask or to seek.) Try to find Naftali's moral quest in Exercise D.

Exercise D

Read the following passage and answer the questions about it using what you have learned in this part of the lesson.

The world was full of wonders and Naftali had the urge to write them down and spread them far and wide over all the cities, towns, and villages.

In Lublin, Naftali went to the bookstores and bought storybooks, but he soon saw that there weren't enough storybooks to be had. The storekeepers said that it didn't pay the printers to print them since they brought in so little money. But could everything be measured by money? There were children and even grownups everywhere who yearned to hear stories and Naftali decided to tell all that he had heard.

Put an *x* in the box beside the correct answer.

1. Which one of the following best describes Naftali's moral quest?

   ☐ a. He sought to become a wealthy bookseller.

   ☐ b. He sought more knowledge for himself.

   ☐ c. He sought an answer to the one true question.

   ☐ d. He sought to spread knowledge everywhere through stories.

2. You have probably heard it said that you can't buy everything in life. This is an important moral lesson. What question does Naftali ask that points to this moral truth? Write the question on the lines below.

   _____

   _____

Use the Answer Key on page 459 to check your answers. Correct any wrong answers and review this part of the lesson if you don't understand why an answer was wrong. Now go on to do the Comprehension Questions.

Comprehension Questions

Recognizing
Words in
Context

1. Coming home with no passengers and no money, Zelig was *despondent*. In other words, he was

   ☐ a. walking.

   ☐ b. unhappy.

   ☐ c. hurrying.

   ☐ d. desperate.

Recognizing
Words in
Context

2. Naftali studied more *diligently* than other children. This means that he

   ☐ a. found studying easier.

   ☐ b. studied harder.

   ☐ c. studied faster.

   ☐ d. was smarter.

Recalling
Facts

3. Who was Reb Zebulun?

   ☐ a. A bookseller

   ☐ b. A coachman

   ☐ c. A rich man

   ☐ d. A printer

4. When did Naftali meet Reb Zebulun?

☐ a. When Naftali was an old man

☐ b. After Naftali became a storyteller

☐ c. After Naftali met Reb Falik

☐ d. When Naftali was a small boy

5. Naftali's father said to him, "A bookseller doesn't make enough to support himself, his family, and a horse besides." Naftali replied, "For me it will be enough." This reply was a guide to Naftali's life. It is stated in another way later in the story with the words

☐ a. "He had become used to wandering."

☐ b. "The world was full of wonders. . . ."

☐ c. "Could everything be measured by money?"

☐ d. "The present is only a moment. . . ."

6. Naftali's ambition was to be a traveling bookseller. This was because he

☐ a. wanted to earn a lot of money.

☐ b. was a very good reader.

☐ c. wanted to do what he enjoyed most.

☐ d. liked horses as his father did.

7. We are told that both children and adults would gather to listen to Naftali's stories, and that people would often invite him into their homes to eat and sleep. These facts suggest that Naftali

☐ a. wished he had a family of his own.

☐ b. was not lonely in his wandering life.

☐ c. didn't like to sleep in his wagon.

☐ d. never had any time to himself.

8. "When a day passes it is no longer there." What does this have to do with storytelling?

☐ a. Storytelling preserves the events of the day.

☐ b. Storytelling helps the days pass by.

☐ c. Storytelling makes the days seem longer.

☐ d. Storytelling keeps you from wasting time.

9. What did Naftali have that he never used?

☐ a. His wagon

☐ b. Money

☐ c. A groshen

☐ d. A whip

10. According to the story, what happens when a person does his work out of love?

☐ a. He remains poor.

☐ b. He becomes a very religious person.

☐ c. He is often made fun of by others.

☐ d. He brings out love in others.

11. Who was Reb Falik?

☐ a. A rich man who loved stories

☐ b. A well-known bookseller

☐ c. A printer in Lublin

☐ d. A world traveler

12. When did Naftali meet Reb Falik?

☐ a. When Naftali was a child

☐ b. When Naftali was an old man

☐ c. When Naftali was starting out as a bookseller

☐ d. On Naftali's return from Israel

13. As he viewed the old oak on Reb Falik's estate, Naftali decided that he wanted to

☐ a. settle down.

☐ b. write his first story.

☐ c. become a printer.

☐ d. bury Sus there.

14. An oak tree drew *sustenance* from Sus's body. *Sustenance* is

☐ a. knowledge to go on living.

☐ b. love that binds friends together.

☐ c. food to maintain life.

☐ d. faith that lasts after death.

15. Which one of the following is an important idea that is often repeated in the story?

☐ a. Life is one long story.

☐ b. Be kind to animals.

☐ c. Beware of imps and evil spirits.

☐ d. Life is good to people who like stories.

Now check your answers using the Answer Key on page 459. Make no mark for right answers. <u>Correct</u> any wrong answers you may have by putting a checkmark (✓) in the box next to the right answer. Count the number of questions you answered correctly and plot the total on the Comprehension Scores graph on page 462.

Next, look at the questions you answered incorrectly. What types of questions were they? Count the number you got wrong of each type and enter the numbers in the spaces below.

Recognizing Words in Context   _____

Recalling Facts   _____

Keeping Events in Order   _____

Making Inferences   _____

Understanding Main Ideas   _____

Now use these numbers to fill in the Comprehension Skills Profile on page 463.

Discussion Guides

The questions below will help you to think about the story and the lesson you have just read. If you don't discuss these questions in class, try to think about them or discuss them with your classmates.

Discussing Folk Stories

1. A feature of many folk stories that is not discussed in the lesson is *wish fulfillment*. This means that someone who wants something very badly wishes for it and gets it. There may be a genie, fairy, imp, god or magician to make the wish come true. What is Naftali's wish, and how does it come true?

2. In part 4 of the lesson you learned that many folk stories tell about a quest. A quest usually involves travel. Describe Naftali's quest in detail. Was he successful in his quest? Explain your opinion.

3. Most folk stories are set in the country among plain country people. How does "Naftali the Storyteller" fit this pattern? Can you think of a folk story that takes place in a city? Can you make one up?

Discussing the Story

4. In the story, Reb Falik says: "What's life, after all? The future isn't here yet and you cannot foresee what it will bring. The present is only a moment and the past is one long story. Those who don't tell stories and don't hear stories live only for that moment, and that isn't enough." Explain what you think Reb Falik means.

5. The story ends with a quotation from the Scriptures (the Bible). What does the quotation mean and how does it apply to the story? (The quotation is from the Second Book of Samuel, Chapter 1, verse 23. David is mourning the death of King Saul and his son Jonathan, who were slain in battle.)

6. Are there people like Naftali in the world? If you don't think there are, explain why not. If you think there are, tell who they are and in what way they are like Naftali. (You can think of groups of people or of organizations rather than just one person.)

Discussing the Author's Work

7. The way Isaac Singer tells this story seems almost childish at times. Still, people of all ages enjoy the story. What is your opinion of the simple way in which the story is told? How would the story change if the language and the situations were more "grown up"?

8. Isaac Singer writes in Yiddish. His work is then translated into English and other languages. A great many of his stories are set among Jewish people in Poland in the last century or before. How different would the story be, do you think, if the people were Polish and Catholic? English and Protestant? Japanese and Buddhist?

9. When Isaac Singer was given the Nobel Prize for Literature in 1978, he was praised for "bringing universal conditions to life." What "universal conditions" does he bring to life in "Naftali the Storyteller and His Horse, Sus"?

Writing Exercise

Find and read another folk story. Then do the following.

1. Retell the story as if the events in it happened to you, your family and your friends.

2. When you have finished, tell in a sentence or two what the moral lesson of your story is.

Unit 10   Judgments and Conclusions:
          Discussing Stories

The Lucid Eye in Silver Town

BY JOHN UPDIKE

About the Illustration

What judgments can
you make about what is
happening in this scene?
Point out some details in
the drawing to support your
response.

Here are some questions to
help you think:

☐ Where is this scene taking
   place?

☐ Of the six people shown
   in this picture, which
   three seem to be the
   main characters?

☐ In what way are the man
   on the left and the man
   on the right different?

☐ What do you think the
   man on the right is
   talking about with
   the boy?

Unit 10

Introduction	What the Story Is About/What the Lesson Is About
Story	The Lucid Eye in Silver Town
Lesson	Judgments and Conclusions: Discussing Stories
Activities	Comprehension Questions/Discussion Guides/Writing Exercise

Introduction

What the Story Is About

New York City has been called many things. It is the Big Apple, with something for everyone. With tongue in cheek, O. Henry, the famous short story writer, called it Baghdad-on-the-subway. Baghdad was a city of great wealth and beauty in the days of the Persian Empire. Author Washington Irving called it Gotham. He took this name from a town in England that is famous in folk tales as a place of fools. John Updike calls it Silver Town.

Jay August and his father come to New York for two reasons. They plan to visit Uncle Quin, father's worldly and well-to-do brother, and they want to buy a book about the work of the Dutch painter Vermeer. "The Vermeer book was my idea," Jay points out, "meeting Uncle Quin was my father's."

The time is 1945. World War II is drawing to a close. The Great Depression of the 1930s has disappeared for most people in the booming war years. But Jay's father is still finding things rough financially. All he has for the trip to New York City are the train tickets and five dollars that is suppose to be for the Vermeer book, if they can find one.

As they enter their teen years, boys tend to have mixed feelings about their fathers. This is very much the case with Jay. His father, Martin August, is a quiet, gentle, agreeable man. His problem seems to be that he has no self-confidence. He gives everyone else credit for being smarter than he is. This includes his wife, his son Jay, who gets perfect grades in school, and his brother Quin, who has become wealthy. Quin and Jay are "go-getters," according to the father. He is not. And this attitude infuriates Jay. He wishes his father would not be so hard on himself.

The story is not an exciting one. It is more a story that makes you think about life and about people. It contains more ideas than actions. Jay and his father go to see a rich man in a great city—Silver Town. Jay is growing up, and his father wants him to see something more of the world than the small town in which he lives. He wants to show him the city and introduce him to a man who has "accomplished" things in the world—his uncle Quin. It should be like a trip to fabulous Baghdad. But it does not turn out that way. *Why* it doesn't turn out well is what you should try to decide as you read the story.

Authors often write stories that contain facts and experiences from their own lives. There are many similarities between John Updike, the author of "The Lucid Eye in Silver Town," and Jay, the main character in the story. Like Jay, Updike comes from a small town in Pennsylvania. Jay is thirteen at the time of the story, which is 1945. John Updike was born in 1932, so he was also thirteen in 1945. Like Jay, Updike was a brilliant scholar and has an interest in art.

Updike has written many award-winning novels, short stories and poems. He is best known for his novels *Rabbit Run, Rabbit Redux,* and *Rabbit Is Rich.*

What the Lesson Is About

The lesson that follows the story is about making judgments and drawing conclusions about stories. In order to discuss a story, you must have made certain judgments and drawn certain conclusions about it. You have been doing this throughout this book and probably with every story you have ever read, for that matter.

In thinking about a story, you first decide whether or not you like the story. You should have reasons for the way you feel, of course. You think about the characters, about the settings and how they affect you, and about the meanings of the conflicts and the action in the story.

Then you assemble in your mind the many facts and details that the author has presented. From these facts and details you form ideas about the meaning of the story and its importance or value. These ideas are inferences that you make from the story. And from the inferences you form opinions—judgments and conclusions—about the characters and the action in the story, and about what the story has to say—the theme.

The following questions will help you to focus on making judgments and drawing conclusions as you read "The Lucid Eye in Silver Town."

1. The word *lucid* means very clear. It also means easily or clearly understood. A *lucid eye*, then, sees things clearly and with understanding. Does Jay in the story have a lucid eye? Does he see and understand everything clearly? Are there some things he does not see and does not understand?

2. Martin and Quin August are brothers. What details can you find in the story that help you form an opinion of the kinds of men the two brothers are?

3. Jay does not seem much impressed with his rich Uncle Quin. Why do you think Jay and Uncle Quin don't get along very well?

4. There is a scene in the story in which Martin August (Jay's father) is saying good-bye to his brother Quin. What can you conclude about the feelings between the two brothers at this point?

The Lucid Eye in Silver Town

John Updike

The first time I visited New York City, I was thirteen and went with my father. I went to meet my Uncle Quin and to buy a book about Vermeer. The Vermeer book was my idea, and my mother's; meeting Uncle Quin was my father's. A generation ago, my uncle had vanished in the direction of Chicago and become, apparently, rich; in the last week he had come east on business and I had graduated from the eighth grade with perfect marks. My father claimed that I and his brother were the smartest people he had ever met— "go-getters," he called us, with perhaps more irony than at the time I gave him credit for—and in his visionary way he suddenly, irresistibly felt that now was the time for us to meet. New York in those days was seven dollars away; we measured everything, distance and time, in money then. World War II was almost over but we were still living in the Depression. My father and I set off with the return tickets and a five-dollar bill in his pocket. The five dollars was for the book.

My mother, on the railway platform, suddenly exclaimed, "I *hate* the Augusts." This surprised me, because we were all Augusts—I was an August, my father was an August, Uncle Quincy was an August, and she, I had thought, was an August.

My father gazed serenely over her head and said, "You have every reason to. I wouldn't blame you if you took a gun and shot us all. Except for Quin and your son. They're the only ones of us ever had any get up and git." Nothing was more infuriating about my father than his way of agreeing.

Uncle Quin didn't meet us at Pennsylvania Station. If my father was disappointed, he didn't reveal it to me. It was after one o'clock and all we had for lunch were two candy bars. By walking what seemed to me a very long way on pavements only a little broader than those of my home town, and not so clean, we reached the hotel, which seemed to sprout somehow from Grand Central Station. The lobby smelled of perfume. After the clerk had phoned Quincy August that a man who said he was his brother was at the desk, an elevator took us to the twentieth floor. Inside the room sat three men, each in a gray or blue suit with freshly pressed pants and garters peeping from under the cuffs when they crossed their legs. The men were not quite interchangeable. One had a caterpillar-shaped moustache, one had tangled blond eyebrows like my father's, and the third had a drink in his hand—the others had drinks, too, but were not gripping them so tightly.

"Gentlemen, I'd like you to meet my brother Marty and his young son," Uncle Quin said.

"The kid's name is Jay," my father added, shaking hands with each of the two men, staring them in the eye. I imitated my father, and the moustached man, not expecting my firm handshake and stare, said, "Why, hello there, Jay!"

"Marty, would you and the boy like to freshen up? The facilities are through the door and to the left."

"Thank you, Quin. I believe we will. Excuse me, gentlemen."

"Certainly."

"Certainly."

My father and I went into the bedroom of the suite. The furniture was square and new and all the same shade of maroon. On the bed was an opened suitcase, also new. The clean, expensive smells of leather and lotion were beautiful to me. Uncle Quin's underwear looked silk and was full of fleurs-de-lis. When I was through in the lavatory, I made for the living room, to rejoin Uncle Quin and his friends.

"Hold it," my father said. "Let's wait in here."

"Won't that look rude?"

"No. It's what Quin wants."

"Now Daddy, don't be ridiculous. He'll think we've died in here."

"No he won't, not my brother. He's working some deal. He doesn't want to be bothered. I know how my brother works: he got us in here so we'd stay in here."

"*Really*, Pop. You're such a schemer." But I did not want to go in there without him. I looked around the room for something to read. There was nothing, not even a newspaper, except a shiny little pamphlet about the hotel itself. I wondered when we would get a chance to look for the Vermeer book. I wondered what the men in the next room were talking about. I wondered why Uncle Quin was so short, when my father was so tall. By leaning out of the window, I could see taxicabs maneuvering like windup toys.

My father came and stood beside me. "Don't lean out too far."

I edged out inches farther and took a big bite of the high, cold air, spiced by the distant street noises. "Look at the green cab cut in front of the yellow," I said. "Should they be making U-turns on that street?"

"In New York it's OK. Survival of the fittest is the only law here."

"Isn't that the Chrysler Building?"

"Yes, isn't it graceful though? It always reminds me of the queen of the chessboard."

"What's the one beside it?"

"I don't know. Some big gravestone. The one deep in back, from this window, is the Woolworth Building. For years it was the tallest building in the world."

As, side by side at the window, we talked, I was surprised that my father could answer so many of my questions. As a young man, before I was born, he had traveled, looking for work; this was not *his* first trip to New York. Excited by my new respect, I longed to say something to remold that calm, beaten face.

"Do you really think he meant for us to stay out here?" I asked.

"Quin is a go-getter," he said, gazing over my head. "I admire him. Anything he wanted, from little on up, he went after it. Slam. Bang. His thinking is miles ahead of mine— just like your mother's. You can feel them pull out ahead of you." He moved his hands, palms down, like two taxis, the left quickly pulling ahead of the right. "You're the same way."

"Sure, sure." My impatience was not merely embarrassment at being praised; I was irritated that he considered Uncle Quin as smart as myself. At that point in my life I was sure that only stupid people took an interest in money.

When Uncle Quin finally entered the bedroom, he said, "Martin, I hoped you and the boy would come out and join us."

"Hell, I didn't want to butt in. You and those men were talking business."

"Lucas and Roebuck and I? Now, Marty, it was nothing that my own brother couldn't hear. Just a minor matter of adjustment. Both these men are fine men. Very important in their own fields. I'm disappointed that you couldn't see more of them. Believe me, I hadn't meant for you to hide in here. Now what kind of drink would you like?"

"I don't care. I drink very little any more."

"Scotch-and-water, Marty?"

"Swell."

"And the boy? What about some ginger ale, young man? Or would you like milk?"

"The ginger ale," I said.

"There was a day, you know, when your father could drink any two men under the table."

As I remember it, a waiter brought the drinks to the room, and while we were drinking them I asked if we were going to spend all afternoon in this room. Uncle Quin didn't seem to hear, but five minutes later he suggested that the boy might like to take a look around the city—Gotham, he called it. Baghdad-on-the-Subway. My father said that that would be a once-in-a-lifetime treat for the kid. He always called me "the kid" when I was sick or had lost at something or was angry—when he felt sorry for me, in short. The three of us went down in the elevator and took a taxi ride down Broadway, or up Broadway—I wasn't sure. "This is what they call the Great White Way," Uncle Quin said several times. Once he apologized, "In daytime it's just another street." The trip didn't seem so much designed for sightseeing as for getting Uncle Quin to the Pickernut Club, a little restaurant set in a block of similar canopied places. I remember we stepped down into it and it was dark inside. A piano was playing *There's a Small Hotel*.

"He shouldn't do that," Uncle Quin said. Then he waved to the man behind the piano. "How are you, Freddie? How are the kids?"

"Fine, Mr. August, fine," Freddie said, bobbing his head and smiling and not missing a note.

"That's Quin's song," my father said to me as we wriggled our way into a dark curved seat at a round table.

I didn't say anything, but Uncle Quin, overhearing some disapproval in my silence, said, "Freddie's a first-rate man. He has a boy going to Colgate this autumn."

I asked, "Is that really your song?"

Uncle Quin grinned and put his warm broad hand on my shoulder; I hated, at that age, being touched. "I let them think it is," he said, oddly purring. "To me, songs are like young girls. They're all pretty."

A waiter in a red coat scurried up. "Mr. August! Back from the West? How are you, Mr. August?"

"Getting by, Jerome, getting by. Jerome, I'd like you to meet my kid brother, Martin."

"How do you do, Mr. Martin. Are you paying New York a visit? Or do you live here?"

My father quickly shook hands with Jerome, somewhat

to Jerome's surprise. "I'm just up for the afternoon, thank you. I live in a hick town in Pennsylvania you never heard of."

"I see, sir. A quick visit."

"This is the first time in six years that I've had a chance to see my brother."

"Yes, we've seen very little of him these past years. He's a man we can never see too much of, isn't that right?"

Uncle Quin interrupted. "This is my nephew Jay."

"How do you like the big city, Jay?"

"Fine." I didn't duplicate my father's mistake of offering to shake hands.

"Why, Jerome," Uncle Quin said. "My brother and I would like to have a Scotch-on-the-rocks. The boy would like a ginger ale."

"No, wait," I said. "What kinds of ice cream do you have?"

"Vanilla and chocolate, sir."

I hesitated. I could scarcely believe it, when the cheap drugstore at home had fifteen flavors.

"I'm afraid it's not a very big selection," Jerome said.

"I guess vanilla."

"Yes, sir. One plate of vanilla."

When my ice cream came it was a golf ball in a flat silver dish; it kept spinning away as I dug at it with my spoon. Uncle Quin watched me and asked, "Is there anything especially you'd like to do?"

"The kid'd like to get into a bookstore," my father said.

"A bookstore. What sort of book, Jay?"

I said, "I'd like to look for a good book of Vermeer."

"Vermeer," Uncle Quin pronounced slowly, relishing the r's, pretending to give the matter thought. "Dutch School."

"He's Dutch, yes."

"For my own money, Jay, the French are the people to beat. We have four Degas ballet dancers in our living room in Chicago, and I could sit and look at one of them for hours. I think it's wonderful, the feeling for balance the man had."

"Yeah, but don't Degas' paintings always remind you of

colored drawings? For actually *looking* at things in terms of paint, for the lucid eye, I think Vermeer makes Degas look sick."

Uncle Quin said nothing, and my father, after an anxious glance across the table, said, "That's the way he and his mother talk all the time. It's all beyond me. I can't understand a thing they say."

"Your mother is encouraging you to be a painter, is she, Jay?" Uncle Quin's smile was very wide and his cheeks were pushed out as if each held a candy.

"Sure, I suppose she is."

"Your mother is a very wonderful woman, Jay," Uncle Quin said.

It was such an embarrassing remark, and so much depended upon your definition of "wonderful," that I dug at my ice cream, and my father asked Uncle Quin about his own wife, Tessie. When we left, Uncle Quin signed the check with his name and the name of some company. It was close to five o'clock.

My uncle didn't know much about the location of bookstores in New York—his last fifteen years had been spent in Chicago—but he thought that if we went to Forty-second Street and Sixth Avenue we should find something. The cab driver let us out beside a park that acted as kind of a backyard for the Public Library. It looked so inviting, so agreeably dusty, with the pigeons and the men nodding on the benches and the office girls in their taut summer dresses, that without thinking, I led the two men into it. Shimmering buildings arrowed upward and glinted through the treetops. This was New York, I felt: the silver town. Towers of ambition rose, crystalline, within me. "If you stand here," my father said, "you can see the Empire State." I went and stood beneath my father's arm and followed with my eyes the direction of it. Something sharp and hard fell into my right eye. I ducked my head and blinked; it was painful.

"What's the trouble?" Uncle Quin's voice asked.

My father said, "The poor kid's got something into his eye. He has the worst luck that way of anybody I ever knew."

The thing seemed to have life. It bit. "Ow," I said, angry enough to cry.

"If we can get him out of the wind," my father's voice said, "maybe I can see it."

"No, now, Marty, use your head. Never fool with the eyes or ears. The hotel is within two blocks. Can you walk two blocks, Jay?"

"I'm blind, not lame," I snapped.

"He has a ready wit," Uncle Quin said.

Between the two men, shielding my eye with a hand, I walked to the hotel. From time to time, one of them would take my other hand, or put one of theirs on my shoulder, but I would walk faster, and the hands would drop away. I hoped our entrance into the hotel lobby would not be too conspicuous; I took my hand from my eye and walked erect, defying the impulse to stoop. Except for the one lid being shut and possibly my face being red, I imagined I looked passably suave. However, my guardians lost no time betraying me. Not only did they walk at my heels, as if I might topple any instant, but my father told one old bum sitting in the lobby, "Poor kid got something in his eye," and Uncle Quin, passing the desk, called, "Send up a doctor to Twenty-eleven."

"You shouldn't have done that, Quin," my father said in the elevator. "I can get it out, now that he's out of the wind. This is happening all the time. The kid's eyes are too far front."

"Never fool with the eyes, Martin. They are your most precious tool in life."

"It'll work out," I said, though I didn't believe it would. It felt like a steel chip, deeply embedded.

Up in the room, Uncle Quin made me lie down on the bed. My father, a clean handkerchief wadded in his hand so that one corner stuck out, approached me, but it hurt so much to open the eye that I repulsed him. "Don't torment me," I said, twisting my face away. "What good does it do? The doctor'll be up."

Regretfully my father put the handkerchief back into his pocket.

The doctor was a soft-handed man with little to say to anybody; he wasn't pretending to be the family doctor. He rolled my lower eyelid on a thin stick, jabbed with a Q-tip, and showed me, on the end of the Q-tip, an eyelash. He dropped three drops of yellow fluid into the eye to remove any chance of infection. The fluid stung, and I shut my eyes, leaning back into the pillow, glad it was over. When I opened them, my father was passing a bill into the doctor's hand. The doctor thanked him, winked at me, and left. Uncle Quin came out of the bathroom.

"Well, young man, how are you feeling now?" he asked.

"Fine."

"It was just an eyelash," my father said.

"*Just* an eyelash! Well I know how an eyelash can feel like a razor blade in there. But, now that the young invalid is recovered, we can think of dinner."

"No, I really appreciate your kindness, Quin, but we must be getting back to the sticks. I have an eight-o'clock meeting I should be at."

"I'm extremely sorry to hear that. What sort of meeting, Marty?"

"A church council."

"So you're still doing church work. Well, God bless you for it."

"Grace wanted me to ask you if you couldn't possibly come over some day. We'll put you up overnight. It would be a real treat for her to see you again."

Uncle Quin reached up and put his arm around his younger brother's shoulders. "Martin, I'd like that better than anything in the world. But I am solid with appointments, and I must head west this Thursday. They don't let me have a minute's repose. Nothing would please my heart better than to share a quiet day with you and Grace in your home. Please give her my love, and tell her what a wonderful boy she is raising. The two of you are raising."

My father promised, "I'll do that." And, after a little more fuss, we left.

"The child better?" the old man in the lobby called to us on the way out.

"It was just an eyelash, thank you, sir," my father said.

When we got outside, I wondered if there were any bookstores still open.

"We have no money."

"None at all?"

"The doctor charged five dollars. That's how much it costs in New York to get something in your eye."

"I didn't do it on purpose. Do you think I pulled out the eyelash and stuck it in there myself? I didn't tell you to call the doctor."

"I know that."

"Couldn't we just go into a bookstore and look a minute?"

"We haven't time, Jay."

But when we reached Pennsylvania Station, it was over thirty minutes until the next train left. As we sat on a bench, my father smiled reminiscently. "Boy, he's smart, isn't he? His thinking is sixty light-years ahead of mine."

"Whose?"

"My brother. Notice the way he hid in the bathroom until the doctor was gone? That's how to make money. The rich man collects dollar bills like the stamp collector collects stamps. I knew he'd do it. I knew it when he told the clerk to send up a doctor that I'd have to pay for it."

"Well, why *should* he pay for it? *You* were the person to pay for it."

"That's right. Why should he?" My father settled back, his eyes forward, his hands crossed and limp in his lap. The skin beneath his chin was loose; his temples seemed concave. The liquor was probably disagreeing with him. "That's why he's where he is now, and that's why I am where I am."

The seed of my anger seemed to be a desire to recall him to himself, to scold him out of being old and tired. "Well, why'd you bring along only five dollars? You might have known something would happen."

"You're right, Jay. I should have brought more."

"Look. Right over there is an open bookstore. Now if you had brought *ten* dollars——"

"Is it open? I don't think so. They just left the lights in the window on."

"What if it isn't? What does it matter to us? Anyway, what kind of art book can you get for five dollars? Color plates cost money. How much do you think a decent book of Vermeer costs? It'd be cheap at fifteen dollars, even secondhand, with the pages all crummy and full of spilled coffee." I kept on, shrilly flailing the passive and infuriating figure of my father, until we left the city. Once we were on the homeward train, my tantrum ended; it had been a kind of ritual, for both of us, and he had endured my screams complacently, nodding assent, like a midwife assisting at the birth of family pride. Years passed before I needed to go to New York again.

Judgments and Conclusions: Discussing Stories

No doubt you have had many discussions about the stories in this book by now. We hope you have enjoyed the discussions and that you have learned something from them. In this lesson you will be asked to think about some of the reasons *why* people discuss stories, and about *how* they go about discussing them. You will also learn how to make judgments about stories and how you can apply a story experience to your own life.

People discuss stories, novels, plays and movies for a number of reasons and in a number of ways. Teachers discuss stories with their students. Friends discuss stories with one another for pleasure. Newspaper writers discuss new books and movies for their readers by writing reviews. Scholars analyze stories for important ideas. Discussing stories is not just a school exercise. It's something you will do, something you will learn from, for the rest of your life.

A discussion is a search for answers to certain questions. Is the story enjoyable? Why did I like it? Is the author a skillful writer? Are the ideas behind the story interesting to think about? Are they of value? Do I agree with them? Why do the characters behave the way they do? There are many other questions that can be asked as well, as you have seen in other lessons.

Discussion takes stories beyond mere entertainment. It makes them a learning experience. Even if you only *think* about a story after reading it, you are, in a way, discussing it with yourself. You can compare the story experience with experiences in your own life. You can make judgments. You can come to conclusions. And in this way you can learn something new from each story you read.

People who read a great deal and who try to learn from what they read are usually successful people. But they don't *just* read. They think about what they read and they decide how the ideas they find in their reading fit into the general scheme of life.

In this lesson, you will look at one good way to think about a story and discuss it. It consists of these four steps:

1 Putting yourself in the story situation.

2 Putting facts and details together.

3 Discussing the story.

4 Making judgments and drawing conclusions.

A story is an experience. It is something that happens to you in your mind, through reading. So, just as you think about experiences that happen in real life, you can also think about the experience of a story.

Putting Yourself in the Story Situation

But before the story can become an experience for you, you must place yourself within the story situation. You may recall that in earlier lessons this was referred to as "sharing" in the story. You share in a story with the help of the author's skill and your own imagination. By way of review, here's what happens:

Setting. You "see" in your mind's eye where the story takes place. You can understand what it feels like to be in the situation that the author describes.

Characters. You picture what the characters must look like. You understand how the characters feel. You identify with the main character of the story.

Plot. You feel involved in the situation, then in the conflict and the action. Your feelings deepen as the conflict grows. You feel excitement, sorrow, tension, or relief. You feel whatever the author wants you to feel.

Having shared in the experience of the story, you can think about it and talk about it. The first thing you are likely to discuss is the "sense of being there." This is very much a matter of *feeling*. How does the setting make you feel? How do you feel about the characters? And how does the action make you feel? Try discussing your feelings about this passage from "The Lucid Eye in Silver Town."

Uncle Quin didn't meet us at Pennsylvania Station. If my father was disappointed, he didn't reveal it to me. It was after one o'clock and all we had for lunch were two candy bars. By walking what seemed to me a very long way on pavements only a little broader than those of my home town, and not so clean, we reached the hotel, which seemed to sprout somehow from Grand Central Station. The lobby smelled of perfume. After the clerk had phoned Quincy August that a man who said he was his brother was at the desk, an elevator took us to the twentieth floor. Inside the room sat three men, each in a gray or blue suit with freshly pressed pants and garters peeping from under the cuffs when they crossed their legs. The men were not quite interchangeable.

Jay is seeing New York City for the first time. It is a new experience for him. And, through him, it becomes a new experience for the reader. To begin a discussion of the story, you can ask yourself these questions:

How do you feel about the big city and the hotel as Jay describes them?   (Setting)

How does the author make you feel about the father, the hotel clerk, and the men in the room?   (Characters)

How does the action of the story make you feel at this point?   (Plot)

Not everyone will have the same answers to these questions. Each reader will feel somewhat different. This is what makes a discussion. Here is one way of looking at the passage:

Setting. The streets are not much wider than those at home, and they're not as clean. Jay's tone suggests that he is not very impressed by the big city. Because Jay is the main character, you tend to see things and feel about them as he does. You may change your mind later, as you get to know Jay better, but at this point you are led to feel that perhaps New York City is not so great after all. The hotel smells of perfume. Jay doesn't comment further on this. It is a detail that draws you closer to the story because it involves another one of your senses—your sense of smell.

Characters. Jay is no more impressed with the people than he is with the city. He has not given us a very flattering view of his father. The hotel clerk is rude. (The clerk reports to Uncle Quin "that a man who *said* he was his brother was at the desk." His tone rudely suggests that Jay's father couldn't possibly be Quin's brother.)

The men in the room, including Uncle Quin, are "not quite interchangeable." This means that they look very much alike: they are all wearing suits that are similar, and they all wear garters to hold up their socks. (It was fashionable for well-dressed men to wear garters in the 1940s.)

So far, Jay has expressed disapproval of everyone. The only one he has had a good word for, in fact, is himself. He let you know early in the story that his father thinks he is a "go-getter" and that he has graduated from eighth grade with perfect marks. This presents something of a problem for a reader. You want to sympathize with Jay's feelings because he is the main character—you want to identify with him—but at the same time you may wonder whether or not you really like a boy who seems to have nothing good to say about anyone or anything.

Plot and Action. One of the best ways to become involved in the action of a story is to try to imagine yourself in the same situation as the main character. To do this, stop and ask yourself, "What is the situation?" Then summarize what has happened so far, *placing yourself* in the role of one of the characters. For example, what is going on in this passage, from Jay's point of view? If you were to think of yourself as Jay, your thoughts might go something like this:

> I am a thirteen-year-old boy who has just arrived in New York with my father. No one has come to meet us at the station. We are apparently going to meet my uncle, whom I don't know, *before* we look for the book I want to buy. It is past lunchtime and all we have had to eat are candy bars. After a long walk we arrive at a large hotel. I meet three well-dressed strangers. One is my Uncle Quin. I know my father wants me to be impressed by all this, but I'm not. I think I see things as they really are. To me the city is dirty, the hotel looks grotesque—it seems "to sprout somehow from Grand Central Station"—and the men are all alike. I am not impressed by their well-tailored suits.

Now stand back from the situation again and ask yourself, "Is this how I would react to a similar situation?" Whether the answer is yes or no, you will have opened the door to many more questions about what is taking place in the story. They are the same questions that come to mind when you are involved in a situation in real life.

Why does Jay behave the way he does? Why does he see things as he does? Is his view of the world and the people around him a correct view? Or is his view of the world slanted or prejudiced in some way?

How you answer these questions depends on several things. It depends on the kind of person you are yourself. It depends on whether or not you have had experiences that are similar to those in the story—traveling to a strange place, meeting new people. And it depends on how much the author of the story has affected your thinking through his artistry—by the way in which he has painted the scene and the characters with words.

There are usually no pat answers to questions raised by a story. Neither are there pat answers to many real-life situations. There are only options—choices. But by thinking carefully about a situation and the ideas presented in a story, you enable yourself to see the choices that are available. And, from the choices, you try to choose the answers that you think are correct. This is making judgments and drawing conclusions. It is forming an opinion.

Exercise A

Read the following passage and answer the questions about it using what you have learned in this part of the lesson.

My father and I went into the bedroom of the suite. The furniture was square and new and all the same shade of maroon. On the bed was an opened suitcase, also new. The clean, expensive smells of leather and lotion were beautiful to me. Uncle Quin's underwear looked silk and was full of fleurs-de-lis. When I was through in the lavatory, I made for the living room, to rejoin Uncle Quin and his friends.

"Hold it," my father said. "Let's wait in here."

"Won't that look rude?"

"No. It's what Quin wants."

"Now Daddy, don't be ridiculous. He'll think we've died in here."

"No he won't, not my brother. He's working some deal. He doesn't want to be bothered. I know how my brother works: he got us in here so we'd stay in here."

"*Really*, Pop. You're such a schemer." But I did not want to go in there without him. I looked around the room for something to read. There was nothing, not even a newspaper, except a shiny little pamphlet about the hotel itself.

Put an *x* in the box beside the correct answer.

1. Imagine you are Jay's father. You have come to meet your brother, whom you haven't seen in years. He is wealthy while you are poor. He is talking with two men, and you think he is working on an important business deal. You decide to stay in the bedroom, out of the way. Which one of the following reasons might best explain your decision not to go back in the living room where the businessmen are?

   ☐ a. You are afraid of your brother and of the men.

   ☐ b. You are nervous and uncertain about how to act and about what is expected of you, and you think you are being tactful.

   ☐ c. You are hostile and don't want anything to do with your brother and his friends.

   ☐ d. You have no interest in your brother's wheeling and dealing, so you just stay out of the scene.

2. The author helps you to place yourself in the story situation by reporting the sights and smells that the characters encounter. Jay sees things clearly and vividly (lucidly). On the lines below, list at least one sight and one smell described in the passage that help you to see things and feel about them as Jay does.

   _____

   _____

   _____

Now check your answers using the Answer Key on page 460. Correct any wrong answers and review this part of the lesson if you don't understand why an answer was wrong.

2 Putting Facts and Details Together— Making Inferences

When you have a new experience, the first thing you do is size up the situation. There are many things you need to know, among them: What am I dealing with? Am I safe? Are the people to be trusted? Will I be happy here? Will I be bored? Will trouble develop later? How must I act?

You pick up the information you need to answer these questions from both large and small details. Imagine, for example, that you arrive at a party where you don't know anyone very well. You are greeted at the door by the host. He takes you inside, offers you something to eat, and introduces you to several friendly people who include you in their conversation. There is music playing and people are dancing and laughing. "Nice crowd," you conclude. "I think I'm going to have a good time."

You have put all the facts and details together and made a judgment. Your reasoning told you what the details meant. You *inferred* certain meanings from what you saw, based on your knowledge and experience. Inferences are based on the facts and details you have before you. Making inferences is like being a detective. You make certain judgments and conclusions based on clues you have gathered.

You do the same thing when you read. It doesn't matter if it is a story, a newspaper article or a passage in a history textbook. It all works the same way. In "The Lucid Eye in Silver Town" you make inferences about father and Uncle Quin from facts and details provided by the author. Putting clues and impressions together, you also form ideas about Jay. The author has carefully chosen the facts and details that he has included in the story in order to lead you to certain conclusions about the characters in the story and to communicate particular ideas to you. At some point in your reading, you naturally begin to wonder what the author is trying to tell you through the story. Once again, you examine the facts and details in order to make a decision.

In the story, the author is describing the meeting of three people—Jay, Martin August and Quin August. Jay is the one with the *lucid eye*. He is the one for whom details of setting stand out clearly and sharply, like the details in a Vermeer painting. The author calls your attention to this in the way Jay notices details: it is Jay who describes to us the way the men in the hotel room hold their glasses and how their sock garters show. He describes how the city looks from the hotel window, how the buildings "arrowed upward and glinted through the treetops. This was

New York," he says, "the silver town." Another detail that allows us to infer that Jay is the one with the lucid eye is that later in the story, when discussing art with his uncle, he says, "For actually *looking* at things in terms of paint, for the lucid eye, I think Vermeer makes Degas look sick."

But is Jay's eye quite so lucid when it comes to understanding people? Is he as good at seeing and understanding the differences between himself, his father and his Uncle Quin as he is at seeing the differences between a Degas and a Vermeer painting, or at seeing things? This is one of the things you may want to decide from evidence contained in other details in the story.

You base most of your thinking and your discussions about a story on the inferences you are able to make. Making inferences is "reading between the lines." You make an inference when you understand something that has been implied, or hinted at, but not stated directly. You look at facts that are given or at the actions of characters, and you judge their meanings or significances. What inferences can you make about each of the characters from the details in this passage?

> [Jay asks his father about staying in the bedroom]
> "Do you really think he meant for us to stay out here?" I asked.
>
> "Quin is a go-getter," he said, gazing over my head. "I admire him. Anything he wanted, from little on up, he went after it. Slam. Bang. His thinking is miles ahead of mine— just like your mother's. You can feel them pull out ahead of you." . . .
>
> When Uncle Quin finally entered the bedroom, he said, "Martin, I hoped you and the boy would come out and join us."
>
> "Hell, I didn't want to butt in. You and those men were talking business."
>
> "Lucas and Roebuck and I? Now, Marty, it was nothing that my own brother couldn't hear."

You may infer from Jay's question that he doubts his father's judgment. "Do you really think he meant for us to stay out here?" he asks.

Why, you must ask yourself, does father insist on hiding in the bedroom? You will probably conclude that he is timid or that he feels inferior. That being the case, why is he that way? Did Uncle Quin really mean for them to stay in the bedroom, or was he just politely inviting them to refresh themselves, as a good host usually does? Is Jay seeing Uncle Quin and the situation clearly, while his father is allowing his own feelings of inadequacy to interfere with clear judgment? Perhaps other clues in the story will answer these questions. Perhaps not. They are interesting ideas to think about and discuss.

Now see what inferences you can make from the details provided in the passage in Exercise B.

Exercise B

Read the following passage and answer the questions about it using what you have learned in this part of the lesson.

A waiter in a red coat scurried up. "Mr. August! Back from the West? How are you, Mr. August?"

"Getting by, Jerome, getting by. Jerome, I'd like you to meet my kid brother, Martin."

"How do you do, Mr. Martin. Are you paying New York a visit? Or do you live here?"

My father quickly shook hands with Jerome, somewhat to Jerome's surprise. "I'm just up for the afternoon, thank you. I live in a hick town in Pennsylvania you never heard of."

"I see, sir. A quick visit." . . .

Uncle Quin interrupted. "This is my nephew Jay."

"How do you like the big city, Jay?"

"Fine." I didn't duplicate my father's mistake of offering to shake hands.

Put an *x* in the box beside the correct answer.

1. Quin is addressed as Mr. August. Father is called Mr. Martin. The waiter is called Jerome, and Jay is called simply Jay. What can you infer from these little details about the way in which the characters address one another?

   ☐ a. There is a social order here. Some people rate more respect than others.

   ☐ b. Even though this is an expensive restaurant, the atmosphere is easy and informal.

□ c. Uncle Quin is a person whom everyone admires and respects.

□ d. Everyone in this restaurant is addressed in a formal manner.

2. If you examine all the facts and details in this passage, you may infer that Jay is more aware of what is considered "correct" in this restaurant than his father is. What small actions by father and Jay show this?

_____

_____

_____

Now check your answers using the Answer Key on page 460. Correct any wrong answers and review this part of the lesson if you don't understand why an answer was wrong.

Discussing Stories

3 Discussing the Story

Very often when a teacher says, "Now let's discuss the story you have just read," there is a deadly silence. People who can ordinarily talk for hours suddenly find their mouths zippered shut. If you are one of these people who have a hard time thinking about how to talk about a story, try thinking of the story as an experience you have just had. Then talk about it as you would talk about anything else that has happened to you. If you have read the story carefully, you have all the facts at hand. You "know" the people in the story and what has happened to them.

The easiest way to start a discussion is to say whether or not you liked the story. This is as simple as answering the question, Did you have a good time? when you return from a trip. Then you can go on to discuss specific things about the story. Read the following list to see the kinds of things you can discuss about any story.

Did you like the story? Start with the overall impression you got from the story. What did you like about it? What didn't you like? Were you able to get involved in the story experience? *Always try to give a reason for your opinion.* Include your reasons for liking or disliking certain characters, settings, actions or the author's style of writing.

Discuss the conflicts and actions. What happens in the story? What is the main thing that is going on? How do the characters respond to what happens in the story? What are the major problems that they must face?

Discuss the characters. The people—the characters—are the most interesting element of any story, just as people are the most interesting element in life. Discussing characters can be fascinating. It is like discussing different kinds of personalities that you may meet. What do you think of the characters? Whom do you like or dislike? WHY do you feel the way you do about the characters?

Discuss the ideas presented in the story. As you discuss the characters, actions and conflicts, you will naturally start talking about the ideas that are found in the story, for actions cannot take place without ideas to base them on. In "The Lucid Eye in Silver Town," for example, what is the relationship between Jay and his father? How do they feel toward each other? What makes Jay so sour at times, and so arrogant? Why does the father accept all of Jay's outbursts so calmly? Why do you think John Updike titled the story "The Lucid Eye in Silver Town"? Does Jay see things entirely clearly at the time in which the story takes place, or does he see the whole incident more clearly when he looks back on it as an adult, which is when he is telling the story of his trip to New York? (The narrator of the story, as you may have noticed, is an older Jay looking back on his first visit to New York City. Does he see the incident more clearly, now that he is mature, than he did as a rather selfish young boy?)

Apply the story experience to your own life. Talk about the story in terms of its relationship to real life. What have you learned from this experience that you have shared with Martin, Quin and Jay August? Can the ideas in the story be applied to situations you might encounter in your own life? Do they compare in any way with situations you yourself have already encountered?

Present your judgments and conclusions. By this point you have discussed the story in great detail. You are ready to sum up, or draw conclusions. Ask yourself again, "Did I like the story?" When you began your discussion with this question, the answer you gave was probably not much more than a *feeling* you had for the story. Now, after thinking about the story carefully and in detail, you can give what is known as an *informed* opinion—an opinion based on knowledge and thought. You have made judgments and come to certain conclusions.

Let's apply some of these discussion elements to the following passage:

> . . . I asked if we were going to spend all afternoon in this room. Uncle Quin didn't seem to hear, but five minutes later he suggested that the boy might like to take a look around the city. . . . My father said that that would be a once-in-a-lifetime treat for the kid. He always called me "the kid" when I was sick or had lost at something or was angry— when he felt sorry for me, in short. The three of us went down in the elevator and took a taxi ride down Broadway, or up Broadway—I wasn't sure. "This is what they call the Great White Way," Uncle Quin said several times. Once he apologized, "In daytime it's just another street." The trip didn't seem so much designed for sightseeing as for getting

Uncle Quin to the Pickernut Club, a little restaurant set in a
block of similar canopied places. I remember we stepped
down into it and it was dark inside. A piano was playing
There's a Small Hotel.

"He shouldn't do that," Uncle Quin said. Then he waved
to the man behind the piano. . . .

"That's Quin's song," my father said to me as we wriggled
our way into a dark curved seat at a round table.

I didn't say anything, but Uncle Quin, overhearing some
disapproval in my silence, said, "Freddie's a first-rate man."

The conflict and action. Jay bluntly suggests that they are spending
too much time in the hotel room. So, Uncle Quin suggests "a look around
the city." The "look around" turns out to be a taxi ride to the Pickernut
Club, a restaurant where Uncle Quin is well known, for more drinking—
just what they had been doing in the hotel room. As they enter, they are
greeted by the piano player playing Quin's favorite song for him.

In this scene the characters seem uncomfortable together. Put yourself in the place of each of the characters in turn. How would *you* feel in
this situation? How would you act?

Jay seems to be in conflict with his uncle. He doesn't like the way he
acts, the fact that he has taken them to this restaurant instead for a
real sightseeing trip.

The characters. Uncle Quin tries to take charge, because he is the
host. He tries to act worldly and knowledgeable about the city. Jay's
father is passive and agreeable to any suggestions, as usual. He calls
Jay "the kid," something Jay says he does when he is feeling sorry for
him. So, he must be feeling sorry for Jay. Why? Jay is bored and impatient. He wants to see something of the city. He is not impressed by
his uncle, as we can infer from the "disapproval" in his silence when
his father comments that the piano player is playing Quin's song.

Uncle Quin and father seem to want to please each other and Jay.
But they don't quite know how to go about it. Uncle Quin, after all, is
really a stranger to Jay and his father. None of them appear to have
much in common. Their interests are very different. For his part, Jay
seems determined not to be pleased by anything his father and Quin
want to do. He wants to look for a book, and that keeps being put off.

Is Jay being too sour and too critical of the adults? Is his father being
too agreeable, too passive, once again? There are several possibilities
that you might consider. Is Uncle Quin trying to show off a bit, to

impress Jay and his father? Or does he truly think that he is enter-taining his guests? Perhaps Quin just doesn't quite know what to do with his brother and Jay, and he's doing the best that he can in a bad situation.

The ideas. The author wants you to think about the uncomfortable situation in which these three characters have placed themselves. People often act in strange ways when they are trying to be sociable. This is especially true when the people involved are strangers to one another or have nothing in common. How *should* people act in such situations? What would be the consequences if everyone were to express his true feelings, as Jay does? What happens when people hide their feelings, as father does? And what about the man who is somewhere in the middle, as Uncle Quin is?

Applying the story experience. As you place yourself in the story situation, you are, in a very real way, undergoing an experience in life yourself. The situation in which the characters in the story find them-selves is a very common one. By experiencing the situation through a story, you can learn from it without being hurt by it.

What *do* you learn from the experiences of these three people?

Judgments and conclusions. When you discuss the actions, the characters and the ideas in the story, you naturally make judgments. Your judgments are based on evidence you find in the story and on your thoughts about this evidence. You also make judgments based on the ideas that you hear others express in the discussion process.

The various judgments you make are resolutions to the questions that have been raised by the story. You decide, from all the choices that are possible, what you think and how you feel about the story as a whole, the individual characters, the actions and the ideas that have been presented. These are your conclusions. Other people may approach the story from different personal experiences, from a different point of view, and may come to different conclusions.

You may come to several conclusions. Decisions about stories, like decisions about people in real life, are not always cut and dried. They are not always clearly one way or the other. Characters can have a number of different aspects to their personalities, just as people do. You may like some things about them and dislike others. You may conclude that a situation may be looked at in more than one way, just as you can in real-life situations. Answers are not always clearly given, in stories or in life.

Exercise C

Read the following passage and answer the questions about it using what you have learned in this part of the lesson.

As we sat on a bench, my father smiled reminiscently.

"Boy, he's smart, isn't he? His thinking is sixty light-years ahead of mine."

"Whose?"

"My brother. Notice the way he hid in the bathroom until the doctor was gone? That's how to make money. The rich man collects dollar bills like the stamp collector collects stamps. I knew he'd do it. I knew it when he told the clerk to send up a doctor that I'd have to pay for it."

"Well, why *should* he pay for it? *You* were the person to pay for it."

"That's right. Why should he?" My father settled back, his eyes forward, his hands crossed and limp in his lap. The skin beneath his chin was loose; his temples seemed concave. The liquor was probably disagreeing with him. "That's why he's where he is now, and that's why I am where I am."

The seed of my anger seemed to be a desire to recall him to himself, to scold him out of being old and tired. "Well, why'd you bring along only five dollars? You might have known something would happen."

"You're right, Jay. I should have brought more."

Put an *x* in the box beside the correct answer.

1. Which one of the following expressions best represents the main aspect of father's thinking?

   ☐ a. If I try harder, I'll succeed.

   ☐ b. Someday I'll be like my brother Quin.

   ☐ c. Everyone else is brighter and quicker than I am.

   ☐ d. It doesn't pay to be kind or thoughtful.

2. Father appears to be trying to teach Jay that it was smart of Quin to avoid paying the doctor by ducking into the bathroom. What does Jay say that shows that he doesn't agree with his father's thinking?

_____

_____

_____

Now check your answers using the Answer Key on page 460. Correct any wrong answers and review this part of the lesson if you don't understand why an answer was wrong.

4 Making Judgments and Drawing Conclusions

"Judgments" and "conclusions" are words that tend to make reading sound very technical. Don't let the words give you that impression. As we have said, you make judgments and conclusions all the time. It is a mental process that goes on every minute of your life. It is as automatic as breathing. When you see a tree in your path, you conclude that you must walk around it. When you look at the time on your watch, you judge how much time you have to get to school. You put arithmetic facts together and conclude the right answer. You taste a new food and judge whether you like it or not. You then decide, or conclude, whether or not you will eat it.

The more experience you have in life, the better your judgments and conclusions become. This is because experiences give you more facts on which to base your judgments. This is the main purpose of education. It gives you information you need to make good judgments and sound conclusions in new situations as they come along. Reading provides you with information and introduces you to experiences that you couldn't, or wouldn't want to, get any other way. And these experiences help you in making decisions in your life.

Making judgments and drawing conclusions are not really "steps" you take in reading a story; you do these things both *as* you read and *after* you have finished reading. You made a judgment and came to a conclusion every time you answered a question in this book or in a class discussion. You can't talk about setting without judging where it is or what time a scene or story is placed in. You can't talk about characters without making judgments about them. Upon completing a story, you can look back at all the facts and details you have read and make judgments about the story as a whole. You can decide, or conclude, whether or not the story was a good one, as far as you are concerned.

The social situation presented in "The Lucid Eye in Silver Town" is a very common one. People often find themselves in uncomfortable situations, where they don't really know what is expected of them and they have little in common with the people they are with. And everyone goes through a time when he or she stops seeing things as a child and begins to see the world in a different way, as Jay does in this story. He is seeing a different part of the world from the one in which he has been brought up, and he is seeing his father from a new perspective. He may be comparing him with his uncle, who is at home with the ways of the city. You will undoubtedly find yourself in a similar social situation someday, if you haven't already. This "universality" is what makes the story an enduring one—one that people in different places and different times can understand and share in. Perhaps after reading this story you will better understand this kind of situation when you find yourself in it.

What judgments and conclusions can you make from this passage in the story:

> "But, now that the young invalid is recovered, we can think of dinner."
>
> "No, I really appreciate your kindness, Quin, but we must be getting back to the sticks. I have an eight-o'clock meeting I should be at."
>
> "I'm extremely sorry to hear that. What sort of meeting, Marty?"
>
> "A church council."
>
> "So you're still doing church work. Well, God bless you for it."
>
> "Grace wanted me to ask you if you couldn't possibly come over some day. We'll put you up overnight. It would be a real treat for her to see you again."
>
> Uncle Quin reached up and put his arm around his younger brother's shoulders. "Martin, I'd like that better than anything in the world. But I am solid with appointments, and I must head west this Thursday. They don't let me have a minute's repose. Nothing would please my heart better than to share a quiet day with you and Grace in your home. Please give her my love, and tell her what a wonderful boy she is raising. The two of you are raising."

What we have in this scene is people making polite excuses to one another. If father really wanted to have dinner with Quin, his "meeting" wouldn't matter, he would skip it. So, you can conclude that father wants to leave. In the same way, you may conclude that Quin could very well visit his brother's home if he wanted to. He is a successful businessman who can most likely take time off whenever he wants to. But he really doesn't want to make the visit. "I'd like that better than anything in the world," he says. "Nothing would please my heart better than to share a quiet day with you and Grace in your home." This is just the kind of talk that people use when they are being polite to each other but not saying what they honestly mean. You can conclude that Quin is as uncomfortable as everyone else with this visit and is glad to see it end.

Does this kind of falseness apply to your life? Of course it does. People are always saying things they don't mean, in order to be polite. It's sometimes good to know how to do this yourself. And it's good to be able to judge the truth behind someone else's "socially acceptable" white lies.

Exercise D

Read the following passage and answer the questions about it using what you have learned in this part of the lesson.

"Look. Right over there is an open bookstore. Now if you had brought *ten* dollars— —"

"Is it open? I don't think so. They just left the lights in the window on."

"What if it isn't? What does it matter to us? Anyway, what kind of art book can you get for five dollars? Color plates cost money. How much do you think a decent book of Vermeer costs? It'd be cheap at fifteen dollars, even secondhand, with the pages all crummy and full of spilled coffee." I kept on, shrilly flailing the passive and infuriating figure of my father, until we left the city. Once we were on the homeward train, my tantrum ended; it had been a kind of ritual, for both of us, and he had endured my screams complacently, nodding assent, like a midwife assisting at the birth of family pride. Years passed before I needed to go to New York again.

Put an *x* in the box beside the correct answer.

1. Here, and in several other places in the story, Jay tells you why he gets so angry with his father. It is because his father is so

   ☐ a. passive.

   ☐ b. impulsive.

   ☐ c. impatient.

   ☐ d. unintelligent.

2. What remark leads you to understand that Jay learned an important lesson on this visit to "Silver Town," a lesson that stayed with him for a long time? Write the sentence on the lines below.

   _____

   _____

Use the Answer Key on page 460 to check your answers. Correct any wrong answers and review this part of the lesson if you don't understand why an answer was wrong. Now go on to do the Comprehension Questions.

Comprehension Questions

Answer these questions without looking back at the story. Choose the best answer to each question and put an x in the box beside it.

Recalling
Facts

1. Which one of the following statements best describes the financial condition of Jay's family?

   ☐ a. They were fairly well-off.

   ☐ b. They had to make every dollar count.

   ☐ c. They lived in extreme poverty.

   ☐ d. They had a lot of money but wouldn't spend it.

Keeping
Events in
Order

2. At what point in the story does Jay feel a new respect for his father?

   ☐ a. When Jay and his father lean out the hotel window together and talk about New York.

   ☐ b. When his father shakes hands with the waiter.

   ☐ c. When his father tries to examine his eye.

   ☐ d. When his father pays the doctor.

Understanding
Main Ideas

3. Which one of the following quotations represents Jay's strongest feelings toward his father in this story?

   ☐ a. "*Really*, Pop. You're such a schemer."

   ☐ b. "I *hate* the Augusts."

   ☐ c. "Don't torment me. . . . What good does it do? The doctor'll be up."

   ☐ d. " . . . I longed to say something to remold that calm, beaten face."

4. **Martin August thinks his brother Quin is smart. He says to Jay, "You're the same way." What does Jay think?**

☐ a. Jay thinks he is smarter than Uncle Quin.

☐ b. Jay agrees with his father on this point.

☐ c. Jay thinks Uncle Quin is smarter.

☐ d. Jay thinks his father is the smartest one of all.

5. **In the hotel room, Quin orders drinks for himself, his brother and Jay. He again orders for all of them in the restaurant, ordering a ginger ale for Jay. Jay says, "No, wait," and he orders ice cream instead. Why does he do this?**

☐ a. He wants to see what the waiter will say.

☐ b. He wants to be like his father.

☐ c. He wants to get ice cream in a silver dish.

☐ d. He wants to do his own ordering.

6. **We don't see much of Jay's mother. But what we do know suggests that she**

☐ a. is happy and content with her life.

☐ b. hopes Jay will be just like his father.

☐ c. encourages her son to "make something of himself."

☐ d. feels a little bit in awe of her husband's family.

7. **When does Jay get the chance to look for a bookstore?**

☐ a. As soon as he and his father arrive in New York

☐ b. Right after Quin's business meeting is over

☐ c. After leaving the Pickernut Club

☐ d. While he and his father wait for the train home

8. There are only two brief happy moments in this story. They both involve Jay and seem to relate to the same thing. What is the one thing that makes Jay happy on this visit?

☐ a. Meeting the people of New York

☐ b. Eating at fine restaurants in New York

☐ c. Looking at the buildings of New York

☐ d. Riding through New York in taxi cabs

9. At one point in the story, New York truly seems like a silver town to Jay. Which one of the following excerpts from the story marks that time?

☐ a. "My father and I set off with the return tickets and a five-dollar bill in his pocket. The five dollars was for the book."

☐ b. "Shimmering buildings arrowed upward and glinted through the treetops. . . . Towers of ambition rose, crystalline, within me."

☐ c. "By walking . . . on pavements only a little broader than those of my home town . . . we reached the hotel, which seemed to sprout somehow from Grand Central Station."

☐ d. "On the bed was an opened suitcase, also new. The clean, expensive smells of leather and lotion were beautiful to me."

10. What happened to Jay as he gazed at the Empire State Building?

☐ a. Uncle Quin said, "This is known as Gotham."

☐ b. His father said they had to leave.

☐ c. His uncle spotted a bookstore.

☐ d. Something fell in his eye.

11. Returning to the hotel, Jay did not want to be *con-spicuous*. In other words, he didn't want to be

   ☐ a. heard.

   ☐ b. helped.

   ☐ c. noticed.

   ☐ d. forced.

12. As Jay entered the hotel, with his face red and one eye closed, he tried to look *suave*. *Suave* means

   ☐ a. smooth and cool.

   ☐ b. aggressive and in charge.

   ☐ c. pitiful and suffering.

   ☐ d. handsome and attractive.

13. Who ordered the doctor?

   ☐ a. Martin

   ☐ b. Quin

   ☐ c. Jay

   ☐ d. The hotel clerk

14. Who paid for the doctor?

   ☐ a. Martin

   ☐ b. Quin

   ☐ c. Jay

   ☐ d. The hotel clerk

15. Waiting in the railroad station, Jay kept on *"shrilly flailing"* his father. In other words, Jay was

☐ a. waving his arms about, which embarrassed his father.

☐ b. arguing with his father, who couldn't stand being argued with.

☐ c. screaming at his father in a high-pitched voice, as though beating him.

☐ d. crying because of his disappointment, and this hurt his father.

Now check your answers using the Answer Key on page 460. Make no mark for right answers. <u>Correct</u> any wrong answers you may have by putting a checkmark (✓) in the box next to the right answer. Count the number of questions you answered correctly and plot the total on the Comprehension Scores graph on page 462.

Next, look at the questions you answered incorrectly. What types of questions were they? Count the number you got wrong of each type and enter the numbers in the spaces below.

Recognizing Words in Context   _____

Recalling Facts   _____

Keeping Events in Order   _____

Making Inferences   _____

Understanding Main Ideas   _____

Now use these numbers to fill in the Comprehension Skills Profile on page 463.

Discussion Guides

The questions below will help you to think about the story and the lesson you have just read. If you don't discuss these questions in class, try to think about them or discuss them with your classmates.

Making Judgments and Drawing Conclusions

1. What can you infer about Uncle Quin's drinking habits? Use facts and details from the story to support your inference.

2. At the beginning of the story, mother surprised Jay by saying, "I *hate* the Augusts." Now that you have become acquainted with three of the Augusts, why do you think she said this?

3. What are Jay's feelings toward his father? Find details in the story to support your conclusions.

Discussing the Story

4. The story takes place in New York City in about 1945. Why does the story have meaning for you, even though it is a later time and you may never have been to New York?

5. Once Jay says of his father, "I longed to say something to remold that calm, beaten face." Another time he says he had "a desire to recall him to himself, to scold him out of being old and tired." But Jay never did say anything to help his father. Why not, do you think?

6. The story ends with Jay screaming in anger at his father in the train station. Then the older Jay, the narrator who is looking back, says, "it had been a kind of ritual, for both of us." Then he calls it "the birth of family pride." What do you think he meant by these remarks?

Discussing the Author's Work

7. In the story, Jay is thirteen. The narrator—the person telling the story—is an older Jay. How do you think this fact affects the reader's view of the incidents described in the story? How would the story have been different if Jay had been telling the story just after it happened? What comments and observations that are in the story could not, or probably would not, have been included?

8. The author lets you know that Jay is a very bright thirteen-year-old. How does he do this?

9. John Updike is a very well-known author, so his work has been discussed by many people. These people formed their opinions of Updike's work in much the same way you formed your opinions in working with "The Lucid Eye in Silver Town."

See what has been said about John Updike in *Contemporary Authors* (new revision series, Volume 4). This is a reference book that is like an encyclopedia, with discussions of hundreds of modern writers. Most medium-sized and larger libraries have these volumes. Ask the librarian for help.

How do your opinions of John Updike's work compare to those in *Contemporary Authors*?

Writing Exercise

In fifty words or less, complete each of the following statements about "The Lucid Eye in Silver Town." (You must use *at least* twenty-five words.)

Explain the Conflicts and Actions

1. The story is about a boy named Jay who . . .

2. The story is about Martin August who . . .

3. The story is about Quin August who . . .

Explain Your Feelings

Fill in each blank with the feeling you had for the character and then complete the statement, as you did the ones on the left.

4. The feeling I had for Jay was _____

_____ because . . .

5. The feeling I had for Martin August was _____

_____ because . . .

6. The feeling I had for Quin August was _____

_____ because . . .

Answer Key

Unit 1: **First Confession**

The Short Story

Exercise A

1. d

2. And all because of that old woman!

Exercise B

1. d

2. She became the raging malicious devil she really was.

Exercise C

1. a

2. Talking to the priest upside-down; Jackie falling off his perch

Exercise D

1. b

2. Nora is not very good, as her actions have shown. And Jackie is not a terrible sinner. He is no better or worse than anyone else—including Nora.

Comprehension Questions

1. d
2. c
3. b
4. b
5. c

6. a
7. c
8. a
9. c
10. c

11. a
12. b
13. a
14. c
15. a

Unit 2: **To Build a Fire**

Plot

Exercise A

1. b

2. It did not lead him to meditate upon his frailty as a creature of temperature, and upon man's frailty in general, able only to live within certain narrow limits of heat and cold.

Exercise B

1. d

2. He should have made a fire.

Exercise C

1. a

2. It was his last panic.

Exercise D

1. c

2. The brief day drew to a close in a long, slow twilight.

Comprehension Questions

1. b	6. d	11. b
2. d	7. a	12. d
3. a	8. c	13. c
4. a	9. c	14. a
5. b	10. a	15. b

Unit 3: **Raymond's Run**

Character

Exercise A

1. c

2. What a character looks like: Rosie who is as fat as I am skinny
What Squeaky thinks: people ain't grateful; talks about me like a dog; has a big mouth; is too stupid

Exercise B

1. d

2. So me and Raymond smile at each other and he says "Gidyap" to his team and I continue with my breathing exercises, strolling down Broadway toward the icey man on 145th with not a care in the world cause I am Miss Quicksilver herself.

Exercise C

1. a

2. a. Mr. Pearson is made to seem clumsy and foolish looking.
   b. Mr. Pearson seems to suggest he wants Squeaky to purposely lose the race.

Exercise D

1. a

2. smile

Comprehension Questions

1. d	6. c	11. d
2. a	7. b	12. c
3. c	8. a	13. d
4. b	9. a	14. c
5. a	10. d	15. b

Unit 4: **Chocolate Pudding**

Setting ———————————————————————

Exercise A

1. c

2. chocolate pudding

Exercise B

1. d

2. View 1: safe, enclosed,
         protected
   View 2: frail, weather-beaten,
         flimsy

Exercise C

1. b

2. the school grounds, Middle
   Square, Stony Acres

Exercise D

1. a

2. Teddy's fur-lined jacket

Comprehension Questions ———————————————

1. c	6. d	11. d
2. d	7. a	12. b
3. b	8. c	13. a
4. c	9. b	14. a
5. a	10. c	15. c

Unit 5: **The Moustache**

Theme _____

Exercise A

1. a

2. a wax museum

Exercise C

1. c

2. she calls his grandmother "dear"; she winks; she talks to him as if his grandmother wasn't there; her "patient" smile

Exercise B

1. d

2. I was too proud.

Exercise D

1. b

2. Hey, Mom, you and Dad really love each other, don't you? I mean—there's nothing to forgive between you, is there?

Comprehension Questions _____

1. d

2. a

3. c

4. a

5. c

6. d

7. a

8. d

9. a

10. a

11. c

12. b

13. d

14. b

15. c

Unit 6: **Another April**

Use of Language

Exercise A

1. d

2. what kind of a looking person

Exercise B

1. a

2. blue April wind; blue April sky. It was just blue space and little white clouds floated upon this blue.

Exercise C

1. c

2. as big and as round as a flour barrel; as big 'round his pipestem legs as emptied meal sacks; like sled runners

Exercise D

1. d

2. the wind play with his white whiskers

Comprehension Questions

1. d
2. a
3. c
4. b
5. d

6. c
7. d
8. b
9. b
10. d

11. a
12. a
13. c
14. d
15. a

Unit 7: **Sucker**

Tone and Mood

Exercise A

1. a

2. Passage A: (1) His voice was fast; His voice was excited and he kept on talking fast. (2) it was a good feeling; so seriously; warm and close
   Passage B: (1) waiting expression on his face; I'd maybe answer him rough-like (2) I was so worried; he began to get on my nerves

Exercise B

1. d

2. His eyes got narrow and his fists shut; There was a hard look to his eyes; He just sat there with those eyes on me; his face was hard and didn't move

Exercise C

1. a

2. quiet, dark, cold

Exercise D

1. c

2. There was something in me and I couldn't help myself. Words came without me knowing what they would be.

Comprehension Questions

1. b	6. b	11. d
2. d	7. b	12. c
3. a	8. d	13. c
4. c	9. a	14. a
5. a	10. a	15. b

Unit 8: **A Sound of Thunder**

Science Fiction

Exercise A

1. c

2. They were in an old time, a very old time indeed . . . . Christ isn't born yet. Moses has not gone to the mountain to talk with God. The Pyramids are still in the earth, waiting to be cut out and put up. Alexander, Caesar, Napoleon, Hitler—none of them exists. That is the jungle of sixty million two thousand and fifty-five years before President Keith. (Any two of these sentences constitute a correct answer.)

Exercise B

1. a

2. Some dinosaurs have two brains, one in the head, another far down the spinal column.

Exercise D

1. b

2. It was like standing by a wrecked locomotive or a steam shovel at quitting time, all valves being released or levered tight.

Exercise C

1. d

2. Who knows? Who really can say he knows?

Comprehension Questions

1. d	6. a	11. a
2. c	7. d	12. c
3. a	8. c	13. b
4. b	9. c	14. c
5. b	10. a	15. d

Unit 9: Naftali the Storyteller and His Horse, Sus

The Folk Story

Exercise A

1. c

2. If stories weren't told or books weren't written, man would live like the beasts, only for the day.

Exercise B

1. a

2. The whole earth, all the stars, all the planets, all the comets represent within them one divine history, one source of life, one endless and wondrous story that only God knows in its entirety.

Exercise C

1. b

2. reading

Exercise D

1. d

2. But could everything be measured by money?

Comprehension Questions

1. b	6. c	11. a
2. b	7. b	12. b
3. a	8. a	13. a
4. d	9. d	14. c
5. c	10. d	15. a

Unit 10: **The Lucid Eye in Silver Town**

Judgments and Conclusions: Discussing Stories _____

Exercise A

1. b

2. Sights: new square maroon furniture; new suitcase; Quin's fine underwear; no reading material except a shiny pamphlet
Smells: clean, expensive smells of leather and lotion

Exercise B

1. a

2. Father shakes hands with the waiter; Jay doesn't.

Exercise C

1. c

2. Well, why *should* he pay for it? *You* were the person to pay for it.

Exercise D

1. a

2. Years passed before I needed to go to New York again.

Comprehension Questions _____

1. b
2. a
3. d
4. a
5. d

6. c
7. c
8. c
9. b
10. d

11. c
12. a
13. b
14. a
15. c

Comprehension
Scores Graph
&
Comprehension
Skills Profile

Comprehension Scores

Use this graph to plot your comprehension scores. At the top of the graph are the names of the stories in the book. To mark your score for a unit, find the name of the story you just read and follow the line beneath it down until it crosses the line for the number of questions you got right. Put an *x* where the lines meet. As you mark your score for each unit, graph your progress by drawing a line to connect the *x*'s. The numbers on the right show your comprehension percentage score.

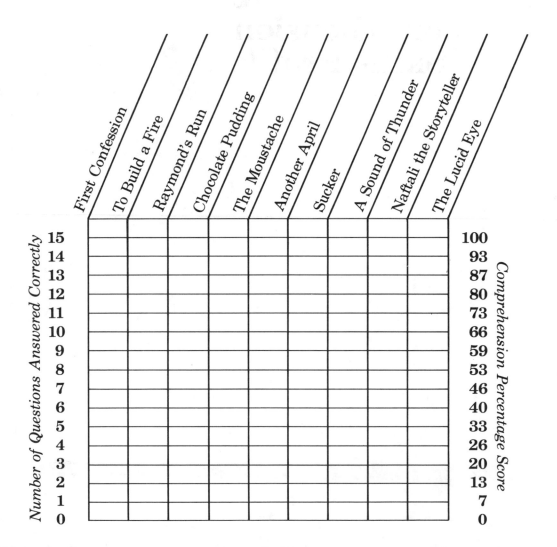

Comprehension Skills Profile

Use this profile to see which comprehension skills you need to work on. Each unit contains three questions in each of five comprehension skills areas. These skills areas are printed at the top of the profile. Each covers three columns of boxes. Fill in one box for each question you got wrong in a particular comprehension category, next to the number of the appropriate unit. As you complete each unit in the book, the profile will show you which kinds of questions give you trouble. Your teacher may want to give you extra help with these skills.

	Categories of Comprehension Skills														
	Recognizing Words in Context			Recalling Facts			Keeping Events in Order			Making Inferences			Understanding Main Ideas		
Unit 1 First Confession															
Unit 2 To Build a Fire															
Unit 3 Raymond's Run															
Unit 4 Chocolate Pudding															
Unit 5 The Moustache															
Unit 6 Another April															
Unit 7 Sucker															
Unit 8 A Sound of Thunder															
Unit 9 Naftali the Storyteller															
Unit 10 The Lucid Eye															